God flooded the earth to annihilate humanity's sins. What if that sinful race didn't die when floodwaters covered them but instead adapted to breathe water?

Under the depths of the ocean one boy has raised himself, until the day when he meets a dark-skinned man with news that will change the lives of his civilization forever.

Now he must save his people from another empire of water dwellers bent on enslaving the oceans and torturing his peaceful realm.

Yet another question is posed as he learns that his people are descended from humans that lived on the land above the ocean; a people that were destroyed by floods made by the rage of God.

If they have to, in order to escape, will they be able to breathe air and join whatever is left of the world above the waters?

What would they find there? Is the mythological Noah still alive?

The Ark of Humanity

Scott J. Toney

Breakwater Harbor Books, Inc.
Scott J. Toney, Founder
poeticliscence@hotmail.com

First Paperback Printing, February 2011

"And God saw the earth, and behold, it was corrupt; for all flesh had corrupted their way upon the earth. And God said to Noah, 'I have determined to make an end to all flesh; for the earth is filled with violence through them; behold I will destroy them with the earth. Make yourself an ark of gopher wood; make rooms in the ark and cover it inside and out with pitch...

'For behold, I will bring a flood of waters upon the earth, to destroy all flesh in which is the breath of life from under heaven; everything that is on the earth shall die. But I will establish my covenant with you; and you shall come into the ark, you, your sons, your wife, and your sons' wives with you. And of every living thing of flesh, you shall bring two of every living sort in the ark, to keep them alive with you; they shall be male and female. Of the birds according to their kinds, and of the animals according to their kinds of every creeping thing of the ground according to its kind, two of every sort shall come in to you, to keep them alive.'

Noah did this; he did all that God commanded him.

Then the lord said to Noah, 'Go into the ark, you and all your household, for I have seen that you are righteous before me in this generation...

'For in seven days I will send rain upon the earth forty days and forty nights; and every living thing that I have made I will blot out from the face of the ground.'

And the waters prevailed so mightily upon the earth that all the high mountains under the whole heaven were covered. And all flesh died that moved upon the earth, birds, cattle, beasts, all swarming creatures that swarm upon the earth, and every man; everything on the dry land in whose nostrils was the breath of life died."

- The Book of Genesis

But those beings whose home was the waters lived, as did those who fled to the waters instead of away from them.

Dedications

This story is dedicated to Paul Towne, my Grandfather, and a man who taught me through the way he lived his life to persevere through all adversity, and to be a good man while doing so.

It is also dedicated to Mr. Gehtes, a teacher who taught me that the path to God comes to us in mysterious ways, that we can bring good to this world through each avenue we choose and that in all religions of the world there are truths which we all share.

Acknowledgements

Thank you, Gerry, for all your hard work in editing and for your dedication to making this work the best that it could be. You taught me how to bring a finished product into being.

Thanks also to David Towne, for all the hard work editing this book and also for being an Uncle who cares and who took the time to teach his nephews how great an Uncle can be.

Without my parents, instilling in me from a young age to follow my dreams, and Mark, a man who has truly taught me what being a man means, I would not have finished this book. It is also friends like Nick, Jen and Dave, with their encouragement, which convinced me to write on.

Above all else I am thankful to, and for, my wife and daughter. This book is worth nothing without a love like ours. Each day I am blessed to wake up in a place more magical than Camelot, more beautiful then Ireland and filled with more love than I could ever have dreamed of or wished for. Laura, I know what a lucky man I am.

1

Beginnings
Orion's Birth
In the depths beneath the sea

To many men _Orion's Birth_ was a place hushed; plagued within their thoughts, vanquished from their words, but Maanta was not many men. In truth he was not a man at all but rather something of a boy and even amongst his peers was observed as more strange than not. The most normal of his bizarre traits was the fact that his body had not particularly agreed with him when he decided that it should lengthen and evolve into a man. So many of his peers in the _Meridian Hearth Sands_ had grown many minnow lengths in the recent past's sun illumination risings and fallings.   Their chests broadened, muscles gained definition, and their vocal cords no longer produced sounds the pitch of whale songs but instead evolved into tones more like those of walruses.

*

Crescent sheens of pale yellow sun illumination in _Orion's Birth_'s northern flowing currents rippled and flowed across Maanta's slim, pale legs and amongst the ocean's sweet liquid breeze giving a crescent pastel glow to the multicolored fins on either side of Maanta's ankles. These warm curtains of light delicately played across Maanta's body before finding rest upon the surrounding oceanic sands; his chest a canvas for their wavering, his eyes a pure opal dreaming longingly of the oceanic births above.

His slim, white fingertips sifted meticulously through the soft earth as he gazed towards *Orion's* oceanic sky. Maanta's frail insecurities showed not in this majestic place. This was his place. This was his home.

I wonder what all of this means, Maanta thought as he breathed in the brisk midday passing currents.

All about *Orion's Birth,* bubbling plumes shimmering silver, emerald, and other swiveling hues swam intertwining towards the sea births overhead. This transparent liquid was long feared by his race and forbidden from their *Sands.*

In youth before his mother's death, Maanta was taught this belief. Amongst his mother's kelp-melded cove, embedded along the *East Shale Wall,* she forbade things to his mind. The myth of the transparent fluid was just one of these sewn within his thoughts. Her sweet scent of jelly flora still fresh upon his mind, her words simmering upon his tongue...

"Junge Fisch", she had said, *"Many fathoms past whence aqua fabrics first roamed the world, whence mortals breathed their beginnings, we existed of the transparent womb. Our elder ones traversed many wheres above these seas and partook much of those wheres fruits. Seas were not the places in which those ancestors dwelled. And so it was for many years that men ate northern meats and northern fruits and cherished the world of sand.*

Then one day a dark being fell from beyond the northern land plummeting deep within north's soil, for in this sand, air, we did breathe, and Gelu kept all where sands did meet the water's shore. Gelu had shunned the dark one and so gave him forth the ancestors to do with as they wished.

With coming tides came knowledge from the dark man, allowing our ancestors to grow north fields vaster than an oceanic chasm's deepest deep and providing them with gems in such amounts that greed o'er took their souls. And so it was, that man took in Gelu's drowned son and many shrines were erected in his glorification. The dark one was pleased and soot and shade disgraced the sand.

Gelu forsake our ancestors for this and so, as he had drowned the dark one he soon would drown our peoples. Telling only the pure of heart, Noa, of his plans Gelu forsook the realm of men commanding the currents which we breathe into our gills to devour all the northern sands giving birth to our new world.

Legend has it that the dark one still dwells somewhere beneath our depths shunned by our people for all time's realm. Few of our people adapted to the ocean breath and it is told that if any man doth breathe north fluid once more his soul shall cease to pulse."

Maanta's mother had finished this particular haunting tale with a warning to never approach the deadly fluid which pulsed within *Orion's Birth*'s walls. Of course this was all the more reason for Maanta to seek out the fluid. Because of this very tale – whether it held true merit or not Maanta did not know - the people of the *Meridian Hearth Sands* dared not venture past the mystic blue glowing runed walls. Maanta was the only one to have entered within this place for many tides and was shunned for doing so.

Water currents swam between his slim, pale back and the clay oceanic earth beneath him. Closing his eyes, Maanta submerged his fingertips within the cool clay, embracing the currents rippling beneath his body. When he closed his eyes like this he almost felt as if he were a Manta Ray and not just a Maanta boy, with his swiveling body braced close to the sands and kelp ocean floor. He imagined he was a ray combing the depths for food and exploring the world, speaking to the fish as he pulsed along. He imagined the sunlight warming over his closed eyelids to be molten crevices in the crust of the *Meridian Hearth Sands,* illuminating his trail to future seaweed fields and blackened volcanic chasm delves.

A school of glimmering silver fish swam in unison across his long bluish gray fins, tickling them. The fish swam swiftly and with graceful ease through the water until the oceanic horizon swallowed their path. While immersing his thoughts in the cast of imaginary lava webs and swaying oceanic vegetation, Maanta awoke. One lone ripple peacefully swept itself across his daydream, then another, and then another until every precious flowing droplet of his imagined illusion shivered into a blur.

*

Cool water calmly embraced Maanta's opal eyes as *Orion's Birth*'s makings wove his thoughts from their dream scape and once more into reality. The continuous marble runed wall, which was built long ago to assist *Orion's Birth* in performing whatever task it might have been created to perform, had begun to echo its melodic song in skipping waves across the inner sanctum. Here Maanta laid, his pale, trembling fingers grasping soft sand earth while he had dreamt his daydream. Swarming, transparent bubble liquid plumes rose from the inner room sands and from the very sands beneath where Maanta had hovered and slept just moments prior.

They dance like northern silver fish schools, Maanta thought while watching as the bubbles played in a waltz towards their new home with the rest of their fluid's family on the ocean's surface.

Relinquishing his embrace from the ocean's floor, Maanta used his ankle fins and cupped webbed fingers to swim his way up and over the inner *Orion's Birth* wall. Along his ascent away, he wove fancy, precise somersaults and flips through the inner room's bubble tapestry and even managed the last minute rescue of a pearl white snail from the sands a few feet from the wall. His latest treasure was tucked delicately in a shale and whale hide satchel his mother had gifted him some time ago before her passing. The tiny visitor would be safe here until Maanta could find a more suitable place to set his newfound friend down.

Once far enough away from the happenings in *Orion's Birth,* Maanta curled a half turn in the ocean's waters to peer back on this place he so loved.

Orion's Birth consisted of three oval walls, two made up of oceanic stone consumed by a millennia of kelp, coral and anemone inhabitation, and one inner wall of pure shimmering white marble splattered with glowing runes the size of a young whale's fin and glowing with the soft, seemingly beaconing glow of *north*'s light constellations. Their calm, entrancing beams glimmered off the coral covered walls sprinkling yellows, reds and oranges throughout the pulsing, drifting depths. The outer walls touching the ocean floor draped an outstretched rainbow of beauty across the near seaweed drifting sands. Four outstretched pillars in the center of the final ring stood as titans and draped a shadow down on the surrounding sands. Their outstretched arms reached up as far as eyes could see.

Instantaneously in a vast plume, Orion's Birth's center filled with clear liquid which vaulted upwards pressing in rolling currents against the ocean's upper film. Filaments of creamy, light brown sand drifted slowly down. Neon streamers of light also danced before Maanta's eyes. He had seen this display so many times before yet was always mystified by the sight. He knew it was deadly if you got caught up in its plume, however it was also magnificently intricate and amazing. The currents were coming, and now it was time for his wild ride back to the *Meridian Hearth Sands*.

Maanta grinned with anticipation. Dipping swiftly down, he swam quickly and with ease, tensing his muscles like a harpoon through the ocean depths. He knew what he would discover upon reaching the ocean floor.

His sleek, webbed fingers quickly slipped around Archa's smooth fins. Maanta braced for what was soon to come.

Archa was warmed by her friend Maanta's body once more close along her back. Her deep dolphin eyes swept the yonder aquatic traveling realm in preparation, partaking of the calm before the storm.

*

Swift ocean currents surged down the towering, transparent fluid column's outer walls, swarming towards the ocean's floor. A flurry of sand stirred as the currents dashed and swept with tornadic whirlpool speeds for the remainder of the ocean's expanse, carrying many creatures and sands far, far from their homes.

The pair, Maanta and Archa, caught the pummeling current with swift, masterful ease, disappearing from *Orion's Birth*, destined for *Meridia*. Maanta softly kissed the dolphin's smooth forehead and hugged close to his friend. The two... a harpoon in the ocean's breeze.

2

<u>Swim the Way</u>

Swimming in the waters away from Orion's Birth

Faster and faster Maanta and his slick-backed companion swam, swift currents pushing their ever increasing pace, passing various sea creatures and plant life as they approached them with blurring speed.

While being swept through the cool depths, Maanta found himself pondering what old Amaranth might have gotten himself into back home in Meridia with his mystical trinkets and kelp logs. *Amaranth probably lay across a smooth oceanic slab somewhere beside flowing molten streams, dipping his corundum scribing claw into the luminescent lava currents and then scalding historic preaching upon a leaf of kelp parchment.*

What the bizarre old man ever found so fascinating about long mucked historic writings by even older dead scribes totally escaped Maanta's comprehension. It was the numerous shimmering trinkets in Amaranth's hollowed-out cove on The East Shale Wall that kept Maanta hovering in mid-swim outside Amaranth's windows when the waters went dark, with anticipation of what magics might unfold. Nothing ever happened of interest, but Maanta was sure that if he waited long enough, surely a fang-toothed ocean worm spewing black poisonous ooze or one of many other frightening creatures from the olden days would appear.

Maybe tonight will be the night, Maanta thought to himself as Archa dove just below an approaching driftwood column. Ducking, its bark barely skimmed Maanta's curly brown hair as the two swept by.

Maanta loved this wild ride with all of its swift approaching perils and heart pulsing speeds. There was something invigorating about being swept along by a swirling current that you couldn't control and just accepting the dangers of the world and attempting to overcome them. Maanta thought of The Meridian Hearth Sands as a place where nothing of any interest could ever be. No wars were ever fought or even skirmishes for that matter. An abundance of fish was gifted in adoration of King Nicholea Rocaran from the people of Meridia, and with the weekly festivals to Gelu, with all of their drink and merriment, Maanta was left to his own devices when it came down to actually entertaining himself.

*

Many light sheddings of time past and the waters paled in their reflections from the ocean's crest far above where Maanta glided. Famished, both from the many whale-lengths swim and from missing mid-day-meal while basking in Orion's Birth, Maanta determined that there would be no harm in departing from the swift current stream. Surely some scrumptious, shelled, critter-crawlers dwelt on the oceanic floor just waiting to be caught.

Maanta's soft touch caressed the side of Archa's head giving her the command to slowly descend from the pulsing current which swept them along. She dove from the current breeze using its push, pressing against her tailfin to masterfully ease herself and Maanta gently down. In a single motion her pale companion flipped backwards from his perch, skimming the ocean's floor. His body shimmered in trickling lights drifting from above, stirring sands which rested just below his flowing form.

As he swept, transparent beings stirred from their well hidden resting places. If a person knew what he was searching for he could see these teeny creatures scurrying just beneath the ocean's sands. Maanta swam a half circle and cupped a few of the intricate creatures in his hands, using his webbed fingertips as a net. He was being careful to only take what was needed for his dusk-meal.

"Maanta," his mother had once said, "only partake of that which will replenish your health until next-eating. Those beings who share our oceanic home are Gelu's children also and are to be cherished and loved as you would care for your kin. We must partake of them to stay strong but that does not mean we should mindlessly disrespect their lives. To forget Gelu's love for them would be to gouge our very souls."

Maanta found these words to make much sense and so was careful to only take what was needed from the sands with which Gelu had blessed him.

He prepared the critter-crawlers by cracking a malta shell which was stored in a seaweed strap along his left wrist. Glowing crimson ooze seeped from the shell, pouring out and over a ring of cragged stones, sizzling as its warmth embraced the ocean's cool waters. Maanta rummaged through his shale satchel for the heating net, which he had snatched from a vender in the selling place. Once found, he situated the critter-crawlers in the web of seaweed knots and then floated them above the warming fluid to give them just the right delicate, stewed, warm taste.

Scraping their shells across a cragged stone revealed a delicate red and pearl hued edible delight inside. Maanta prepared a meal of the critter-crawlers mixed with seaweed strands and powder made of coral remains for himself and his companion. Archa ate first, as all ridden friends should, as they give most of the effort on trips such as this. After he had seen to Archa, Maanta was content to savor the remains of the food. Its taste was sweet and coolly graced his mouth's palate as it went to its new dwelling place in his rumbling stomach.

Maanta smiled as the last sliver of seaweed swiveled through his pursed lips. He hadn't truly realized how hungry he had been until he had spied the critter-crawlers in the sands. Rested and fed, Maanta was ready once more to take to the task of adventuring home.

Cupping his fingertips once more, he swept under Archa's belly and perched upon her sleek back.

"Ooooahooo," Maanta sang to Archa in her dolphin tongue asking to go home.

"Help m-m-m-e..." The ocean spewed a haunting whispering response.

Maanta shivered with unease. His webbed fingers gripped at Archa's sides causing her to rear in discomfort. She tossed him from her back off into a rising cove wall above where they had been delighting on dusk-meal just moments before. He clasped his pale back with his hand and felt over a scattered, rough blood patch left from his collision with the stone. It was just a wound. It would heal.

What had spoken to him, whispering in such pained unease? Should he flee for his life or go investigating off into the ocean's quickly blackening obsidian hue to discover what had spoken to him? These questions danced through his thoughts as if they mattered. Inside, Maanta knew that he could never turn away from an intriguing moment of unknowing. He also could never forgive himself if he thought he might have left a person in the cold Meridian outersands to be devoured by lurking many-toothed harkfish or to starve in wounded misery.

Not too far off on the ocean floor something stirred. A black muscular arm convulsed beneath a large moss covered stone.

"Heeeeeeelp..." the voice beckoned again.

Maanta swam with all the force that could be summoned from his soul. His thoughts leapt far beyond his body to assist this fellow man, his heart booming with the unknown. Maanta gasped as he neared where the voice had emulated. Deep crimson droplets hovered and swayed where the twitching hand raked at the sands from beneath its stone-pinned resting place. Maanta, repulsed by the crushed being's blood, breathed in a vast inhale of fresh oceanic water and dove through the crimson murk, curving his hands along the pinning stone's underbelly.

His small arms shimmered in the setting northlight. They were shaking as he attempted with all of his mustered strength to lift up the stone and rescue the thing beneath, his joints burning for the cause. A bitter salty taste passed through lips and into lungs as he came to the realization that he couldn't lift this mighty stone alone. The stone was simply too weighty for anyone, let alone a weak merboy, to lift without help. In his heart though, he couldn't give up. There had to be some hope.

And then it came to him as if some prayer had been answered. From the corner of his eye Maanta spied a whale rib bone, encrusted to the ocean floor beneath his very toes. Using a nearby shell to pry the bone free, Maanta diligently scraped all sands away from its edges. With a smooth tug at the bone, swift suction filled the void where it had once been, giving Maanta just what he hoped was needed to accomplish his task.

"Sir if you can hear me," Maanta spoke toward beneath the stone, "swim with all your soul allows when I lift the stone up and away from you."

"H-H-H-e-l..." The voice simply murmured in return.

Shafting the sleek whale rib beneath the stone, Maanta dug his feet beneath the ocean's sands and pushed down as far as his muscles would allow. He screamed as his muscles burned in agony. He braced the stone up with the whale bone mere minnow lengths higher than it had been moments before.

A hulkish, ragged, dark-skinned man swam dazedly out of the open crevice, his clothes tattered and muscles shredded with blood. A deep gash along his shoulder bled more intensely then the rest of his wounds. A long, gray beard swayed from the stranger's chin as his massive body went limp amongst the ocean's breeze.

Relieving himself of the limb, stone and the infinitely searing pain, Maanta now turned his curiosity toward this new and mysterious companion. From where had he come and where was his destination? What could have happened to have left him in such dire agony? All would have to wait until the dark-colored man awoke.

Maanta wrapped the man's wounds in seaweed bandages and waited in curious anticipation. Archa joined his side.

*

Several light darkenings of time passed. All the while Maanta took in the appearance of this new and foreign man. Golden cuffs and trinkets adorned his body. In several places streams of separating and intertwining gold appeared to have been scorched into flesh, joining body and the currency into one. Contrasted against the man's dark brown skin this golden, tattooed tapestry looked delicately beautiful. One stream of likewise golden bead drops trickled a ring across his otherwise barren forehead.

Was this man of royal blood? Maanta wondered. He had never seen any man or woman quite as decorated and could not imagine that any person without royal blood could afford to display himself like this. There was one thing though that caused him to doubt this conclusion. Along with the golden splendor adorning his body, this man was also marked in another fashion. Harshly scorched lines made out an eerie eye brand along the bare of his back.

Maanta had heard word of men who had enslaved others beyond The Meridia Hearth Sands in an effort to gain power and prestige. The King would not permit such practices within his *Sands*.

It was rumored that the enslaved ones were branded much like this but surely, Maanta conceived, a slave would not be permitted so close to Meridia. And how could a slave amass such a vast array of fortune?
*

The strange man's eyes opened to the world of the real once more, pure white spheres peering as if through the curtain of Maanta's soul. Disturbing yet peaceful was his stare to look upon.

"Good day young one," the man huffed in his brash low tone. "I do not know all of which has occurred to me but somehow feel I as if I owe you that which is many thanks."

"I only did what any other would do." Maanta smiled, happy that the man had appreciated him. "It was my pleasure. You have a long gash along your shoulder. If you would like, I know of a place in Meridia where you might get that looked at and healed." A small potions cove existed on the outskirts of Meridia. He had taken rest there many a time himself, needing healings after his trips to the Meridian outersands.

"So soon to offer one's assistance to a stranger that one barely knows?" The man asked. "I could be a thief or one in seek of others for enslaving."

"As for thievery," Maanta grinned, "you should be more cautious of me than I of you, seeing as I am just a poor, clearly tatter-clothed boy and you are draped in fine golden gems." Thoughts came to him for a moment about the possibility of the stranger being one who gathers slaves. The man could have been a slave once who had been honored with the privilege of seeking out others to enslave. Certainly it would account for his eye scorch and for the abundance of gold shimmering his skin. Well, if the man was out to enslave young, weak, scatterbrained mer boys, it had become far too late for Maanta to avoid that misfortune.

Maanta nervously twisted a wayward flowing seaweed strand, stretching it upon his fingertips. "A man who was felled by slowly falling ocean stones surely would not be swift enough to capture a young one such as me."

"And it appears wit accompanies courage as another trait which is yours. My name," the man smiled a warm grinning smile, "would be Sift. Seeing as you are the rescuer of that which is my life I am supposing that you are owed as much. Perhaps if friends we will be," the man slowly closed and opened his left eye, "some day my last name will follow. If you would listen I would tell of who I am and what it is that brings me here needing, how is it you said, needing of the assistance of scatterbrained mer boys."

The northern lights had faded and only the faintest of definitions could be made out by both men's eyes. Maanta cracked a malta shell, scattering its glowing red ooze across the ocean's floor, as they hovered above in the oceanic currents. If he was to be listening to a tale, Maanta had decided that he would do it by malta glow. Sweet gemlike crimson glowingly trickled across Maanta, Archa, and Sift's bodies. Somewhere off in the distance a whale sang.

"My mother always told me never to speak with strangers," Maanta grinned. "I've never understood that rule. It's a pleasure to meet you, Sift. You can call me Maanta and I am afraid that I don't know my last name and so you also may never know. Please, I would love to hear some of who and what you've been."

"As for my beginnings and youthhood in the ocean's currents, I'm afraid that those tales will have to wait for days not so close to passing to their ends. I come from a place far away from these sands known by a name that you have probably never heard. My people were enslaved by others in that place. I, with my brothers and sisters, was scorch branded by my lord and sent scavenging through the molten creviced depths beneath the sand and stone floor. Not as sensitive to that which would be malta burns, my peoples fell to many monstrosities.

"Throughout the years kin which was mine fell to tortures of the depths. Many of my family found themselves sold to other lords many leagues away. Before my very eyes the father I knew's body shriveled and scorched to ash, melding along two pressing volcanic walls. The slave watchmen just laughed at his shriveled corpse and insisted that us enslaved ones scrape his putrid dead form from the volcanic walls to peddle in the market for its minerals. Vividly remember I this once and of many more horrific times. My father's face still haunts dreams which are mine, his features twisted in boiling agony. So sad it is that such things in our world have come into being."

Maanta shivered in the cool waters. Tiny goose bumps of disturbed disbelief held him still.

Sift plucked a tiny shimmering fish from above and cradled it between his hands and fingertips. "And so it was that loneliness did take my soul. I became hard like the molten ooze after cooling and morphing to stone. Thus it was for many north light passings that I had lost who I was.

"One ocean-darkness I fell to sleeping, incased within net cagings, breathing into my gills the bloody scent of those around me. And I awoke with blurred sight in the arms of one dark cloaked man somewhere along our city's outskirts. Poisoned must I have been. *'Flee and never return to this land,'* the cloaked one proclaimed, his deep opal eyes, surging with the glimmer of an eternal flame which evaporates the ocean's depths.

"Sleep overtook my mind and upon awakening took I the advice, swimming deep away from that which was my home. Other brave souls have joined my side. Together, scavenge we the depths in watch for those which have lost their paths and might wish to be our brethren." While saying this last part a certain calming softness swept his voice, as if speaking of a home.

Sift un-cupped his strong yet somehow delicate hands and looked upwards, warmly smiling as the little shimmering fish swam happily away.

"What brings you so close to Meridia if I might ask?" Maanta asked.

"That, I am afraid, is a subject of which I can not say but a promise young Maanta I shall give you. Before the rest of Meridia shall know, I shall be sharing with you that which brings me to this place. There is nothing within me to be fearing of."

The man's pearl white eyes glanced at something within the darkness depths as he said this. What was there? Why wouldn't this man tell him about his reasons for being so close to Meridia, Maanta pondered, and for that matter what had brought Sift to his near death encounter needing assistance? These questions and many more riddled Maanta's thoughts. There was so much more to ask and with deeper darkness looming in, so little time to do so.

"Lola!" The mahogany colored man bellowed out, waving his arms in gleeful excitement at something unseen and unknown.

A smooth something pressed at Maanta's pale back, almost nudging him as Archa did when feeding time came and he had not yet given her food. But this something nudging was nudging his whole back and was definitely too large to be his sleek, smooth ocean companion.

A large eye, emerald in hue and with the look of a pale mirrored pane, stared back at Maanta as he half swirled in the currents, causing his heart to gulp at the thought of being nudged by such a bizarre creature.

With two dolphin length fins outstretching from either side, this fish hovered, staring through its emerald globes and causing Maanta to realize that here was truly something the likes of which he had never seen. To think in all of the places that he had been and all of the adventures that he had been on there were still creatures out there that Maanta did not know existed. Shimmering sleek fins the size of Meridian warrior shields cascaded down the creature's sides also and melded at the underbelly in a sort of sterling spike. A swaying green angel fin briskly cascaded from the creature's back, dancing in the water's breeze.

"Some companion you turned out to be, fish!" Sift jokingly grumbled out, swimming over to where this unique fish glided.

Still stunned from the unexpected encounter, Maanta watched as Sift patted on the fish's sleek scales in greeting.

"A boulder from up high fells your friend," he waved his hands frantically at the fish, "and all that you can do is flounder about? And I thought you and I to be soul mates of a kind. See what happens if a boulder topples you my friend or if hunger overwhelms the belly of a fellow man and he wishes to purchase you." He slapped the fish's side and teased it with a goofy glare.

Lola looked back at the man as if to say, *Silly little man how would you get home if you'd dare let such things happen to me?* Her eyes mockingly glimmered in the crimson malta stone's luminescence.

"As you may very well have come to guessing," Sift smiled back at Maanta, apparently quite pleased with the look of surprise which had been on his face just moments prior, "this is my companion of traveling, Lola."

"It's good to know that I wasn't about to become someone's nightsnack," Maanta replied, "but seeing as you're wounded and the darkness soon will descend to pitch black, we'd better make our way back towards Meridia. Will you be alright to ride?"

"Surely you jest?" The dark skinned man swam and gripped two stones upon the silver reflective fish's backside. "Wounded though I may be, one doesn't live in ways such as I and be unable to ride and do what one must. Thank you for your help young Maanta. If you would still take me, I would be pleased to go to the place in Meridia where you have spoken of, so that I may be healed."

Archa dipped from the ocean above, gliding beneath Maanta's fingertips. He met her fins and lifted himself to her back then patted her neck calmly to show the loving of a dear friend.

"Follow me," he grinned, happy to be off again on yet another adventure through the depths, and sounded the tones which he had grown to know so well, "Ooooahooo!"

The foursome swept off through the pitch night appearing to passer fish eyes as phantasms sifting currents through the seas.

A low blue sapphire hue shone down from ocean's crest above; draping all things below the crest within the ocean depths in dark gray haunting mist specks. Night fish glowed like stars, lightly shimmering the belly of the ocean, and somewhere off in the distance malta streams smoothly tangled their webs across all mercreatures' sight.

3

Night Guest
Cardonea Tower

Her eyes shimmered with soft beauty in the musky oceanic night from where she floated in her tower rising above the ocean floor.

Two walls of ivory-flicked shale rose from the depths in the distance and high above where even her tower's height reached, curving like two lids across the building's iris.

Dwelling within these walls lived her people and her father's people. In the coal dark night, malta glows glistening from both the East and West Shale Wall's inner cavern dwellings comforted and warmed her. The lights from their warm malta kindling seemed to waltz from place to place glistening the leagues of aquatic ocean between her and all that her eyes could see.

It was here, while her thoughts drifted in this soft, soothing trance of illuminating opal sight, that something of interest caught her eye.

Somewhere off in the depths, below her tower's rising walls, a ghastly pale albino boy hugging a dolphin's back skimmed Meridea's floor. She could hear the dolphin's almost inaudible calls in the distance. This bizarre pair was followed by a massive fluorescent hued fish and a man, whose skin appeared to be that of pitch night. But both entities were impossible. Neither could exist.

The first was impossible because seeing a dolphin so far down in the Meridian depths was unfathomable. Dolphins couldn't breathe for long without the transparent fluid which was so abundant above and close to the ocean's crest. And there was none to be found in the depths which were home to Meridia, certainly not in enough abundance to sustain such a creature of beauty as the dolphin.

The second because…

…because no man that she had ever heard tale of bore skin the hue of pitch oceanic night. No man had flesh of black.

Glimmering light spilled out from the East Shale Wall's doorways and windows, shimmering like shell gloss across the sands and coral where these travelers swam. She wondered if her sight and thoughts were deceiving her or if this duo of travelers was actually real.

Whatever the two were, one thing was certain. They were beautiful. The pale boy flung his thin arms in wide motions while puffing out his chest as though speaking to the other man, perhaps blustering on about the city's walls or tales that he had heard of things within them. The boy's left leg tightened to the dolphin's side as they swept down to the oceanic floor. His arm swept below where she knew a snail garden lay, his fingers gently releasing something small in amongst the kelp and snail domain.

Rising from the downward swoop, a long shaft of coral stretched forth from the boy's fingertips and plunged into the sands below, spewing forth a tail of whipped sand in a playful, swirling breeze.

This night parade of two, the pale boy clasping to his dolphin companion and the stern-faced, dark-skinned man with his large fluorescent fish beneath him, glided stealthily along the East Shale Wall, illuminated in malta light as they drifted from her sight.

Long, ruby locks flowed across Anna's youthful form and into the currents' breeze as she floated for moments after the small parade's passing, her thoughts lost completely on what the presence of these two unusual travelers might mean.

She had looked upon the two from a distance, it was true, but still the young boy's face played in her mind. There had been something lively in his smile and in the way that he frolicked in the currents that awakened something in her. What that thing that gave her goosebumps could be though, Anna could not say.

She yawned as a cool breeze of water wove over her. Lazily, she glided with her ankle and wrist fins over to her place of resting and curled up in a warm cover of prepared whale skins, kelp strands and various minerals which would keep the warmth in as dreams wandered in her mind.

Anna's green eyes softly shut as reflections of the ocean birth's stars sprinkled a mind-enthralling tapestry within her thoughts.

*   *   *

With one wide swerve of the arm Maanta waved to Sift and watched as the dark man, shimmering with gold adornments, jetted on the back of Lola toward the glowing coral potions cove along the East Shale Wall where Maanta had directed him. When morning arose he would check on this new friend.

"Ooooahooo," Maanta sang to Archa, telling her to go and rest ahead of him in their shale-wall cove dwelling. The night was still young with more exploring left to do.

Warm, crimson light from The East Shale Wall draped amongst the darkness, reminding Maanta of times long past as he cupped the cool waters in his webbed fingertips. Illumination lights let his thoughts wander away to other days, days when his mother still was alive.

When he was a child she would wrap him up in kelp and cradle him in her arms while drifting in the currents next to their own little stone malta pit. She would hum or sing a lullaby to him while carefully tracing his hair with her fingertips. Sometimes if he was lucky she would tell him tales of long ago or even make up tales from the minds of different creatures that made their homes nearby in the Meridian sands.

How nice it would be to feel that warmth again and to relax in the glow of his mother's own malta pit. Maanta could almost smell this past like a sugary, ocean flora scent wafting just past him in the drifting currents. It was as if this scrumptious memory could be found beckoning from the closest cove home and yet was out of reach, forbidden for the eating.

Daydreaming again, Maanta realized as he exited from his thoughts and memories, *and the daytime is nowhere to be found. How bizarre is it when you find yourself daydreaming when the rest of the ocean finds itself in slumber? The rest of the world just doesn't know what it's missing.*

Swooping in one brisk, fluid swirl, Maanta skimmed the gargantuan cove wall of dwelling places towards his final destination before night's rest would be allowed to overtake his body.

Warm, spiraling currents wafted across Maanta's fingertips then wove about his lips as he clutched on a stone windowsill, eyes glimmering with intrigue, peering within the shale crevice home of the wise elder, Amaranth.

Would tonight be the night, Maanta wondered, in which the curiously kind, old man would finally awaken magical serpents dwelling down beneath the depths of Meridia or possibly even summon forth apparitions from Meridian ages long past?

For many a night passing Maanta had peered upon this very dwelling's windowsill in the hopes of viewing things such as this. He had overheard many a tale while in Meridea's marketplace of Amaranth and of his vibrant magical doings but as of that very moment, all which had been awarded Maanta for his sneaky patience were malta-hued nights in which the old man etched with his corundum claw upon various kelp parchments. These were mixed with the occasional night of Amaranth irrationally babbling in song.

Are the tales of Amaranth's doings just that, Maanta wondered, *elaborate myths brought to life by the mis-told recollections of Meridea's inhabitants?*

He had overheard tales of magical technicolor blooms forged instantaneously, brought about by one simple drifting of the old man's fingertips. But the only blooms of brilliance Maanta had seen within the cavern which was Amaranth's dwelling place were sand blooms rippling through the room as kelp parchments unraveled for Amaranth's reading.

Why does the man have to be so bedamned boring? Maanta found himself pondering as his sights and wandering thoughts drifted towards the shelvings and various other unliving inhabitants of the room. Glimmering pink, obsidian, emerald and an assortment of other-hued potions lined the carved-out stone shelving, shimmering their vibrant, reflective glows all over the room and tapering off into the oceanic night.

Hovering above a slate table in the room's center, with his back to Maanta, Amaranth scribed a passage on tender, fresh parchment. Life shone from his eyes in gentle blue sparks. He knew the young one was there, watching in the murky night. Smiling, he smoothly soothed crimson chemical soils in his palms.

Amaranth swiftly swam upright, fists clenched, and flung his fingers free. Vibrant red heat-blooms burst from his palms, sweeping about and fizzling amongst the ocean's depths. Forbidden fluid bubbles scattered, webbing amongst the room and collecting along the cragged shale cavern's ceiling like fish eggs to a coral wall.

Shivers ran up Maanta's spine. What was this thing which he had seen? The stories must be true.

A single warm ash speck from one of the blooms drifted as it cooled, still barely lit with red heat, out Amaranth's shale window entrance and Maanta clasped it in his palm. It faded to pure gray ash as Maanta stuffed this remnant of the beautiful vision in a small folded-seaweed pouch.

*

As the young merboy swam quickly to his cove of resting along the East Shale Wall, Amaranth grinned. He loved watching young merchildren revel in anticipation and awe over simple displays such as this. It was this innocence and unknowing in them that brightened his days, reminding him of a youth long past.

Amaranth set a stone time regulator, his own contraption of mirrors and cranks, in a hole in the wall to let the morn's light shine upon his eyes when the day was still young. He nestled face down, and fins within the water, in the nest of air lining the ceiling above.

*

Amaranth awoke, as night passed, to the pure white glare of a being hovering beneath his eyes.

"Who…" Amaranth began to ask.

"There is much to speak," the thing replied.

4

<u>Arrival</u>
Maanta's room in Meridia

Two nova white eyes glared at him, a chill breath rippling upon his neck, as he lay bonded in molten chains to the darkness, his arms singed and a foreign mind clawing, dragging at his soul. His stomach went clammy with blood's pulse. Maanta was alone, not knowing where, but alone.

"Come to me," the words of a foreign being scathed within his mind. "Come and be adorned."

Maanta would not reply, could not reply.

A chain ripped through his back and ribs, catching in the boney cage, spurting blood and causing pain to reverberate through the whole of him. His chest split, splattering the nova eyes with deep red blood which fizzled upon their touch. The world faded to rippled aquatic daylight.

It was a dream. Thank Gelu it was a dream.

Archa's smooth gray nose bobbed Maanta's side in anxiousness of his awakening, spiraling him gently in an open float amongst the cove dwelling.

Vaulting against the back shale wall, Maanta disrobed his seaweed night-sheet and swam with cupped webbed fingertips toward a collection of small fish eggs he'd gathered a few days before. They browned quickly over a cracked malta shell's molten fluids, holding a saltiness in taste meshed with the sweetness of oceanic flora saps, and served as a delicious daylight meal.

Archa devoured hers as Maanta scrubbed his pale body with sea salts while using his ankle fins to spin close to a suction vent in the ceiling of his cove. The vent took away uncleanliness and provided a humming sensation upon the skin.

He dressed in whale leather, instructed Archa to stay put, and dipped through the window of his East Shale Wall home.

*

The currents caught on his webbed fingertips and sped him inwards toward Meridia's everyday hustle and bustle. He swept past the vibrant multicolored scale-clothed merchants with their exotic fish-filled cages and sea plants of the deep and shallow depths. One of these particular plants caught his eye even in the quickness of his passing. What appeared to be a hybrid plant which he had not seen before, possibly sold to the peddler by a foreign traveler, knotted its notched deep purple tentacles in Meridia's oceanic breeze.

How bizarre, he thought, that he who traveled throughout much of the oceanic births and depths would have never seen any particular plant from any place at all before.

The peddler and his unique plant passed on with the pressing oceanic breeze as Maanta ducked beneath an arched coral column which connected the inner tower to The East Shale Wall. He jetted upward with tensed legs and beating ankle fins and swept through a ring of playing merchildren who were not the least bit concerned with him.

It was the bizarre and favorite game of young merchildren to curve their bodies ever so slightly and chase each other in a ring, using their wrist and ankle fins to keep up in the loop until one of the children would drift out because of the suction that it created. The ring became smaller and did so each time another child was suctioned out. Sometimes when the ring was down to two it would seem as if it was a shimmering blue orb hovering in the waters, mystically resisting the aquatic currents.

Maanta loved to watch as a young Meridian but could never join in, as he possessed webbed fingers instead of wrist fins. This was not simply a rarity among Meridians, it was a never. Maanta felt unique to be the only such as this. Most others thought him weak and a burden to their play groups. That and many things caused him to explore alone.

Currents pushed behind him as he swept his pale, webbed fingers down towards Meridia's potion cove in anticipation of meeting with his newfound friend, Sift, and Sift's riding companion, Lola.

Meridians of all shapes and sizes bustled above and below. A gathering of artisans squeezed different colored inks from fish-scale tubes onto a kelp tapestry, creating a rainbow of colors depicting an oceanic molten eruption. Mer families swept past, dining upon anemone stuffed squid tentacles as they swept into the worship cove for readings taught of Gelu. One rotund, opal-skinned man nearly rammed Maanta with his whale bone Noosechariot, while being pulled towards market by fanglet fish.

Maanta dove below the hollowed out bone contraption, physically pulling himself out of currents that were sucking him towards the Noosechariot's jagged hull.

"Pesky pale child!" The hefty Meridian grunted.

The paleness of his skin, that's all some ever saw. It haunted him, but Maanta knew there was more than milky flesh to his whole, though some never seemed to see this. It singed the soul at times but molded him, he thought, to be just who he was.

That's not true, he thought. *If I were bluer, adorned with wrist fins, the things I've seen would not have come to my eyes and the life I've lived would not be mine. It's the taunting I have to thank for my adventures throughout the depths, because without it I'd have stayed and played with others, being not this me, but more like them.*

It hurt though. It always would.

Sucking water through his lungs and curling down toward the bustling labyrinth potions cove, he dove.

To find a dark-skinned man adorned in gold and scorched tattoos amongst a potions cove of opal Meridians should not be hard, he thought. While sweeping toward the jutting cove of stone, Maanta sighted what appeared to be a vast, barren space in the injured camp of Meridians.

"They're coming to slaughter our women," a man gargled while pivoting past Maanta away from the cove.

Maanta jutted through the depths towards the barren area, where only Sift lay hovering above a rising stone table.

"What have they done?" Maanta gasped as he reached the black skinned man.

Forbidden fluid drifted up from Sift's open lips.

"Nothing have they done, my friend," Sift grinned. "That's not for lack of trying. Since morn broke neither healer nor injured has come close except to gawk at or threaten me. Noticed have I that none here have skin the coloring of mine, or yours for that matter. Probably I would think that is why. Folk fear what is not the usual."

Then how are you healed if none would come near? Maanta wondered. *Where is the gash along your shoulder? And why so alert and lively if none have come with food? I trust you, Sift, but what is it you're hiding?*

"I'm sorry," Maanta said. "They're so scared of anything they haven't known before. A year back the waters became warmer in Meridea's Koffen Caves and cavern fishers haven't adventured close since. Tales of poisonous ink fish breeding in the caves depths, heating their currents, run wild."

And then it happened, a beginning none foresaw but it was just that.

Waves of Meridians that were huddling away from Sift before, swept in scurrying sheets above their heads towards the iris tower of Meridia's center, towards the hearth of Zhar Nicholea, Cardonea Tower. Whispers excitedly passed from lips and none took notice of Maanta or his companion. Not ignoring, only moving on as if leaving once craved minnows for larger fish, perhaps ones with a tangy zest.

"The look in their eyes, like a gossip freshly born," Sift remarked. "Shall we see what's whispered mongst these depths, friend of mine?"

"Sounds good to me," Maanta replied.

"Lola!" Sift lowly bellowed her to his side. He clasped the stones on Lola's side, hoisting himself upon her scales. Maanta, Sift and Lola swept toward the commotion gathering about Cardonea Tower.

* * *

Cardonea Tower

"You must come with us to greet our visitors, Anna!" Zhar Nicholea, Meridia's husky ruler pled with his youngest daughter. His burley crimson beard waved in the currents, pressing to his multicolored, shimmering jellyfish garments. He hovered, mid-float, between Anna's chamber room doorway and the ornate carved windowsill she swam gently in and out of.

"Why should I?" She asked, tossing her arms. "You don't even know these men except that they say they're a lost race of our ancestors. Why must you always flaunt me like a chest of gems? I'm not Zharista. I don't want royalty. I don't want power. I want to be left to live the life of normal Meridians."

He moved slowly through the chamber until they were close, then touched his large, callused hands softly to her rich, blue cheeks, looking deep into those emerald eyes.

"You are like rippling light in night's waters to me, daughter," he said softly, touched with love. "I ask you to come because your warmth brings a clearness of mind and heart to me when I need it the most. Your mother, brother, sisters and you are what gives me strength to not fall into the jaded traps of others, and to do what's right for our kingdom. It is not for these men I ask you to come with me. It is for me."

Tears built in her eyes as he swam from the room, shutting the doorway gently behind him with those massive hands.

Yes, mer people cry too. But their tears cannot be seen and drift into the waters where none will know they ever were. It's just a feeling swelling in their eyes as the currents ripple in.

She knew he'd understand her not wanting to file out in gaudy revelry to meet the visitors. She wanted to go now, to be there by his side, but a strength inside her would not give in. That strength insisted she was right even though she knew it was wrong.

Anna hovered parallel to the window sill, awaiting her family's royal glide to meet the visitors along Meridia's outer rim, watching for her father.

* * *

"What's going on?" Maanta asked, not really expecting an answer, as they pressed through crowds of Meridians engulfing Cardonea Tower in a sphere of befuddlement. Not a sole so much as glanced at Maanta and his companions. They were clamoring towards something close to Meridia's front opening, a rather large crevice separating the East and West Shale walls.

Maanta was forced to squeeze past a man's rotund belly above, a woman's sleek back below, through a mother and her five whining children arguing and hovering together and various other things before seeing what the city had scuttled together to witness.

Cardonea's gargantuan stone drawbridge, draped in seaweed grown above it throughout the ages because most Meridians used windows to enter and leave the tower, waved through the waters, swirling them as it boomed upon the oceanic floor.

Sands whipped up around the fallen stone and swept inwards toward the tower and a man, his wife, their son and two of their daughters, surrounded by eight hulking Meridian guardsmen, drifted slowly through the swirling sands towards the distant wall's crevice. The guards bore armor shaped from giant emerald-crab shells, wielding emerald spheres and shield stones depicting Gelu creating the upper world, in their hands. It was a symbolic waltz of pride.

Nicholea's enormous guards parted the murmuring crowd with stern fists the size of the Zhar's own head. The seriousness imbedded upon their leader's deep blue cheeks and eyes rippled an awakening consciousness within the Meridians, a mutual inward knowledge that their Zhar, with his usual serious and gently kind demeanor, was troubled by something this day he had awoken to.

* * *

Just that morning as the light shown down from the ocean's crest, Nicholea awoke to a messenger boy from a place beyond Meridia's sands. The Zhar's two personal guardsmen swept through his bedchamber entrance, the thin youthful arms of the boy clasped in their fists. But it wasn't the boy's arms, lips, head or torso which caught Nichalea's waterbreath to his throat. It was the fin flapping below the boy's waist. Meridians weren't built like this. Any normal Meridian boy coming with message would be directed to the waiting halls for attention after morning's meal, but because of the boy's uniqueness he was brought directly to the Zhar's attention. What was this boy? Where were his legs and leg fins?

"Release me at once," the boy demanded of the guards, his tense, red eyes fixed on the Zhar. "Be you the leader of these lands?"

The guards hovered, still as floating columns.

"Where is your legs boy?" Nicholea questioned, Zharista Alexandra gently awakening beside him.

"Master Evanshade requests an audience outside the city walls as the midday comes, with news of a race separated from yours years before now. Let me loose or his kindness will turn sour once I tell him of how you've held his own Master's son hostage." Jagged teeth twisted between the boy's lips as churning heat lit within his eyes. "I am Venge. I bring greetings from the sands of Sangfoul."

"Does this Evanshade come in friendship or with destruction?"

"He comes with desire to retwine the friendship of our race's lost ancestors, a true waste of time."

At this, the guards simultaneously tightened their grip and the boy cursed staggeringly, blood drifting from his lower lip as he bit it in rage.

"Let him go," Nicholea quickly said. "I'll meet this Evanshade. Venge, I apologize for any disservice you feel you've been given. I am excited to learn of our brethren race."

Venge cringed at the apology, was escorted by the guards beyond Cardonea Tower and swam, swiftly beating his tailfin, beyond Meridea's walls.

* * *

"Is there wisdom in meeting a man who leads such an indignant boy, out beyond Meridia's walls with only friendship on the mind?" Alexandra drifted towards Nicholea as the procession neared the meeting of the East and West Shale walls, the outskirts of Meridia City. Her curly red hair flowed up and down in the currents, patting the tiny gems glimmering about her pastel pearl dress.

"Truly there is not, my love, but would there not be even less wisdom in not meeting with such a man and leaving all that is unknown to remain unknown? I will not let harm befall you, our son or our daughters. Our guards and Gelu protect us, Meridia's outersands are ours too and not so large a troop could enter them without our knowing. These men we meet surely would not be enough to harm us, be their intentions malice."

"Greetings," a voice then bellowed from beyond the shale walls, "from Sangfoul. I am Evanshade of the guard of Sangfoul and servant of the Lord of the depths.

Three foreign men drifted in the currents before all Meridia, silver fish swirling before them, strapped in black and crimson hued whale hides. Pale, blue-skinned Venge beat his fin on the left, another blue-skinned man swam to the right and a black skinned man, draped with pointed teeth, floated between the two. This third was Evanshade. Fins pulsed where legs would normally be.

Nicholea had heard of black men beyond his waters but had never seen one before and until now was unsure he even believed in such a thing. Even with this newness, Evanshade's warm, mocha eyes looked into the Zhar's own, and a smile on the man's lips brought a trust into Nicholea. For Evanshade was one of those men to whom women found instant attraction and men found instant trust. Venge might be the wickedest youth in all the world's waters, but Nicholea saw something in Evanshade he connected with, a sort of seemingly gentle passion resting in those eyes.

"I am Nicholea, Meridia's Zhar, and this is my Zharista Alexandra, our son Ailoo and daughters Psyol and Lilya. We welcome you to Meridia with many curiosities of your race."

Nicholea's fins pulsed in the currents, drifting him close enough to touch Evanshade. The men of Sangfoul hovered still in the waters, and with the extension of the Zhar's massive yet gentle right hand, Evanshade and Nicholea shook.

"Tonight we shall feast in honor of the re-meeting of two brother races and talk much of our loves, passions and livelihoods Evanshade of Sangfoul. We shall revel and toast to new friendship. Come, to Cardonea Tower."

"Agreed. There is much about these waters I am curious to learn, my friend."

The two parties wove together as one as they swam in the depths through a murmuring wall of Meridians toward Cardonea Tower and its shimmering, reflecting, spherical rise. The goliath-like guards pushed back the hovering crowds for the royal family's protection as they swam.

High above in the tower Anna watched as her father came home, wondering who these half men, half fish beings were and what, if anything, they would come to mean to her life. A certain shame rippled through her because she had been so stubborn with her father about meeting the strangers. If the visitors remained in the tower as night came, she decided she would welcome them and apologize to her father.

* * *

Maanta heard a gruff rumble behind him as the procession neared. It was Sift, and he clasped a fist over Maanta's shoulder and dragged him backwards through the crowd. The boy's ears were battered by the collage of Meridians around him, being clipped and squeezed between them.

The crowd, after being hit first by Sift and then rammed by Maanta against his will, was torn about whether to look at the two's bizarre retreat or the procession of newcomers before them.

"...rumors...the time...too soon...enslaved...no...too soon...," Maanta caught Sift babbling before Maanta's neck twisted awkwardly back as the left side of his skull pounded against a hovering whale-bone chariot. His body ripped from Sift's grasp, swinging beneath the chariot and scattering the shimmering fish which had been carrying the vessel through the waters.

Maanta's merbody sunk toward the ocean's depths with the chariot above it crashing down toward him.

"A boy's trapped below that cart," someone in the gathering bellowed out. Others followed suit. A few in the mass dove to save him.

Sift's wrist and arm fins beat rapidly in the waters as he struggled to catch up. Water pressed his chest, as if attempting to weight him upwards as he swam. And in the corner of his eye he saw something glistening like a scale covered harpoon, jutting toward the cragged sands where Maanta would hit. The thing's back half beat through the waters, leaving a rippling effect behind as it went.

A humming sound resonated as the thing swept beneath the chariot, its back half bumping swiftly against the vessel's bottom.

Sift realized what it was, who the man was as it pulsed toward him swifter than any man of his race swam. His eyes locked Evanshade's stern, deep, peaceful eyes and recognized the fanged teeth worn across the man's necklace as he clasped the pale boy tightly in his arms. Something in Evanshade's face changed as the two men passed in the waters, a dark recognition, and then peacefulness retook his eyes.

The two knew each other from some place, some time, but here amongst the crowd both men knew nothing could be said or done. Like opposing magnetic fields their souls burned, separating them in opposite directions.

Sift swam quickly toward and amongst The East Shale Wall's darkened coves to bide his time.

Pockets of the crowd warmly cheered Evanshade as he returned to the Zhar's party with the pale Maanta resting limp in his arms.

5

Delving In

Cardonea Tower

A strangling, tense sensation struck Maanta's body as he struggled to consciousness, finding himself braced by seaweed to the walls of a spherical stone room.

Where am I? He found himself wondering, still groggy and half unconscious.

The last I remember before this, Zhar Nicholea was swimming with his family and strange men with fins for legs. Then Sift clasped onto my arm, dragging and pummeling me through a crowd.

"Ouch!" He murmured. A swollen bump on his head made him writhe with pain.

And then there was that white mass hurling towards me.

Maanta tugged with his wrists and ankles at his seaweed bonds until they wrested loose from the walls. His eyes began focusing upon illuminated bottles resting in and on the room's various nooks and shelving. A netting of pink and opal gems swayed gently along the room's upper stones. He was in a potions room, one reminding him much of Amaranth's own. He probably was being looked after for whatever had happened to him. But where was the healer? And then he realized the room's walls were the silvery white shade of the pillaring Cardonia Tower. Their hue glistened like that of reflecting pearl. Something must have happened out there with Sift and he had been taken here to heal.

Swiveling in the waters and cupping them in his finger-webs, Maanta swam toward the room's red door. With a push it swung outwards, causing foul waters in the outer halls to rivet past his lips and froth about in the back of his throat. He gagged at the taste. A deep red hue massaged the waters, clotting in the stone floor's crevices.

Maanta's stomach turned as a gurgling sound belched from beyond where he could see in the swirling halls. With swift scoops of his fingertips he swept over Cardonea Tower's master healer, his throat half slit and throbbing in the water. Blood rippled outwards in all directions as the man's eyes glossed over with red.

Maanta's stomach churned. A foul taste rose in his throat.

Something was terribly wrong in this tower, whether it had anything to do with the visitors Nicholea greeted outside the East and West Shale Walls, Sift or something unknown to Maanta. He shivered as he swept through the halls, hugging the ceiling and alert with his eyes wide open, racing to warn Nicholea.

The walls narrowed and widened as Maanta's fins pressed him forward, instincts of urgency searing through his tendons and mind as gutted, speared and even headless bodies of fellow Meridians wallowed and spasmed beneath him in the malta-stone lit halls. Their eyes rolled over with white as they quivered in death below him. Diving down a jutting, downward pathway, darkness swelled in, swallowing Maanta's sight.

Muffled through the walls somewhere close a woman howled in anguish. Maanta felt with his fingertips against the wall from where the noise had come; causing chilled, rough stone to scratch along his flesh. No doorway or opening emerged as the howls died off abruptly. Then down the hallway through the rippling waters a light swiveled up catching his eyes, fading away and dissipating back into darkness. A burnt scent wafting up through the waters from where the light flickered moments earlier rushed shivers across the boy's spine, like a dull knife point dragging across the back of the skull.

Waters washed along Maanta's eyes as he pushed farther through the darkness. The burnt, charred smell grew heavier, choking his throat. He wanted to stop, to find a hollow place in the pitch-black and curl up, outlasting whatever curse had befallen Cardonia Tower. But there would be no rest. The stench of bloody death had submerged itself in the liquid amongst these halls.

It's as if this bloody, burnt stench is itself searching out Cardonia Tower's life to wrench away from it, Maanta thought. *Possibly the dark one from the tales mother used to tell has possessed these waters with his vacant soul. Gelu help me know what to do.*

It was then in the darkness, a darkness which seemed like a deep chasm of dank eternity, that words Maanta's mother had taught him to speak to Gelu in his time of need, resonated in his mind.

"Gelu, who art in the world above," Maanta whispered softly as if to someone close by and yet at the same moment somehow far away. "Hallowed be thy name. By kingdom come thy will be done in the oceans as it is in thy loving heart. Give the ocean's people this day thy daily fish and forgive us our trespasses as we forgive those who trespass against us. Lead us not into temptation, but deliver us from evil. For thine is the kingdom, and the power, and the glory forever and ever. My love to you Lord. Amen."

Maybe it was how the prayer brought him fond memories of his mother's smiles and caring ways of life or maybe it was Gelu himself answering Maanta's prayer, but warmth flowed over him now. He had to press on through the tower in hopes of helping others who might be in need.

And so he swept, quickly swirling with his fins, down the weaving hall of darkness until it opened to a wide room where the burning stench smelled strongest. Maanta couldn't see the room through the darkness, but as he swam he had hugged the walls, watching them expand upon reaching the vast, open space.

Here the waters were warm, almost boiling warm, and a glowing, crimson orb lit the room faintly from the floor deep below him. Maanta dove quickly toward the shimmering light, touching the orb upon reaching it, he recoiled in burning pain. The thing, the size of Maanta's own head, bubbled with molten rock much like the Malta stones he used to simmer fish over in his cove home, but with an intensity and heat far greater than he'd seen such a thing have before.

As the crimson sphere boiled below him, spitting out rank, gaseous fumes, Maanta noticed an age weathered plaque melting in on itself on the molten mass's side.

"BE WARNED," it read, "Molten Flare only for use in dire situations. Gases may be poisonous, but light and stench should attract attention and rescue efforts. Apply a stone mask to your face upon Molten Stone cracking."

Well this stench certainly isn't ignorable, Maanta thought. *I wonder who sent the signal.*

A thought came over him. *What if this is a trap to draw forth any survivors of the massacre? Will this poison kill me or is someone here, waiting in the darkness for the right moment to run me through with their trident?*

A beastly fist, the size of the boy's body if it was rolled into a ball, clenched around Maanta's waist and slammed him against a massive, hard surface hovering in the waters feet away.

Two massive, red eyes, encompassed by what appeared to be a giant's head, slowly pressed in to vision before him, lit by the luminous malta light.

"Silence boy," it lowly whispered. "You're the one they saved outside the tower today aren't you?"

Maanta nodded his head, assuming something like that had happened. His back ached from the collision with whatever the giant's hand was pressing him against.

The giant's eyes blinked slowly in the waters, and a look of sadness came over its features.

"Evanshade, and the other beings with a fin where their legs should be, swam to the tower's meeting hall with Nicholea." His voice deepened while telling his story. It was scratchy as if the tale pained him. "Nicholea had instructed me and the other guards to watch over the family as they spoke in case anything went wrong, and a feast of sea spiced crab was served. The Zhar and the royal family sat in their seaweed hammocks as they told tales of Meridea's past to the foreigners.

"It was intriguing to watch the foreigners' faces as they listened to the tales of our ancestry. While Nicholea told of Noa, the tale of how our people once lived in the world above the waters and about how and why we were punished and forced to live beneath the water's beating waves, Evanshade's eyes flickered with light and a convulsion of the mind could be seen in his features."

The gargantuan sea guard's Adam's apple gulped deeply in his throat. His eyelids shut as bloody bubbles gurgled through his lips.

"And then we slaughtered them."

*

Dusk, earlier that day...

Sift's fin muscles ached, burned as he swam along The East Shale Wall's darkened crevices further and further away from Evanshade and closer to his destination. Had he been recognized by Evanshade? He swept on for leagues in the depths, darting glances behind him, expecting to find he had been followed, and expecting to find at any moment the pangs of death upon him. A burning, tingling pulse swept through his ankle and wrist fins causing them to go numb and cease beating in exhaustion. His body careened into a rugged stone outcropping before him, sweeping him in a tumbling swirl beneath the stone ledge.

Sift cursed himself, knowing he had become so out of shape relying on Lola to take him everywhere. Where was she? He had sent her away as he and Maanta had neared the crowds surrounding Cardonia Tower, but why hadn't she sensed something was wrong with him? Surely she'd come searching for him, wanting to be by his side.

As he caressed his leg fins with his massive black hands, Sift mentally willed them to beat again. In the aquatic, light blue daylight something shimmered in a small cove room above him in The East Shale Wall. Sift saw this and his thoughts warmed. This was where he had been swimming toward vigorously.

There was only a small distance farther to go, and then there would be someone he could share his thoughts with, no matter how dreadful he knew those thoughts to be. As the pulse of his fins moved him briskly in the waters toward the small Meridian wall home, something bumped hard into his back.

He swirled in the waters in nervous anticipation. A large, slim, colorful fish stared back.

"Lola!" His low voice bounded out into the waters as he wrapped his large arms around her scaly body.

The fish nudged him lovingly with her head, a look like a smile shining in her glimmering, emerald eyes. Sift then clasped his hands upon the gripping stones along Lola's back, caressing her scales as he sat, and the two swept together through the waters toward the shale cove home close by.

As they came upon the opening Lola swirled slightly below it, as she was too large to enter. With the beating of his fins Sift raised upwards, hovering into the home of a sapphire blue skinned, gangly, old man who scampered to and fro from kelp parchment to kelp parchment covering the cove's walls. The man's slim fingers swept along lines written upon them. A light blue glow lit gently in his eyes.

"They've arrived Amaranth," Sift spoke quickly to the man.

"I thought we had more time," the gangly man replied. "I've found nothing written amongst our scholars' kelp scrolls or the scripts of before our time telling of another race with serpentine fins where legs should be. You said there would be more time before their coming."

"Tail fins they have must allow them to move quicker than us. Arrived have they as three, without fish or whales to pull them along. If these beings can move with swiftness as such then perhaps many others upon us could be before even night falls." Sift himself cringed as the words crept along his lips. These had been the same beings who held him in captive enslavement years before. He knew the wrath their tortures reaped on the body and then on the mind for years afterwards, as in his own mind.

"In speaking to you last night told you I did of the young boy in my tribe who spied on their race for us, telling us of their plans to slaughter and enslave Meridia."

"Yes," Amaranth replied, seeing there was more in the man's eyes he had to tell.

"What was spoken not from my lips to your ears was of the enslavement all of my people have endured in times before this. Our tribe is a tribe of escapees from their oceanic enslavement camps.

"This mark," Sift swirled around indicating the eye branding singed upon his back, "is the evil ones' marking of ownership they have of us. They keep my race in nets when using them not, to mine resources from the molten rock along the ocean crust. As elderly grow old and feeble, often the evil ones' skewer flesh of theirs with tridents and press them up against the lava crevices, laughing as the flesh of our elders boils and simmers into the life-swallowing molten walls.

"Such peaceful a civilization as Meridia, no army or history of war having had, is doomed. Little time is there left. As many Meridians as possible must be warned and brought to our tribe's waters where learn they can the ways of battle to retake their waters."

"To convince my people to leave their home waters, where many have never ventured beyond, will be difficult." Amaranth's eyes glowed a dark blue now. "Much of Meridia knows and trusts me though, and so there is hope of convincing many Meridians to follow.

"There is just one thing. A person of noir skin such as yourself has never ventured into our depths and many would be wary to follow you. They could even fear you and instead place their trust in the serpent-finned beings. Possibly for now I should gather up my fellow Meridians and lead them to meet you further off in the waters depths."

"Very well, but my people all noir skinned are, and yours are blue except for the young Maanta from what I've seen. Deal we must with this in time. Where do we meet?"

"Do you know of any place close to these waters?"

"Believe I Maanta called it Orion's Birth, a place along the outskirts of Meridia where oxygen bubbles boil beneath the ocean floor, rising through a stone temple toward the crest of the waters above. I've seen it from a distance and easily could I find it again."

"Our people," Amaranth cringed, "are scared of that place. It is sacred because it is said that is where we descended through the waters when Gelu shunned us from the land and air above. We are connected to Gelu there more than anywhere else in these depths. But people fear the 'forbidden fluid' air, which bubbles up from the earth there. They believe that because it is what our ancestors breathed in the world above, it will suffocate us.

"I will meet you there before darkness falls tomorrow with as many Meridians as will follow me but only outside the stone chapel's walls. They will not enter where the forbidden fluid swells and ripples towards the ocean surface."

"Agreed. And then I will lead you to my lands where best can we plan how to help Meridia. Hurt was Maanta while we were fleeing the crowds surrounding the serpent finned peoples' arrival, and taken to Cardonea Tower for healing. Surely danger he is in there. Try will I to find him and bring him to reunite with us."

"Take great care of him, Sift. He has a unique heart and at times is like a grandson to me."

"I will. Until meet we again, my friend."

"Something tells me that this day, when we remember it, will seem like leagues of time away. A grievous darkness is cloaking itself upon us."

6

Meridia Adrift

Cardonea Tower, in the darkness

The Present

Blood curdled from the sea guard's lips and a wound upon his side as he gripped Maanta tightly in his goliath fist. Bloody tears swept above the man's eyelids and filtered off into the darkness of the huge castle room's waters.

"I felt Evanshade's eyes scavenging inside my mind as Nicholea told him all about our people and our world. Evanshade's mind caged me in mine." The guard's eyes convulsed. "There were four of us there, enough guards to protect our Zhar and his family, enough to kill them. My fist lifted first, moving as if controlled by something beyond me, and clenched upon Nicholea's throat. I could feel the base of his skull poke against my hand as it cracked like a shell in my fist, and yet his eyes still moved and he still managed to gurgle out to his family 'swim.'

"Orachus, another guard, thrust a rod of iron in the Zharista's spine and bent her backwards with his fists, cracking her in two. Orpan and Falink, the other two guards, broke off the children's limbs before Nicholea as he wriggled for freedom in my grasp. All the while Evanshade and his company smiled on the Zhar as if taunting him from across the room.

My soul died as I watched my own hand forcing Nicholea to watch the death of his family. And then my left hand rose, clasping my sword, and swept through his neck, slicing it and beheading him with such force that the iron lodged through my armor and into my side. The decapitated body slumped as the head spun in the waters. I could feel Evanshade letting loose my mind but somehow I could not regain control of my body.

"The boy, Venge, then prodded us with a poison tipped spear, his eyes flickering as he did so and as my mind slipped to darkness. Venge ground his sharp, fanged teeth together creating a shrill noise like bone on a shale wall. They left us for dead, off possibly to pillage Cardonea Tower or Meridia itself, but I awoke.

"I formed the light of the chamber's giant malta shell to draw someone here, to tell them this."

"What?" Maanta asked.

"She never came to greet them and no-one mentioned her name so the foreign ones do not know." The guard swung his hand toward a hole in the wall. "Out that window and off into another one close by, Meridea's new Zharista, Anna, lives."

The guard's fist loosed Maanta and his body went limp in the waters, as if he had completed destiny and now could rest in the afterlife. As Maanta swept toward the window he looked back at the dead guard whose body had been used to mutilate his own Zhar. There in the murky, red darkness the bodies of eight others clung to the room's corners as the limbs of the children floated past, limply in the current.

*

Anna's eyes shimmered in her room's reflective shell mirror as she looked upon herself glistening from head to toe in sparkling jewels and the highest quality oceanic kelp fabric.

"I'll go," she spoke to herself. "If this is what Papa wants then I'll go to the festival hall tonight with him and meet the newcomers after they've finished with all the formalities. But I'll keep a watchful eye on them, too."

She clipped her hair together in the back with her yellow hair clip and went to dab on eye colorings while looking close into her reflection.

Thud!

A noise sounded against her door.

Thud!

"I'll be out soon Papa," Anna responded thinking Nicholea had come to get her for the festivities.

Silence. Anna slipped gem-covered rings upon her toes.

Thud! Thud! The noise came again.

"Coming Papa!" As she spun toward the stone door Anna peered out at the night waters. Light beams from far above skipped across the waters and oceanic floor. Her memories took her to when she was younger and would play tag with her father, pretending that if you swam into the light then you would be "it." She always knew though that if she swam into the light, all she'd have to do was give her father a certain smile that she had perfected well to melt his heart and he would agree to be "it" once more.

Anna's hand gripped the door's stone handle firmly and as she opened it, her skin chilled. Nicholea's red bearded head, wrinkled, bloodily mutilated and bodiless, thumped against the door. Minute globules spewed from it into the currents.

Murky crimson washed through the door's opening as Anna felt her heart stop and then beat rapidly.

Somewhere in the distance she heard someone calling for her, some noise attempting to get her attention. Her knowledge of this noise swept away as quickly as it had come.

"NO!" She screeched, tearing gems from her shimmering garments in horrified anger. "NOOO!" She swept into the hall to search out the rest of her family, and if not for them then for revenge.

The person who called for her before made himself known again but was ignored. Anna's fins whipped faster then she'd ever moved them before as her pastel blue body draped in jewels cut forward through red murk toward her mother's quarters.

Darkness swelled in from the walls as she swept the corridors. The stench of death lingered in her nostrils as bodies of others she had once shared the tower with hovered before and behind her path.

Anna's torso and legs pumped up and down for speed. Faster and faster the darkness swept past, a turn, a twist, more darkness. Pearls, inlayed within the shale walls, watched her like eyes glimmering through the pitch.

Something beckoned softly from the darkness for her, a beast she thought, come to bring death. It bit at her heels causing her to convulse and loose herself of its grasp.

A pearl white hand grasped her shoulder as she moved in the currents. The pale opaque ghost was somehow comforting. Why was she not afraid of it she wondered? Where had she seen it before?

"They're dead. Your family is dead." Its slim, pale webbed fingers loosed her arm as it spoke.

*

Deep within the darkness of one of Cardonea Tower's halls Maanta first was attracted to the Zharista's beauty. Even traumatized and delusional from the shock of her father's death, Anna's deep emerald eyes carried a kind of knowledge and truth which caught him in a blush. Her pale blue skin reminded him of the sky in the world above, which he had seen once upon daring to venture close towards the ocean's surface. He could love her, Maanta realized in that moment, but what she needed now was a friend.

"Ghost," she whispered at him, shutting herself off from realities. "I saw you the night before the strangers came, traveling with the dark skinned man, dark skin just like the leader of the strangers. You are an apparition, come to save my family, but now have found there's only me."

"Zharista I..." Maanta began.

"The Zharista is my mother, Ghost; I am still merely the daughter of the Zhar."

"I am not a ghost. I am a boy, a Meridian boy who somehow woke up inside this tower which seems to be wrapped in chaos. One of your family's guards described to me how your family was murdered. He led me to you and told me you were alive."

"If you're not an apparition then how did you find me amongst this labyrinth of halls?"

It hasn't been easy, he thought to himself.

"I saw you open your door as I swam through your window to warn you about the massacre. When I called to you, you wouldn't listen and I've been following you through the darkness, bellowing out your name, ever since."

Anna pursed her lips at him and whispered, "Ghost."

Well if she thinks I'm a ghost, he thought, *then so be it. We've got to get out of here before the foreigners come through again and discover us.*

"Maanta's my name, not Ghost, but no matter who you think I am we need to leave this tower and find safety."

"Why didn't you appear in time to save my family, Ghost? We're all dead you know, slaughtered."

There isn't time for this now, Maanta thought as his webbed hand clasped on her arm's soft skin. *We have to escape.*

To where, he didn't know, but the muscles in his pale limbs flexed while adrenaline fueled the escape. At first Anna's weight was a strain on his body, but after a few whale's lengths she began to swim on her own behind him as if she were in a trance just mimicking his movements. Anna's eyes stared blankly ahead.

Maanta found the darkness and gore numbing as he rushed toward Anna's window and the end of it all, or toward clean waters at-least. His skin pricked, while the hollow echo of nothing but their own movements resonated in his ears. It was too silent. Such a tremendous tragedy was occurring and yet the waters stood calm. And then a soft yet distant sound, something like the cooling of molten lava crept into his ears.

"Ssssssss," A noise came from the end of the corridor behind them as they neared Anna's room.

Maanta swirled to look back on a slim, tailfinned boy, and his burning red eyes illuminating the dark. Venge had been searching the tower for anyone still living. Anna faced her doorway while hovering, as if trapped in ambivalence.

"More fun for me," Venge grinned.

In the time it takes for a breath to elapse his tail swooshed in the waters and covered the spans between them. Ripples rolled over on themselves behind him as he thrust a spear toward Maanta.

Maanta dodged it, feeling the cold, gray tip barely catch in his shoulder while zipping past.

He's fast, Maanta realized, *quicker than any Meridian.*

Maanta turned to flee, grasping Anna's arm and barreling toward her room, but looming above them was the fang-toothed Venge. He dove and clasped his fist upon Anna's throat, raising it towards his sharp fangs to gnaw into her. Cracking, his lips stretched along his teeth.

Swirling and then thrusting his legs into Venge, Maanta retaliated before Anna could be bitten. Venge dove for Maanta and grabbed the back of his skull, plunging his face toward the bottom of the cragged stone hall.

And then in the back of Maanta's sight, something dark swept in from the window, thrashing Venge's side, somersaulting his body sideways against a flowing kelp tapestry depicting the anointing of the first Zhar. Venge let loose Maanta's hair as he was hit.

As Maanta turned towards the scene above him a large noir skinned man floated, fists ready, glaring with dark hatred at the fang-toothed Venge.

"Sift, isn't it?" The fanged one questioned while licking his own blood from his lips. "How did you escape?"

"He let me out." The runes across Sift's body illuminated as he answered.

"Who?" The red in Venge's eyes curled.

"Someone whose soul, darkened has become, since then. That is all," Slowly Sift drifted forward. "Which one are you?"

"I am Venge, the son of the dark one. You know the one I speak of. He wants you, you and all these dirty mutts to enslave," A white fire burned in the center of the boy's eyes.

"You, your father and your entire race, meet you will, your ends and face Gelu one day, boy. I pray a hand in it I will have." Sift swept swiftly toward Venge but the boy whipped his tailfin once and was gone, lost in the darkness.

"Sssssssss…" The boy hissed while swimming away.

Pursuing Venge wasn't an option for Sift, Maanta realized, to do so would be to leave him and Anna alone again and who knew what else might find them in this darkness.

"Are you harmed, young Maanta?" Sift questioned.

"My neck is a little sore, but aside from that all seems to be well. How did you find me?"

"Your dolphin scented you out and led me to you. Beyond the window is where she waits."

Just beyond Anna's window Maanta could barely make out Archa's smooth, bobbing head, her eyes looking for him over her sleek nose, waiting patiently for him to join her.

It seemed to Maanta as if he had a question for every moment which had passed since he had last seen Sift. How did he get to Cardonea Tower? What had happened to him to put him in the potions room? Who was Venge? How did Sift know the boy's father? Did the chaos in Meridia have anything to do with why Sift had come here? There were so many more questions.

Maanta looked into Sift's heavy eyes. His posture shrank as a look of weariness overcame him.

"Who is your female companion?" Sift asked. He swam before her and glanced upon her blank stare. "She looks as if mentally in another place."

"Angel," Anna whispered, jutting her head forward as she did so, waving crimson curly locks too and fro. Her soft blue fingertips lifted to Sift's cheeks, "of death."

"At least you're an Angel," Maanta remarked sarcastically as Sift turned to him in wonderment. "She thinks I'm a ghost who came to save her family. She watched us as we arrived the other night and I guess you're the angel of death. She's delusional."

"Clearly. Whose family is she of?"

"Zhar Nicholea's, and they're all dead except her, slaughtered at the hands of their own guards as the foreigners possessed the guards' minds. She's Zharista now but won't believe it."

"And disillusion possesses the mind which is hers because of this?"

"That and because she found out about it when discovering the Zhar's decapitated head knocking upon her door."

"Such shame is it that ones as young as you and she should such harsh death witness. And no time there is to rest, to work from her this madness. We must escape Meridea's misfortune and meet with Amaranth within the outskirts Orion's Birth."

Maanta gusted to the waters before Sift and Anna now. "How do you know of Amaranth? What have you been hiding from me?"

"Not hiding have I been anything. Thought I that there would be more time before the dark ones would arrive to explain that which has been happening. Our night of arrival I sought out Amaranth and spoke with him of the coming foreigners and possible danger which they might bring. One of our own people once knew him and spoke to me to confide in him first. This is why I came, to warn your people, but we underestimated the dark ones' speed."

"Who are they, Sift?"

"They are the race who enslave my people young, Maanta. Evanshade, the one who led them here, seared my back with the marking of the eye himself."

"And how did I get to Cardonea Tower?"

"There is no time. I will speak all you wish to know to you as we flee this place but Meridia is dying and the dark ones are searching for others to bring death to."

Anna's eyes grew large. "Death! Take me to the waters of the un-living, Angel, where I might find my family."

Maanta could feel irritation building inside himself, lost in this madness with a beautiful girl who wouldn't believe the truth. "He's not an angel of death and I'm not a ghost!" He rolled his eyes over at Sift. "We'll leave along the darkened crevices along the bottom of The West Shale Wall. I used to sneak away that way once night fell, as a youth before my mother passed. I can ride Archa and you Lola but how will we bring Anna?"

"Ghost," Anna whispered. "You are not needed. You have failed my family and I must travel with Death now."

Maanta smiled. "I think I'll come along, thanks."

Sift looked to Maanta as he spoke in a low voice, his eyes reminding the boy not to show rudeness to the Zharista, as he might regret it once she woke from her spell. "She can be braced in front of me while riding Lola. Lola has strength enough to carry both."

The waters beyond Anna's window seemed to breathe a frosty chill over the tower as the three passed through it and onto their journey. Archa's smooth head and back slid beneath Maanta as he led them. She dove swiftly down the tower towards the oceanic coral flora below. Its rough, colorful foliage wove about the tower as they met it and dove amongst its labyrinth of crevices.

Lola's delicate, shimmering scales whipped along the tower's outer wall as she met Sift who pulled himself upon her, embracing Anna closely in front of him, and nudged the massive fish downward after Maanta.

As Sift joined him, Maanta gazed through a webbing of holes in the orange coral above his eyes' sight. Cardonea Tower's slim spindle of glowing silvery white rose above toward the ocean's surface. *I've always thought of this as the iris of a great eye watching and protecting the waters close by,* Maanta thought. *Now it resembles more a great worm fleeing for the births above.*

Tail finned creatures swept o'er the tower's shimmering radiance, dark silhouettes across the oceanic night-lights above. Some stabbed at silhouettes of Meridians with things unseen. Others swept in and out of the tower's entrances, pillaging its valuables. Silhouettes of Meridians also hovered, slain faceless blotches, speckling the waters above.

"They swept in." Sift turned to him while the party wove amongst the coral and kelp weavings toward the dark hollow crevices of The West Shale Wall. "As darkness fell, a tsunami of tail finned men swept o'er The East and West Shale Walls, pillaging the home coves and bringing death to your people. I told Amaranth of Evanshade's arrival and so he warned fellow Meridians who trusted him, fleeing with them before the brutalities, but so many were lost."

"AaaaaHoooo," Maanta cupped his mouth close to Archa's ear hole telling her to scoop within the West Shale Wall's crevices from the vibrant coral.

Three dark walls surrounded them as they looked toward the waters and tower they fled. Barely visible stone whipped by in the darkness.

"What will we do?" Emptiness and vulnerability swelled within Maanta. He had never felt a strong attachment to Meridia or his fellow Meridians after his mother had died, but now that his world appeared to slip beyond his grasp, Maanta found a love for things he had been distancing himself from. He had always reveled in nature, sounds, scents and his own daydreams but overlooked the city's workings themselves. He began missing the burnt scent of the Meridian water heaters as they fed kelp to the molten pit along the oceanic floor beneath his cove home. He thought of the market place with its hovering food and craft stands, the Meridians laughing, talking or sometimes grumbling while bumping into one another as they shopped. Who would feed the small fish who begged for scraps now that the Meridians were leaving?

Sixteen years had passed in his lifetime, barely enough to experience all he should experience here, Maanta thought.

"Things, your people will learn from us, and together both our peoples shall retake your realm," Sift spoke. "Do not fear my friend, we will retake Meridia and come to the single finned ones' place of living also to un-slave my brethren."

But what of the things they've taken from us for all time?
Maanta thought. *What of Anna's family? What of our way of life?*
Will the things that made us happy ever be here again? Will we even
experience the same sorrows we once did?

While sweeping closer toward Meridia's outskirts,
Maanta noticed a young girl about his age pressing her slim
back along the wall's darkness. Her eyes glared out towards
the city's center with an alertness flickering in them.

"Young one!" Sift bellowed to her. "We're leaving the
city to meet others. Come with us and a rescuing you will find
from these tortures which have befallen Meridia."

Maanta recognized her then. "Illala," he called out. "It's
Maanta from your classes at Meridian Hearth School. Come
with us. They're destroying Meridia. There's nothing left for
us here."

"I'll come if you'll have me but first I must tell you
something."

"There can't be anything that would make us leave you
behind. Hurry. We must escape before being seen."

"I was sleeping when the scale tailed creatures dove
through the holes in my family's cove home walls," Illala said.
"I awoke to the wails of my mother in the other room as they
tortured her. My brother and father were then choked in the
waters outside our cove, where I discovered them while
escaping, blood spewing from their lips.

"Their leader came to the back room where I had been
resting after he was done with my father. His dark skin shone
as his deep eyes looked upon me. He could see the fear in my
eyes and at the same time an attraction to me could be seen
within his. Whispers then brushed through his lips.

"'I told my men your death would come at the hand of
me alone, young woman; but fear not I have no intentions of
relinquishing such beauty. You must scream though and act
as if I have seized the life from your soul. My name is
Evanshade,' he said. 'Remember me.'

"I shivered, as I feared him and what he had done to my family, and yet somehow felt attracted to him at the same time. How could this man who was rescuing me be the same who sabotaged Meridia and ended my families' lives? 'AHHHHH!' I screamed.

"I escaped once they left and have been watching him and his people with fear and wonderment ever since."

"How could you be attracted to a man who slaughtered your family and is destroying our home?" Maanta's stomach churned. Did he even want someone with any feeling but hatred for the tail finned men with him? Could someone like her possibly turn on them someday and even bring Evanshade to them? A look in Sift's eyes told Maanta that Sift knew what he was thinking.

Anna sat like a doll, wordless and staring forward, in front of Sift on Lola's back.

Sift spoke to Illala. "There is something in this Evanshade's eyes, young one, which brings the emotions of trust and love. Know not I why he has spared you but make no mistaking him anything but an evil being. Also scorn yourself not for feeling longing for him, for he has entranced many with his stare before. It matters not how you feel. If you wish it, you will find a welcoming to our journeying party."

"Thank you for your understanding. What was your name, sir?" Illala asked.

"Sift, Miss, a pleasure to meet you."

"I'll join you," A high-pitched whistle leapt through Illala's lips as a small fish a fourth of Lola's height and length swam from coral weavings nearby. It nudged the girl's fingertips playfully. "And Lisaly shall carry me. I must confess though part of why I'm agreeing to leave so willingly is because I see there will be safeness with your group and yet you seem to have much you could tell me of the beings of Evanshade's race."

"There is certainly much to share with you and all Meridians, young one, and all you wish to ask I will answer," Sift spoke. "We must flee now though, as surely the single finned ones will find and be upon us if lingering in Meridia we are."

A boom careened through the waters as shards of stone flicked from the Shale Wall opposite them where the intruders blasted through its' storage chambers. Startled by the sudden noise, Archa swept forward toward the city's outskirts.

"That settles it," Maanta smiled and looked back towards his companions following swiftly in pursuit. He wove his arm as if daring them to catch up. *Hopefully Sift's right to trust her,* he thought. *To leave someone I've known behind when she needed us would lead to a dark descent of the mind, but bringing her with us could prove a decision defeating the purpose of our escape.*

Archa, Lisaly and Lola hugged tightly to the wall as they swept toward Meridia's ominous city border, their riders clinging close upon their backs. The cool waters rushing past played and swiveled upon Maanta's webbed fingertips reminding him of days when he'd drift through the city with Archa, off venturing toward the unknown.

Here's an adventure I never thought we would experience together Archa, he thought. *How bizarre that so many of our adventures were to escape Meridia and now we embark on one to hopefully someday retake this place.*

Sheens of light rippled along the pale skinned boy sweeping away from Meridea's Eye, Cardonea Tower and The East and West Shale Walls. As he sped toward Orion's Birth to reunite with his people, the boy didn't turn to see his home and the destruction befalling it.

I'll think of it the way it was before the tail finned beings came, he thought. *And our people will return to reclaim this land and bring it to the way it once was.*

The company swept onward and at the tail of them all a girl, Illala, looked back not upon Meridia but desiring a man whose eyes were Evanshade's.
*

Two crimson eyes glared upon them from a dark area in the kelp and coral woven flora, silently following.

7

Adrift

Waters far outside Meridia

As dark night lingered on in the depths the small company found the exhaustion of an emotionally wearying day weighing on their bodies and minds. More then once Maanta's eyelids succumbed to heaviness as his mind slipped into temporary sleep, only to be jostled awake by the feeling of slipping backwards off Archa's back into the water's currents.

Through squinted eyes upon awakening from the short rest the third or forth time, he couldn't remember, Maanta noticed something which brought warmth to him. A sleek stone outcropping jutted up from the oceanic floor below them. His heart jumped with happiness as he recognized it as one of the places he had discovered and rested in on his wanderings with Archa outside Meridia.

"Here we can rest in security!" He called back to his companions, knowing they could use a break before continuing. *More then anything I need a break,* he thought. *I'm the only one who knows the way and if I keep falling asleep on Archa like this we'll never get there.*

A puzzled look crept upon Illala's face. "We'll be safe in the open ocean next to a smooth stone mound? Maanta what do you take us for? Shouldn't we just continue to Orion's Birth?"

"Things often are not as they do seem in the waters beyond the realms of oceanic dwellings," Sift turned to her. "Something is telling me Maanta's stone twill be a blessing quite worth relishing."

"I've explored all of these depths," Maanta continued. "I know their bearings and their secrets. Follow me."

He nudged Archa's smooth gray side with his left foot and dove swiftly with her to the far bottom of the stone hill. Floating from her back he scooped his body downward toward the place where the stone appeared to meet with kelp along the sea floor. Sift and Illala were close behind. Anna sat poised, eyes closed, upon Lola.

Maanta's webbed fingertips pried at the seaweed upon the stone revealing an opening a little more then the height and width of Archa.

"Because of how smooth and stern the stone looks no-one will suspect a secret opening in the bottom of it and there is room enough for all but Lola inside." Maanta saw a hungry expression lingering in Sift's eyes. "And small cavern crabs dwell within also."

There would be no better place, they agreed, to rest before continuing on to Orion's Birth. Any of the single-finned beings who came searching would hardly recognize Lola if she rested close by to the stone mound. She could also serve as a watcher to warn them if need be.

"Watch out for giant octopi," Sift grinned as he stripped Lola of her riding garb, so she would appear to be an ordinary fish, and patted her scales.

Archa and Lisaly swept beneath the stone elegantly before their riders. Illala followed closely and then Sift, with Anna mimicking his movements, followed him.

"It's beautiful!" Maanta could hear Illala exclaiming from inside. "And warm."

Sheer black darkness swept around him as he himself entered. He curled his body back to re-cover the opening with kelp and then swam along in the pitch dark. A turn here, a turn there and the water began to warm. A glowing hot-molten light shimmered up from the room below him where the others were already getting comfortable. A small lava stream swept within the room. Maanta knew that the others would like that. This place provided warmth, food and a kind of comforting temporary home for the night rest.

Sift formed a net from kelp and rustled up crustaceans from the cave. He placed them in it and they simmered over the flowing molten stream. The creatures popped and sizzled while changing to a dark rust color. Sift's massive hands plucked the first critter from its net cooking chamber.

"Scrumptious," he exclaimed after crunching on the first one, savoring its' salty-sweet taste as it fell upon the taste buds.

Maanta and Illala partook of the small morsels while Sift snapped the shell from one of the crustaceans and swam towards Anna.

"Here." He held the food up for her to eat. "Exhausted you must be after all that has happened today."

She stared at him blankly, her precious emerald eyes looking gently into his. "I am dead. And soon I will join my family. There is no need to eat, no reason to nourish a soul without life."

"You are not dead," Sift said to her. "Men from foreign lands, slaughtered have they your family and brought destruction upon your world, but life there still beats in your chest. Literal death hath not yet come and mental death can only arrive if giving in you are to its' callings. Together we will survive this tragedy which befalls us. Vibrant life there will be once more if faith and time you give the world to repair its misfortunes."

"How can I live without my family? What kind of existence is that?" She asked.

"They are with you in spirit, young one, and always will be. I too have lost my family. My mother, I never knew; and I myself saw the father which is mine murdered by the same race of creatures who have come to your Meridia. I know not much of your people's 'one God' Gelu. But my race has its own religion and we believe that as death takes the relatives and friends which are ours, their souls travel as kin with our own souls, protecting us until we ourselves meet death. Sometimes they act as spirits to protect us. You see, to me my father and your family are with us here in this hidden cavern, providing us the loving strength needed to see us through."

The light of hope sparked in Anna's eyes as he spoke of this. "We believe that Gelu is always with us much like that and that our dead look down at us from a place called heaven, a beautiful place where the waters and souls swim clean and pure. Do you know your religion to be true?"

Sift smiled, happy to see Anna returning to her senses. "In truth I know very little but it is what I believe and where I place my faith. I feel my father with me when I'm sad. Possibly the truth lies somewhere between what is our religion and yours. Possibly it is the same in different words."

"Whatever the truth is thank you for helping bring hope to this day of misery." Anna cupped a crustacean in her fingers and passed it through her lips, enjoying the simple delicacy. "Thank you for helping rescue me."

The two swam toward Maanta and Illala, taking turns reaching within the kelp net web and savoring the remaining edibles.

As they floated along the cavern walls that night, preparing to enter the night's world of dreams, Maanta looked to his companions, a group of friends of circumstance. What would this makeshift tribe experience together, he wondered? How were the rest of Meridia's survivors reacting?

"I'm sorry," Maanta whispered to Anna who was floating close by. He thought her precious red hair flowing in the calm current was so beautiful. "I shouldn't have been rude to you back in the tower."

"Don't worry about it." Anna opened her eyes to look upon him. He was handsome, she thought, in a quirky kind of way. "I barely remember any of what happened between us back there. Thank you for finding me."

Even then when you were distraught, you were beautiful, Maanta thought but couldn't bring himself to tell her. Surely she wouldn't want to hear things like that on a day like this.

"You seemed like you weren't yourself and I didn't have any patience with you."

"How dare you!" She smiled. "You were worried about being found out and killed and you didn't take the time to coax me from whatever distortion my mind was going through. I tell you, the next time you've gone loopy and we're being pursued I won't take the time to reason with you either. Deal?"

"Deal!" He felt a little better now after Anna's little bout of sarcasm.

From across the warm cavern Sift opened an eye as he listened in to the young ones getting to know each other.

"Where did you live in our waters?" Anna asked.

"I lived with my mother along The East Shale Wall before she passed and I never knew my father. He died of a heart sickness before my birthing. And so as they are both now gone I live along The East Shale wall alone, or I guess I did until today." Something about being there with her took the harshness of that reality temporarily away. "I love our Meridia. Do you know, I never realized how the peace we experienced there was so valuable until today."

Tears from Anna's eyes drifted into the waters. "Father always said that peace and love were treasures worth more than any other. He always did his best to provide us with that world we had in Meridia I think. And yet here we find ourselves being pushed to warring times without the peace he provided."

"Zhar Nicholea was a fantastic man." Maanta looked to her. "At least there is one thing that he valued that those beings cannot take from us - love. We can carry a love for all things with us wherever we go. He nurtured that in your family and our culture and we must remember to hold on to that and remind our people of its importance when we reunite with them."

Sift grinned from across the room as he recognized maturity in the boy's words. He knew that would help Maanta to survive the troublesome times to come.

Something inside Maanta was yearning to change the subject, wanting to find a topic fun but simple, to get to know Anna better with. The day had been tragic but surely the night didn't have to end like that.

"Have you ever seen the daylight twinkling down from the ocean's crest as it rises in the morning, in the waters beyond Meridia?" He asked figuring she had probably spent most of her life within the city walls like most Meridians.

"I've only ever seen the sunrise from Cardonea Tower." She smiled. "Why? Are you telling me the sunrises are different out here?"

"Oh they're so much more beautiful out here. The molten heaters within The East and West Shale walls cause the waters above Meridia to filter off some of the rising daylight. The rising daylight colors are vibrant and crisp beyond the walls."

"Do you think we could awaken in time to watch the next morning's sunrise?" She asked.

"Young ones, time for resting it has become," Sift called from across the room before closing his eyes to sleep. He decided he would enjoy a little bit of the pestering adult role. Never having children of his own, maybe he would take these orphaned three under his wing and attempt to teach them ways of the world they'd not yet known. "The morn will soon arrive and no rest will you have found."

Anna's crimson locks drift gently. "Would you want to?" She whispered.

"That sounds enchanting," Maanta whispered back. "Good night."

"Good night."

And the two held hands while closing their eyes and letting the world of dreams sweep them away.

A duet of deep crimson eyes seared the waters as they scoured the depths near the stone hiding-place, searching out their prey. Lola scuttled beyond the sight of the eyes' grasp behind a patch of coral in the waters.

* * *

"Anna," Maanta shook her gently in the waters as he whispered to her. "Wake up it's time for the daylight's rising."

"What?" She mumbled, still sleepy eyed. "There's no sun. It's so dark."

"We have to go now if we want to catch the lights as they arrive to the waters."

"Ok," Anna whispered, a little more awake now. "Should we wake Sift and Illala?"

"Let them rest. We'll come back for them." Maanta dove below to where the molten stream wove across the cavern floor and plucked a few leftover crustaceans from the cooking net they were heated in the night before. Anna wove a comb Sift had taken from her room through her hair while Maanta munched on the first of the crunchy morsels. "Want some?" He held them out to her as she took two and ate them.

Anna and Maanta swam and wove their bodies through the dark pathway connecting the cavern to the outer waters. They searched for the entrance hole with their fingertips and together swept away the sands and seaweed concealing the opening. Maanta dove up and out first with a swift spin, happy to be in open waters once more and to see that the light had not yet risen.

Not a word was spoken as the companions perched themselves upon the stone mound waiting for the sun to rise. Maanta stretched his back and arms out along the cool stone, resting his head upon a patch of moss. Anna's arms splayed back while her eyes looked wonderingly at the oceanic surface above.

A wash of cool purple and then maroon blossomed upon the waters above before rippling to peach-apricot hues. Pure yellow and cool orange then danced a paralleling ballet through the waters, a vision formed while shimmering across the waves above.

A sigh slipped from Anna's lips. "It's so pure."

The two watched the colors glisten and dance above them in silence for lingering moments, the kind of moments a person remembers their whole life as crisp as if they were just then living them, before Maanta spoke.

"I've never shared this with someone before. Often I would stay out beyond Meridia's walls to see the morning rise but I've never shared this with anyone but Archa."

A pure light blue shimmered down; settling in the depths as the sun fully rose above.

Anna scooped upwards and spun, whipping the currents about her sleek blue form. "We should watch the sunrise together wherever we go. I wonder if it's different in all the world's lands."

"I can think of no better companion to do that with." Maanta smiled as he lay on the stone, watching her swim and spin above him. He got to thinking then of how this good moment had come from the last days' disaster. *How many more good experiences will come out of that tragedy?* He pondered. *And what horrors are still to befall us in its wake?*

He realized then, as he lay there basking in the sunrise and pondering life, that they had both missed something. His features flushed to a stone chill. "Where's Lola? I haven't sighted her since we exited the cavern."

"Nor have I." Anna swam around the stone mound and spun up sands upon the oceanic floor while searching for the large fish.

Maanta darted beside her. "Surely if the single-finned ones had found and killed her we would have heard them. Maybe something spooked her so she swept off to hide."

"We should awaken Sift," Anna said as she swam within the stone cavern, Maanta closely following.

"UH!" Sift moaned and shook violently, as if in shock as the pair woke him. And as his milky eyes opened to look upon them he realized where he was.

Illala awoke silently because of the commotion across the cavern.

"Lola's gone." Anna shook Sift, rousing him further to his senses. "We awoke to watch the sun rise and she's nowhere to be seen."

"Lola would not be leaving the closeness of these cavern walls unless trouble there has come. Swiftness and watchfulness must we travel with this day, and with urgency search to find her." Sift moved quickly, stuffing belongings in their seaweed and whale-hide pouches and collecting the remaining crustaceans from the prior night's dusk meal to replenish the group's bodies with later. "Come.

We must move," he spoke as the others finished their own readying. Sift's legs moved upward and downward while darting toward the cavern exit hole. His body, so thick and muscular, barely fit through. The others with their companions scuttled out one by one.

"LOLA!" Sift bellowed forth. "LOLA!" He swirled and swept to the stone mound's opposite side. "LOOOOOLAAAAAA!"

Sure enough the shimmering fish appeared in the distance from behind a stone outcropping, hovering close to the ocean floor while approaching them.

"What is bothering you friend?" Sift questioned as Lola arrived. A look of fear hung upon her eyes.

"Wrongness has found us here," Sift spoke as he harnessed Lola and floated up and upon her. "Maanta how is the distance from here to Orion's Birth?"

"We're a half day away if the waters are calm." He caressed Archa's smooth head while sitting upon her. Illala swept upon Lisaly and Anna sat upon Lola behind Sift.

"Swiftly we must move," Sift looked to the pale skinned Maanta as he said this. In Sift's eyes the boy thought he recognized more then a hint of worry.

*

The party swam close to one another while quickly pressing through the waters, dark cliffs of coral-blanketed mountainous rock looming shadows down from above. And a silence echoed in the sights and sounds of the world around them. The water's breeze was still and calm and nothing moved as they swept by. No sounds could be heard and no creatures, even tiny bottom-dwellers, seamed to exist except themselves.

"Why is it so silent?" Anna asked the question they had all been thinking. "It's as if the ocean's soul has left this place."

Sift turned back to her. "Possibly the ocean's creatures sense something we do not." As he said this his sight moved from her eyes to the distance behind her. Even in that vastness nothing broke the stillness. And then something, sounding as if it were coming from far in the distance behind them, hummed gently in his ears.

"Something's coming, young ones," he warned them while turning again to see if he could see the thing approaching. It had the shape of one of the tail finned beings and swept so swiftly toward them that within seconds it darted from the point of being almost non-visible to looming down above them. Sift swam up from Lola's back and latched to the being's tail fin. "Venge!" He cursed.

"Let loose my fin. I'm not here for you," the boy gargled and spat into the waters through sharp gritted teeth, his crimson eyes beaming into Sift's own. "It's the girl I'm interested in."

Sift's arm muscles flexed as he spun, fighting against Venge's powerful tail in the currents. The boy struck at Sift with his sharp whale-bone knife as the noir skinned man attempted to dash him into nearby rock cliffs. "Swim!" He shouted to his companions. "Find you, I will, amongst the waters further on."

He climbed up the boy's fin and latched his grasp to the boy's neck, driving him toward the sands below. And in the final moment before impact with the oceanic floor Venge thrust with his tail against the sands below, thrashing Sift upon the sands instead, causing him to loose his grip upon Venge's neck.

The remaining threesome hadn't fled and instead watched the commotion, uncertain of what to do.

Venge rose and pushed swiftly away from Sift, lobbing his tailfin against the man's chest while propelling himself upwards.

"Protect Anna!" Sift called out to the others. "He wants her."

Heartbeats seemed to arrive in a slow motion barrage in Maanta's chest as he rode Archa swiftly to Anna's side, grasping a long sharp stone shard from the oceanic floor as he reached her. A heat burned from behind his eyes while glaring at Venge rushing towards them. "I won't let you have her," he spoke before noticing something off about Venge's movements.

The fiery eyed Venge gargled a sinister laugh while infatuating his sight not upon Anna but instead on Illala a ways behind her. Maanta had been attempting to protect Anna and Sift was headed for them now but before their eyes Venge gushed above and behind them, quicker than Maanta could turn to see, wrapping his arms across Illala's waist and ripping her from Lisaly's back.

"Wrong girl!" He called out to Sift above Illala's shrieks and calls for help.

The waters seemed a solid mass slowing Maanta as he braced his hand to Archa's smooth forehead telling her to pursue Venge. Archa and Lola thrust forward, carrying Maanta and Anna to Illala's aid. With the sight of this Venge beat his powerful tailfin once and, as if he had ceased to have ever come, disappeared to nothing amongst the oceanic fathoms behind them.

"Follow him! Sift come atop Lola with me," Anna called to Sift and then looked back upon the man, a cold hardened look of despair portraying itself upon his features.

"No use there is in doing such a thing Anna. Too quick he is and too many places there would be for searching within these waters." Mentally Sift cursed himself for not gripping tighter to the boy and for not stopping him from stealing off with Illala.

"Well I'm Zharista now and I say we can't just give up searching for Illala regardless of if we think it would be impossible to find her," Anna said. "There are so few of my people left. We must not give up on her."

"It's useless. We'll never find her."

"Then be alone as a man who has lost his hope. Maanta, will you come with me?"

"Wait," Sift spoke, his wrist and leg fins gliding him towards her now. "If death had been Venge's purpose in taking Illala then here her life he would have struck from her. A different quest he must have in mind. As in the past I have said I know where his race of beings lives. Surely they are going there and there we will also travel to halt them from injuring your and my peoples anymore. Pledge I this to you. There we will find and rescue her. Here there is no use."

Maanta looked upon Lisaly, Illala's fish, as Sift spoke, a being without its companion.

"We will find her." The pale skinned boy looked into Anna's eyes. "I promise I will be there when we do and won't rest until she's found."

"Ok, but I'm not stopping until we find her again and I'm holding both of you to your word."

Sift felt the cool waters play across his lips. "To you Anna my soul is pledged until Illala we have saved and the realm which was once your family's we have restored. May my trust and friendship be yours."

As Sift spoke Maanta reassured Anna by placing his hand on hers. Before him the cool bright blue light of midday darkened to a deeper shade, heading toward nighttime hours once more.

"We need to move if we're to reach Orion's Birth before darkness falls." Maanta looked again to Anna's pure eyes as Sift wove through the waters and settled upon Lola behind her. "I know it will be hard to do but maybe you should ride Lisaly. She's a friendly and trustable companion. You need something to move more quickly upon and surely Illala wouldn't wish us to leave her companion behind."

"I was thinking the same thing although I feel kind of bad about it all the same." Anna's fins rose her from Lola's back of glistening multicolored scales before she swam to Lisaly. The smaller fish wriggled and jerked as Anna tried to sit upon her but with soothing words and gentle caresses of the hand, Lisaly calmed and let Anna upon her. "She misses Illala but I think she'll be alright."

"Follow my lead." Maanta sped forward upon Archa's smooth back, watching tiny sand grains beneath him mesh together into a blurred tapestry below.

Anna followed closely, her red curls rippling in the currents, and Sift moved alert and close behind her. What had happened once with Illala, the group would not allow to happen again.

Peering from cavern holes and coral weavings below, Maanta saw small fish looking upon them and moving about. *Venge must be far off now because they no longer sense him and have resumed their oceanic rituals,* he thought. A shark glided below them, causing the party to swim above slightly in avoidance of it. A family of pink shimmering jellyfish glided beside them for a while as they swept onwards.

Gelu bless Illala, Maanta thought. *The world is moving on without her.*

8

To the twist of Twilight

Open water beyond Meridia

The currents whirled past her body, howling like the sound of shells held close to the ears. Illala's tears churned in the waters about her and swept within her throat as Venge grasped tight to her body, pummeling her through the oceanic depths.

His irises radiated crimson, mocking her as she looked into them. All the while the coming currents burned and stung her eyes as approaching water bashed against them.

Why have you taken me? She wanted to ask him. *Where are we going? Am I going to die?* But with such swiftness Venge swam, all that came from her lips was a choking gargle.

"I'll bet you're wondering why I came for you, why I tracked you to these sands beyond Meridia?" A cracked, sly smile crept upon Venge's slimy lips as a sandy oceanic fog spun around him and Illala. "Evanshade sent for you."

Without a second to react, or even register what was said, Illala saw a massive log whip through the murky sands out of nowhere and felt a thump against her skull as Venge spun and plunged her head against it. The girl's body hung limp in Venge's arms as he spun, pivoted and quickened faster toward Meridia's Cardonea Tower.

*

Slowly the lightness of consciousness swam within Illala's eyes once more. Small blurs spun across her sight, like stars reflecting through the ocean's surface, and the room she found herself in came to focus. The vast walls were white cool stone decorated with sapphires and tapestries formed from golden gems pressed within them. Above her Illala took in a ceiling dome high above and around. About her was a scribing desk, large shell mirror, a single window, gem jewelry, scribe scrolls, a shell horn music player and a black skinned man with deep pure opal eyes staring gently within her own. A single tailfin beat beneath him.

Evanshade. She knew it at once to be him, the man who had brought such darkness to her family, her people, and yet brought such warmth to her heart just with a look from his eyes.

"Are you alright?" He questioned while beating his masculine and strong tailfin before her. "I told Venge to not harm you, and see he has disobeyed. He will pay for that."

A pulse behind her eyes beat roughly from where Venge had spun her into the log. "My head's a little sore. Why did you have him come and take me from my friends?"

"When I was young I had a family," Evanshade began. "When I was with them I felt warmth and love. They filled me with a feeling that I had not felt since their perishing, had not felt until I lay my eyes upon yours last night during the mayhem of the siege. I felt warm when we looked to each other. I feel warm now."

"Somehow I do, too." Illala smiled slightly towards him. *But I shouldn't,* she thought. *You murdered my family and have torn my world apart. A piece of me hates you for that. And yet the rest of me looks into those deep eyes and is attracted to you. How can I be attracted to a man like you?*

"I think there's just something unmistakably true about me and you. That's why I sent for you," Evanshade said. "Because, no matter the things I have done, I want to feel that warmth with you for as long as I can. I am a terrible man. I won't deny that but I will never be bad to you. I would never do a disservice to this warmth like that."

"How could you kill my family and friends and then expect me to just be swept away and want to be with you?" An angry heat burned from Illala's eyes now. "How do I know you wouldn't do the same to me if I angered you?"

"I spared your life once before and if I could take back the destruction my people have caused your world I would. Someone with such beauty as yours does not deserve to have something like this done to them."

"And my people, all of Meridia deserved this?" She was furious now. "How could I ever love a man like you?"

"It wasn't just me. I was following orders, and if I would have disobeyed then someone would have slain me, taken my place and done the same thing. I would not be here with you and things would still be the way they are. You would probably be dead."

"Some things are worth giving up everything for." The waters seemed to chill about the room for Illala. And then warmth bloomed in her fingertips as Evanshade touched his hand to hers.

"I would never force you to stay with me," he spoke. "I'll even accompany you back to your friends if you wish to leave. Though I would love to know you better and spend our lives together, warming each other's days and nights."

Something then formed in Illala's mind. *Here's my chance,* she thought. *I'll tell him I'm leaving and to take me back to the others. There would be four of us and one of him. They could take him and punish him for what he has done. If they don't kill him then maybe he can be convinced to stay with us and help retake Meridia. We could still be together if he lives.* After all he had done surely she could betray him. She would tell him to accompany her to the others. It would be for the good of both of their lives.

Her eyes stared at the patterned stone floor below. Evanshade's warm hand touched hers. "I'll stay with you." She looked into his eyes. "Don't ever hurt me."

"I won't," his voice held sincerity.

Their lips met and then held a passionate kiss as the warmth of their bodies touched. His hands held her waist. Hers slid down, barely touching his scaly tailfin, causing her to realize how little she truly understood of the man. His lips were embracing, and yet foreign.

He kissed her hand and bowed while swimming toward the room's door. "I have to attend to my soldiers and the remains of the city but I'll be back as night falls. I will never keep you against your will. If you ever wish to leave just let me know. Thank you," he smiled and paused, "for being with me."

The large ornate stone door opened with a pull of Evanshade's hand, causing waters to weave inwards from the hall before rushing back out as the door pressed closed behind him.

In the wake of Evanshade's departure Illala noticed a light crimson hue seeping past the windowsill and moving like a serpent along the stone ceiling above. Her ankle and wrist fins carried her to the opening as curiosity churned inside her, longing to know where the light originated from.

The East Shale Wall spanned before her along Meridia's ocean floor. To her horror, she saw chained Meridians carving out the stone and sand below, revealing a molten cavern crevice where she had known the marketplace to once be. A Meridian man faltered in his shoveling of the earth and a guard speared him in the back of the skull, sending his face into the searing molten ooze.

What have I done? Illala huddled in the shadowed upper corner of her room after covering up the window with a kelp blanket. *What have I done?*

***

...and at the same moment off on the outskirts of Orion's Birth.

"They're so beautiful..." Anna gasped as the details of Orion's Birth's gargantuan archaic shimmering stone walls came into focus before her. "I've heard of their beauty but never have seen them before." A light like the colors of the inside of a seashell seemed to hover over the place.

"I've always loved lying in the sands along the walls' center and staring up at the ocean surface above," Maanta spoke to her while taking in the beauty of the place he loved so much once more.

"Is it true that the forbidden fluid air flows from those sands in the center of this place?" Anna asked.

Puffing up his slim pale chest Maanta pretended to be brave. "It does. But if you know when it comes it's easy to escape from."

"There, in the outskirts along the far side of the walls." Sift thrust his massive arm forward while pointing at small things moving to and fro in the distance before them. "There we shall Amaranth and the others be finding."

As they approached Amaranth and his companions, the destruction the tailfinned beings had reaped in Meridia showed its evidence once more. Trios and couples of Meridians scattered across the barren waters before them, appearing to be but a husk of the population the city had once bore witness to. A worn looking Amaranth approached them, swimming with some exhaustion which must have lain itself upon him since his arrival.

"There are but ninety-three of us remaining," Amaranth spoke. "Around 3,000 of our people lived and thrived in Meridia. These few were leery to follow me when I warned them of the oncoming slaughter but as it started they were quick to group and flee from their homes. I fear now though that fear has overcome them. Here we are stranded in the barren depths with broken families and little means of survival. They have lost their spirits and fear the tailfinned beings following us."

Sift placed his large hand on Amaranth's weary shoulder. "As I have said, part am I, of a civilization of friends out here in the open waters who are wishing to lend our allegiance to those apposing the tailfinned beings. Teachings we shall undertake for your people to show them ways of self protection and battling. Our two cultures shall retake Meridia, bringing happiness to your peoples' faces once more."

Amaranth's deep old eyes turned up, peering into Sift's. "They will be fearful of your peoples' dark skin. They wish for their world back but especially now, fear what they do not know."

"In time both our peoples must find a way to look past the differences which are skin color to come together as one and defeat our common enemy," Sift said. "My people reside leagues to the north away from this place and their assistance twould be a great help on our travel there. As the morn light shimmers through the waters above in the tomorrow believe I that we should send young Maanta on Lola's back to my realm with a request for warriors to assist us in our traveling to there.

"Lola is swift and knowing of the way. Young Maanta is brave and a frequent wanderer of unknown waters and so he will be safe and able. I would go myself but to leave you without a warrior here to protect these people twould be wrong. They lived in peace before two nights past and cannot yet defend themselves."

Amaranth thought for a moment. "And what of Maanta's safety? He is but a boy. What if he, instead of us, is attacked by the tailfinned beings?"

At that moment a low bellowing hum of whale noises echoed from the waters above. As Sift and Amaranth were deep in conversation Maanta had noticed a giant whale moving slowly there. He had gone to kill it so that his people would have something to eat. Speeding toward it on the back of Archa, he speared it in the back of the skull in an attempt to take it down and was now attempting to guide it toward an oceanic cliff by tugging on the lodged spear. The whale moaned again, thrusting its body back and forth in an attempt to throw the boy.

"Possesses he a quick wit, agility and knowledge of the vast outer waters which not many of your people have attained," Sift spoke with certainty while watching the boy's abilities and his battle against the great whale's strength. "Not many can take down a whale alone."

Amaranth opened his lips as if to call for some of the stronger young Meridians close by to assist Maanta.

"No," Sift spoke. "By doing this himself he learns certainty of his own strength."

The two watched while above, a boy, their friend Maanta, flexed his muscles in an attempt to topple this goliath of a whale. Slowly he drove it toward the cliff, all the while calling for Archa to help move the creature where he wanted it to go. Another loud whale moan bellowed in the depths as the creature collided amongst the cragged cliff and dark gray stone floor, finally arriving to its place of perishing.

"I suppose you're right." Amaranth watched in amazement. "Maanta will be more than able, or at least as able as any of us would be."

The whole camp was watching now as Maanta said a prayer over the dead whale, remounted Archa, spun in the waters and jutted toward his friends once more.

"This will be enough food to hold us over for a few days." He looked at them with a reflection of pride upon his face for what he had been able to accomplish for his depleted people. "It's sad though that such a majestic creature has to die in order for us to eat."

"Yes it is sad." Amaranth smiled at Maanta. "But it is also Gelu's plan that we should use these animals for our nourishment. I'm sure our people will gratefully accept this gift of life Gelu has provided us. There is a pool of molten flowing rock near by where we can eat and make preparations for the days to come."

"Why haven't our people camped within Orion's Birth's walls for protection from the elements and from our enemy?" Maanta was befuddled, knowing that the places' rising stone walls could provide a good temporary home until they could travel on to Sift's realm.

"They fear the air flowing from Orion's Birth's center and they fear the stories of its poisonous ways," Amaranth spoke.

"But air only bubbles-up from the inner ring of wall. There is no air in the outer rings. Surely they will understand that and know that they will be safer there then in open water."

"We will speak of this and many other things tonight, young Maanta, as we partake of your catch, but first Sift and I have a proposition for you. We wish for you to travel to Sift's people on Lola's back to ask them for assistance in traveling to their realm. We need Sift here, in case we are attacked again, or else he himself would do this. Will you go?"

An adventure, Maanta thought. *This will be a new place with new exciting people and happenings. But do I really need more adventures now. I almost wish they all would stop so I could rest a while.* "When would I leave?"

"Tomorrow as the morning's light first plays across the ocean's crest."

"And how would I get there? I've never been to the place where his people are."

"Knows the way, Lola does," Sift smiled as he spoke. "With assuredness I speak to you that she is all the direction you shall require. Certainties have I also that they will be recognizing her as she arrives. My people shall know who has sent you."

Gelu help there not to be any tragedies befalling me on this adventure, as there have been on the others recently, Maanta thought to Gelu in his head. "I will go," he spoke, "but I will miss my fellow Meridians."

The darkness from above slowly swept within the ocean's waters as the group rested before night-meal. Maanta and Anna wrapped themselves in kelp blankets other Meridians had brought with them and napped, huddling close together for warmth. Their riding companions fed on small fish bobbing around a nearby coral reef and Sift helped Amaranth and other members of the larger group prepare the fallen whale for night-meal. Meticulously they cut out pieces of meat, warmed and cooked them over the close-by pool of molten rock.

As the night succumbed to pitch darkness, the remaining Meridians and the tall dark Sift met to eat.

Amaranth's wise weary eyes looked over the crowd as he hovered in the waters before them, molten light shimmering across his form. "Before we partake of this night meal we must give thanks for what has been provided us." A soft silence fell over the waters and all but Sift bowed heads and shut eyes.

"Dear Gelu, thank you for all you have given us even in these darkest of hours when many of us surely doubt you. We know our sadness pains you and your pain saddens us in return. For you care for us in such greatness that you deserve the ultimate happiness. We find that in these last few days we have depended on the glimmers of light you provide us to give us the smiles we require to move on. This food, this glimmer of light, is a blessing you've sent us. May this whale which has perished for us to live, be blessed with a glorious existence in the heavens. We love you as we have always loved you. May we and all people be worthy of your blessings. Amen."

While divvying up the pieces of whale a warm, solemn, content feeling fell about them.

A cool red glow lit their expressions as they dined on whale and spoke, all lost in small conversations irrelevant to the tragedies they had experienced a few nights past. This was the first real meal most had had and they were escaping to happier worlds of companionship and tale-telling. Maanta stared within the glowing lava leaping from molten stone to stone in the pit. He could not escape reality as the others did. There was no time to rest. He would be off again tomorrow on a league of adventure all his own.

"Take care of yourself on your journey." Anna looked into his eyes, a hint of worry dancing in the back of her own. "I've just barely gotten to know you and somehow it feels as though you are the closest thing to family I have left."

"I'll be careful." He touched her soft hands. "And I'll miss you."

She smiled and blushed and the night went on with the two holding hands, watching as the molten stones burned on. They would sleep side by side again this night holding hands and savoring their slumber, knowing they would be apart in days and nights to come.

***

...and as they slept, across the ocean's waters in a small room of Cardonea Tower...

Illala slumbered, curled up in kelp sheets and a blanket of shark skin, tossing restlessly in this chilly tower room. Her eyes burned with inner despair as she slept. A warm hand then touched her, softly a warm body arrived. Evanshade woke her gently and kissed her on the lips. He said he missed her during the day. Suddenly the chill in her soul warmed again. The two made love, real love, before warmly snuggling and slumbering together as the night passed on.

In the room below, not the width of three bricks below, a faceless man screamed into a steal mask fashioned to his face. His teeth ground on a plate strapped between them.

9

Crescent Dusk

Orion's Birth

Maanta's heart beat heavily in the morning as he awoke, a clear clementine glow illuminating the water's surface above him and somehow Anna's hand still resting softly in his own. *I wish I could wake her so that we could share this sunrise together,* he thought. *But I can't. She's too beautiful while she sleeps and she needs her rest after the days we've had. I wouldn't want to wake her from what looks to be such a peaceful slumber.*

Anna's head tilted beautifully to the side as small yellow fish scampered by above her.

He had been startled awake. He knew this, but at the same time it hadn't been a panicky startle. A zesty fish scent swept across his nostrils. *Where's that scent coming from?* He wondered.

"Do you preference the scent of spiced squid?" Sift whispered while floating beside and above him in the waters, careful not to wake Anna. "When closeness to the nostrils comes, awaken any beast it can. But such smallness was the piece I swept across your nose to awaken you."

"What happened to the good old fashioned shaking?" Maanta whispered back, grinning.

"Such a spiced scent will keep your senses alert for much time, more then any simple shaking," The large man returned the smile. "Come. There is much traveling to be had this day. With luck and early leavings of this place my realm might you find before the darkness falls."

Maanta swam away gently from Anna, careful not to awaken her with his movements or the rippling of the waters his movements left behind. The currents somersaulted beneath his cupped webbed hands, pressing him in Sift's direction, toward where the riding companions were resting. He looked back once more upon Anna and smiled while swimming away.

Archa, Lola, Lisaly and the other riding fish dove and spun in the waters, as if playing a chasing game with each other, as Sift and Maanta dove down toward them from above. Archa nudged Lola's side with her smooth dolphin head and Lola in return sped quickly forward and back, gently whisking Archa's nose with her waving fish tail.

"AAAOOO!" Archa beamed in reply, spinning in a circle around the large fish.

"Lola!" Sift beckoned to his riding companion. She glided swiftly to his side. "You must be taking our young friend Maanta to our living waters now." His large hands gently brushed back and forth on the fish's vibrant scales. "Arrive him safely to our home Lovely Lola. Missing you shall I be while you are away."

As Sift said his goodbyes to Lola, Maanta also gave a temporary farewell to Archa, kissing her smooth round head and feeling her skinny long mouth nudge roughly upon his palm while she ate salty crustaceans he had kept from the feast the night before. She nudged the last crispy morsel from his pale webbed fingertips, quickly devouring it away. "AO, AO!" She opened her mouth wide, bobbing it while smiling.

Sift stuffed something, bundled tight in kelp, into a pouch along Lola's side. "Last night, as to sleep you went, spiced and saved some leftover whale meat I did for you. Its spices shall keep it safeness to eat in days to come, and preserve a little tender tastiness as well." He spun a tiny dark morsel of something between his lips. "And have dried I some miniature morsels also for Lola to savor." Another of the small dried morsels passed from Sift's large dark fingers to Maanta's pale ones.

The boy peeled it in half for smaller portions and was mentally salivating while partaking of the salty treats. "Thank you. This is delicious. I'm sure Lola and I will appreciate this many times during our journey. Take care of Archa for me while I am away."

"I will. Do the same yourself with Lola, my friend. And take care while riding. The strength which possesses, Lola does, is far greater than that of most companions."

"What do I do when I arrive to your people? Whom should I ask for?"

"As for words which use you should, they shall come to you. And for asking for someone with whom to speak, simply say to anyone that Sift has sent for them. For you see although my people have no leader, I am an elder and one whom they look up to most. Now you must leave for the journey this shall be before the sunlight arises higher overhead."

I wonder how well Lola will accept me as a new riding companion, Maanta pondered while petting her vibrant scales. He kissed Archa's forehead once more, spun freely in the waters embracing his own movements and slowly floated down upon Lola's back. As he clenched his slim legs tight to her muscular sides he felt a strong respect for the strength of this fish beneath him. His webbed fists braced tightly to the holding stones Sift had placed along Lola's front side. *I wonder what riding with her will be like. How will it be different then riding with Archa?*

Sift smiled sternly. "Fare thee well, young Maanta."

"Fare thee well your self friend." With this Maanta pressed his heels to Lola's sides, letting her know it was time to leave. It was as if a giant muscle shot forth carrying him from beneath. Lola's strength became obvious as she burst him forth through the depths. He held his body close to her form so as not to be whipped off in the counter-flowing currents about her.

Faster and faster she sped, blurring all existence from vision. It was as if a smudged cloud masked all things. Lola quickened more still and the waters around him seemed to blank to gray. And then a hissing entered his hearing.

"Sssssssssss." The waters barely tipped upon his earlobes while zipping by. "Sssssssssss."

This is enough to be maddening, Maanta thought to himself in the almost silence. *I don't know how Sift can stand to travel like this. He must have been holding back while riding with us before.* Lola's back bucked and sloped upward causing the boy to grasp even tighter to the riding stones. His legs almost choked at the fish's sides now. *I don't know why I was being so careful when nudging her forward before. It seems as if she barely even knows I'm here with her.* She thrust down again, to the left and right, quickly pivoting at times full circle causing Maanta to almost lose his grip and spin off into the empty water abyss.

With time though, hours it seemed, Maanta adjusted and became used to her movements. The hissing and blurry world took him mentally to a place where he was quite accustomed to being, a daydream.

Within the Daydream

Two nova white eyes glared at him, a chill breath rippling upon his neck, as he lay bonded in molten chains to the darkness, his arms singed and a foreign mind clawing, dragging at his soul. His stomach went clammy with blood's pulse. Maanta was alone, not knowing where, but alone. Somehow this was familiar. Where was he?

"Come to me," the spoken sounds burned within his mind. "Come and be adorned."

"Who's there?" Maanta replied. "What do you want of me?"

"I am power. I am strength. I am darkness." Sizzling, the nova eyes glared through him as the words were spoken from the darkness beyond them.

"What do you want of me?"

"I am lust. I am hatred. I am fire."

A shiver swept through Maanta's body, sliced upon his skin. What truly was this thing speaking to him? What was happening?

"I am denial. I am jealousy. I am fear. Do you fear me?" It spoke in low ominous tones. "Come to me! Come and be adorned."

Maanta huddled in a corner of the darkness with the light of the reflecting nova eyes shimmering across his face, unable to speak. Waters began to sizzle about him, forming boils upon his flesh. Tears flowed from his open eyes as his eyes themselves cooked like eggs and burst into the open darkness.

The boy's chest split, splattering the nova eyes with deep red blood which fizzled upon their touch, and the world faded to rippled aquatic daylight.

Maanta convulsed while awakening from the daymare, floating in open waters as Lola nudged roughly at his sides. Whatever that thing had been in his dream, he had no desire to see it again. "Did you throw me in the waters as I slept, lovely Lola?" He smiled to her; thankful she had noticed him missing and had come back for him.

To his surprise the daylight seemed to be nearing its end along the waters above, playing in pink hued colors now. He would have to rest here tonight, on a plain of open stone. Dark, glowing-eyed eels dipped and swooped after smaller fish in the far waters beyond.

"Thank goodness for our leftover whale meat, eh girl? Do you think it will taste as good now as it did in the morn's light?"

Lola spun in the waters with apparent happiness and hunger. As he took the meat from its bag his mouth watered at the scent of spiced meat. Lola partook of the dried portions Sift had taken such care of preparing and the boy heated his meat cube over an open malta shell, browning it ever so slightly.

As he chewed it he reveled at the way it melted in his mouth.

***

...fathoms away in one of many hearth rooms of Cardonea Tower...

The room was barren of mortal life other than Illala's own, as it had been since her awakening this morning when Evanshade was nowhere to be found. It was silent, and dark, and cold, but outside in the waters beyond she heard screams.

After what they had done together last night how could he just leave all day without even a kiss goodbye. In the corner of the room, setting upon a small ornate pearl desk he had left her smoked salmon, hardened seaweed and cubes of something sweet to eat. She had let it sit there, nibbling on the seaweed from time to time, but too depressed to eat much and longing for his attention.

She hovered in a lonely lost state as goose-bumps rose upon her body. Below her then a soft stone grinding noise began. Diving, her fingertips searched the smooth stone floor. Vibrating in her touch a single shale brick ground up and out of the floor and following it was a single hand, grasping in the open waters before her as if for breath. Its fingertips were pulpy, bloodying waters about them. Illala's throat gurgled in repulsion.

It was a metallic voice which came next, as if it had come from teeth being ground against an iron plaque. "Save me!" The strong hand grasped upon her thin wrist. "They've imprisoned me in this darkness. Free me!"

"Who are you?" She responded. "Pull back your arm, and show your face through the hole to me."

The massive hand released her, scraping the holes cragged sides while descending. The pained metallic voice returned. "I saw you through a hole in my cell's wall as you arrived the other night. I am a Meridian, as you yourself appear to be."

Illala gasped while looking through the hole upon the man's almost featureless metal-clad face. His blue flesh stretched and melted across his head, bruising in places and deeply gashing in others. His nose looked to have been torn off somehow, his lips stuck together in places around a metal contraption clasped upon his head and his eyes squinted. "What happened to your face?" She asked trying not to hurt his feelings by sounding totally disgusted.

Coughing up something from his lips the man's head shook violently. "The day they took this realm I was made with others to dig and open up the lava flows below Meridia. As the molten streams bubbled upon the sands they laughed at me, pressing my face and body into its flow. I am outwardly but a shell of the man once known as Odyssey. But inwardly I am a stronger man then they shall ever know." As if in a nervous twitch the man's head shook again.

How can I love a man who leads others in doing this to my people? Illala thought to herself. "Do you have any ideas for how I could free you? I know we are in Cardonea Tower but don't know much about its inner workings."

"There is..." The man spoke then swiftly hushed, a look of terror playing on his deformed face.

It was then that the world played itself in slow motion before Illala's sight. She wished to speak or interfere in some way but lost all voice in her throat, her body going stone still as the noise of an opening door echoed within the man's room below. Odyssey dove from view as Evanshade glided where Odyssey had just been.

"Have you lost your wits with your appearances you poor soul?" Evanshade thrust a pointed bone club against Odyssey's fleshy form causing the sound of weeping to softly fill the room. "Your babblings resonate unintelligible sounds within the outer halls. There is no one here with you, you poor creature. Do yourself a favor and silence those lips before the guards do so themselves. Soon as you are healed, you will work with the molten streams again."

"...no..." Odyssey mumbled and Evanshade struck the bone upon his shoulder, blood rippling out from where it was thrust and clotting in the stagnant waters. The hull of the man was overtaken by limp unconsciousness.

Illala went cold while looking upon the man she loved's grin.

"Don't worry." Evanshade spun to leave the unconscious man in cold blankness. "You won't be alone. We've discovered your runaway fellow Meridians along the outskirts of Orion's Birth. Soon they will return to slave by your side." He spat in the waters. "Do you think they've missed me?" The stone door echoed in his departing.

Silence swept through Illala's soul as she came to the full realization of what Evanshade was telling Odyssey. *He's going to capture Maanta and the others and bring them back here to torture,* she thought. Images of Venge swooping from nowhere to capture her, against her and the rest of her traveling party's wills, drowned her mind in dark thoughts. *There will be no escape. There will be no hope for any of them,* and then a darker thought aroused in the mind of Illala while she placed the shale stone in its floor opening. *Should I murder Evanshade as he sleeps tonight? Would that even make a difference?*

Wrapped in seaweed sheets, she hovered in the waters as night came, not asleep, but clenching a sharp bone hair tool, plotting for when Evanshade would join her.

The waters were cool and still as Evanshade entered the room. "I missed you today," he whispered to Illala, careful not to wake her barely crimson-lit form floating wrapped in seaweed sheets in the room's center. "I wish I could have been here with you today. I wish a lot of things." His strong noir hands gently moved her seaweed sheets and then wrapped them once more around them both as he moved his arms around Illala to hold her close.

"No!" Her harsh voice filled his ears while her foot throbbed against his tailfin. "No!"

"Why? What has happened to you?" He asked, worried, but there was no reply. He wrapped his arms around her again, only to be kicked once more. "If I didn't do what is being done to your people it would just be another of my people doing the same."

Hours, it seemed, after Evanshade had made his last attempt to hold her Illala managed to find the world of slumber.

The man she was no longer sure she loved, Evanshade, spent his night staring and lost in thought out the bedroom window upon Meridia's ruined city. Was what he was doing so wrong? If he had not obeyed his master would he not be dead himself? *In the darkness of this night I see Meridia has lost some of its beauty since I first arrived here. They were such a joyous people before we arrived. If we had not come they would be joyous still. And yet then I would not have found Illala.*

In the hours of the night Evanshade found no sleep or solace. But in the wee time before aquatic dawn, in a state of sheer exhaustion, other thoughts entered Evanshade's mind. Regret formed for the ways in which he treated Odyssey. He called Odyssey's guards away for an early morn eat before returning dressed in flowing, disguising black garb and entering the stone prison room.

"Who are you?" Odyssey's gritty metallic voice greeted him. "What do you want of me?" Evanshade grasped Odyssey's shoulder where he had received the beating earlier that night.

"Shhh..." The hidden Evanshade whispered. Would the man attack him if he knew who he was? "They will hear you if you speak loudly. I am a friend. That is all you need know."

"Are you here to rescue me?"

"Here." Evanshade shoved a heavy bundle of kelp and whale meat into the man's hands. "Eat this or hide it before the guards come with your mush. You deserve better food."

"Thank you." The starving weary man tore open his package, getting whale meat beneath his nails while devouring his morn meal.

As Evanshade thrust his tail in the waters and left the room he felt as if a stone struck his heart. "I'm sorry..." he whispered.

Odyssey's grotesque face looked up, covered in food. "What?" But Evanshade had gone.

10

Mesh of Faith

The waters outside Baneal

Morning light shimmered pink and powder blue, rippling through the water births above as Maanta approached a place he assumed was Sift's home realm. It was not a place of elaborate splendor but instead possessed a pure, rough beauty like that of a cooling lava stone.

Towering mud pillars stood above the oceanic floor before him. Black skinned men and women swam from holes dug out of the mighty goliaths, looking like tiny fish in the distance far away. Maanta's heart jumped as he realized he also saw groups of people riding the backs of whales and standing guard about the pillar dwellings. With tiny harpoons mounted upon bows, they appeared to scour the outward waters within their sight.

We should have been prepared like this, alert at all times, Maanta thought. *If we had been more careful maybe we could have protected ourselves, or at least more of us could have escaped.* Water currents licked his shins as Lola slowed beneath him. Their approach to the looming mud towers was quick, and soon four dark skinned men riding fish much like Lola shot forth toward him from holes in close by stone walls.

One man bore a helmet carved from bone and armor done mostly in the same design. "Who are you?" He questioned in a resonating low voice. "For what reason has Lola brought you to us? You must be a friend or else she could never have been convinced to bring you. Is Sift in need of our assistance?"

Another of the men whispered softly. "Is he alive?"

"Do not dare to question your leader's wit and skills," the first man replied as if reprimanding the second. "Rest assured he is alive."

"Don't worry, he's alive," Maanta quickly answered the second man's question. The idea of Sift being dead sent chills over his body. "He came to my people's realm, Meridia, to warn us of the treachery of the tail finned beings, but few of us escaped their wrath in time. Now my people wait, frail and few in a place we call Orion's Birth many leagues distance from here. Sift remained there to defend them while sending me onward to request assistance from you. They need better protection if they are to travel here to your realm."

As the bone, helmeted man took off his helm a look of deep thought and sadness displayed itself like a scar upon his face. "My son died bringing us the information of what was to occur in Meridia and I have feared this whole time that what we had learned had come too late to save that place."

Maanta felt for the man. "I am alive because of what your son has done. It wasn't all for nought. There are others like me at Orion's Birth, but surely the tail finned beings are searching them out as we speak. Surely there are others still alive also in Meridia who need rescuing."

"You are right. In these past days you yourself have endured more than I. We must tally our losses, pray and move forward to prevent the loss of other lives. It seems as if there is little time to spare. The tail finned ones could be upon your people at any moment. Our warriors must assemble and leave for Orion's Birth immediately.

"Cole." He turned to a slim bald man behind him. "Assemble the harpooners and trident wielders and tell them to quickly meet here with their fastest riding fish. We are leaving to rescue Sift. There is much to prepare and little time to do so." And then he turned toward Maanta in a moment of curiosity. "You never gave me your name, boy."

Cole pivoted and shot with his riding fish toward a series of larger holes in the massive brown structures.

"I am Maanta." He shook the man's bone-armored hand.

"Like the manta ray. What a majestic fish. When I escaped Sangfoul, the city where the tail finned ones dwell, I swear I saw one following behind me to this city. It was warming to feel I had company. I am pleased to meet you. You have been given a fantastic name."

"Thank you." Maanta smiled. "I hope I can live up to your appreciation for the animal."

"You came to us alone with nothing but a riding companion to accompany you on this long journey. That is a good beginning. Come to think of it, that is how many of us arrived here, on a journey, alone, to escape the race of Sangfoul. My name is Tao." The man's facial features showed he was again thinking of the tragedy befalling Meridia. "How many tail finned beings are there within Meridia's walls?"

"I was unconscious during the siege and witnessed the last of it only from a distance, but Sift seemed to think there were no more then fifty of them. They swept in on us so quickly. Evanshade came first with a boy they call Venge under the guise of peace." Maanta burned hot with anger as images of the evil looking boy sweeping off with Illala came to his mind.

Waters swept about the bone mask façade as the dark skinned man placed it once more over his face. "I hate to say it but you're lucky it was Evanshade and not Venge's father or the Dark One. They are more brutal and wicked than him. That's probably why Venge was sent along, to watch and prod Evanshade. That boy is slick like an eel and bites like a shark."

"As we escaped, Venge took one of our party and swept off with her before we could stop him." *Is Illala even still alive?* Maanta pondered. *Surely there is something more we should have done to rescue her.*

Tao's fists clenched upon his fish's riding stones. "Then they must know where you were going. If they haven't already arrived they could besiege Orion's Birth before nightfall. We must move quicker then I thought. There is no time to talk." Tao's bone-masked eyes shimmered as he spoke to Maanta. "Have you eaten on this journey, boy? I fear there is no time to properly show you our city and to provide you with the nourishment I'm sure you well need."

"I've had some to eat." *But I wouldn't mind a freshly cooked meal,* Maanta thought, his mouth watering as he predicted the various foods he might be served here, had they the time to spare. "The day before I left for your city, I took down a whale for us all to feast upon. Sift wrapped leftovers for me and even dried tasty morsels to tide Lola over."

"A boy as young as you took down a whale on his own?" Disbelief entered Tao's voice.

"Yes. But surely anyone else could have done the same if they had tried."

"That is modesty in your voice, young Maanta. I can see why Sift sent you to us. A soul like yours will be an asset in days to come."

It was surprising, Maanta thought, how quickly Tao and his warriors prepared for the journey. Within the time it took to feed Lola and eat a portion of the whale meat Sift had prepared for him, the trident wielders and harpooners had formed a spherical traveling group all around him. Their riding fish were massive and yet slim like Lola, with a look of wisdom and age in their eyes. Maanta turned to look into the eyes of the riding fish behind him. There was sharpness there like in the eyes of an eel.

There must be ten or more warriors in all directions about me, Maanta thought. *What a force. Surely this will be enough to hold back the tail finned ones. Maybe we can even retake Meridia.*

A boy almost his own age swept about them handing spiced seaweed wrapped pieces of octopus and squid to the warriors, each man or woman thanking and blessing the boy while taking their share.

As the boy reached Maanta he handed him a wrap of each. "Are you the man they're saying has come from a foreign land to ask our help in rescuing his people?" The boy asked in an admiring fashion. "I told my father that I want to come with you to defend your people but he says I'm too young."

Wow, Maanta thought. This was the first time anyone had called him a man. *This boy can't be more then a year or two younger than me. Surely there is so much more for me to experience before I am a man. If I had a father, would he have said I was too young to come here alone and find these people to save us? What would I be like if I was raised with a father, or even if mother was still around?* Maanta had gone wandering off into his own thoughts again, until he caught the boy arguing his case to come along.

"I would be a great help. I mastered the spear many leagues of time ago. See?" A sharp pointed shaft slid from the youth's bag while his small hands grasped it in the water's smooth currents. Forcefully pressing his fingers upon grooves along the shaft he opened it like an umbrella shaft to a larger spear and lunged it, accurately, toward a large stone protruding below. "Surely father will listen to you because you are the one who's come for our help. I know I am young, but I could greatly help your people with my skills."

Maanta knew the boy's father wouldn't change his mind, even if asked to, but he found it humorous that the boy was actually more skilled then he knew most Meridians to be.

The boy looked anxious. "Will you ask him for me? I could even be your personal guard."

There was no way the boy would be given permission to come. *He's more skilled than I myself am, though,* Maanta thought. What could he say to his fellow youth? There was a look in the boy's eyes. He so wanted to come.

But the female warrior behind Maanta, who rode the eel eyed fish, called to the youth. "Do you know, Sebastian, that I talked with your father myself about whether or not to allow you to come. He thought it would be best to have you here while we are away, to help protect our people in case we would be attacked. With the warriors gone you and a few others will be all that's left to protect this place. It is a big responsibility."

"I didn't realize that," the boy said and bowed. "I would be honored to do that for our people." He turned to Maanta again. "It was a pleasure to meet you, sir." And with that, the boy was off again delivering his remaining food parcels.

"You may think that I was pacifying young Sebastian," the stern-faced female warrior spoke to Maanta. "With our warriors leaving to protect your people though, he and a few other skilled youth will be all that's left to protect our own city. He has talents I'd love to have along with us, but there has to be someone left here to protect this place. He is the son of Tao. Either Tao or Sebastian I would gladly have by my side in battle. The son learns from the father."

"How old was Tao's other son when he died?" Maanta's thoughts traveled now. He hoped he wouldn't offend her by being nosy about the man he had just recently met.

"He was but a year older than the boy you have just spoken with, 15."

Maanta was startled. When he had heard of how Tao's son had perished while bringing information back to his people of the tail finned beings' intentions in Meridia, Maanta assumed that the son had been a young man in his twenties. *The differences between my people and Sift's are amazing.* "I had thought he had been much older from the way Sift and Tao spoke of him."

"In many ways he was," the woman's voice had a gentle musky accent to it, Maanta noticed, as she spoke. "Many of our youth are mentally older then their age. They have to be to deal with the tragedies they've witnessed, and constant threat of Sangfoul. That is where the ones you call the 'tail finned beings' are from."

I suppose it makes sense that the youth here would mature faster than in peaceful waters. It's been only days since the people of Sangfoul attacked us and yet it seems as if months have passed.

"The presence of the race of Sangfoul haunts my people," the woman spoke, her eyes hazing over as she thought back to another place and time. "Once, when I was a young girl, they discovered our dwelling caves. You see, before living in this place, we made our homes in carved out oceanic cliff holes. Around the time of my birthing my people had just begun escaping from Sangfoul's slavery, and when I was young, had still not yet established a city.

"The raiding tail finned beings slaughtered most of us, beheading my parents in front of my eyes before I escaped in a small wall crevice in our dwelling. I felt as if I had aged years in that night as I curled in a small stone space in the wall. Haunting whale songs echoed in my ears and my stomach was dry and famished with hunger. I was certain they would find a way through the wall and murder me at any moment. I remember slicing my finger upon the wall and being nauseous from the taste of my blood about me. That's one of the reasons I'm coming along to help your people. I'm tired of seeing youth grow old before their time because of the tortures they've endured."

As she finished what she was saying, Maanta noticed Tao spinning and swirling swiftly upon his riding fish, checking and rechecking his warriors so as to make sure they were prepared for the journey.

"Thank you for coming to aid Meridia," Maanta spoke to the woman as a school of small orange-yellow fish glided past them, tickling his fingers while forming to his palm and curling away.

Tao's voice then echoed in the cool breezy waters through a curved shell. "My people, Once more we have been called upon to fend off the dark evil of Sangfoul's people. This journey is a noble one and must be made swiftly. Guard this foreign boy, Maanta, with your lives and once we reach this place we are heading, a place by the name of Orion's Birth, be cautious of the people of Sangfoul. If they are not there, then they should be shortly. Remember, the souls of our lost loved ones will protect and comfort us on this journey. Take warmth in your heart because of this. I find peace in that my recently passed son, Ailcalm, rides with me."

Please protect us lord, Maanta found himself praying to Gelu. *I know nothing of our dead riding with us but please protect us all.* A small glimmering light in the waters a way off warmed his heart. It reminded him of Gelu. And for some reason, in that moment, it reminded him of Anna as well.

Tao finished his words. "For the kind heart of the heavens, may we succeed! Let us ride!" A wailing sound careened forth from the large shell as Tao's lips pressed upon it, his cheeks puffing with water.

Small fish scattered away in all directions from the noise and the riding companions seemed to hum while slowly moving forward in the gargantuan mass. Lola's slim body rippled quickly beneath Maanta.

With a gust, the sphere of warriors moved forward, shooting with a massive thrust through the ocean. Maanta's cheeks pulsed upon his face as the water pressure streamers produced by the group's movements tangled about him. *We're moving even faster then Lola was moving me on the journey here,* he realized. *I wonder if it has something to do with the fact that we're moving as a group.*

A kind of pressure shield forming at the front of the group then caught his attention. It was as if the speed of their movements was creating a moving barrier between them and the waters and particles before them. Floating seaweed, coral and sand collided with the natural wall and whipped away and beyond them.

"Have you ever seen anything like it?" The woman he had spoken with hollered from behind him to be heard over the careening water sounds. "They call me Leil, by the way. We should arrive by nightfall."

I wonder how the riders and fish up front know where to go through this mesh of colors, Maanta's thoughts wandered. *I wonder if it has anything to do with faith.*

11

Between Moments
Orion's Birth

Midday shone a gloomy light over Orion's Birth's currents on the third day after Meridia's siege. It had been only three days. And yet somehow Anna's family already seemed so far distant, lost from her life. Ages seemed to have passed since her father had last hugged her in his strong arms. Why was it so impossible to remember the way his fingers felt against her hair as he comforted her? What she would give to have her father with her now.

Archa bobbed Anna's arms with her nose, attempting to console the girl whose tears invisibly webbed from her eyes within the waters before her.

Anna found herself here, where the riding companions were being kept, for most of the time since Maanta had left to find Sift's realm. She was torn between sadness for the loss of her family and emptiness in her heart because of the feelings that were growing in her for Maanta. It was odd to explain or even ponder but she had begun to feel as if he might be a member of a new family for her.

Archa bit playfully at her arm and tugged it in the waters, aiming to receive some of the spiced kelp Anna had been twisting methodically between her fingertips. "Here you are, girl."

She released small pieces of kelp into the currents and smiled while watching the dolphin bob and swirl before her to catch its lunch meal. "What does Maanta usually feed you I wonder?" She stared off through the deep blue waters, lost in ponderous thought for a moment. "I wish you could speak. There are so many things I'd like to know about Maanta and surely if you knew how to tell me you'd have something intriguing to say."

"Aaaahoooo!" Archa sang.

It was funny, Anna thought, that Archa possibly had understood her and was trying to communicate back.

"Aaaahoooo!"

And then suddenly it wasn't so cute anymore. It occurred to her that Archa might be attempting to communicate something entirely different as Anna saw dark shadows sweeping toward the main encampment of Meridians. The shadows massed in groups and swarmed in from all directions. Were those tailfins she saw whipping upon their backsides?

"Shhhh!" She harshly whispered to Archa. But it was useless; all of the riding fish about her now were nervous and wailing out their aquatic songs. Thank goodness that at least Archa had caught the hint and quieted down. "Archa, we must hide."

The dolphin bobbed its head knowingly as Anna wrapped her arms around its neck. She hugged close to its form and the two swept low along the ocean's depths. Where was she going to hide? And then she surprised herself while remembering something Maanta had said. Orion's inner walls produced the poisonous fluid, air, and that is why her fellow Meridians were afraid to take shelter there. Would the tail finned race also have fear of this place? Would they be afraid to search there?

She saw it as her only hope and quickly steered Archa toward the one place near the shimmering walls that the tail finned ones had not yet come. They swept within the darkness of Orion's Birth's inner ring, ducking under an outstretched ledge and peered from a crack in the shadowy darkness. Archa's smooth body shivered nervously beside her.

She watched her people scurrying frantically as the Meridian encampment prepared for the attack. Sift eluded the tail finned beings' eyes as they approached, moving his body close to the sands and stealthily within a mass of oceanic vegetation. *Where is he going?* Anna wondered. *Isn't he supposed to be defending our people?* Surely there was something she was missing here.

"Don't scatter!" The elderly but stern looking Amaranth bellowed, his garb flapping in the waters. "They'll only pick us off with their quickness. Grab your defenses and gather here in a group. If we gather in a mass, then they'll have to come at all of us at once. We'll have a chance to make them fight more then one of us at a time."

Desperation played itself out with evidence upon the façades of the exhausted Meridians' bodies. They had lost so much sleep in the past nights while mourning their dead. Men and women alike nervously clamored with shabby weaponry brought in the flight from Meridia and makeshift shielding recently forged from the shell plates of crimson crustaceans.

Two whale lengths before her Anna witnessed a man swiftly harpooned in the back by an approaching tail finned being. The man's jaw bucked upwards as his body was pinned to the ocean floor. Grotesque gurgling noises popped outwards from his lips as his eyes filled with blood and rolled upwards.

"They are upon us! Come Quickly!" Amaranth called again with panic.

Many other of Anna's fellow Meridians were beheaded or harpooned upon the surrounding sands and against Orion's Births' walls before the remaining group came together in a spherical group about Amaranth. The finned creatures' swarming reminded her of a giant serpent and during the commotion she could swear she had also witnessed that wretched boy, Venge, gnawing upon a beheaded man's neck.

A foul taste churned in her throat.

"Come at us then!" Amaranth taunted the intruders forward. "You've come to finish us off, so do so! You'll lose a good many of your number in doing it though, I promise you!"

"Allacaristan!" Amaranth shouted from the mass of weakened Meridians. Dust leapt forth from his fingertips and frothed about the group within the waters, forming a hard shell-like substance upon their weaponry and flesh.

Evanshade emerged, whipping swiftly from his army as he watched this. "If you surrender now, old man, we'll let you live but you must come with and work under us. You will be fed and provided shelter."

"Provided a shelter which is rightfully ours? We will be no-one's slaves, you disillusioned creature. We would rather die a noble death than work as minions for a dark-souled race. Why couldn't you just be content to remain in your realm and live out your lives in peace? What pleasure can there be in tormenting us?"

Evanshade fixed a dark look at Amaranth. "It is not in our right to question the lord of all darkness. We are here because he commands us to be here. As you will come with us, as he commands you to do, also. Otherwise, here you will perish a horrid death in these waters."

Strength and determination took a stand in Amaranth's eyes. "We would welcome death over whatever your dark lord plans for us. Our lord will rescue our souls in the afterlife. If this is to be our final stand, then we will make it here."

"You are a stubborn old man." Pivoting in the currents, Evanshade turned to face his men. "The Meridians choose their destiny. Slay them."

A flurry of harpoons hummed while releasing from the fists of the men of Sangfoul at the floating Meridians. Many raised shields or shifted in effort to dodge the projectiles. A woman with flowing locks dove before her child to shield the young boy.

Though, to her and all but Amaranth's surprise, whatever he had used on them caused the harpoons to ricochet from their shields and flesh. "Do not move," he whispered to them. "If you do your bodies will be exposed once more." His fingertips flicked in the waters while sending several black spheres toward the tail finned creatures who were now rushing at them to kill them with close contact.

Octopus oils spewed forth from the balls, singeing the attackers' corneas and temporarily blinding their sight.

"Let the ones who are friends of mine alone, Evanshade, darkness servant!" Sift called while rapidly approaching upon Lisaly's back, a trident poised within his fist. "For your people owe me a battle, before with them you can duel."

"Sift, my old foe." Evanshade tightly grasped his own trident. "I was wondering when you would resurface after fleeing me in Meridia. Would you too wish to return to servant-hood with these people?"

"You will pay!" Sift solemnly spoke before moving Lisaly toward Evanshade and thrusting his trident into the other man's weapon. Orange and crimson sparks fizzled in the currents as the weapons ground across each other. The two locked in a squealing metallic embrace, their bodies contorting in all directions as they attempted to outwit each other, getting the better of their opponent, but nothing halted the tension-filled display.

Long moments passed as each man gasped for breath, searching for a weakness in the other's battle strategy.

As Evanshade dislodged his trident, lunging it at Sift's skull Sift slipped a sharpened shell from his garments and slashed it into his opponent's chest with his free hand. Blood spewed forth Evanshade's body from the gash, but as the man writhed in pain he managed to strike Lisaly with his trident, sending the riding companion to the aquatic depths and squirming toward inevitable death.

Anna shielded her eyes. All was lost. What was worse was that she had promised herself when Illala was taken that she would protect Lisaly from harm. It was impossible that the fish would survive the spearing.

When Anna took her hands from her eyes to look once more on what was happening, Evanshade was nursing his wounds, Sift was being held captive by three muscular tail finned beings and the remaining Meridians were surrounded and looking fearful of what was to come.

Her heart stood still as she noticed a distraught look now hiding in Amaranth's eyes. When would Maanta return with the men of Sift's realm she wondered? Would they be able to help or falter and themselves be slain?

Evanshade's group and the Meridians were at a standstill now. The beings of Sangfoul wandered in a serpentine whirl about the mass of Meridians, unable to pierce their bodies due to whatever Amaranth had covered them with but they also remained relentless and unwilling to allow the group to escape.

"We originally didn't wish to kill them, anyway," Evanshade spoke in hushed tones with one of his men while blood colored his fingertips from where he clasped his side. "And our sorcerers in Meridia surely can reverse whatever spell this old man has cast upon his people. Let us prod them along on a journey to their homewaters. It will be tedious but there we can un-cast this spell and do with them whatever we will."

The man whom Evanshade had just spoken with swished off to inform his fellows. Soon the Meridians were netted in kelp and were being forced to swim to Meridia and their uncertain futures. Some found their arms tangling to the net's outer sides as they swam.

Sift was strapped with whale hide behind the kelp prison, his arms bound to his legs behind him, his mouth clasped open in a clattering metal contraption. As the group moved away his twitching wide eyes caught Anna's own.

"I can't tell if he's more afraid for himself or for me, left here alone," Anna whispered to Archa. "I don't know who I'm more afraid for. If Maanta returns, we have to find a way to rescue them." She turned away and curled in the fetus position, her long crimson locks clinging to Orion's Birth's inner wall behind her. Moments passed. The silence, she thought, was maddening.

This madness would be what would salvage her soul from the death, which is eternal despair. All about her she searched, certain that at an unexpected moment a tail finned being would swoop down and murder her.

Eventually though, after what seemed like an hour, something beautiful appeared above her eyes. A multicolored sphere, looking like a massive bubble, glistened and quickly rushed by. Inside the massive orb, like illusions, dark skinned men and women rode upon large shimmering fish. Their eyes appeared transfixed on the waters before them. Some bore masks of twisted bone that frightened her but she was warmed by the hope that these might be Sift's fellows.

The waters hummed as the sphere crossed above. She smiled as deep within the orb she noticed Maanta's slim pale body perched upon Lola's slim lengthy one. She waved at him but couldn't tell if he himself had taken notice of her. It would be another moment before the sphere had passed above. Its speed slowed as it did so and by the time it had passed, Anna had perched upon Archa and swept off in the waters following the orb to the place where it would end its journey.

* * *

Within the Sphere

Maanta's eyes squinted as the traveling party's bubble slowed, the things before him becoming less of a shimmering multicolored mesh now and more of a clear view. Eventually the bubble that surrounded the traveling party, as they swept along, dissipated.

"Is this Orion's Birth?" Leil's voice called from behind. "Its walls are so intricately draped with runes. I wonder what they say."

They were just passing Orion's inner walls now. Maanta desperately searched the sands before him, knowing his fellow Meridians should be here and afraid of what had happened to them.

"They were camped here!" Maanta hollered ahead to Tao.

"Then we must find them, and with haste!" Tao lifted his bone mask to be heard more clearly. "The beings of Sangfoul surely have taken them, or else their bodies would still remain. Toward which currents is Meridia?"

"This way!" Maanta swung his pale arm slightly to the side and maneuvered Lola toward the direction as well. He could see nothing unusual there. Had they been captured and were now heading to Meridia? It would make sense but how long had it been since they had been taken?

Tao reared upon his riding companion, riding swiftly upward for a better position, then dove to where he was almost touching the sandy oceanic floor. He clasped a harpoon against his tone arm and swung it forward in the direction of Meridia. "They are there in the far distance hugging the ocean floor as they move! We must maneuver quickly to catch them!"

Before Tao had finished his words the group was off again.

Maanta squinted to see what Tao saw. *The man must have phenomenal sight,* he realized. *I wonder if he had it at birth or has honed it over the years.* Carefully as he moved Maanta searched for what Tao had seen, and then far away on the lower horizon noticed what looked like a serpentine mirage shivering, a minute distant apparition. He had never seen it during the many times he had been here before.

I should have seen that. I should have looked harder. It's not phenomenal sight that Tao has after-all, Maanta decided. *He just pays great attention to detail.* He would work on that in the future. It could prove a necessity one day. *I wonder if that's what makes great people, the dedication and effort they put into things, and not the abilities they are born with or inherit.*

Maanta's group divided and hugged oceanic cliffs and the ocean's bottom while pressing toward their enemies. It would not pay to be seen before reaching the beings of Sangfoul. Their enemies would only evade them with their quickness.

"You are needed for something, young Maanta!" Tao beckoned him from the front of their group.

Maanta whispered to Lola and the two jutted forward until arriving side by side with Tao. "What can I do?" He began to see the forms of his enemies and entrapped friends becoming clearer in the distance before him.

"They are not many leagues from us now," Tao's low voice resonated with both nervousness and excitement. "And if they notice us before we are upon them they'll flee beyond our abilities to catch them again. We must flank them in their front so that they turn to face us. That is where you come in to play."

"Me? What do you want me to do? Who should I follow?"

Tao grinned behind his bone mask as they continually swept onward. "Follow yourself. You know these waters better then I, or any of my fellows, and we need someone to lead a group to cut the beings of Sangfoul off. You are my choice. You must sweep quicker than the rest of us in a wide arch before them and halt them as they flee our pursuit. Leil will follow you, along with five of our best men. I've noticed you and Leil talking. It's good to see you made quick friends."

"Are you sure I'm the right one to lead?" Waters somersaulted upon Maanta's face and passing sands stung his eyes in a gust as he spoke. "Puh! Yuck." He spat out sands whipping into his throat. "I could instruct someone so that they could lead. I'm nowhere near the strongest fighter here."

"Did you decide it was time for a snack my friend?" Tao joked, Maanta still struggling to get the sand from his mouth. "I've made my decision. Do not question me. You are right for this task. I'll speak with the others and they will meet with you here at the head of our group. Besides, when your people see you it will give them courage." And with a swift swish Tao's riding fish took him back to where five bulky riders and Leil had clumped together behind them.

Tao may want me to lead them, Maanta thought. *But what if they don't want to follow my lead? Why would they follow a boy when they are the experienced, elder warriors?*

"I don't understand Tao's choice of you to lead." A large man approached upon his rather chubby fish. "But I trust his decision. Do not worry. I won't allow our mission to go awry."

"You'll be fine." Leil came next with the others, tapping her hand upon his pale back while riding past. "You know these waters better then us. It was a good call."

Tao must have warned them of my apprehension, Maanta pondered. "We'll go this way." He pointed above a rolling wall of coral on their left. "It stretches clear to Meridia. We can remain hidden behind it as we pass where they are." His deep opal eyes looked down to a dagger strapped upon his side.

"That won't get you far." Tao handed him his massive golden trident, its shaft lined and ribbed with various patterns. "You might find this tool handier."

Astonished, Maanta wielded it sternly in his webbed fingertips. "I can't accept such a gift from you. And besides, what will you fight with?"

"I have a spear. And Leil can tell you I am master with it as well. I have many tridents in my home dwelling and this is something you will need if you are to protect yourself. Now leave and listen for my shell call as a signal of attack." Tao gripped Maanta's shoulder sternly. "May your God be with you."

"Follow me." The ghostly white boy directed his troop while sweeping Lola upwards over the coral wall and swiftly dipping low along its other side. They moved stealthily and swiftly as waters blurred before them and the coral looked as if it had become a humming wall of smooth ivory glass.

"Hmmmmmm Hmmmmmm." It sang before something else entered the tune. "Hmmmmmm Hmkeemmjusmmletm."

"Slow down," Maanta whispered behind to the others. "That must be them speaking on the other side of the wall." The coral became cragged coral again as they slowed. Lola took him closer as he cupped his ear to listen.

"We should slaughter them all and use their entrails as fuel for Sangfaul's great furnace," a high-pitched voice shrieked.

"Or feed their innards to those wretched riding companions of theirs!" Another howled.

"No matter how it's done I'd love to hear them scream," the first replied.

And then another voice interrupted, its scratchy tone sending shivers along Maanta's body.

"Shhh!" Venge's distinct twisted voice broke through. "I smell something beyond the wall you fools. Clamp your mouths and be alert. I'll investigate."

Nothing more need be heard as Maanta and his companions swept forward to escape being discovered. The boy's heart stung as if on fire. Waters wiggled along his webbed fingers like fish in a fisherman's net. "There's a shale cove a league down we can hide in before Tao's shell sounds."

As he looked behind he noticed Venge's forehead rising where he had snooped moments before but before Venge could look in their direction the troop was un-seeable, hiding amongst the shale.

Long moments passed as they awaited Tao's call. A deathly silence floated in the waters. Maanta caught himself grinding his nails upon the trident gifted him by Tao, his nerves searching for release.

"Ooooooooooooooo!" The howling of Tao's shell bellowed from where the traveling group had come.

"Now!" Maanta beckoned as he, Leil and the five muscular warriors shot forth toward the shale cove walls. "Rise above the coral there!" Lola twisted to the side, hugging up and over the peak of the coral wall. Maanta hugged her back, closely followed by the others, down in the path of Evanshade and the tail finned beings' retreat from Tao.

Nervous anxiousness simmered along Maanta's muscles as a horde of serpent-backed men rushed toward him. "Halt!" He shouted. "We have come to defend Meridia!"

Evanshade somersaulted with his trident, lunging it outward while bracing it upon his toned arm, pulsing vigorously toward Maanta. The boy's trident sparked, stinging his palm while locking with Evanshade's own weapon. His wrists burned as the man pressed his body down in the currents.

"You?" Evanshade bellowed. "I saved your life outside Cardonea Tower, the one just deed I did in your realm, and this is how I am redeemed? I should have left you to be crushed by the chariot! I'll make up for my mistake here."

Maanta couldn't respond. Too much of his attention needed to be given to the struggle to keep Evanshade from running him through. Slowly he pushed Evanshade up but soon found himself fighting a losing battle again as the man's tailfin rammed into Lola's side causing her to tip sideways. In his side vision he saw Evanshade's trident rushing toward his eyes.

Clang! A foreign weapon stopped it short and Maanta soon noticed it was the rather burly man he had traveled with who had come to his rescue. "I told you I wouldn't let anything happen to you, young one." The large man thrust his weight against Evanshade while swinging a harpoon. Evanshade fled and then spun into the burly warrior before being halted once more.

"Maanta!" Tao beckoned from a whale-length off. "Go to your fellow Meridians. Cut loose their bonds and free Sift so that he may assist us in this battle!" Two enemies were slowly overpowering Tao himself.

With but a moment's search Maanta found the tightly wound kelp netting holding Amaranth and the others captive. As he reached them a woman clasped his arm with her shaky hand. Sobs uncontrollably mumbled from her mouth.

"I'll have you free shortly," he spoke to her before diving deep below. *What to use to break them free? My dagger is too dull. If I had a Malta shell I could burn the kelp off.* A large clamshell lodged between two stones below glimmered light all about. *This will have to do.* After dismounting Lola, his cupped hands swiftly pulsed his body downwards, knocking his heels along the massive shell. A cracking sound echoed while splitting it free where the stones pinched its sides. Grasping the shell he swam to Lola's back and rose with her up to the netting.

"Back away and watch out for the shell's edge," he spoke into the net cage as Meridians quickly swam from where Maanta had begun to cut the shell's sharp side along the kelp. Fraying, the kelp snapped strand by strand. Amaranth met Maanta from the inside, tugging on the kelp to break the strands quickly.

"Thank Gelu you arrived with help," Amaranth spoke. "Who knows what would have awaited us in Meridia. It is sad that we must fear our own home like this."

"I hope some day we can live there in peace again." The boy's sawing tore free another piece of kelp. "Is this enough for your escape?"

"But can we ever feel safe there or any other place again?" Amaranth tugged on the hole in the netting to extend it to its fullest. "I think this will do." Appendage by appendage, he squeezed through the netting. "Follow me!" He called to the others before turning to Maanta. "Thank you. Now free Sift. He's strapped to the back of us."

Maanta didn't know what to expect upon finding Sift bound to the back of the netting. Truthfully, he was shocked the strong man had been captured at all. Sift struck the boy as being someone who'd rather give his last breath fighting than admit defeat. Thoughts of Sift defending him in Meridia against Venge played out in his mind.

As Maanta came to the netting's back he took in the severity of what had been done to Sift following his capture.

Crimson blood curdled along the man's lips where a metallic contraption ground upon his face, contorting his features and bringing on irritation and pus. Black straps of whale carcass bound Sift's arms and legs together on the netting behind him. His skin was torn and bloody from where he had been whipped. His eyes whirled wildly like those of a strangled fish.

It didn't escape Maanta's thoughts while he sawed through the tough whale carcass that this old flesh could be from the whale he himself had slain. *What a horrible thing,* he thought. "What have they done to you?" He asked as a burning sensation sizzled across his muscles, all his force used while ripping the last of the fish flesh apart.

Sift's body writhed in the currents while regaining control of his limbs. His dark hands clasped upon the contraption encompassing his skull and locking his jaws. Vigorously beating its joints with his fists, Sift attempted his own release before realizing it would accomplish nothing. He only brought about further injury.

Maanta pulled out his trident and began locking its longest tip within one of the mask's joints. "Maybe we can stress the metal into breaking," He looked to Sift's eyes for permission to attempt it.

Sift grasped the trident's tip and pushed it away while grunting in agitation. There was something he wanted to communicate. Maanta held out his dagger and Sift eagerly snatched it from the boy's webbed fingertips. Quickly he dug its tip within the mask's joints but the metal only screeched eerily. He lodged it between the small opening at the mask's mouth and tried prying the contraption open before letting out a scream of agony while accidentally catching his tongue on the blade.

"We'll have to find the mask's key," Maanta spoke disappointedly. "But where would it be?"

The question's answer became obvious as Sift caught a glimpse of Evanshade in the edge of his eyesight. A simmering hatred lurked in Sift's eyes as his fists shook, the dagger clutched in his hand. And as Sift's legs pumped vigorously, taking him toward Evanshade, a howl echoed through Sift's lips. The emotions he wished to express spewed forth in eerie reverberation.

"I'll help you!" Maanta called after Sift who was already pivoting past warriors and skirmishes in his path. Maanta quickly reached Sift, thanks to Lola's quick movements, but the face encaged man shot him a look as if to say stay back because this was between him and Evanshade, alone. "At least take Lola back from me." Maanta stroked the riding companion's scales. "You'll need her agility to keep up with Evanshade."

A tail finned man locked in battle near by shot them a glance. "Like this beast of a creature would stand a chance against our leader!"

Sift thrust his dagger in the back of the man's skull causing him to convulse and sink limply in the waters. Maanta swam from Lola's back and Sift took his place before shooting toward Evanshade to take his revenge.

For a long moment Maanta shuddered while watching the dagger-struck man's dying eyes. *Is there any goodness, justness or correctness in any fighting and in what we do here? Is either of our sides right? Sure, these creatures murdered our families and drove us from our homes, but look at this man Sift has taken the life of. What son or daughter is fatherless now because of this death?*

Does that not make any killing of another being an unforgivable sin? And if we don't fight back they will murder and enslave us all. Gelu can love us for nothing we do here. There is much shame in our ways.

You might think that Maanta would follow Sift then, to help him as he said he would, but he didn't. Instead the slim boy dove, swimming as quickly as his leg fins and webbed fingertips would take him from the entangled chaos. He knew he wanted to rescue his fellow Meridians but knew no way of doing it without fighting and killing.

He was a boy, he realized while huddled in a small stone outcropping close by, cool currents whipping across his flesh. Tao had tried to show him he could be a man now but he wasn't. He knew his friends could win without him. And this is what he counted on.

Sobbing, was that sobbing he heard close by? Or was he sobbing and he hadn't known it? No, it was something other then himself. A sweet youthful girl's face with smooth curly red hair falling about it peered around the corner. Her deep emerald eyes peered within his own. Maanta held out his arms and the two closely embraced. "Anna..." he breathed softly, happy to have her near. "Thank Gelu you're ok." Archa's smooth body bobbed around the corner next, her head nudging his elbow with a smile in her eyes. "I missed you too, girl." He stroked her smooth body gently.

Anna told him how they had been ambushed and about how she had hidden in the inner ring of Orion's Birth because of what he had told her about the air there and how others feared it. She told him of Lisaly's death also. "When they took the others I was alone, but eventually I saw you riding Lola above and I had faith things would work out somehow."

"You saw us as we swam past? I wish I would have known so that I could have gone to you." They loosened their embrace and Maanta looked into her soft eyes once more. "I missed you while I was away. I missed everyone I guess. I missed you deep in my heart though."

Anna held close to Maanta's warm body. "I missed you too."

The battle raged a league before them. The two held close, making silent prayers to Gelu that their friends would prevail. Maanta made his own silent prayer that there would be few deaths on both sides.

At that moment in the battle's heart Sift quickly approached where Evanshade was locked in battle with the large man who had rescued Maanta.

Evanshade almost was impaled by the larger man's harpoon as Sift drove his caged head into Evanshade's spine. A spasm crept up his body as a crack resounded within him. Evanshade spun to meet the confrontation and was shocked when Sift managed to block his trident with a mere dagger. "Venge!" He hollered to the boy who was busy mutilating an escaped Meridian. "Come to me. Distract this rotund beast behind me!"

"My name," the large man's sturdy harpoon clashed with Venge's own. "is Hone! And I would have been more merciful than Sift will be with you. He doesn't need my assistance to outwit and overpower the likes of you."

"We'll see if this weak man holds his own." Evanshade smirked while focusing all of his efforts on slaying Sift. "Can you see through that mask you freak?" He taunted his foe while thrusting his trident against Sift's dagger. "It sure would be kind of someone to take that off of you. It's too bad I buried the lock's key below the sands of Orion's Birth. I could always run you through to put you out of your misery though."

The two men confronted each other in intense conflict as small skirmishes flared about them. Each man's muscles tightened and inflamed while twisting, clashing his weapon against the other man's. With each collide of their weapons both men tired, becoming slow and less precise as time passed about them, but never was there contact made with the other man's flesh. Their faces heated with fury and exhaustion.

Opal light trickled down from the ocean's surface and set a frost of light on their bodies as they fought.

And yet, as time went on, Evanshade noted the perishing bodies of his fellow men floating in the waters about them. Tao's men were slowly thinning his men's numbers. Behind him Venge was definitively losing the battle with Hone. If Evanshade survived the battle here and Venge perished, surely Venge's father, Evanshade's superior, would decapitate Evanshade himself.

"Retreat to Meridia!" Evanshade bellowed out while thrusting his trident against Sift's dagger, setting his foe off balance. Instantly the surviving men of Sangfoul pumped their tailfins in the currents, sweeping rapidly out of sight in Meridia's direction. However, instead of retreating, Evanshade swam quickly toward the center of where the conflict had been before clasping one of the Meridian's wrists in his tight fist.

"Help!" Amaranth yelled as Tao, Sift, Hone and the others rushed to his rescue.

"You have not won this conflict!" Evanshade called out through a grimace as they approached him. "You have only prolonged the fates of these Meridians and yourselves. I will send for reinforcements and we will find and capture you all! And Sift, I will personally forge a mask for you to wear the next time we meet."

Sift threw his dagger toward Evanshade but missed his tailfin by a shell's width. Tao and the others darted for Evanshade but with one swift thrust of his tailfin the man was off in the waters, following his men, and dragging Amaranth's struggling body behind him. There was no catching him as he disappeared from sight mere seconds later.

They had rescued most of the surviving Meridians but could they truly consider this victory, Maanta wondered while looking on from his hiding place. With so much death about them from the losses of both sides surely there could be no victory here for anyone. "It's over. They've left." He gently stroked Anna's crimson curls while bracing her in his arms. She hadn't wanted to watch and so he had held her close instead. "Evanshade seems to have captured Amaranth though."

"Someday they'll pay for what they've done to us," Anna cursed through a sob. "They will, even if I have to make them pay by myself." She swam off to join the others.

Vengeance can't be the answer, Maanta thought. *But what is?* "What do we do to save both ourselves and our souls?" He spoke to Archa while floating up and upon her back. It was good to feel her familiar form beneath him once more instead of Lola's awkward slim body. "I wish you could speak." He lovingly kissed her forehead. "Fish don't war and battle in masses like this. Surely you know the answer to my question if you could only say. "Ooooahooo!" He sang to Archa and the two joined Anna and the others in mending wounds and burying the dead in the sands below.

Neither Tao nor any of the others spoke of how Maanta had left them during the battle. He was, however, showered with praise for setting his fellow Meridians free. He assumed they had thought he had stopped fighting out of fear and they had understood because of his youth. Did any of them feel as he did, that they should find a way to end the fighting on both sides? Death sickened him.

Burying the dead was a solemn process. He accidentally touched one of the dead's hands while covering its body with sand and heavy stones. Goosebumps jumped up his arms and down his legs as repulsion frothed in his stomach. He couldn't look in their faces. He didn't want to recognize them and have the reality of the monstrosity that had occurred connect even more in his thoughts.

Once the burial process had been completed, at least thirty men, women and children had been sealed in their watery tombs and every living person who had placed them there was worn and dark-eyed from exhaustion.

As darkness swept through the waters like an oily film, this tired band of Meridians and their saviors would return once more to Orion's Birth, encamping before a long journey to Sift and Tao's home city as morning would break. Small groups broke oyster shells over broken malta stones outside Orion's Birth's walls and spoke of how they would reap their revenge on the beings of Sangfoul, the horrid things they would do to Evanshade, if they ever got their hands on him.

Amaranth and Sift had spoken once of how the skin colors of their peoples might cause them to be leery of each other. The Meridians had soft light blue bodies, contrasting greatly with Sift's people's deep black skin. But their common enemy had brought both groups together without even a second thought of the other group's race.

Maanta huddled with Archa in the darkness against Orion's Birth's outer wall, listening in hidden silence to the words one close-by group of his fellow Meridians spoke.

One tattered and grungy Meridian with a bald head and flowing slim beard cooked a fish above the simmering malta heat. "For what they've done to us, we should behead each and every one of those devils."

"If only we could catch them and stand a chance against their army," A slim woman in pastel shell garb spoke. "But it seems as if we are the ones hunted instead of them."

The first man replied to her. "I've heard that new man, Tao, saying that once we reach his city they will train us to defend ourselves and to fight the beings of Sangfoul. They will join us and we will have our day and our revenge."

This is ridiculous, Maanta thought while petting Archa's back. *No matter what training we receive, we will never be able to defeat the people of Sangfoul. And we have to free Amaranth and the others, but what is all this talk of revenge? If we attack their lands, then surely we will end up killing their innocents and be sinful "devils" ourselves. How do we free our people without killing and without going over the edge and being like them?*

"Their entire race deserves to die for what they've done to us," a youth slightly younger then Maanta said to the others. A woman close by shushed him and told him that surely there were tail finned beings that were good-hearted and that he should watch his tongue, but Maanta was repulsed and fled from his hiding spot to a place where he was certain he'd be alone with his thoughts, Orion's Birth's inner circle.

The runes in the inner circle glowed a sweet rose hue as he arrived and Maanta traced them with the tips of his webbed fingers as he thought. They rippled with vibrant colors. Colors, sounds and movements of inanimate objects fascinated him. Taking in the sights and sounds around him reminded him much of the days when he was alone in his wanderings of the outer-waters. *I felt like such an outcast then,* he thought. *And yet here I am with friends and yearning for peaceful aquatic wanderings.*

A soft sound whispered in his ears next, like seaweed brushing against a reef in the currents. He swung around swiftly in the waters, not so much out of fear for what was making the noise but more out of curiosity. Had something followed him within Orion's Birth's inner circle?

In the watery darkness of night, sight was difficult, but the red glowing runes speckled his surroundings just enough to allow him to make out the beautiful girl before him. Her deep emerald eyes playing with the red light caught his heart and breath in a shiver. *Every time I see her, she looks more beautiful than she has ever looked before,* he thought. *Why is that?* Her flowing curves and soft blue skin entranced him. And those crimson curly locks, why was she so attractive?

Anna twisted her fingers in her hair as it flowed in the currents and smiled at him. "I hope you don't mind my intruding." She came into the light a little more. "I've been looking for you ever since we returned from the battle."

"How could I mind?" Maanta smiled a true smile back at her. "You can intrude on me anytime you like."

"Watch what you wish for." She gave him a flirtatious look while swimming gently about. "I might like it too much and intrude all the time."

"There could be no such thing as too much with you." Maanta tried to flirt back, finding he was a little nervous while doing so.

Anna swam at him, giving him a swift push and pivoting quickly away.

"Oh really?" Maanta sped after her, chasing her in circles for moments, then wrapping his slim, pale arms about her body, bringing her down close to the sands below them. They were so close now. Her warm body snuggled close to his as she looked up into his eyes. Maanta realized that in this moment he didn't care what was going on in the world about him. He had Anna in his arms.

"Maanta," Anna spoke with what seemed to be some sort of purpose to him now. Her voice was soft. "I want you to always remember the way my eyes look tonight. Feel how I feel for you." Maanta was lost in her eyes. "I have a love in me that's growing for you."

A rush of warmth flooded Maanta's soul. "I feel the same thing in me for you." He gently touched her soft cheek, holding her loving look. "I'll never leave you. I'll always be here for you whenever you need me. I promise."

"Don't say things you can't know will be true." Her hand traced upon his. "But thank you. I would love that. If there's one good thing that all these horrible events around us have brought me, it's you. And there's nothing I would give you up for."

He traced his fingers through her hair and along her head as she moved closer still. Their lips were so close now. And even though he had never kissed before, he knew he wanted to with her.

Her warm, soft lips pressed against his, her body forming to his own and warming his. They were mentally one, he realized, in that moment. He would carry this with him forever. His hands held her close along the bare of her back.

Something was happening now though.

What was moving beneath him now, attempting to break up this moment? *Archa? He thought. Stop it! This is really a personal moment that we don't need you for. Do I really have to stop being close with Anna to send you away?*

The thing moved more and more beneath him, pushing upward on his legs and then swarming about his body and above. His legs flipped above his head as he realized what "it" was. A geyser of air thrust Maanta's body upward causing his fingers to claw at Anna's back as the two's lips were ripped apart. "NOOOO!" He screamed, tumbling up in the air burst with no control over his movements. His neck snapped back and thrashed from side to side as he whirled toward the ocean's surface above.

Far below he could hear Anna screaming because of the pain he had caused her with his nails and then bellowing out his name, hoping he would find his way back.

"MAANTA!" Anna screamed. It sounded like a hollow echo now, leagues away. "M..A..A..N..T..A.."

Sheets of the forbidden fluid, air, whirled about him making it impossible to see anything as the burst spat him upward. His eyes burned, water evaporating off them into steam as he tried to open them. He sucked on his fingers, attempting to breath in the water still barely clinging to their forms, but the air proved too much, sweeping past his lips and through his nose in a choking swarm.

Squirming, the gills within his throat sucked and writhed at the foreign substance causing him to suck more for water in futile agony. He choked, trying to scream to Anna, but no noise passed his lips.

The air geyser's walls swirled about him as he cartwheeled in their mist, writhing up and up before rocketing Maanta's pale form high above the ocean within an open mass of the poisonous substance, the night sky.

Hovering there for a moment; he wondered if possibly he would be able to swim in this substance now. *I have to make it back to Anna,* he thought. *I promised I would never leave her. There must be a way back.*

His guts thrust to the stomach as he fell. There is no falling underwater. He had never fallen before and grappled for sanity in the drop, still gagging on the air.

In mere seconds his body cracked against the ocean's top film. Blackness filled his sight as unconsciousness swept in. In the darkness, with pure navy blue night sky within eye's reach above him for the first time in his life, Maanta's body limply bobbed on the edge of ocean and air. His lips sucked at the waters beneath him impulsively, sustaining life in his slim form at least for a short time.

On a nearby shore a wrinkled old man twirled his long gray beard, staring at the stars and humming softly to himself.

12

Light Beginning

Meridia

In Cardonea Tower, at the very moment Maanta burst into the skies above, a young girl, Illala, hovered in the waters of her room, staring out her window at the fresh molten streams illuminating the darkness beneath the tower walls. The waters tasted bitter on her palate. *Where is Evanshade?* The thought rushed over her as a slim, white fish swam before her. *Has he gone to attack my people? He's been away all day.* Not that she really wanted to see him after witnessing him beat the deformed man in the cell below her. But knowing he'd been away so long had her worried about the things he was up to.

I don't know how to feel for him. When he's with me I grow toward loving him. I long to spend more time together. He's sweet and loving and kind. But when I start to give in to love I think of how he helped his people kill my family and led them to slaughter my people. How could I ever love such a dark-souled man?

When he gave her the option to leave, she realized, she should have left. How could this ever work? He seemed to regret what his people had done, and yet was too much of a coward to fight against his people and work to restore the Meridians to their realm.

A haunting moan reverberated through the floor below. *Odyssey's moan,* Illala realized. The night's darkness was consuming her and the scarred face of the imprisoned man hovered, an illusion in her thoughts. *I can't stay here with a man who lets things like the torturing of Odyssey happen around him.* She dove swiftly toward the floor, toward the shale brick that the man had removed before speaking with her. *I have to speak with Odyssey before I can leave, try to discover a way of rescuing him.* Her sleek slim nails grabbed at the shale brick's grooves, prying it loose once more from the flooring.

A sharp grinding noise shrieked in the silence as her fingertips clenched the raised stone in their grasp, almost lifting it completely from its hole. It was heavy but she could lift it. Odyssey's moans seamed closer now. "Help me with the brick!" She attempted to call to him below as the man's moaning ceased. But nothing happened. There was no attempt to push it upward from below. Was he so restrained now that he could not reach the port of their communication?

With her muscles flexed and body strained Illala slid the shale brick up from its setting only to watch it float back down quickly into place as she involuntarily flinched because of a nausea and pain suddenly swarming in her stomach. The brick's sides roughly rubbed against her fingertips while slipping away. Her youthful body curled in the fetal position while her hands massaged her sides in an attempt to relieve the discomfort. *What's making me feel like this?* She wondered. *Has someone poisoned my food?*

As the pain subsided another possibility played in her thoughts. "Could it be?" She gasped softly aloud. "There's one way of knowing for sure," her whisper seemed to hover in the silence and an anxious dread buried within her.

Her fingertips found an intricate stone case in a corner of the room and fumbled to open the shell within its hold. As the shell cracked and split, yellow ooze within seemed to stick to the darkness about it, giving the shell a mystic essence.

While closing her eyes she clasped the shell in her right hand, gliding it along her lower region. As Illala's eyes opened, orange ooze replaced where yellow once was.

Happiness and horror embraced in the moment as tears of joy and sadness streamed forth from her eyes.

There would be no leaving Evanshade.

I am pregnant with his child, Illala's thoughts trailed into silent night.

13

As one
Orion's Birth

Orion's Birth's inner ring seemed a silent tomb after Maanta had ripped away from Anna's grasp. She wailed and screamed for him in helpless dismay for long moments after watching him tumble upward in the air column toward the world above. Quickly her fins carried her after him but he was gone.

As the last of the air dissipated she found a lost sensation filling her soul. Surprisingly, the painful scrapes Maanta had left with his nails while ripping away from her, were the only comforting things she could find at all. They were proof that he had been there.

Anna might have drifted off into loneliness then, as she once had done before, if it wasn't for something Maanta had once shared with her about the aftermath of Orion's Birth's air eruptions. She had no time for feeling lost. She had to act.

"After the Birth's forbidden fluid eruptions, they rarely happen," Maanta had reassured her, "massive oceanic currents careen down the Birth's walls in a beautiful hail, sweeping everything in their path far from the Birth's walls. Many times Archa has embraced those currents with me on her, riding us all the way to Meridia."

The last place I want to go right now, Anna realized, *is Meridia.* The others wouldn't know of the coming currents unless she warned them and quickly.

"Archa!" She called, hoping the riding companion would come and take her to the others, but the smooth backed creature was nowhere to be found. "Maybe she's followed Maanta to wherever he has gone," she spoke to herself while her fins and movements carried her quickly above Orion's Birth's walls in a massive upward then downward swoop. Her back stung as she moved. *With Archa's help, hopefully he'll find his way back to us.*

A colorful conch shell shimmered beneath her as she dove within the group of Meridians and Sift's people to warn them. Her slim, pastel blue fingers quickly brushed the sands collecting on it away. With a gliding motion, she lifted the shell's small end to her lips.

"Huddle beside Orion's Birth's outer wall!" Her voice careened through the shell horn startling many of the group about her, causing them to jerk and swerve toward her in curiosity. "Go!" She shouted, as they slowly moved and listened to her. "Orion's Birth has spewed air toward the ocean's crest, taking Maanta with it, and soon rushing currents will sweep these waters, driving all in their path far away!"

With more haste the group swept against the wall, attempting to bury themselves within the sands there. A de-masked Sift bolted on Lola's back to Anna's side as she joined the others, huddling in the sands and grasping tightly to a sunken tree limb almost completely lodged within the sand.

Sift's face was worn red from where the mask had ground against it, but it was good to see the man out of his face prison once more. "Beat it with a stone, Tao did, until cracked it away," Sift spoke in his low tone, knowing her thoughts. "Maanta's been taken away? Since the mask has been removed, for him I've been searching. Have no worries though, young one. He will return to us. Of this I have faith."

In the darkness about them silence settled in. It had been far too long since the bursting column of air. Soon the currents would be upon them. A rumble resonated in the pitch black waters above.

"Brace tightly," Sift spoke beneath his breath.

Swift ocean currents burst from above as if out of nothing, dashing down Orion's Birth's towering outer walls above them, swarming toward the ocean's floor. Anna shivered in anticipation. Her eyes closed tightly while her hands clasped to the sunken limb. In her hard grasp the wood felt as if it would collapse in on itself at any moment. The soggy bark molded upon her fingers.

An airy, crackly sound deafened her hearing, as she felt just the softest of spiraling currents weaving about her body. *The sound hums as if there were hands held and pressed to my ears,* she thought before opening her eyes to sight amore. Swift currents leapt over her to the sands before her in a rushing, curved wall. A kaleidoscope of greens and browns, interwoven in the sweeping waters as kelp, sand and other oceanic gems, swept away in the underwater waterfall.

Plop! A small red something hopped out from the currents, swirling mid-float before her.

"Place it between your lips and eat," Sift's deep voice startled her. "From the upper world they are and," he smiled hungrily, "delicious! Swirling currents must have captured it from the realm of air."

The cherry-red thing slipped in her fingertips as Anna plucked it from the waters. And that's exactly what it was, a cherry.

Diving waters swept before her as she bit into the fruit, releasing its juice into a sweet cocktail that rippled on her palate. *Mmmm,* she thought before biting at the seed and pondering curiously as to what it was.

Pft! Spitting forth her soft lips a seed leapt within the sweeping currents, rushing off into disappearance. Juices from the fruit's body coolly massaged Anna's throat while her tongue pressed it against the inside of her cheek. *How is something like this created?* She pondered, having never eaten a fruit before. *Why doesn't anything like this grow here?* She chewed it some more before swallowing the succulent morsel.

Long moments of humming, rushing silence passed as the sweeping currents before them cantered against the ocean floor, leaping outward and away.

Mmmmmmmmmmmm, the deep noise bumped in Anna's ears, *Mmmmmmmmmmmm.*

Morning sunlight sheens trickled down from above after hours of throbbing blurry waters.

The currents passed and calmed to a breezy flow.

Anna and Sift would gather a band of five to search out Maanta. They skimmed the waters above and around Orion's Birth for leagues with no success until darkness approached the waters once more. Archa also was nowhere to be found.

"We have to return to our home to tell my people what has happened here," Tao spoke to Anna after their final comb of the surrounding waters. "They could be in danger without us there to protect them. Surely the beings of Sangfoul will amass against us."

"And what of Maanta?" Anna's exhausted eyes stared through the waters and the day's dwindling light. "How do I leave a boy who rescued me from the dark fate of the rest of my family? How do I leave someone who has stood by my side, befriended me and who I care for as if he were my own blood?" Her tired eyes became excited while catching on a swirling shadow in the distance, then calmed in sadness while the girl realized she had not seen Maanta, but instead, had been made a fool by tricks of light.

"Do I let the last member of my family slip once more from my life?" She sighed. "And does Meridia's Zharista have such a coarse heart that she leaves her most treasured friend alone in this darkness?" In the darkness, as she had searched for Maanta, the fact that she was all that was left of her family had eaten at her. She had made a defiant stand against her father the day he died by proclaiming that she was not yet the Zharista, her mother was. And yet here she was, her mother dead, and the title passed on.

Her entire family was dead, and here she was, the final living heir. "How can a Zharista feel so frail? I am helpless in finding my friend."

"I wish I had your strength." Tao hugged her as they floated in the waters. It reminded Anna of her father's strong embrace. "You have the strength of faith where I have lost all hope of finding Maanta. I am the weak one here. Sometimes the truest strength comes from a person's faith in something, even through all despair." He looked into her eyes, almost failing to say what was next to come, because of his dread of hurting her. "We have to go though or else my own family and home might fall without my people there to protect it."

"Then leave me behind with a few others to find him and we will come once he returns."

"We came here to find you and we won't leave without you." Tao's caring eyes turned stern now. "And what would you do if Evanshade and his warriors returned here?"

Anna pulled away from him, floating back just slightly in the waters, and gave him a defiant look as if to say she would stand in her position no matter what he said.

"Let's compromise." Tao pointed his muscular arm toward the place where his home was, far away in the distance. "We'll return to my home waters, rest our bodies and minds for a few days and then you, Sift and a group of warriors can return here to search for Maanta.

"The boy will be fine until then. He is strong, resilient and intelligent. From what I know of him he can hold his own in these waters. And there's something else I haven't thought of until this moment, Maanta is the only Meridian who has been to our home. I have faith that he would be able to find it again on his own."

Anna was silent, contemplating something. "If Sift leaves Lola for Maanta to ride back to your city on, then I will go with you. Your traveling companions move so swiftly that I don't know if he himself remembers the way, but I have confidence that if he returns, Lola will find him and bring him to us."

Tao smiled a deep smile and motioned an arm in the waters above. "Sift!" He bellowed out an echoing boon for the man.

Sift whooshed down from a coral alcove far above upon Lola's back. The long sleek fish shimmered radiantly as swiveling currents curled behind her.

Has Sift been watching us from above this whole time? Anna wondered.

Tao swam in the waters back to Anna. "You always fight to take a little more for your cause don't you, young one?" He flicked his index finger in a swift motion to give his words emphasis. "I respect that."

"What need are you having of me, Tao?" Sift asked.

"Night-time is quickly falling upon us my friend, and as we have spoken in private, we must set a course for our home so we may provide protection for our people in case there is a retaliatory attack on us there from the creatures of Sangfaul. And yet it is difficult to abandon hope of finding young Maanta near Orion's Birth's waters. I have spoken with Zharista Anna about these matters also and she places one request if we are to return to our city with her by our side."

"What asking do you have for us, Anna?" Sift's expression smoothed into a friendlier look as he spoke to her.

It comforted Anna to know that in such short time she had formed a relationship with this foreign man where he felt comfortable enough to relax around her. She hoped he would grant her request. "It's more of a question for you." It was hard to ask Sift to part with Lola again so soon after they had reunited. *He shows more compassion to Lola then I think some men ever have shown their wives,* she thought. "I would feel more secure leaving our search for Maanta here if I knew he could find his way to us if he returns. Would you leave Lola here for a short while to guide him if he makes his way back to Orion's Birth? I know she would watch for him and take good care of him."

Anna looked at Sift with youthful eyes that make the heart want to give them whatever it is they want. Mentally she prepared herself for the "no" which would inevitably come. Why would Sift part with the riding companion whom he'd been parted from for so long?

A long moment passed.

"Yes," the deep voice resonated from Sift's lips. Beads bobbed upon the man's neck in the oceanic currents as he kissed Lola's head scales. "The words of which you speak make sense, Anna. If Maanta is close by, Lola shall find him and to our side return him."

Anna sighed. "Thank you. Maanta feels so much like family to me now. I just can't leave him alone. You don't know how much this means to me. How will Lola know to stay?"

"Lola." Sift lifted his stern dark hand from her scales. "Heard have you what we say?"

"Ooooiii..." The noise echoed from the large creature's petite lips.

"Wait will you here for Maanta and return him to us? Come to your side, I will, if you do not come to us in ten light rising and fallings."

"Ooooiii..."

"It is settled. She will stay." Sift smiled proudly. "My Lola is a smart fish. All that is, she understands."

Anna was impressed. "And this is why I have faith in her to return him to us."

The aqua-crimson sunlight dimmed in the oceans above and Tao was anxious to return home. "Then it is settled," he spoke. "We leave for Baneal as quickly as we can get our peoples mustered. There we can revive ourselves, train the Meridians to defend their people, and plan for our revenge on the beings of Sangfoul. They have committed enough atrocities on both our races to deserve the repercussions."

Revenge. The word didn't sound harsh in any of the three's ears. It sounded only just. But how would killing settle in their stomachs, or their nightmares, from the souls they took? How would these realities affect them, affect Anna?

The youthful warmth froze a bit in Anna's eyes as *revenge* echoed in her thoughts. "Those beasts deserve what destruction we will bring them." Coldly she glared upon blank ocean waters. "We will train, and for my father's death, they all will perish."

An hour later the remaining Meridians huddled in a hovering group with Sift's dark skinned people, preparing for the trip to Baneal.

"My people and Meridian friends, we do not all ride upon the swift moving fish of Baneal in this journey home." Tao floated in the group's center, garbed in his luminescent bone mask and armor. "For this reason we must travel slower and with more wariness. Slim yourselves out into a thin procession and hug tightly to the depth's mountainous stone outcroppings.

"The soldiers of Sangfoul may await us in this journey's passageways so keep an open eye for them always. Also be watchful in the waters behind you for they may try to follow us and discover our home. Remember, the souls of our lost loved ones will protect and comfort us on this journey. Take warmth in your heart because of this. Once again I tell you I find peace in that my recently passed son, Ailcalm, rides with me. That we have survived this past battle is proof that our deceased loved ones ride and battle with us, giving us strength."

A long soft silence passed through the mass then. As Tao's words touched the hearts of his fellow people and placed their souls deep in thought, the Meridians gave lost glances to each other, thinking it strange that anyone would think that their dead loved ones were with them.

Neither race could understand the other one's religion, Anna realized, as she caught her fellow Meridians giving each other bizarre glances. She herself hadn't understood when she had discussed the very thing with Sift. *This will drive a small rift between our two peoples,* she thought, realizing that even the smallest of rifts could open to a canyon someday. *There has to be a way to seal this rift closed before it even opens.*

A soft voice, Anna's, rose like the soft calls of a whale, and all others there hushed and tuned their hearing to listen close to her words. "We have come together as two races into one. We were not two separate creatures who have now joined in a common cause. Instead think of our two groups as siblings who had never met but are tied by blood. We have found our brothers and sisters. Together we fit like the grooves of oceanic walls which were once joined as one, and are one again. My heart beats in the chest of each of you as your hearts beat in mine.

"And my fellow Meridians, think of this when you think of the religion of our new siblings. They feel as if the souls of their dead fight and live alongside them. Do we not feel the same? Does Gelu not say that even though we can not see him, he is always with and inside us? Your deceased mothers and fathers, do you not feel them at times watching over you from the home of Gelu himself? When I think of our religion and our companion's religion I also see two siblings who once shared the same parent. I propose to you that our two religions have adapted from one religion which is truth. We should all enrich our lives and faith with knowledge learned from each other."

A school of crimson fish swiveled through the group as Anna's words stopped, leaving hushed silence about the waters. She laid her hand upon one's slick, scaly back, feeling it swivel past her. Its playful movements brought her a smile.

She caught a look in Tao's eyes.

He was pleased that she had found a way to bring the two groups more united in spirit. "The Zharista speaks wisely!" His deep voice reverberated from beneath his ornamented bone mask. "My son, Ailcalm must be with this Gelu of which she speaks and also by my side. As I am sure her deceased parents, brothers and sisters are with her in this very journey."

A heaviness weighed in her chest as Anna heard Tao's words.

Tao thrust forward in the currents upon his riding fish while waving an arm toward the distant waters. "As one we ride to Baneal!"

Anna's toes tingled in the currents as the group rushed single file behind their leader. The group's movements sent odd ripples in the waters and she quickly fell in with Sift toward the back of the procession.

In the shadows beneath an outcropped stone wall the serpentine line of multicolored fish and large and small merpeople disappeared. Dust rippled as the only evidence of their stealth journey.

All was silent aside from the usual moaning of oceanic creatures, but if thoughts could be heard, Anna's thoughts might have stood out from the rest. Her eyes swelled. It was too much to bear. *Does Maanta also travel with my soul and reside with Gelu?*

Only Lola remained in Orion's Birth, hunting for the lost boy.

14

The Currents Above
On land

"Japeth, Shem, over there a man drowns in the water along our shore!" A deep old voice resonating with strength commanded two of his sons. "We must try to rescue him. Drag him forth from the water!" The old man stood, garbed in earthen-toned robes as his long gray beard whipped in the swift breeze.

Four light brown, muscular arms clasped upon the convulsing pale body of a dying boy, dragging him in the currents toward shore. The whites of the boy's eyes flashed in his head as he thrust his lips into the salty ocean, sucking in the liquid.

"What's he doing?" shouted Japeth, twisting his muscles in an attempt to lift the boy from the ocean.

"He's delirious!" Shem called before clutching the boy's hair with his large hand and thrusting the boy's head up from the water.

Maanta's gills collapsed in on themselves as he arose to consciousness once more. Air swept through him as he attempted to scream but the poisonous substance kept his noise to a cracked choke. The air seared his insides as he fought whatever force was restraining his movements.

His eyes opened and the sun's scorching beams blinded him, causing him to see multicolored spots before darkness overtook his vision. Whatever beast had its grasp on him tugged him further into the venomous air.

...save self... The thought barely rushed past his mind as the pain of existing encumbered him.

The lifesaving water currents were so shallow now as he ripped his hair from the thing's grasp and savored the liquid in his lips. Clawing, his fingers latched in on the underwater beach sands in an attempt to gain control of his movements. But the sands only stirred, collecting along his gills and choking him in another way.

"He's dying!" A voice bellowed past Maanta's ears. "Toss him to shore so we may push the water from his lungs!"

His body and thoughts violently shook as the beast lifted him above the ocean, his life source, and imbedded him in a hot burning sheet of sand. He tried to swim upward in the poisonous air substance but could get nowhere. What was that force pushing down on him? The beast had seemed to let loose of him but still he could not swim away.

Water evaporated from his pores. Every one of them sizzled and died in the sun's heat, collapsing in on themselves. It was as if a billion heated small pins dug minute grooves in his moist body. The boy's webbed hands pushed back on his flesh in an attempt to keep the moisture from rushing away.

From nowhere, it seemed, a fist lunged into his chest, pumping against it vigorously while vacuuming the water up from his lips. His neck's inner gills ripped from the throat's wall and spat from his lips into the air above before wiggling and dying on his chest. Maanta's thoughts collapsed in on themselves and unconsciousness overtook him once more.

"He's calmer now brother," a voice spoke in the silence of Maanta's mind. "And look, his chest rises and falls."

"Carry him to the guest room in our home," the old voice spoke in the distance. "There we shall nurse him to health."

Darkness... the world was pitch now, black as an oil plume. Maanta couldn't conjure sufficient strength in his muscles to move, even lift his eyelids. He couldn't help but feel a vacant staleness in his flesh. Any of his remaining fish-like scales had shriveled like dried rose buds on his limbs and now rest there like scabs. His eyelids sweltered and sat heavily on their sockets as a sunbeam from somewhere in the vast expanse of existence shown down on their outer skin.

Just as the boy thought he would evaporate away and cease to exist in this bizarre new reality, a firm yet wrinkled hand clasped his own which lay limp beside him. Also, from above, another strong hand placed a cool, moist cloth upon his forehead and eyes. Cool water from the cloth trickled down along his cracked lips, sliding in a spiral down his throat.

Whoever possessed the two strong yet wrinkly hands hummed a gentle melody while tending Maanta's fever.

For hours the man patiently changed the cool cloth with others.

At sparse moments he would place slivers of salmon within the boy's lips and Maanta would eventually swallow them down. The salty oceanic morsels slowly were revitalizing his muscles.

The last cool cloth was lifted from Maanta's forehead and the strong hand released his own as the humming faded a bit but still came from close by.

The fish brought some strength to Maanta's body. He yearned for more cool moisture from the cloths. And so with every reserve of strength Maanta lifted his eyelids.

Blinding light flooded in but as his irises adjusted Maanta dropped his sight on the strong but elderly fellow staring at him and rocking in a wooden chair while humming across the clay-walled room.

A genuine smile passed across the old man's bearded lips. "God blesses you, boy. Whatever dropped you in the ocean to drown, surely God's grace is the true reason you've survived. We figured you for almost dead the first two weeks after we rescued you from the ocean's grasp. And these past three haven't been much better. Would you like some more fish I wonder?"

Maanta tipped his head once forward and back against an earth toned pillow.

"Well, I'm not one to deny someone good hearty food." He passed three more pieces of salmon slowly through Maanta's pale lips.

Each swallow burned but revitalized. Maanta opened his lips to speak but couldn't find the way to shape words through the air clogging his lungs. Instead he choked and spat out a piece of the fish.

"Rest, young one." The old man stroked his hair. "There will be plenty of time for talking once you are fully healed. I have no doubt you have interesting stories to share with my family and me."

Maanta succumbed once more to the oily depths of deep sleep. There was reassuring warmth there beside him now though. Something joined him in the dark unconsciousness, swimming for him through the waters, helping to churn the depths of unconsciousness by his side. *God*, was the only thought which possessed his mind while rafting toward the world of dreams.

Time passed. Maanta's mind closed. No thoughts existed. Then in loud booming echoes thoughts returned.

thump,   thump.......thump,   thump.......thump,
thump.......thump, thump... Sight came to Maanta easier this
time as his eyes spread wide in the burning, singeing air.
Sharp golden sunshine flushed within his sight as an outside
breeze licked at his face. He was in what appeared to be a half
shell of ceramic, his legs thrashing, free of his mind's control,
in a thin bath of dirty water about him.

"Brace the boy's legs to the tub Japeth!!!" A deep
mature voice that Maanta vaguely recognized shouted from
behind him. "He must be bathed! His stench is foul!"

Water... Maanta's thoughts raced as he realized the
substance was beneath him. *Water!* He thrust his head beneath
the thin level of dirty tub water, attempting to breathe it
through his gills. But his gills were gone. He gagged on the
once life-blessing substance. *What's... h... appening?* His
thoughts burped and skipped. *What... h... ave they... d... one?*

"Grab his skull and lift it above the water Shem!" The
light-brown skinned Japeth hollered at the man who had just
spoken behind Maanta.

Shem cupped the boy's thrashing head in two massive
hands and thrust it above the dirty bath. "This is useless,
brother. I don't know why but the boy appears to be trying to
drown himself. If we're busy holding his limbs in place and
keeping his head above water we'll never get him washed."

Maanta's eyes flicked violently in his skull as darkness
once again consumed him. *Water...* his thoughts trailed off.

"Let us lift him from the bath then, brother, and try
again later when he is more subdued," Japeth spoke with calm
and yet a hint of irritation.

The two brothers grabbed Maanta's limbs and jerked
him quickly up out of the outdoor bath before Shem draped
the boy over his shoulders. Slowly he would carry the boy
until carefully laying Maanta out on the bed the family
provided him.

The boy's body was limp and sank gently within the feather stuffed resting place. All consciousness had left as he had lifted from the shallow tub waters Maanta mistook for salvation.

In the dank darkness of Maanta's lost mind the soft breath of one word caught his thoughts, *God*. The pureness of the word skimmed like a breeze on the ocean, constantly soft and just above the waters but unattainable to all those who live within the sea. *But the sea and the waters have deserted me,* his mind rambled in the nothing. *And yet I still live somehow in this bizarre place that I sometimes awaken to. Am I breathing in the air?*

"Freedom from the waters is yours if you only accept it and believe in me," a voice whispered in the hollow darkness, a warming light emulating around its words. **"There is forgiveness for your people's sins."**

"NO! COME TO ME *beneath the depths*," another voice, enticing yet sinister, intruded.

Blank nothing came like a kiss to Maanta's drifting thoughts. It extinguished his mind, preventing him from thinking through what was meant by the two voices which had joined him.

The twitching void of nothing covered him like a thick, dark mud, consuming him in its embrace.

Darkness.

Nothing.

A softly hummed melody caressed Maanta's hearing and livened his heart. The darkness of his dream-state shifted from deep black noir to a light sandy hue. Once more he felt the presence of a moist rag being held to his forehead by a strong, comforting hand.

His eyes no longer burned when he opened them to the daylight filtering through the windows of the room. His body did not ache, nor did his flesh sting with purging evaporation from the air. In a deep comforting breath he inhaled the air about him and filled his lungs full, lungs he never knew existed until this very breath.

As Maanta exhaled that first full breath his sight set slowly on the face of an elderly man beside him who was holding the moist cloth to his forehead.

The man's features were old and wrinkled but exuded life as he smiled warmly at the boy. "You look more alive today, boy, than you have ever since we rescued you." The man's beard jiggled up and down as he spoke. "Maybe this time we'll be able to keep you from relapsing into unconsciousness again. Tell me, boy. Do you have a name?"

"........." Maanta's lips moved but still he could not find the way to form speech out of water.

"That's alright. It will come to you in time." The man's wrinkled hand rested on Maanta's to comfort him.

"...mkft..." Maanta struggled to speak in the air. "...Maanta."

"Maanta." The old man's grin widened. "That's an interesting name. I've never heard anything like it before. Your name reminds me much of what we all are... Man. You're speaking now, and that's a good sign. How far down the coast does your family dwell young Maanta?"

"...ckt...ckt...ckt..." The boy couldn't bring speech to his lips again. His body shook with agitation.

The old man brought a wrinkled finger to his lips. "Shhh... There will be plenty of time for you to talk later. If it hurts to do so now do not hurt your throat. Let's see. We need to devise some way of keeping you conscious. Do you like stories?"

Maanta managed a smile. The last story he had been told was from his mother long ago. After that he had resorted to creating stories to tell himself.

"I'll take that smile as a yes." The old man ran his fingers through his beard as if in deep thought. "This is a true story, of my life.

"Once, a long, long time ago, I was a young child who lived in a small thatch house on the rim of a vast sea. My parents farmed for a living and I assumed them perfect, as most children assume their parents to be during the early part of their lives. I had friends, a deep faith, family and all was well in our happy community. It remained that way for years until, during a deep crimson sunrise; a man fell from the sky and careened into the beach. We thought he was a star. All of the local families who saw the falling man rushed to see what had crashed into our shore.

"I'll never forget his features, the aura he exuded. Serenity encompassed him. In a massive crater on our shore the blond haired, blue eyed man stood with a brisk smile on his face, clothed in blue and white silk. He stared through the clouds above as if to mock something, or someone."

The old man slipped a dried, salted pumpkin seed between his lips and flipped it with his tongue methodically. "And I swear to you. The first time I saw him, the man had wings, wide flowing wings that stretched in the air to shroud my eyes from half the ocean before me. They sparkled in the sunrise, whipping and curling in the wind. And then as my people laid their first steps to his crater the man's wings disappeared, evaporating into the clouds. No one ever spoke of his wings except me. Were they ever there? Where did they go?

"I never entered that crater, was unnerved by the unnatural occurrences about me. But instead I watched as my people flocked to the man like a herd of sheep to a shepherd, or a wolf in a fancy robe. I never heard the exchange of words between him and my people that day but as he spoke the man's eyes flicked every few moments from a cool blue to a deep heart-purging orange.

"I was 18 when the man hurled upon us from the sky and would age 582 years before my last experience with him would place its footprint on my life. He called himself Lucifer and claimed himself a fallen angel of heaven.

"If he had fallen from heaven then surely he had not tripped, God must have thrust him out, for in his time with us he taught my community to sleep with each other's wives and husbands, steal each other's food, poison each other's crops, to rape our children and murder our neighbors. One time, I even overheard the soft voiced man convincing a young man to take his own life. Kilol was the boy's name and his neck would be in a self-hung noose by sun's set.

"I tried and tried to show my people the evilness of Lucifer's ways but they would hear no sense. They were blinded by greed and lust, desires that could only be quenched by things he had brought to my people's souls.

"And then the day came when the final straw fell into place, it seems, in the 'fallen angel's' plan. I awoke in the sweltering heat of a summer's morning to look out my window on an idol carved in the man's likeness. Kissing its form were four of the highest ranking families in my village. Lucifer himself stood behind the unholy falsification, his fiery eyes glaring at mine, peering into my soul.

"In that moment I closed my eyes and prayed to God to relieve my people of that man and bring a world to us once more where we would be free of the sins he brought to us.

"In the darkness of my mind a deep, calming voice, echoed. *'I have heard your prayer son of Adam. I have determined to make an end to all flesh; for the earth is filled with violence through them; behold I will destroy them with the earth. Make yourself an ark of gopher wood; make rooms in the ark and cover it inside and out with pitch.'*

"'*For behold, I will bring a flood of waters upon the earth, to destroy all flesh in which is the breath of life from under heaven; everything that is on the earth shall die. But I will establish my covenant with you; and you shall come into the ark, you, your sons, your wife, and your sons' wives with you. And of every living thing of flesh, you shall bring two of every living sort in the ark, to keep them alive with you; they shall be male and female. Of the birds according to their kinds, and of the animals according to their kinds of every creeping thing of the ground according to its kind, two of every sort shall come in to you, to keep them alive.'*

"It is impossible to explain how I knew, but it was God's voice and so I did as he instructed. When the ark was complete, it was 450 feet long, 75 feet wide and 45 feet high with three decks spanning from side to side. I had never seen a vessel so massive. And now a question resonated in my thoughts, how would I gather two of every kind of animal from the earth for my boat? There was no need to ponder this though, for as soon as I lowered the ark's loading ramp its first time, I noticed something moving in the brush of the beach before me.

"One nose, then another popped through the brushy leaves. All the many animals of the earth came, two-by-two, down the beach and into the ark. I've never seen such a sight in my life and probably never will again. Two snow-white bunnies led first, their soft fur glistening in the sun and their cute button noses twitching as they hopped happily along. Two jet-black panthers followed closely behind, their muscles flexing majestically with each step. Two grisly bears were third, grunting and moaning as they swatted at the moist sands below them as they walked.

"God must have brought the many creatures from all over the world into that procession, for every form of creature was there from koala bears, kangaroos and giraffes to polar bears, otters and monarch butterflies. The last animal to come in the group I thought would snap the ark's deck in half. Two gargantuan wrinkly gray elephants shook the earth beneath us as they sauntered onto the ark's ramp, their bellies swaying slightly as the ramp flexed beneath each massive step. When they had all boarded my sons and I loaded pounds upon pounds of meat, vegetables, fruit and grain we had gathered to keep the animals and ourselves fed.

"As we stood some distance away admiring our work a voice once again echoed in my thoughts. *'Go into the ark, you and all your household, for I have seen that you are righteous before me in this generation. For in seven days I will send rain upon the earth forty days and forty nights; and every living thing that I have made I will blot out from the face of the ground.'*

"By night's end I and my family had moved all of our personal possessions and us upon the ark. My wife strung fresh cut flowers from deck to deck all about the boat in an attempt to cut back on the wet animal smell. In the days to come, my fellow people would come to mock us and point out what a foolish thing we had done. I even told them about the great flood God was sending us to wipe out the vast sins of our world but they merely took me for a crazy old man.

"Those final seven days as the rains came and refused to stop, the only man which said nothing to me was Lucifer himself. As we waited for the flood to come he stood on the beach below us, staring up into our eyes, with a wide grin on his face, those deep eyes of his flickering with flame in the nights. What a possessed creature was Lucifer. He aged not one day since he had first come to us but his eyes ignited more and more with crimson with each new soul he took.

"'God is sending a flood to wash away all of the sins you have brought upon us!' I called down to him.

"A wolf howled in the distance but from his lips there was no reply.

"On the seventh day the waters rose beneath us, not slowly, but in a surge lifting our ark to the very heights of the sky. It was the most bizarre thing though, just before the world flooded Lucifer led many of my civilization into the ocean beside us, causing them to disappear beneath the depths before the flood. He joined them and as God's maelstrom hit, the remnants of my people screamed in agony as they drowned. The raging waves around us seemed a mass of red and green, red blood of the earth's creatures and green of the earth's vegetation. The sky was black with disappointment and rage. There would be no more blue sky or ocean that day, the color of peace and calm. The carcass of a dead ape drifted below my window in the chaos. I was saddened that this creature had to die because of humanity's sins.

"The first night was no easier on the heart. For an entire day, as the maelstrom raged, the cries of the earth's people and animals could be heard wailing and being snuffed out across the globe.

"For thirty-nine more days and nights, the maelstrom roared, and what we heard after those days was worse; silence. When the rain stopped and waters calmed, all the animals on the ark stopped their moaning, chirping and roaring and we heard nothing in the distance on the open waters. Eerie, hollow blankness lay upon us.

"'Where is the world?' My son, Japeth, would turn to me and ask.

"'It is on the ark with us,' I would tell him. But it hurt my soul to know that my people, no matter how sinful they had become, had all perished in the world behind us. The air itself smelled stale, lifeless. God must have felt my heart and smelt what I smelt in that moment for after I breathed the stagnant air a great wind blew about us which smelled of honeysuckle. There will be life to the earth again, God was promising us.

"At the end of a hundred and fifty days the waters had abated and in the seventh month on the seventeenth day the waters had receded enough that our ark came to rest upon the mountains of Ar'arat. The waters continued to abate until the tenth month. On the first day of the flood's tenth month, we could see the tops of the Ar'arat Mountains about us. Still, I knew there would be no hope in searching for land.

"After forty more days I called my sons and our wives to my side. 'Shem, Japeth, Ham,' I said. 'The earth is once more revealing itself to us. Look at the beautiful brown mountains bobbing up from beneath the ocean around us and stretching like legs below the ark. Boys, find me a bird that we can release to see if the waters have subsided from the face of the ground.'

"Japeth and Ham had become quite fond of a raven they named Zemer and so we sent Zemer forth to see if the waters had dried up enough anywhere on the earth for us to leave our ark and live on the earth once more. Zemer's deep black wings carried her quickly from the ark but she disappeared in the winds and never returned to us again. It is my hope she discovered land and had just not known to return.

"The next day I sent forth a dove, a favorite of my own, who would often eat sunflower seeds gently from my hands, and in the evening she returned to me with no sign of finding dry land.

"Seven days later, again, I sent the dove out of the ark and as the sunset played a tranquil pink across the sky she returned to me, and lo, in her mouth was a freshly plucked olive leaf. This could mean nothing less than that the waters had subsided from the earth beneath us.

"Seven more days I waited and sent out my dove again and she did not return to us anymore. To join her, I let loose her mate.

That night as I lay in the darkness saying my prayers with my wife already fast asleep on my chest, God's voice echoed once more in my mind. *'Go from the ark, you and your wife, and your sons and your sons' wives with you. Bring forth with you every living thing that is with you of all flesh-birds and animals and every creeping thing that creeps on the earth-that they may breed abundantly on the earth, and be fruitful and multiply on the earth.'*

"And, as the next morning came, I stood looking from our ark's deck, down the steep face of Ar'arat's mountainside which stretched off into the mist beneath us. 'How far down the slope is level ground?' I gasped to my wife beside me. 'Surely the elephants and giraffes can't maneuver the slope beneath us, nor can the seals or platypuses.'

"Japeth called me to his side from behind us then and told me of a plan he had been concocting since our first day wedged upon Ar'arat's peaks. As evening came, we would put it into effect.

"The wind blew crisply at our backs as my three sons and I stood stiffly on our ark's back deck, nervous about what we would soon attempt. Japeth turned to me with a grin. 'Praise the Lord for he has kept us safe thus far.'

"I grasped his hand firmly in my own. 'And praise him as he protects all of us on our journey to level ground. Do not fear my sons, for in what we do, God is by our side.' The animals were secured below deck. Our wives were calming the creatures' nerves and all of us were saying silent prayers to God to bind us in safety.

"As Japeth and Ham tied two thick ropes in triple knots to the deck's inlaid posts, Ham sliced his palm on a splintered beam, causing crimson blood to drip from his hand. Ham and Japeth grasped the ropes and leapt off the deck's edge into the swirling fog below, their ropes left tightly creaking against the deck. Ham's hand had bloodstained the rope where he had touched it, churning my stomach with its sight. A man should never lose a son before his own death and Ham's blood brought the very real possibility to my thoughts of losing my sons and our wives. 'Keep a tight grasp on Ham's rope,' I spoke to Shem. 'I'll hold tight to Japeth's. We don't know when they'll need us to pull them aboard.'

"Japeth would later tell me that as they leapt into the fog his heart was crushed in his chest as he saw Ham beside him smash into the ark's bottom hull. But Ham held on, both brothers' hands clasping tightly to separate ropes as they swung freely above the vast drop of Ar'arat's mountainside beneath them. Swinging back and forth, they built enough momentum to reach the bottom of the hull once more and lodge their stone pickaxes into its' dense underbelly. 'There!' Japeth freed a hand, pointing before him to where the rugged slope clutched our ark against its terrain. 'We must free the ark of Ar'arat's grasp!' Japeth and Ham tied the ropes to their waists and drew two more pickaxes to help them on their way to where the stone met the boat.

"When they reached their spot the boys kept one axe each lodged in the boat's hull while using their second to hack and pry at the places where the Ar'arat held us in its' clutch. Stones broke free, careening in echoes down the mountainside.

"I heard a scream of frustration while up on deck as Japeth lodged his second ax with a swift stroke between the rocks and the ark. Moments later, Ham would dislodge the ark from Ar'arat and the ark teetered forward, slowly at first. 'Pull us up father!' I heard him bellow from below.

"The muscles in my forearms seared in pain as I yanked one arm-length after another of Japeth's rope upon the deck. Beside me Shem's face reddened as he did the same for Ham. 'Pull! Pull!' I screamed as the Ark's bow sank forward in a swift tilt, kicking its backside up in an attempt to buck us. I went sliding into the post where Japeth had tied his rope. As our ark crashed into and slid down the mountainside Japeth fell in over the backside and against the post and me.

"I whipped a glance at Shem who was curled across from us against the post Ham had sliced his hand on. A blood speckled rope end flew in the wind the ark produced as the ark bucked down the mountainside. 'Ham!' I hollered helplessly.

"With my nails I clung to grooves in the ark's floorboards, pulling myself up the ark's back deck to get a look back at the terrain rumbling behind us in hopes of catching a glimpse of Ham safely there and away from the careening boat. Nothing. Nothing was in the boat's wake but a blur of stones, mud and dried-up seaweed.

"I wept tears into the swirling winds and beside my hand a pickaxe crashed into the wooden railing. Another thrashed into the rail beside my other hand and in exhaustion Ham's eyes rose over the side and met mine. As I clasped his two hands he fainted in my grasp and with all my might I thrust him aboard. We both careened down the deck into Japeth before being pulled in the ark itself by our wives.

"Without our wives, after all we had done to free the ark and return to safety, we probably would have all been swept overboard again in a matter of moments and been crushed by the debris the ark churned in its wake.

"Darkness swirled in a blur beneath my eyelids as consciousness returned to me. Nausea sank in my belly as I opened my eyes to see the ark's inner deck sloping greatly downward below me. The sweet scent of flora wafted through my nostrils as my wife's arm held me close to her. *She has the most beautiful, soft strong arms,*' I remember thinking. I had never known her to wear this particular floral scent before. What was that scent?

"And then, while staring toward the corner of our slanted deck past a huddled group of pigs, chickens and goats struggling to stand, a sight caught my eyes that set my heart racing. Beautiful blue, yellow and amber flowers pressed up through a hole in the ark's side that was rubbed bare in our rush down the mountainside.

"I turned to my wife and my family behind her as I sat up on the sloped deck. 'Thanks to the glory of God we have all survived the flood,' I said. I could feel God also there beside me. 'May we continue to serve him as good people throughout our days.'

"No sun has shown as warm and bright in my days as the sun which greeted us as we left our ark. The high-up deck door now rested directly beside the lush green and floral earth so that all we need do to leave the ark was walk from its door to the earth about us. All flowers of the world grew in the field there and blossomed before us, daffodils, lilacs, sunflowers, dandelions, tulips, honeysuckle and many others blessed our senses.

"While leading the animals two by two from the ark I looked up as the birds flew free from the ark's windows in a fountain of color above. I thought I saw two doves meet them in the distance, but in the radiant sunlight as I focused on them, my eyes blurred to see only pure white light.

"That first night as the sun set in the distance we built an alter to the Lord, praising him for his blessings by burning scented planks of wood we had brought with us from home in the fire-pit.

"A low warm voice spoke to all of us then between the sunset and spark of firelight. *'I will never again curse the ground because of man, for the imagination of man's heart is evil from his youth; neither will I ever again destroy every living creature as I have done. While the earth remains, seedtime and harvest, cold and heat, summer and winter, day and night, shall not cease. Be fruitful and multiply, and fill the earth.*

"*'Behold, I establish my covenant with you and your descendants after you, and with every living creature that is with you, the birds, the cattle, and every living beast of the ark with you, as many as came out of the ark. I establish my covenant with you, that never again shall all flesh be cut off by the waters of a flood, and never again shall there be a flood to destroy the earth.*

"*'This is the sign of the covenant which I make between me and you and every living creature that is with you, for all future generations. I set my bow in the cloud, and it shall be a sign of the covenant between me and the earth. When I bring clouds over the earth and the bow is seen in the clouds, I will remember my covenant*

*which is between me and you and every living creature of all flesh;
and the waters shall never again become a flood to destroy all flesh.*

*"'When the bow is in the clouds, I will look upon it and
remember the everlasting covenant between God and every living
creature of all flesh that is upon the earth. This is the sign of the
covenant which I have established between me and all flesh that is
upon the earth.'*

"That is the last time I have truly heard God's spoken word
in my ears. And yet, so many times I hear him calling me through
the tree's breeze or across the ocean's waves."

The old man sat, silently staring as if lost in a dream, at
the wall behind Maanta. His long gray beard rested knotted
up in the old man's fingertips. He wrestled to untangle it.

What a bizarre tale, Maanta thought while staring deep
into the man's eyes. *But then so much of this world of air is bizarre
to me.* His thoughts carried him then to how the tale began, the
flood, the drowned people and the person who descended
upon the village from up above. There was something familiar
about it, all which rested on his tongue's tip. *No! It can't be!* He
thought. "kkssst... What ssss... is kft... your pft...name?"
Maanta held back the urge to cough up blood which churned
in the back of his throat while he spoke. The air burned and
coiled upon the sores where his gills once were.

The elderly man's wrinkled eyes withdrew from their
dream state and refocused on the reality about him. He smiled
at Maanta, a warm smile that a parent would give you. "There
I go, telling a story before properly introducing myself. My
name is Noah."

How can that be? Maanta's mind raced. *His story is so
close to the tale mother used to tell me, and his name so similar to
the man's name she spoke of. But we have been generations in the
waters since that happening.* He would have to find a way to
speak. Maanta fought back the urge to choke on his own
throat. "kkssstfffk..."

Noah saw him struggling. "Calm yourself, boy. There will be plenty of time for talking later once you have healed more."

"kkcftkt... Noah? kft... That can't be." Maanta could feel his throat adapting to the air. "kkssst... My mother once told me stories kft... much like the one you just told me. A man in them was called Noa and he khhhst... spoke with Gelu before the great drowning of my people. But it has been leagues since we have adapted beneath the depths. How could you be that man and still have life? How old are you, Noah?"

The old man raised his eyebrows in an inquisitive look at the boy, himself both baffled and curious. "I am 926 years of age, young Maanta, and I swear to you all I have spoken to you is the truth. God has blessed me with long life. I assume your people don't live quite as long where you are from. And you say you were born of the people who drowned beneath the waters on the day God flooded the earth? This confuses me and yet also explains much. When my sons first found you in the ocean you were thrusting your face into the water as if gasping for breath.

"I also thought it odd that I did not recognize you because all men and women on earth are descendants of me and I believed I knew them all. But when God spoke to me he said that every living thing on earth would perish. How could that be true and you be alive?"

Long moments of silence passed as Noah and Maanta thought.

Maanta pulled strength into his throat once more. "khh... Is it possible that God meant earth, as in soil? For you yourselves lived because you were on the ark and away from the flood and storm. And the fish also lived and they were animals of the earth, but did not come on the ark. What if the people who were on the land when the flood came died, but those fishing on their boats and swimming in the waters adapted to become sea creatures when the waters swallowed them up?"

Noah grinned. "It must be so, because I can't deny that you are alive and sit here before me. God never ceases to surprise me with his wondrous deeds. Even in his hour of fiercest anger he blessed the people of earth with another chance. And I see he was not wrong in doing so. You truly have a kind, warm spirit. Tell me of your world, Maanta. What has happened to the families of the village I once knew?"

As warm sheens of luminous sunlight shown through the room's windows, Maanta told Noah all of what he knew about his people's beginnings beneath the waves. He spoke about how his people learned to cultivate the ocean floor, producing their own seasonings with minerals found in sea plants and drying out saltwater in small caverns beneath the ocean where air pockets collected. Maanta's descriptions of Amaranth's mysterious experiments brought Noah a raised eyebrow.

"He sounds like a sorcerer," Noah interrupted. "Many people would think him an evil man where I am from."

Maanta reassured his new friend that Amaranth was as good a friend as any could ask for and that he had one of the purest hearts he knew of. When the boy spoke of Sift's people, Noah told him that he himself had once had a best friend with dark skin such as this.

"I am warmed to hear their people still survive," Noah grinned.

This led to talk about how Sift's people had been enslaved by the dark-souled race of tail finned people. When Maanta spoke of how Evanshade had led the tail finned ones to Cardonea Tower to massacre the Zhar and Maanta's fellow Meridians, the boy gushed desperate tears of sadness. This new world above the waves was fantastic, but he missed his realm beneath the waves, a way of life and people that would be forever lost to him. Even if he could adapt to breathe water again, his world had been forever changed by the massacre.

Noah simply pulled the boy close in his strong arms and let Maanta's tears flow down his shoulder. As Maanta sat up once more and collected himself, Noah called into the halls of the quaint beach house. "Japeth? Shem? Are you here? Come, the boy has awoken!"

A tall, lanky and yet muscular man skidded through the doorway moments later. "Father, Shem is out helping tend Ham's fields and cattle but I am here." The man thrust his hands to his sides. "Well, I see you've finally awoken. Took you long enough! They call me Japeth."

Japeth has a firm handshake, Maanta noted as they greeted. "Pleased to meet you. My name's Maanta. Thanks for pulling me ashore."

"Let me tell you, you didn't make it any easy task with all that squirming. I could have sworn you wanted to drown." Japeth turned abruptly toward Noah. "Do you need something of me father?"

Noah's strong wrinkled hands cupped one of his son's. "Young Maanta must be starved. In the months he's been in our care we've been able to keep little more then water and slivers of fish in his stomach. Let's fix him a feast of steak, potatoes and corn to revitalize his body."

Japeth's mouth salivated a little at the thought. "I'll get right on it father. I'll pull the food from our salt shelter and have it cooked before you know it," Japeth smirked toward Maanta. "You don't know the feast you're in for boy! Father makes the best seasonings."

Noah turned back to his son. "The proof is in the cooking not in the speaking."

"A wise man speaks wise words father."

As Japeth left the room Maanta's stomach let loose a growl. *I hadn't realized how hunger was overtaking me until he mentioned food,* Maanta thought. *I wonder what steakpotatoes are. And corn? It sounds like some bizarre horned fish.* "Were they dangerous to capture?"

"Pft!" Noah almost laughed but caught himself. How was the boy to know what these things were? "No. Steak is a meat that comes from cows, docile animals that we raise in our fields."

That still didn't answer his question about the corn animals but Maanta decided he'd have to discover the answer for himself.

"Japeth is very skilled at cooking. And he's had plenty of practice cooking for our wives and his children, although my wife passed many years ago. Generations upon generations have been born since the flood waters abated. And Japeth has cooked and taught our descendents to cook for many years. " Noah refocused his attention on Maanta. "I've no doubt he'll fix us up a delicious dish."

"I can't wait to try land food." Maanta rubbed his stomach and grinned. "I'm starved!"

Noah's facial features took on a sterner look. "We might as well discuss what your people are going through as we wait. It seems to me that your people have one of two ways they'll react to the massacre. And the path they appear to be going down bothers me because it could lead them to the same dark place that brought humanity into God's disfavor in the first place.

"With the help of Sift's people they seem to be planning retaliation against the tail finned ones. Your fellow Meridians are angry and bitter and crave revenge for what has been done to them. The problem with hate is that it breeds more hate and a path of destruction and slaughter will form an endless loop across the seas if this happens. One people will retaliate against the other until neither group will remember why they started fighting in the first place. Hate is sin no mater what a person's reasons for hate are, and no good can come from sin."

Maanta's mind grew dense and darkness pulsed in around his sight. The pressure of breathing air and speaking through un-gilled breath caused him to feel woozy once more. *Don't do it Maanta,* he mentally encouraged himself. *If you pass into dream state now, who knows how long it will be until you regain consciousness again.* The darkness dispersed as his sight gained clarity once more.

"Are you alright?" Noah asked after seeing the boy's irises bob like bulbs of air in his eye sockets.

"I'll be alright. It felt as if unconsciousness was coming for me again for a moment. You speak of two journeys my fellow Meridians might choose between. This makes much sense. When we were fleeing from Meridia, my people kept speaking of how they would return to Meridia to free our captured people and kill the tail finned people who slaughtered us. Freeing our captured people is something we must do. Killing all the tail finned people we find there is something that I started thinking about though.

"If we do that, we will be no better than them. Surely the people we would kill have spouses and children of their own. Even if the ones we killed were evil to the soul, surely their families that would suffer cannot all be bad. As the Meridians about me discussed more and more what they would do once they had learned to be warriors from Sift's people, I began to ask myself what Gelu would want us to do. I can't imagine the creator of all earthen and oceanic things would take pleasure in any one of his people taking the life of any other of his people."

"And so you see which path your people must take if they are to retain the inherent goodness which was given them since God drowned the Earth, but granted them another chance." Noah sighed deeply. "God says that if someone hits you or does you harm you are to turn the other cheek and not seek revenge. For what we do to our fellow man we do to him. If you hit another man or woman, even in retaliation, it is as if you have just punched God himself. Not a wise move I'd say."

Maanta shifted on the bed to peer behind him now, toward the ocean shimmering with sunlight behind him. "And now that my lungs breathe only air, there is no way for me to return to persuade them against the path they will inevitably follow. What will come of my people? With all the chances Gelu has given us, will he possibly be able to forgive us again?"

The steamy seasoned scent of freshly grilled meat, potatoes and corn embraced the room where Noah and Maanta sat. And even in the seriousness of the moment, both men salivated and could almost taste the aroma in the air.

Trying to get out his thoughts before the food arrived to immerse his senses, Noah spoke. "God has said that he will never again destroy every living creature, because the imagination of man's heart is evil from his youth. God will never again destroy the world. The thing to fear then instead is that man will destroy himself. If the Meridians are hateful enough, then they will in effect destroy who they once were. The goodness they once were will become only a memory."

Maanta opened his mouth to speak but stopped as Japeth waltzed into the room carrying three clay plates serving as the shelves for three delectable meals. "The steaks are medium father, enough to stop them from mooing but not enough to knock out the flavor," Japeth proudly smiled. "And between the steaks and corn I think I dabbled in every seasoning we have."

As Japeth handed Maanta his plate the boy took a deep breath of aroma. His eyes slowly took in the dish. Steak and potatoes were apparently two separate things. The steak's medium brown color was full and juicy, speckled with seasonings. It had a deep savory flavor as he cut a piece and passed it through his lips. His stomach was warm with the taste. Maanta copied the way Noah and Japeth cut through their potatoes and a warm steam rose from its inside through the air. Its pure rich taste was soft in his mouth.

Somehow, Maanta got to the corn creature before the others. It was long, golden yellow and appeared to have a shell consisting of small pieces. Japeth had also speckled the golden creature with seasoning. The utensils didn't work. The shell refused to cut past the small pieces and the pieces themselves burst as if they were some sort of defense mechanism for the deceased creature. *Does it crack like a crab?* Maanta pondered. He lifted it in his hands to crack the shell. It was slippery in their grasp.

"Now you've got it, Maanta!" Japeth joked as he lifted his corn. "Darn good meal if I say so myself! Who was the cook again?"

"Thanks, Japeth," Maanta spoke. "I definitely won't mind discovering the foods of the land above water." Maanta pushed his two hands apart as they held the corncob in an attempt to crack it in half. Instantly the cob slipped from their grasp, somersaulting in the air before swirling in the corner on the floor, making a popping sound as it landed.

All three men broke out in laughter.

Japeth handed Maanta his corncob with a smirk. "Try again. Don't let this one slip away."

A dolphin's call resonated in the breeze from the waters along the shore.

15

Twitching Froth

days earlier in Meridia's enslavement camps

The only light the elderly slave had to see by was that of an iridescent deep water fish he had clutched in his deformed fist as it scampered by in the waters before he entered the caves. Coal black darkness blanketed the boiling waters around his wounded and worn, frail mer-body. In the five months since his capture, Amaranth had been reduced to a fragment of what he once was, forced to pry free and capture drying malta shells from the sweltering aquatic mines beneath Meridia. Skin peeled loose from his body where lava thrashed from the walls and scoured him.

Soon the tail finned men from Sangfoul would dub him no longer useful and extinguish his life flame. His left leg thumped numbly against the cavern wall. It had become a sort of companion for him as it followed him around, his body no longer able to feel its presence. Globules of blood bubbled from his lips and he licked them up with his tongue, quickly swallowing them. *Salt,* he thought, *I need it.*

"...where are you now..." He whispered as his crooked fingertips caressed the chilled stone cavern wall before him, searching for some crevice he had once known to be there.

"oooooo" Something cooed from the other side of the wall, in an undiscovered cavern beyond his own.

"...ahay..." The shell of Amaranth grinned as shattered teeth played in his expression. "...and in this dawning hour, before the death partakes of something, shall I give thee to bring thy master's make..."

"oooooo" The thing sang back.

"...with swiftness find thy master for in him lay savings stakes..." Amaranth's crooked fingers frantically searched his whale-leather clad body for something he barely knew was there. The boiling waters licked his form. His knuckle popped and echoed as he loosed something from his clothes and stuffed it through the wall's crevice. "...shall journey have thou at now friend..." Amaranth muttered.

Nothing replied, only currents along the ears.

Currents swept past his bloodshot eyes, as slowly Amaranth maneuvered his way back to the main mining room. With only one working leg-fin he spun as he went, his leg thumping each time it clubbed the wall. "...companion..." He whispered to it. "...less the make noise..." The sound echoed through the cavern's hull.

Deep red light bloomed before him as the mining room neared. Tiny crimson streams of lava trickled loose from the walls, scorching his boiled, peeling flesh. A man inside the room ahead wailed as the guards beheaded him for being unable to work. *Me left not long,* the shell of Amaranth thought to itself.

A coral club boomed against his skull and all red became darkness. All sound became silence. All thoughts eclipsed.

Cardonea Tower

Morn's light lit the ocean's surface a crisp fiery hue as Illala awoke to the new day. She swirled in the waters to unwrap the sleeping kelp that kept the cool of night away. That color, the crisp flame light, paralleled her life as of late she thought.

Here was the beauty of the crimson sunrise, a parallel of her newfound life and sense of family with Evanshade, a parallel of the gift of the child that had been growing inside her for five months now. Her belly had puffed up like a blowfish. And as she rested she felt the baby kicking at her stomach and even thought sometimes she could feel its heartbeat.

Then there was the eerie flame hue this particular sunrise took on. It reminded Illala of the tragedy all about her that was the very reason she had come to know the things she was growing to love.

When Evanshade was with her, there in her room in Cardonea Tower which remained the only place she had been since her arrival back home, he showered her with loving words and warmth that she had never known in a man before. He constantly told her of his excitement in that soon she would give birth to their child.

"Soon I will give up my life as a warrior and we will be free to live where we please in the open waters and raise our family," Evanshade had said. But surely the people of Sangfoul would come after him for leaving their ranks, or her own fellow Meridians would take his life for leading the attack on their people. Or maybe Illala herself would take Evanshade's life in the end. After all, he stood by as his warriors slew her parents and siblings. She had grown to love him but deep inside a hatred burned for what he had taken from her.

A constant reminder of the tragedy surrounding her life loomed in the room below. Once the man who called himself Odyssey had been imprisoned there, but Illala had not heard his moans or spoken to him in many light rising and fallings. As the months of her pregnancy passed, Illala's senses enhanced. Evanshade appeared not to notice but she constantly scented the smell of rotting below. Odyssey's corpse was there, she knew, rotting in its own mire, spewing its toxins.

I failed to find Odyssey freedom and now each day I am haunted by his body's stench, Illala thought while looking upon the eerie sunrise dancing upon the ocean's surface above.

Something then interrupted her morning thoughts.

Thump! The floor beneath her faintly sang. *Thump! Thump!*

Urgently she swam to the chilly floor below where she knew she'd find the familiar brick she'd lift to see what was happening beneath her. The brick's edges gripped tight in her fingertips' grasp, grinding on her nails as it attempted to slip away. With all her strength Illala loosed the brick from the floor's grasp, her pregnant body gliding backward in the waters as the brick dislodged. Some of the rank odor that emulated from the room below seemed to be dissipating.

Illala quickly maneuvered herself so she could see into the room below. "Odyssey?" She whispered through the opening. "Do you live? I could have sworn you dead."

"...odyssey..." A whisper replied.

It was the whisper of an unfamiliar voice. Something jerked and swerved in the room below, serpent like in nature.

"Who are you?" Illala spoke louder now. "And where is Odyssey?"

"...and as naming one thing of lays away another takes its form..." the voice spoke. "...fitting name of odyssey and so now am of i..."

As the thing babbled on Illala's eyes adjusted. As it spoke the thing batted a glowing fish, like a cat playing with its toy. The deformed creature jerked and squirmed, its knuckles popping as it pawed the lifeless fish. Boils broke about the malnourished man's face.

Illala shuddered with repulsion and quickly slid the brick into its hole. *They must have disposed of Odyssey's body to make room to imprison another of their slaves too deformed to work,* she thought. *I don't recognize him. Thank goodness he is no-one I have ever known.*

As much as she tried to deny it, there was something familiar about the old deformed creature. But whatever it was that Illala recognized, the being's true self had obviously passed from its mind long before entering the rank cell below.

16

A reunion, A climb, The aurora
On land

The voice resonating in his ears instantly brought Maanta back to a place and time he assumed lost to himself.

"Ooooahooo!" The sweet voice of Archa flowed across the open oceanic breeze from the close-by shore.

Thud!

Maanta's second ear of corn careened into the wood floor below as he stood upright and half ran, half attempted to swim out the doorway and to the ocean beyond. This attempt ended with a thud of Maanta's own, as his body also dropped quickly to the hard floor below, his arms squirming beneath his body as though they were the limbs of a squished spider. The boy grunted in anguish.

"What is he trying to do now?" Japeth stared, befuddled, not knowing that Maanta was from the ocean and had never walked before.

"I don't know," Noah replied before placing his arms beneath Maanta's now still arms and lifting him upright. "What has stirred you, Maanta? What do you need of us?"

Tears streamed down Maanta's face before being soaked up by the garments he had been dressed in. He tried to achieve a stable setting with his feet on the ground. His legs only quivered beneath him.

"Ooooahooo!" Archa's song beat again in the air.

"That voice," Maanta turned to meet Noah's eyes. "That voice is the voice of a dolphin friend of mine from the waters below. She's calling for me. It's hard to explain, but we understand each other. If I can't rejoin her beneath the waves, I must let her know what has happened here." Maanta flinched while twisting his ankle in an attempt to stand. "Can you help me to her side?"

"We'll carry you down to see what this is all about," Noah said as Japeth shot him a bizarre glance. "Japeth, pick the boy up and follow me to the water's edge."

Japeth braced Maanta and thrust him into his arms. "You sure are an odd one, boy."

Noah was already on the sands outside, but called back. "Maanta is a merperson from beneath the waves. You'd best quit insulting him. If you tried to breathe and swim deep in the ocean's depths, I'm sure you'd have difficulties too."

As he carried Maanta across the shimmering, soft beach, Japeth pondered his father's words. He also pondered whether his father could be losing his wits.

Maanta paid no mind to what Japeth had said to him or even what Noah had returned with. In truth, the boy hadn't heard a word. He was excited because of the knowledge that soon he would be by Archa's side again.

Archa's smooth head bobbed in the ocean as she sang again and again to Maanta. *She's so beautiful,* Maanta thought to himself. He hadn't seen her in so long that this vision of her was more enhanced than any he had had of her before. In ribbons from above, the sunlight gleamed across her smooth head. Rippling waters glistened to the farthest reaches of the ocean beyond.

"Put me in the waters," Maanta told Japeth, as the ocean rose and retreated again upon the man's toes.

Japeth gave Noah a questioning look and Noah responded. "Do as he says."

Japeth waded out a bit more and as the waters reached a foot deep the tall muscular man gently set the boy into the ocean. As Maanta swam out to the dolphin both Japeth and Noah realized that the ocean must be his natural habitat, for with fishlike strength, he glided to the animal's side. "He moves like an eel," Japeth spoke.

Archa nudged Maanta with her nose as he approached, sending him tumbling in place. He laughed and jumped back toward her.

"I missed you, girl!" Maanta hugged her neck and gently kissed her on the forehead. "How did you find me?"

"Arch Arch!" She bobbed her head and sang to him. "Arch Arch!" And with a swoop of her head and spraying of water she tossed something from her mouth against his forehead.

Maanta grasped the slim brown tubular thing as it began sinking. "A kelp scroll?" He uttered in disbelief. "You carried this in your mouth all the way from the ocean's depths?" The scroll was the length of Maanta's palm and its slimy coating caused it to almost slip from Maanta's grasp as he undid the seaweed ties holding it shut. As the seaweed plopped and sank past Maanta's beating feet below, the slimy kelp scroll unwound quickly and flopped open in the sunlight.

Maanta's eyes flashed to the bottom of the script. "Amaranth," he breathed. Of course it was Amaranth. There was no other who knew better how to use a corundum-scribing tool. The boy's eyes quickly swept to the script's beginning as he laid it out upon Archa's glistening back to better read. The handwriting almost shivered on the scroll, as if the writer had unsteady hands, but Maanta knew this to be untrue of Amaranth.

Maanta,

I scribe you from a cavern deep beneath Meridia where the warriors of Sangfoul force our race to mine lava. A bleak existence and starvation consume us here.

The guards speak of Sift and the others preparing for an attack to rescue us. They laugh because it is true that no force of even trained Meridians would have a prayer of overtaking them.

I have found hope in this bleak existence, though. A cool brace of currents embraced my body as I chiseled open a vein of lava two days ago. I followed that stream of cool breath through the boiling depths until it led me to an open crevice in the cavern wall. A soft cooing noise resonated there. Perhaps by fate, perhaps by chance, it was Archa on the other side. In her, hope was rediscovered.

She has told me how Orion's Birth jettisoned you to the shores above, how you are being cared for by the people there. You are unconscious, she says, but has seen you consuming air as they bathe you.

Rumors have swept Meridia for centuries, that if we gave our selves to the world of air above, we would adapt to breathe the substance again. So we arrive at hope.

Few know this, but beneath Meridia's lava caverns lay a vast empty cavern of crystal and air.

The chance to free ourselves lies in releasing this cavern of air. Both the enslaved Meridians and warriors of Sangfoul would scatter in hysteria and give not a thought to a thing but their own flesh.

However, I cannot free this gargantuan egg of air myself. It lies too deep beneath me and I am heavily guarded. I need your hands to release it. The cavern of crystal and air connects to a tunnel, which I believe to stretch to the vast realm of land dwellers above. You must discover this cavern and discern a way to release the air into Meridia.

You will not drown as water displaces air amongst the crystalline encasement. Have you never wondered how Archa could breathe both water and air? Dolphins are not deep-sea creatures, and yet she has been with you for years.

This is because when you were but a youth, I tested a theory on Archa.

I once discovered small creatures, which consume water but spew out air when they take what they need from the water itself. They are sticky and malleable and remain wherever one places them. I placed them within Archa's breathing hole and found they produce enough air for her to breathe deep beneath the depths.

I have wrapped a few in this kelp scroll for your use in aquatic breathing.

When Archa believes you are close to consciousness, I will send this to you. Until then, I wait.

Amaranth

The corundum scribing didn't end there. Instead, on the very bottom of the scroll words were scribbled in chaotically, as if as an afterthought.

leagues of time the wavings took as binding of the mind loose shook and now in death or sanity in leaving take, upon arrival not left shall thus I make

"What in the world does he mean by those final words?" Maanta spoke lowly to himself. "It's as if before finally giving the scroll to Archa, he added a final message. But it's unintelligible. His sanity must have slipped between the two writings."

Maanta hadn't seen it at first, but the final words had been written on a folded over piece of scroll from the backside of the page. The folded over piece clung crisply to the front side, so as to blend in. Now the folded over piece pulsed, an eerie rhythmic heartbeat.

"What?" Maanta gasped, lifting the scroll away from Archa's smooth back and holding it up to the sunlight to better analyze.

"Is everything   alright?" Noah called from the beach.

"I'm alright. Thanks." With the scroll held between him and the sun Maanta could make out pulsing veins between the folded over flap of scroll. His pale fingertips peeled loose the folded flap to discover two slim pale-blue jelly creatures stuck between the crease. "These must be the air-creating creatures Amaranth said he would send." The sight of the creatures sent shivers up his body, giving him goose bumps.

They reminded him of symbiosis. He had no desire to be interdependent on another species. "And who knows what service they would attempt to use my body for." Maanta shuddered. "But Archa seems well and they are in her. I'll wait until I need them in the crystal cavern to use them." It was a risk he would have to take to rescue his people.

While bringing the scroll down from the sunlight, he tore the piece of kelp scroll where the transparent creatures clung, off of the main script. In a tight ball he wrapped them, their own bodies serving as the sticky surface to keep the ball sealed shut.

Pulse pulse. Pulse pulse. The creatures beat in his palm as Maanta tucked them into his pant pocket which was soaked beneath the ocean now. Air bubbled up from where they were and collected on the water about him. *It's bizarre to feel them pulse against my leg,* he thought. *I'll have to find a place to store them in Noah's house so I won't have to feel their pulse constantly. I wonder what that will feel like in my mouth.* The thought was unsettling. After rolling up the remaining scroll he stuffed it in his other pocket.

"Archa," he spoke to the dolphin now. "Thank you for carrying me this message from beneath the depths. I have longed to know what has become of you since our separation and yearned to find a way back beneath the depths again. You have brought both things to me.

"The others on land are waiting for me, but stay close in the days to come so we can share our companionship. When I discover the way to the crystalline air egg beneath Meridia, I'll tell you, so that we can meet there beneath the depths."

She nudged him gently with her nose before swimming swiftly around him in a circle.

"Aaaahoooo!" Maanta sang in Archa's language before kissing her gently on her forehead. "I love you, my friend. It's good to have you by my side again."

"Oooooahhhooooo!" Archa bobbed and replied before dipping and swooping off into the depths below, in search of fish to devour now that her journey was complete.

The sun above shone down in streams of glimmering light that flickered on the rippling waters before Maanta. The sunlight warmed his body, causing a sense of calm to soothe his thoughts. How bizarre it was to think that, when he first arrived here, his flesh burned at the air's touch, and his body had cried out in anguish in the heat. Now he cherished the air and sunlight as it warmed his body.

With a pivot and swoop in the waters Maanta swam back to shore with fluid ease. Noah and Japeth watched in awe as Maanta bobbed and swirled in the ocean as he returned.

"That must be what we look like to him on land," Noah spoke to Japeth while his eyes remained fixed on the boy. "Who was the scroll from?" He called out to Maanta as the boy neared them.

After a bursting leap and splash Maanta skimmed the water's surface until he reached the beach and crawled to the sandy shore. "It was a message from Amaranth. He sends news of his knowledge of my people and has requested something of me. Once we are inside, I'd like to discuss it with Japeth and yourself, and ask about your knowledge on something."

"I have a better idea." Noah clasped Maanta's outstretched hand in his own and helped the boy stand shakily on the moist sands beneath his toes. "Within the hour the sun will begin to set. Let us light a flame in the kindling of my fire pit and discuss the scroll by a warm beach fire as we listen to the tide roll in."

...

That night, as the sun cast a pumpkin-orange hue across the sky in its setting, the three reread the scroll with tongues of flame flickering in the ocean breeze before them. An owl's hoot echoed in the distance.

When the scroll was done, Maanta lifted his head away from its words to look into Noah's eyes through the flickering flames of warmth before him. "The tunnel Amaranth speaks of, do you know where I might find it? I have no idea how I would begin to look for such a thing, especially because I don't even know how to properly get around out of water yet."

"Hmm," Noah thought. "Nothing comes to mind. Japeth what are your thoughts?"

Japeth pulled a small chunk of meat he had been roasting in the fire off of a stick and popped it in his mouth, chewing it, and swallowing. "I'm just starting to understand who you are and the world you come from, Maanta." He took a sip from a clay bowl filled with coconut juice he had close by. "But when you came to the place in the scroll where Amaranth spoke of the tunnel which connected to our world I was reminded of something.

"Hundreds of years ago, when I went out to explore this land with Shem, we came upon a cavern in Ar'arat's base whose mouth rose four of my height above us. A cool breeze surrounded us as we explored its insides. The sound you hear when you press a seashell to your ear resonated in the air. It delves deep into the mountainside and curls downward slowly the deeper it goes. We explored the cavern's depths for days until discovering a drop-off in the tunnel we could not pass or descend.

"When we reached this spot Shem dropped a torch down into the hollow drop. The flame swirled as it fell until it was nothing but the faintest of dots, like a tiny star in the vast sea of the sky. Eventually it disappeared, and never did we hear the sound of it hitting bottom. If there is a tunnel which leads below the ocean's depths then surely that place holds what you look for."

Maanta took the clay bowl of coconut juice from Japeth's fingertips and took a long swallow, embracing the succulent sweetness of the juice as it cooled down his throat. "This cavern sounds like the place I need to explore before anywhere else. With any luck it will lead me to the crystalline egg of air." The sun's setting glow was a low hue of crimson-orange as it allowed pitch darkness to consume it along the horizon. Maanta looked down at his legs as ignited ash flicked from the fire before him. "And yet I cannot stand without someone by my side hoisting me up. How will I ever manage a cavern where men of land could not reach its depths?"

Noah looked up through the sky, his beard illuminated by the glow of firelight. "No matter what my sons have not been able to do, the Lord will find a way for you to reach the deepest depths of the cavern of which Japeth speaks." Noah lowered his eyes once more to look through the fire at Maanta's legs. "And you will walk my boy. You will run. You will jog. You will skip. We will teach you and show you the way to do those and many other things. You may now have troubles maneuvering on dry land, but after witnessing your grace and speed in the waters just beyond our shore, I know that you will quickly master the ways of moving on land. We will have you walking by tomorrow's twilight."

...

As Maanta lay nestled on a bed of covered straw that night, his body quickly conformed to the world of nightly slumber. Starlight shone through the window close by and rest upon his closed eyelids. Worries about how he would learn to maneuver the world of land and air encompassed his dreams, as well as something else he had fallen into slumber while thinking of.

"Anna..." he called out more then once into the darkness as he slept.

...

By the next day's end Noah and Japeth had taught Maanta to walk with little shakiness in his legs, and by the week's end he was jogging in short spurts, often from the shoreline to the beach house and back. The following week they taught him to hike up steep cliffs and had him running through fields of flowing, grassy terrain.

Maanta amazed himself with the quickness in which he picked up these skills. He had thought they would take him years to master, but with every step he took or movement he made, he noticed his muscles perfecting minute responses his body needed to make to accomplish them. His strength was also revitalized by the many new foods that he feasted on. The tastes of mango, tomatoes, oranges, spiced chicken, omelets, spices, onions and peppers sparked and rippled upon his palate. It is possible that because his body was so rejuvenated, he adapted so quickly.

By month's end Japeth and Shem would take him to the very foot of Ar'arat Mountain. Its bulky, ridged-stone terrain jutted and curved as it spired through the sky above.

Japeth spoke to Maanta as all three men stood beside the great limb of Ar'arat in a breeze, which whipped around its stony hulk. "If you are to scale the endless pit of the cavern which leads beneath the ocean depths, then surely you must first possess the skill to climb up and down Ar'arat's peak." The three tied an extensive braided rope between them and strapped shoes with spikes to their feet. Japeth handed three metallic picks to Maanta, instructing him to place them in a cowhide belt Noah had crafted for him.

As they hiked up the slope of Ar'arat's lesser grade, Maanta concentrated on the high sloped stone peak before him. He had climbed high stone walls which Japeth had constructed near the shore, but Ar'arat seemed to stretch into the heavens overhead, and vast spans of stone appeared smooth and un-creviced above him. The breaths he took in about him tasted like tulips on his tongue.

"May God bless us," the dark haired, staunch Shem seriously spoke before beginning his ascent up the rising stone before him. His fingers grasped each crevice with masterful ease. Tiny pebbles and dust fled down the mountainside as he ascended.

"I'll be right behind you," Japeth spoke as he urged Maanta to go next. "If we climb like this, then if you lose your grasp on the stone, Shem's strength will hold you up as the rope pulls on his back. And with me beneath you, I can watch you and instruct you where to place your holds."

The stone was cold on Maanta's fingers as he found his first holds. His muscles strained and burned as he pulled his torso to meet his hands and then found new holds to wedge his hands on above. His leg muscles strained as they supported him and lifted his body from behind. Maanta was grateful for his shoe spikes. They at least helped ease what he knew would have been a much more difficult ascent without them.

He thought it would grow more difficult, but he climbed Ar'arat's face with more ease as time went by. The act of finding new holds and releasing old ones fell into a rhythm, with the occasional comment from Japeth as to a better hold to take. His muscles still burned, but were becoming numb to the sensation after never having relief from strain since he had started out. The wind sang in the breeze as he climbed, and the heat his body created as he worked his muscles warmed him. Sunlight laid its blanket upon his back.

A third of the way up the mountain, Maanta noticed Shem disappearing into an outcropping of stone above. "Shem!" He called up the ridged stonewall. "Are you alright?"

Shem's stern, dark-haired face reappeared over the ledge, grinning down at Maanta and Japeth. "Here is a flat ledge of Ar'arat for us to rest before continuing our climb. Surely you both are exhausted!"

"I don't know about Maanta, but my muscles could use the rest," Japeth wasted no time in replying before giving a gentle yank on the rope attached to Maanta from below. "Come on, boy! I've packed some delicious tidbits for us to eat once we get there!"

"Do that again and I may just fall on top of you!" Maanta called down. A brisk wind whisked along his backside as he pulled himself up on the ledge. It was at least ten feet deep and sheltered from the gusts of air by walls of stone on both sides of its in-cut floor. Maanta turned around to look at the land far below as Japeth finished his climb. They weren't yet halfway up the mountainside and already the trees below looked like the tops of broccoli afloat in a green and brown soup. Fog drifted like a serpent in outcroppings of trees below.

Japeth, on the ledge now, fished with his massive hands for something in his leather pack. "Bite into this." He handed numerous blue spheres to Maanta before doing the same for his brother.

Without hesitation Maanta popped one into his mouth and bit into the fruit. It burst into his cheeks as taste-bud sparking juice slid down his throat. Maanta ate the rest of the blueberries in one giant mouthful. "They're delicious," he said as he finished chewing. Maanta was famished now and he hadn't known it until he began to eat. *I hope there's more where those came from*, he thought. His legs burned from the strenuous climb.

Next, Japeth pulled a small loaf of wheat bread from his sack. Oats lined its crust. After breaking it in thirds, he handed the portions to the others and the party sat and leaned against the stone walls while chewing the soft bread.

As Japeth's hands retracted from the pack for the third time, long slim brown things braced between his fingertips. "Take two." He handed some to Maanta who looked at them inquisitively. "It's dried and salted deer meat that has been preserved so it won't go bad as we carry it. It's tough. Chew it slowly."

Maanta bit into a piece, pulling half of it apart from the rest of the stick. He ground the dried meat loose in his teeth as a salty rich flavor nipped at his taste buds. The remaining meat was devoured quickly.

Shem stood and prepared to continue the climb as he chewed his final piece. "We should press on in order to reach the next stopping place before nightfall." He extended his thick arm into the breeze beyond the ledge's wall. "The wind has slowed. We shall have no trouble continuing our climb." Shem removed his climbing picks from his utility belt and began climbing the rising stone above as Maanta and Japeth stood and prepared to do the same.

My muscles are so sore, Maanta thought. *I wonder why I hadn't noticed them aching while we climbed before.*

Japeth placed something in Maanta's palm as the boy pulled out his picks before following Shem. "You seemed to like these a lot."

Maanta opened his hand to find three small blueberries rolling around. "Thanks." He popped them one by one past his lips before continuing the climb. "I wish I could share the delicious treats of my world with you." Maanta's arms strained as he began scaling Ar'arat once more.

Japeth followed close behind. "After freeing your people from Meridia's molten mines, you'll have to return to us to share the treats of your world and visit then."

"That is a day I look forward to greatly." Maanta held himself up on the mountainside and carefully stored the picks once more on his belt. He preferred feeling the stone on his fingertips. He felt closer to the mountain that way, like he had more of a say in how Ar'arat treated him.

The day's remaining climb smoothly passed as light transformed into a collage of darkness and spattered stars. Two-thirds up Ar'arat, they slumbered on a large outstretched cliff. A full moon gleamed bright in the distance. *I wish there were walls of stone to block the winds here,* Maanta thought, half asleep, as goose bumps rippled across his body.

Chilled air swirled about them the closer to the peak the group had come. Together they huddled for warmth, shivering in their sleep.

Maanta awoke to the condensation of a cloud about them misting on his forehead. Droplets of moisture beaded, trickling down his cheeks. Wiping his face and looking off the cliff as he stood, Maanta glanced toward the earth below. He could see nothing through the cloud about him. All was coated in rolling fog, which swayed trickling streamers of sunlight in its breath.

They dined on bread, bananas and dried deer as the fog and clouds scurried away from the morning sun. Land appeared in flecks and speckles through the dissipating clouds as they prepared to climb once more.

"Be careful as you grasp the stone this morning," Shem spoke to Maanta, before ascending toward the mountain's peak. "The morning's moisture has begun to dry but much of the stone will still be wet. As we get higher up, we might even encounter frost. Take your time and watch where I place my picks and hands. It may be best to follow in the grooves I take."

"Thanks for the advice." Maanta tied the braided rope tight to himself. "I'll be sure to watch your holds."

Japeth made a mocking facial expression as he looked to Shem. "What no words of wisdom for me, brother?"

Shem turned toward the steep rock wall, placing his picks in rather large open grooves. "I don't fear for you, brother! If you fall off the mountain, the hot air you're full of will merely cause you to float toward the sky."

Maanta got a chuckle out of their bantering.

Japeth smirked, then shot back. "If that's true then you'd drop like a stone if you fell."

As the party ascended up Ar'arat's high peak the dew on the mountain evaporated as steam into the sky. Holds became less slippery, although the air took on increasingly chilly temperatures as they climbed.

As midday approached, Maanta passed through the froth of a puffy frigid cloud. Frost crept on the mountainous stone it clung to, causing Maanta's fingers to slip in places, as he grabbed for holds. The blood in his fingertips was going numb.

"Use your picks to climb with and the next time we stop I'll pull gloves out of my pack for you to warm your fingers with," Japeth hollered from below.

He must be feeling the chill in his fingertips, too, Maanta thought as he found a strong hold to take with his left hand and reached for his picks with his right. Using picks instead of his hands didn't help the chill much, but gave tighter holds in the frost than his numb fingers did.

Above, as he climbed, the cloud opened up to pastel sunlight. The puffy cloud broke about his nose and face as he pulled himself through its upper crest. Maanta took a moment to look out over the line of clouds reflecting the sunlight about him. *It is one of the most beautiful things I have ever seen. To think, not a year ago I lived beneath the waves in Meridia and had not dreamt of ever knowing the realm above the waves.*

He looked to his hands, where the finger-webs had once been. Ridged scars curved down his fingers' sides now. Truly, he had come a long way. A brisk gust of frigid air whipped about him.

"Come on now, boy! We're almost at the peak," Japeth called from beneath him as he arrived at Maanta's spiked feet.

Back from his realm of thoughts, Maanta pressed ahead, picking groove after groove as he ascended Ar'arat. And then wandering thoughts returned. *I wonder what has happened to Anna,* he thought, her soft, pale blue skin and beautiful pure eyes drifting as images in his mind. *Does she even remember me? I'll never forget when I first laid eyes on her beauty. Even when she was mentally slipping away, I fell for her.*

Shem had been calling for him while he was lost in his daydream.

Maanta shook himself out of his thoughts. His pick thrust against an icy slab, scraping off into open air. His body released from the mountainous rise, whirling out of the sunlight and past gusts of cloud below him.

Japeth shouted as Maanta's body flailed past. "Hold tight, brother! Maanta lost his holds and is careening away." The rope clenched tight around the brothers' waists as Maanta halted, spinning in the air somewhere beneath Japeth.

"How's he holding up?" Shem's deep voice shouted down. "The rope is holding here! I hope we've tied good knots!"

"For now he's fine!" Japeth hollered back. "My rope's holding strong as he spins beneath me, beside a gap in the rock. We need to get him back on the mountain wall." Japeth looked below him at a spinning, stunned and shaking Maanta. Fog and cloud whirled about him. "Are you alright, boy?"

Maanta nodded his head nervously up and down.

"You're lucky Shem ties a good rope," Japeth hollered down once more. "You have to get back to the mountain wall before the rope gives! I saw your picks hurl past as you fell! I have extras I'll lower down to you! Once you have them swing yourself against the mountain wall and clasp yourself once more to its stone!"

"Alright," Maanta barely murmured back, still stunned from the fall. Moments later as Maanta looked up through the clouds he could see two stone picks being lowered through the mists on a string Japeth was slowly sending his way. He unclasped them and braced them in his fists as the rope which connected him to Japeth and Shem slowed its spinning. Maanta mustered his courage and forced himself to mentally deal with the reality he was experiencing. *If I swing toward the mountain too fast, or stay off of its stone much longer, the rope will snap and I'll careen down to Ar'arat's foot,* he thought. *Then I won't live to see my people freed.* "I have the picks!" He hollered for Japeth and Shem. "I'm going to attempt to swing for the wall!"

Up above, Japeth looked to Shem. "Hold tight, brother! Maanta's swinging for the mountain!"

Maanta made slow movements toward and away from the wall, the world shaking back and forth beneath him. The rope creaked while tightening above.

"AAAHHH," Japeth grunted as he supported Maanta's movements with his straining muscles.

Slowly, Ar'arat's stone came closer and closer to Maanta's picks. Maanta stretched to catch in a groove in the rock but the groove broke loose as momentum swung him away. With two more swings Maanta tried again, this time catching both his picks in grooves along the rising mountain wall. He thrust his spiked cleats into the mountainside with a wrenching of stomach muscle and was once more being held up by his own force. "Phew!" He breathed in relief. As he climbed, the rope slumped above him.

"He's done it!" Japeth shouted to his brother.

"Thank goodness!" Shem bellowed down. "I didn't know how much longer we could support both his and our weight!"

Japeth waited for Maanta to catch up to him once more before speaking. "Pay more attention to what you're doing," he spoke to Maanta as the boy passed along his side."

"Don't worry," Maanta said as he climbed past, heavily breathing. "One fall was enough to catch my attention." His heart was still racing. Reaching Ar'arat's peak and embracing brief relaxation was a moment which couldn't arrive too soon.

As noon arrived to the misty chilled world above the clouds, Maanta's stone picks met the peak of Ar'arat. Muscles tightened and strained in Maanta's limbs as he lifted himself off the mountain wall and into the crater which was Ar'arat's peak. He laid there, eyes closed on the frost glinting stone, resting for the first time since his fall. The crater's curved form embraced him as his muscles relaxed and his heart slowed its pulse.

"Can you believe it has been hundreds of years since our ark first perched here in the flood?" Shem asked his brother as Japeth pulled himself onto the mountain's tip. "I can still remember the waters glistening for eons before us as the ark rocked on the very stone where we now stand."

Japeth placed his arm around Shem and lifted Maanta with his other arm to show the boy the vast sky about them. "We have gone so many places, Shem, and witnessed so many things. And yet, no matter what we achieved after the flood, it all leads back to here. A new world began on this peak. The things we experienced, which brought us here, showed us that we have strong enough wills that we may achieve whatever we desire."

"I wish father could climb Ar'arat and share this with us," Shem spoke while looking in awe out at the flowing airscape before them. The sun beat, a hallucinogenic yellow orb, across the sky.

"As do I," Japeth turned to see the entire sky. "And yet, in his old age, father could never make this journey."

Maanta looked out in awe. "Thank you for sharing this with me. I am honored to stand by your side." He had no words to describe it, but as he looked up, rippling majestic ribbons of color wove and shimmered in the sky above. Such a beautiful sight had not caught his eyes before.

"Do not thank us." Japeth looked up in awe. "Thank God. He has brought us here many a time. He has created this world. For us to not share it with you, would be selfish."

"What do you call these lights?" Maanta asked, pointing to the purples, oranges, reds, greens and blues rippling above.

"Aurora borealis," Shem smiled, as he too gazed upon their beauty.

Lunch, that day beneath the weaving, shimmering lights of sky, was a feast of strawberries, blueberries, bananas and pomegranate companioned with wheat bread and sticks of salted meat. Maanta savored each taste on his palate. His close call with death and the beauty about him intensified the entirety of his senses.

Maanta finished his food before the others, and sat, staring off into the luminescent sky about him, his back to Japeth and Shem. His lips moved but made no sound as he gazed upon the ripples of light in the upper sky. He had been reciting a poem he had just written in his mind as he gazed upon the brilliant lights above. Without knowing it he softly began to recite it aloud.

"Friendship
finds its future
in the love
which one thus binds
finds its everlasting aura
in the bathe
of together finds
in my forever quest
both passion and friendship are sealed
and when friends' togetherness is opened
an aurora borealis
reveals."

"You speak beautiful words, Maanta." Shem grasped the boy's shoulder with his hand. "Perhaps you would share them with Noah when we see him again. Even though he cannot be here, you can share a piece of this place's beauty with him."

"I will gladly remember it for him." Maanta took a long look out upon the ribbons of multicolored sky, the shimmering, beating sun and the swirls of frosty clouds, before closing his eyes and committing both them and his poem to memory.

The group would descent Ar'arat's great slope within two days time with no more falls or difficulties with their goings. As Maanta reached Ar'arat's base he looked up at the vast spire above and realized he had completed his quest with many things he had not taken up Ar'arat with him. There was his newfound strong friendship with Japeth and Shem to be thankful for, a new confidence that he could scale the cavern's pits to the air and crystal cavern below Meridia, and the beauty of the aurora he had forever embraced in his mind.

"How amazing it would be to spend days on Ar'arat's peak, taking in the aurora's light ribbons and the sky about us." Maanta stared up Ar'arat's stone spire to where it disappeared in puffy clouds above. "But it would be too cold to stay there long and my people need me beneath the waters."

Japeth punched him on the shoulder and began walking away from Ar'arat before handing Maanta the last handful of blueberries he had brought with them on the climb. "Then that settles it. We must make many trips to Ar'arat's peak once you return from Meridia. Perhaps we could bring the girl you were thinking of when you fell, with us."

Maanta jogged up to Japeth and Shem, who were walking side by side now. "How do you know I was thinking of a girl?"

Japeth grinned as Maanta popped a blueberry in his mouth. "There is always a girl."

17

Departing
The Shore

Maanta could taste the salt of the ocean on his lips as he stood where the ocean meets sand's edge. It was early morning, just past sunrise, and a fog of salty mist swirled across the waters outstretching before him. "AaaaaaHooooo!" He sang out into the pastel orange sunlight rippling across the ocean's crest.

From the barely seeable distance a dolphin bobbed and hopped from the ocean to the air and back again toward him. Light gleamed from its backside. As she neared him Archa bobbed her head and made welcoming noises to him in the breeze. "Arch Arch, Arch Arch."

The cool waters on his feet as he walked into the ocean toward her made him yearn to rejoin her once more beneath the depths. But he knew he couldn't return to the world of water in this way, by her side. The only way to release the air pocket beneath Meridia, and free his enslaved people, would be to take the cavernous tunnels beneath Ar'arat's base to the world of water he so loved.

He extended his hand out above the rippling tide. Archa's smooth forehead met it quickly and he stroked her smooth nose. "I love you girl," he spoke to her with the love of a best friend. "I can't wait to rejoin you beneath the depths."

"Arch Arch." She did a jump and splash in the waves curling shoreward before him.

Archa swam to his side and he stroked her smooth fin. Maanta fed her a fish he had brought from Noah's home. "Today is the day, girl. We're heading into the tunnels beneath Ar'arat to the crystalline egg of air beneath Meridia."

"Arch Arch." She bobbed her head in understanding.

"It should only be a matter of days before we reach that place. I need you to be waiting for me, between the East and West

Shale Walls of Meridia, when I release the air pocket. I don't know what readjusting to breathing water again might do to me. I know though, that if you are there and I pass out, you will find me and take me to my fellow Meridians."

Maanta's shoulders were warm in the sunlight. He kissed Archa on the forehead and petted her head once more. "Be there waiting for me, girl, and I will rejoin you once more beneath the depths."

"AhhhHooo!" Archa called into the air as she swam circles about Maanta. She nudged his leg abruptly before disappearing beneath the waves.

She will be there, Maanta thought. *Even if I had never told her, she would know where I was going and would find me.*

A voice called from the house above the beach. "The packs are prepared and we are ready for our journey in the tunnels beneath Ar'arat!" Japeth beckoned. "As soon as you have finished speaking with the dolphin, we should leave to get an early start!"

Maanta turned and ran up the beach, sand spraying behind him from his toes. "She is already gone, on her way to wait for me in Meridia, and I am ready to get on our way to the cavern's opening. I just have to retrieve something from the house first." He sped up past Japeth and through the main doorway towards the house dining room.

On a large oak table rest a massive clay pot filled with ocean water. The two jelly creatures Amaranth had sent him stuck to its bottom, constantly spewing out air because of the water they consumed. Bubbles collected on the top of the bowl in froth.

He reached his hand into the bowl and was surprised to find the water abnormally warm to the touch. The sticky creatures peeled from the bowl's depths into his palms and he wrapped them in pieces of seaweed he had also kept in the bowl to keep them moist.

If the creatures turned water into air, he had thought, than surely they needed water, if not at least moisture, to survive. He stuffed the pulsing seaweed wrapped creatures into his pocket and began walking toward the front door to join Japeth outside.

"Be safe," Noah spoke from behind him as he walked.

Maanta raced back to the elderly man who had helped him adapt to the realm of air and embraced him warmly. "I will be back, Noah."

"May God bless you in your quest and give you the strength to live in the ways he asks us to live." Noah grinned and gave him another hug. "I anxiously await you again, young man."

"Thank you for all you have done for me and shown me. Oh wait…" Maanta fumbled in his back pocket for something. "This is for you." A folded piece of parchment rested in his hand. He passed it into Noah's fingers. "I thought up this poem on the peak of Ar'arat. It reminds me of the friendship that your family and I share." Maanta gave Noah one final embrace before joining Japeth outside.

The parchment unwrapped slowly and with small crackles in Noah's hands. He read it with great interest. Maanta's voice resonated in his mind.

"Friendship
finds its future
in the love
which one thus binds
finds its everlasting aura
in the bathe
of together finds
in my forever quest
both passion and friendship are sealed
and when friends' togetherness is opened
an aurora borealis
reveals.

"Noah, you have been both friend and family to me since pulling me from the waters. I have never told you this, but I have never known my father. In you I have found a man I wish my father would be. You are kind, loving, understanding and patient. Since I have met you, you and your sons have been by my side at every turn. It will be a blessing to see you again when I return from Meridia. Thank you for making me feel a part of your family."

A single tear traced down Noah's wrinkled cheek. He folded the parchment, placed it on the table and watched out the window as Maanta and Japeth walked side by side toward the cavern in the side of Ar'arat.

18

To Free the Forbidden Fluid
At Cavern's Entrance

"Together we have witnessed the peak of this great goliath," Japeth spoke as he, Shem and Maanta stood with packs on their backs and lit torches in their hands before the mouth of a gargantuan cave in the side of Ar'arat. "Now we will embark on a journey to the uncharted realm of its very depths. Watch your footing. Listen carefully. Beware and respectful of whatever creatures may dwell here."

The midday sun beat exhaustingly overhead as they stepped into the cool darkness of the cave, leaving the sun's sweltering glow behind.

After their first thirty or so steps, Maanta turned around and could barely see the hint of sunlight behind them. His torch crackled above. Echoing droplets of water, dripping from stalactites yards overhead, resonated in the vast cavernous expanse. Japeth led the group. Shem was in back.

"Ouch!" Maanta exclaimed as his foot twisted in a slight drop of stone.

"Are you alright?" Shem spoke from behind, placing his massive arm beneath Maanta's armpit to help him regain his full support.

"I should be alright as long as I keep a better eye on where I step," Maanta replied.

Time seemed to stretch eternally in the darkness as they followed a course, rocky, earth-made trail through moist tunnels leading downward.

In the pitch black about their glowing torches, Maanta thought he saw demons slithering on the walls in the distance, waiting for the company to loose their flames so that they could approach and consume them. Something swooped from above, brushing his ear. He questioned the others, but no one else had seen or felt it.

The darkness led on.

In an effort to liven up their journey, Japeth taught Maanta a melody which Noah had taught Japeth and his brothers as youths. Its lively highs and lows lifted the boy's spirits. Long lengths of time passed, and even after Japeth and Shem had quit the melody, Maanta hummed it gently.

"Shhh!" Japeth let out from the front.

"I was trying to…" Maanta spoke before Japeth cut him off.

"Shhh!"

A faint noise hummed in Maanta's ears. It approached them quickly from the front.

"Duck. Something's coming," Japeth spoke, before urgently kneeling low to the moist cavern floor.

Maanta and Shem followed his lead, their torches flickering above their crouching bodies.

The humming beat louder now in Maanta's eardrums, every second's noise resonating twice as loud as the last in the darkness. Shrieks scathed in echoes against the cavern walls.

"What are they?" Maanta whispered to the brothers.

A gust of wind swept above him as Maanta was almost deafened by a humming and shrieking noise consuming the space about him. Shadows whipped and beat his face and skin. Something crashed into Shem's torch before knocking it from his hand. The creature itself ignited before careening in screams to the cavern floor behind them.

The shrieking went away, the humming dissipated and silence consumed the pitch darkness once more. The creature that had ignited on Shem's torch lay squirming and crippled as the flames exhausted about it.

"What is it?" Maanta questioned as he and the brothers neared its smoldering carcass. The stench of burnt hair caressed the air.

Shem kneeled, picked up his torch and ignited it anew on Maanta's own. "It's a bat, a winged rodent that can bite, but is annoying more than anything. They clutch the roofs of caves and are filthy creatures." Shem pinched its charred, crisp wings with his free hand, holding it up to the dim torchlight. Smoke wafted from its carcass.

"They're actually quite tasty," Japeth chuckled from behind Maanta and Shem. "And this morsel comes fully cooked."

"Feel free, brother." Shem passed the charred bird-rodent to Japeth. "I wouldn't take a bite out of that stank filth for anything you could offer me."

"Suit yourself." Japeth cracked the bats head off along with its wings and feet before tossing the limbs off into unreachable parts of the cavernous path. "Any extra protein for this exhausting journey is welcome to come my way. And you Maanta, will you partake of this creature with me?"

"Mother always said to try everything once." Maanta made a queasy face as Japeth ripped the bat's charred body in half and handed him some to try.

Shem unlatched his leather pack and pulled out something. "I'll stick to dried deer and berries, thanks." He bit into a strawberry. "Mmmm. You know it's not too late to do the same, Maanta."

Maanta shut his eyes and bit off a piece of the bat, pulling meat away from bone. It was a bit salty and burnt, but possessed a rich flavor. He would need his strength in days to come. He decided he had made the right choice. "It's tastes alright." He took another bite.

"Brother, have you ever even tried bat?" Japeth gnawed into his piece, chewed it and swallowed. "It wouldn't hurt you to try a few different things."

After partaking of their meals, the troop was on their way once more.

The darkness seemed to pulse about them now. *What other strange creatures make their homes amongst these halls?* Maanta thought.

The trail became steeper and steeper in the pitch, chilled dark. Once Shem slipped and Maanta caught him as he slid down the sharp slope.

The blank nothing before them seemed to shiver in the cold of his breath. "How long have we been moving?" Maanta's calves ached and above all, his arms were sore from holding the heavy torch.

"Halt!" Japeth held his free hand back toward Maanta to stop his movements while waving his torch before him. A sheer stone wall rose upward against the torchlight, blocking their way. With a swoop, Japeth moved his torch along where the ground should stretch before him. Its flame lighted nothing, only darkness held by a curved edge of stone. "We've arrived. The endless pit drops here. We will rest in this place now, and upon awakening, descend into its depths."

After partaking of a few morsels and boiled cave-water for drinking they took their rest next to the cold, seemingly bottomless hole. The light of Japeth's torch shivered as it leaned against the cavern walls nearby.

Maanta's eyes closed, his head propped upon a raised, moist stone, as dreams overtook his mind.

As he awoke, Maanta shivered. The torchlight had extinguished during their slumber and the cavern swept with bitter chill. All was pitch black.

Slowly he moved his hands to massage his toes, stinging with the bite of cold. His nose dripped and was chill as well, as were his fingers. "It's so cold." He shivered in the darkness.

"Wha…?" Japeth's voice groggily returned.

Maanta pulled his clothes tight around him before breathing into his hands. "The flame's gone out." He shivered. "The air descends with such chill."

"So it has," Shem, apparently already awake, responded. "I didn't wish to wake you, Japeth, but you've got the tools to light a fire to warm us and to relight our torches, in your pack."

Maanta could hear a rustling and something being passed from Japeth to Shem in the darkness.

"Thanks," Shem replied as he retrieved the unknown things. "I'll tell you what I'm doing as I do it, Maanta. You might need this skill."

"What did he pass you?" Maanta asked curiously while warming his chilled toes with his hands once more.

"Sticks, for starting a fire with, and dry leaves for kindling," the noise of Shem stacking sticks and leaves could be heard in the darkness as he spoke. "You rub the sticks vigorously together until the friction of their rubbing creates flame. Then you move the flame from your sticks to other dried sticks and leaves below and softly blow the tiny flame to spread it amongst the kindling."

In the dark silence Maanta could hear sticks rubbing together beside him. Long moments passed and he began to think Shem's hands would tire before the sticks would ignite.

A spark of crimson flicked in the pitch-black air before disappearing once more amongst the darkness it had been birthed from. Another flick of fire jumped from the rubbing sticks, then another.

Shem's breath could be heard as he blew on the tiny flames.

A small red flame rose now from the sticks as they rubbed. Slowly it moved downward until it reached dried leaves and sticks propped up against each other, engulfing the leaves in quick, consuming flame. The small fire rippled up the sticks about it until it put off a soft glow that silhouetted its maker's face.

Shem warmed his hands over the fire and motioned for Japeth and Maanta to join him close to its warmth. "We will light our torches from its flame once we have warmed our selves and nourished our bodies." Shem pulled more meat and fruit from his pack for them to eat and passed it to the others.

They devoured it hungrily.

After they had finished their meal, Maanta looked up at the brothers. "Where do we go from here? I know that neither of you has ventured past this point. As far as we know, this pit truly is bottomless. What if it doesn't lead to the crystalline cavern of air, after all?"

Japeth grasped the boy's hand. "Have faith, Maanta. God has led us on the right path to your people's freedom. The crystalline cavern is at the bottom of this pit, I assure you."

"So how do we proceed?" Maanta stretched his feet close to the flame. He could feel the bones in his toes warming.

Japeth pulled a massive braided rope from his pack. It sat heavily in his lap. "We begin by knotting this rope a few times around this large stalagmite." He patted the stalagmite beside him as if it were a pet. "Then we'll drop the rope's length down the pit and pray it gets us as far as we need to descend.

"Once we reach the end of its length, we'll have to devise a fresh plan from there. Shem will remain here to watch the knot and help us if we need his assistance. Shem, we may need you to unknot the rope from the stalagmite and drop it down to us if we can't reach the bottom of the pit with this single length.

"Also, we won't be able to carry lit torches with us as we descend, but we'll strap them in our packs in case we should need them later."

A few moments of rest passed before Japeth knotted his rope to the stalagmite. He rose slowly, tossing the remaining rope into the pitch-dark void. Both Japeth and Maanta strapped their torches in their packs along with food Shem had taken from his own pack to give them.

"Listen, in case we have need of you, brother," Japeth hugged Shem lovingly before grasping the rope in his fists and beginning his descent into the consuming darkness. "May God watch over us in these depths to which we descend."

Maanta shook Shem's hand. "Thank you for all you have done for me. I look forward to scaling Ar'arat's peak with you once I return. You have become like a brother to me."

Shem walked closer to Maanta and hugged him. "Be safe in your quest."

As Maanta turned to begin his descent into the pit, a shiver rippled through him. The darkness of the hole was all consuming. When he peered down the hole, Japeth was already beyond sight.

"Are you coming or are you just going to stare at me?" Japeth's voice resonated from close below, but Maanta's sight could not focus on him in the nothingness.

The rope braced tight in Maanta's fists, burning his skin as he gripped the tight braid, and with three breaths the darkness had swallowed him into its throat.

The pit's wall was cool and cragged to the touch. Moving slowly and bracing with their legs, Japeth and Maanta lowered hand under hand, downward. Damp moisture clung to the rope, causing them to slip in places, while lowering handgrips.

"I wonder how deep it descends," Maanta spoke.

Japeth's voice climbed upward from below. "Deeper than we could imagine, I fear. But we will reach its depths."

Down and down they descended. Far above, the faint hue of Shem's fire swayed in the pit's entrance, a space that appeared to be no larger then a pebble.

Time seemed to span eternity.

Maanta shifted his head, looking upward as he descended. The distant firelight had disappeared.

The pit narrowed so much, that for a good distance, Maanta's body could barely move through it. In this small length of space Maanta let loose of the rope and merely used his hands to push himself downward through the hole.

A gentle, whispering breath of warm air, warbled up from below as the pit widened once more and Maanta re-grasped the rope.

Japeth startled Maanta as he spoke. "There's a ledge here. We'll soon be running out of rope. We should stop, collect our thoughts and strength and decide how to proceed."

After a few moments more of descending the rope, Maanta's feet found a solid surface beneath him. He held a tight grip to the rope as he felt Japeth there, beside him in the blackness. *There can be no telling how large or small the outstretching stone beneath me is,* Maanta thought. *I'll hold tight to the rope incase I need it.*

"We should run out of rope soon," Japeth's words came from right next to Maanta's ear. "There is no telling how far this chasm descends. I have an idea. I'll call up for Shem to untie the rope and drop it to us and then we'll retie the rope to this outstretch of stone in the wall. If we do this, then you will be able to descend at least the length of the rope again. With luck, that will get you to the pit's ending. You'll need to descend the next length alone though, because I'll need to stand here and watch the rope."

"But, without the rope tied to where Shem is, how will you return?" Maanta knew that he would have no need of a way to return to the land above, but Japeth could not enter the waters and breathe them into his lungs as Maanta planned to do.

"I am a skilled climber and have brought my picks." The darkness was silent for a moment, as if Japeth was in thought. "Do not worry about me. And besides, if I needed him to, I could get Shem to fetch another rope and lower it to me."

"It sounds like a solid plan then," Maanta said, but he knew he would worry for Japeth until he met with him on land again.

Maanta could feel Japeth tugging up and down on the rope through his own grip on its braids.

"BROTHER!!!" Japeth hollered through the hole above. "UNTIE THE ROPE AND LET IT FALL TO US!!!"

Nothing. Silence. Darkness.

"Can he hear us?" Maanta spoke.

"BROTHER!!!" Japeth bellowed. "IF YOU CAN HEAR US, LET THE ROPE FALL!!!"

The rope went limp in their hands. Seconds passed. One. Two. Three. Four. Five… Nine long seconds passed as they stood on a slim cliff in the depths of darkness, clutching to a limp rope.

Whoosh! The rope swept past them, wafting a gush of cool air. Maanta held tight to the rope's end. It tightened and hung from his hands. His body rocked forward as the rope's weight tugged in his hands, but Japeth braced him upward.

"I guess he can hear us," Maanta whispered. "I felt myself sweeping off the edge for a second there."

Maanta could feel Japeth kneeling carefully in the dark, tying the rope to the outstretched ledge beneath them. As Japeth stood, he pulled fruit from his pack and shared it with the boy.

Cool strawberry juices caressed Maanta's throat. The warm winds he had felt earlier were blowing upwards again. *Why would a cave have warm winds?* He wondered.

As they stood close on the small ledge, Japeth began to speak. "There is something I have not told you about a thing you carry in your pack. I have placed a sack of powder there, which explodes, destroying everything around it, once ignited.

"When you are in the crystal cavern of air, you will need a way to crack the crystal and release the air into Meridia. This powder is your solution. Pour it in a pile in the cavern floor, at a distance create fire like Shem has shown you to do, light your torch and toss it upon the powder.

"Cover your ears. An explosion will rock the crystal and waters will flood the cavern as the air pushes through Meridia. Watch for falling stones as the explosion goes off." Japeth gave Maanta a hug. "May your quest bring your people happiness once more and bring you back to us one day. As you descend the depths, I will be here if you are in need of me."

Maanta's soul warmed with Japeth's words. "Thank you for everything you have done for me and sacrificed, to help me on my way. Once my people are freed and calmer days have found their way to the world beneath the waves, I look forward to seeing you once more." He smiled in the darkness. "This time, my visit will be a little better planned, though."

"I look forward to that day," Japeth sighed. "I suppose you should be on your way now. Be safe."

"I will."

Maanta teetered on the outstretched limb of stone beneath him as he reached for the rope dangling from the knot around it. His body tipped and fell before he could grasp the rope, plunging him quickly downward. Hands clasped at vacant air. Heart raced. Mind panicked.

Darkness flushed upward about his irises.

His hands felt as if ripped by fire when finding the rope braid, but he was safely hanging from it once more. "I'm alright!" He yelled, half panting for breath, up to Japeth.

"Stop daydreaming about young ladies," Japeth shouted, "and concentrate on your descent!"

Maanta smirked and gave a silent laugh. *That was close,* he thought. *If I lose my grip here I won't have Japeth and Shem to rescue me.* He was alone now. It was a reality he would have to face.

Down he descended on the rope in the black shadows of nothing. The cave walls no longer were close enough to be felt about his body. The only things that remained of his companions here were his rope and pack. One thing's weight pulled him downward. The other held him up.

With closed eyes he descended for a vast stretch of time. He opened them and the darkness remained the same.

ksssssssssssssss

He could swear he heard bugs scurrying on the cavern walls somewhere close by. As quick as possible he descended until the noise stopped. Something pricked and scurried across the back of his neck.

Crunch! He smacked it with a hand while bracing to the rope with the other. The thing tumbled down his back and into the depths below.

Another gust of warm air puffed about him.

"What is that?" He whispered.

Further into the depths he went, paranoid by each sound and quiver of the air.

Hours passed which seemed like days. Drips from the rocks above trickled down his forehead. The air grew warmer and warmer.

Grip after grip, braid after braid the rope rubbed against his hands as Maanta met the shadows below. His feet clenched the rope as he moved, and then it was gone. Only his hands held on. The rope's length had been exhausted. *How far down is the cavern floor?* He pondered, remembering Japeth's description of the pit as endless.

He panicked. He did not want to be alone anymore. Not even the rope would stay by his side. "JAPETH!" he bellowed upward. "I HAVE REACHED THE ROPE'S END!"

Nothing. Silence. Moments passed.

A humming sound flittered in his ears. *No.* He thought. *No!*

The humming increased as ear-scathing screeches broke in.

He closed his eyes. A consuming wave of bats flushed all about him, their wings beating his face and body. A few attempted to bite him as they passed. Their screeches pierced his thoughts. His body pimpled with goosebumps.

Their wings beat against him in an embracing horde. Then, in a breath they were gone, fluttering up toward another vast span of cavern air. The humming noise dissipated before succumbing to silence once more. His legs hung limp and braced to nothing beneath him.

I have come this far, he thought as he hung at the end of his rope. *My people need me. If I turn back and return to the world above, never releasing the cavern of air, my people may never be freed. They will perish in mutilated agony.* While dangling, he made a decision. After the end of the rope there would be a world to live. He would make it to free his people. *I just need faith,* he thought.

His fingertips released the rope's intricate braid as another warm gust of air puffed about him. Plunging downward, his body became one with the darkness, its winds blowing puffs within his clothes. And then the darkness released him against a smooth, slanted wall. Breath burst from his lips in the collision.

Maanta swept, always facing upward, down the smooth surface as it bumped up and down beneath him. He pressed his palms against the surface to better steady his descent, and was baffled. The surface was warm.

The surface dropped suddenly, releasing him in open air.

Crash!

His body smacked against another smooth substance. He slid to a halt. The floor beneath him radiated heat. *Where have I sent myself?* He thought, with the soothing warm floor below him. *What do I do from here?* Something poked him in the back from his pack. *Of course!*

With haste he pulled out some of the sticks and leaves Japeth had packed for him. With great care, he placed the kindling before him and began rubbing two of the larger sticks together.

A single flame sparked off the sticks and the darkness appeared to light with stars about him, before disappearing again as the spark died. A lick of flame lit where the sticks rubbed and larger stars reappeared. Maanta moved the tongue of flame slowly down against the kindling. It ignited in a rush of light, consuming the entire smooth cavern.

There were thousands of reflections of the fire in the vast crystal cavern about him, almost overwhelming the space with light. It stretched half a mile high and wide. His irises shrunk as sight adjusted to shimmering blue, pink, purple, yellow, white and orange hues reflecting through the crystal encasement.

"I'm here," he breathed, in awe of its beauty. "The depths of Ar'arat possess their own aurora."

He should have eaten. He should have slept. He should have planned. But the crystal cavern trapped him in its beauty, causing him to think of none of these things for long moments.

When his own thoughts returned to him, Maanta realized he had no time to waste. For every moment he postponed releasing the air into Meridia, his fellow Meridians were enduring torture.

He lifted a vast leather pouch from his pack and brought it several yards away from the fire before dumping it out on the shimmering floor beneath him. The black grains the pouch spewed seemed to obliterate and poison the crystal's glow.

Returning close to the fire, he reached his arm into his pack and withdrew the oceanic creatures Amaranth had sent him. The seaweed about them crumbled, dry and brittle, and swayed like falling leaves down to pink reflecting crystal below. The creatures' pulses swept a mental shiver along his spine.

They beat like miniature hearts in his outstretched hand, their veins pulsing as they sucked moisture from his palm. *They are so starved for fluid to breathe and turn into air,* Maanta thought. He was afraid of what they would do to him when he placed them in his mouth. It was too late to worry about that now, though. Without them, he would drown.

He placed them on the two outstretched fingers of each hand, brought his fingers to the corners of his lips, and placed them in the insides of his moist cheeks. The symbiotic creatures instantly sucked to his cheek walls, draining the moisture from his mouth and converting it into air. He coughed, spat, choked.

Dizzy breaths cracked through him, as the room appeared to spin in his mind. The crystal was a haunting sheen of ice. The entirety of his cheeks chapped as the symbiotic creatures sucked away.

Have to have water, he thought, clumsily grabbing his torch from his pack and igniting it ablaze in the fire before him. He dropped it to the crystal floor in the dizzy haze, but quickly picked it up again, bobbling the torch blaze in the air.

With a swift thrust, he lobbed the torch toward the black powder he had poured upon the reflective floor.

Dizzy exhaustion felled Maanta to the crystal beneath him.

BOOM!!! An explosion consumed the room, almost reaching to Maanta's legs. Flames and smoke bellowed forth. The complete encasement of crystal shattered in mirror sized jagged panes. The ceiling tumbled down, piece by piece from above. *THOOM! THOOM!* The fragments shattered the crystalline floor as gushing water poured down after them. Maanta's lips pressed to the crystal floor as water filled the cavern. With each suck of water, gathering there, the symbiotic creatures left his cheeks alone and went more for the waters he was consuming.

THOOM! THOOM! THOOM! THOOM! Fragments from the ceiling crashed down, splashing the collecting water up into the air.

Water consumed the fire Maanta had built. The cavern went dark.

If I'm not crushed by falling pieces of crystal, then I'll swim up to Meridia once the cavern fills with water, Maanta thought. He laid his body beneath the collecting waters, breathing the liquid into his lips softly and listening above him in the darkness as the ceiling fell like asteroids into the rising currents.

THOOM! THOOM!

Stars reappeared in the heights above. Their molten glow seeped and formed the outline of the cracks in the crystalline egg before flowing down through the holes in the ceiling and simmering where it mixed with water and air.

A droplet of orange star plopped in the waters beside him and floated downward until resting on his arm.

"Ouch!" Maanta cursed. The lava scorched a mark just above his hand.

THOOM!

The cavern's center crashed down into the deep waters as lava and water gushed behind it. Maanta swam for the edge of the cavern, where nothing had yet fallen. Waves and splashing currents pressed against him.

Within a matter of moments, the cavern filled with gushing water and lava, the lava sizzling and blackening in the water's embrace.

All air was gone.

An orange spider web of molten lava illuminated the swirling blue waters before him.

<u>19</u>

Breaths Before

Baneal, a day before

Sweat drifted from the pores in Anna's forehead into the oceanic currents resting about her. She spun and did a loop in the waters beyond Baneal's mud pillar homes as a trident thrust where she had just been.

With the trident clutched sternly in her hands, Anna's attacker grinned deviously before thrusting for her again.

Anna took her own trident, spun it in the currents, and lodged it in her attacker's weapon as the curly, longhaired, female attacker flung forward.

Their weapons locked in embrace, spinning them clockwise up and down in the waters. The attacker dislodged her trident and struck Anna's trident once more, in an attempt to dislodge the weapon.

Spinning the prongs of her trident, Anna dislodged the attacker's weapon instead. Anna swam with all her might after the fleeing opponent, chasing her around two mud pillar homes before cornering her against a rock outcropping and the ground.

With a swift thrust Anna plunged her trident away from her hands and toward the curly haired attacker, pinning the girl's right, upward-stretched arm, and neck against the ocean floor below.

Anna smiled.

The other girl began to laugh. "One of these days I'll beat you, you know," Anna's new friend, Millay, joked with her. "Are you going to get this thing off of me, or should I start calling for help from someone else?"

"You had me scared for a second there." Anna grinned as she dove down to release her friend from her trident's grasp. She had met Millay in the months that had passed since the Meridians had come to Baneal with Sift and his people. Here they had been trained by their new dark-skinned friends and practiced in bouts with each other to perfect the tactics they were taught. Anna usually prevailed when the two fought but they had both improved immensely with time.

Anna gripped the trident's long shaft and tugged on it to release it from the ocean floor. Something sharp pressed slightly into her back, releasing the smallest droplet of blood.

"In a battle there is more then one opponent. Just remember that," a young male voice exclaimed from behind her. "Always remain alert."

Anna looked to Millay, rolling her eyes as she did so. "Sebastian?"

"How'd you guess?" Millay shrugged her free shoulder. "I thought you'd get more excitement in discovering him behind you then you would if I were to give away his location."

Tao's son Sebastian had been helping the girls train, partly in an attempt to help them progress, mostly because he was a young boy coming of age who was just becoming interested in girls.

Sebastian pulled the longest point of his trident away from Anna's back. "Tag. You're it!"

"You wouldn't have beaten me if I'd have known you were there," Anna smirked. "Care to have a fair, one on one match?" She dislodged her trident from the ocean floor, unpinning Millay and bracing it in attack position toward Sebastian.

Sebastian jutted backward in the waters, positioning his trident offensively also. "Touché!"

He thrust for her, aiming for her waist, but Anna quickly spun away. She returned immediately, striking his trident as he spun to meet her.

Clang! Clang! Clang! The weapons collided over and over again in the swift flowing, light blue waters.

Anna dove beneath Sebastian, thrusting her trident up. He bobbed upward and met her trident with his own. With his strength he drove her toward the sea floor. His dark muscles tensed as he moved with her, all the while staying above her body. "You would beat me one on one?" He mocked.

Anna's beautiful form swam swiftly to the ocean floor. She bent her knees as her feet touched the sands below, lifted-off upward with a swift flex of her legs and shot behind Sebastian before he knew what was happening. With a downward thrust she pinned Sebastian to the ocean floor, his trident locked in hers as he squirmed to push her up.

A clapping sound came from behind the skirmish. "Well done, young ones! Well done!" Tao exclaimed as he hovered in the waters above them. "I almost wish I didn't have to interrupt the excitement, but it's time for our final nightly feast before our leaving for Meridia tomorrow morning. Sift and all the others are waiting for us in the great hall of dining."

Anna released Sebastian from her trident's clutches and he swam off after his father toward the meeting hall.

"I would have beaten you!" Sebastian called back as he swam. "Rematch?"

"We'll see about that." Anna called after him, rolling her eyes at Millay.

The two girls hugged the ocean floor as they swam, side by side, toward the dining hall.

The bizarre thing about Baneal, Anna thought, was the way the vast city was constructed. It was built as if it were not a vast city at all, but rather only a few mere mud pillar homes stretching toward the ocean's surface that happened to be positioned in the same place. The true vastness of Baneal, however, existed in dugout catacombs beneath the rising pillars.

Anna and Millay swept around the base of a mud pillar, then another, and down a vast dark crevice in the ground.

Voices echoed up from the distance below them as they swam downward, passing illuminated corridors on both sides. After a series of curves and turns, the girls entered the vast dining area through an opening along its roof. Various hues of jellyfish hovered in the waters, illuminating the cool cavern.

The girls swiftly dove, taking their seats next to Sebastian, who was eagerly awaiting his meal.

"Took you long enough!" Sebastian exclaimed.

A few moments later one of the dining hall's cooks swam above them, letting trays of food glide down to them from above.

Anna reached up and grabbed hers, bringing it to settle down on the coral table before her. The meal of richly seasoned shark-steak and kelp looked scrumptious. She waited for Millay and Sebastian to grab theirs also before cutting into the tender shark.

Men and women with spears poked the illuminated jellyfish, directing them toward a stage before the gathering, where Tao and Sift tread water, in what had just been darkness.

Tao cracked a malta shell before him on the ground, its insides spilling molten ooze. He did this when he wished to get the attention of the room.

"People of Baneal and Meridia," Tao began, his armor glistening in the glow of the jellyfish. His hand clenched in the waters above. "We have trained in the art of battle for months for one purpose, to reclaim Meridia and free the Meridians enslaved there. The beings from Sangfoul have tormented our peoples for long enough. Tomorrow they will torment us no more!"

Cheers swept through the dining audience. A group of Meridians, close by, banged their hands on the table.

Tao hushed them with a swift movement of his hand. "For far too long they have enslaved us, slaughtered us, and caged us in both Sangfoul and Meridia! As morning light collects on the water's surface above, we will leave on our journey. Pack what you need. Harness your riding-fish. By nightfall we will collect our revenge!"

The crowd roared as Tao smiled before them. He bowed and swam back in the waters, allowing Sift room to swim foreword and take center stage.

The room resumed their eating; except for Anna and a few others, they quit paying attention to what was playing out before them.

"I fear though that forget we may something, as free the people of Meridia we do," Sift spoke in strong, but not loud tones. "These men of Sangfoul, families they have also of their own. We do, what done must be, but do it not cruelly, for their families will remember what done we have to them, and forget what done they have to us. If for any reason, standing, we slaughter them as they have us, in truth we be but their equals."

Anna thought about what Sift said as the others ate around her. Sift was difficult to understand at times, but what he said made sense. She would remember that the people she fought had souls and families when fighting for her people's freedom tomorrow, but realized that most people by her side may not. *What will the following days bring?* She thought to herself.

Sebastian pinched her side. "Pass the flavoring jellies?" He grinned.

20

A Loss
Baneal

The shimmering light of sunrise had barely stretched its morning arms across the ocean's surface above; as already the people of Baneal and Meridia hovered in traveling formation in the waters of Baneal.

Hundreds of them, garbed in glistening shell shielding and tough dark leather, perched in a sphere formation on the backs of slim, large Baneal riding fish. Tridents, spears, knives and swords were the weapons strapped to their sides. Each man and woman wore his or her own stern, determined facial features. They had trained for months for this day.

Anticipation rippled in the currents. The fish swimming close-by avoided and swam around the group, sensing the emotions that seeped their scent through the people's pores.

Every man, woman and child was with them. Not a soul would stay behind.

Tao and Sift led.

Tao pivoted on the large shimmering fish he was riding, facing the group. His voice echoed through the cool, breezy waters, through a curved shell he held to his lips. "My people, today we ride to Meridia on a mission of rescue. For months we have trained for the task, and on this day we shall not be denied."

A roar boomed through the crowd.

"With noble hearts we shall free our people and chase the scum of Sangfoul from our waters. We shall fight so fiercely that they shall never again return to torment us!"

The crowd cheered. The riding-fish startled in the noise.

"The people of Baneal and Meridia will live together in harmony, protecting each other, caring for each other, and becoming one people. And, in time, we shall travel to Sangfoul itself to free the enslaved people of Baneal. Together we shall triumph! We will not rest until all wrongs committed by the tail finned race are righted! We shall have our revenge!"

The crowd roared for long moments. There was no hushing them.

"People of Baneal, remember the souls of our lost loved ones will protect and comfort us on this journey. Take warmth in your heart because of this. I know that Ailcalm, my deceased son, rides by my side.

"People of Meridia, I have learned much in past months about your Gelu. May he also watch over us and keep us from harm." Tao finished his words. "For the kind heart of the heavens, may we succeed! Let us ride!" A mammoth wailing sound careened forth from the large shell as Tao's lips pressed upon it, his cheeks puffing with water.

Small fish scattered away in all directions from the noise, and the riding companions seemed to hum while slowly moving forward, in the gargantuan mass.

With a gust, the sphere of warriors moved forward, like a crossbow arrow at the instant of its firing.

Baneal stood in its wake, hollow pillars and vacant water. Somewhere in the distance a whale sang. The currents were chill and swift, but no-one was there to witness it.

Within the Sphere

Anna's husky new riding companion shook beneath her as they surged forward in the gargantuan mass. She had never been a part of one of Baneal's traveling spheres before, and was baffled by its sights and sounds as they swept with increasing speed.

For vast lengths in all directions about her, people rode, keeping exact pace with her on their riding-fish. One could have sworn that they were going nowhere, simply swimming in place. If it weren't for the floating seaweed, coral and sands careening into the natural wall of the traveling sphere before her, she would have sworn they were fixed in place.

Greens, blues and browns meshed and rippled on the sphere's outer sides, the particles careening past as they swept forward.

Anna gripped her riding-fish tighter and looked to her right to Millay, who seemed also to be holding onto her riding-fish for dear life. "Is this as much fun as you thought it would be?" She shouted to Millay in an effort to be heard over the loud humming in the sphere.

"We should do it again sometime!" Millay shouted back and cracked a smile while hugging her face against her riding fish.

Both of the girls' curly ruby locks waved in the sweeping currents.

Hours passed and the two girls rode their riding-fish close, for company on the journey.

Anna became lost in thought. Her eyes glazed with vague hollowness, as her thoughts were lost elsewhere.

Millay glanced over to her. "What are you thinking?"

Anna shook her head and came out of her thoughts. "You would think that the deaths of my family would be on my mind as we ride to free my people, and yet it is Maanta who haunts my thoughts."

Millay hadn't known Maanta personally but had seen him at a distance in Orion's Birth. "He was a handsome boy!"

"Is," Anna corrected her, "a little lanky, but there is something embracing and handsome about the purity that seems to be in his eyes. He has such a strong soul."

There was silence for a moment as both girls thought.

Millay unclenched a hand from her riding-fish and held it to Anna's own beside her. "It pains me to say, but surely he is no longer among the living. Lola and Sift found no trace of him around Orion's Birth. And he could have come to us in Baneal, because he had been there before, but he never came."

"He is alive," Anna said; half lost in thought and half mentally by Millay's side. "I can feel it in my mind. But that doubt of what outwardly seems to be is what haunts me. I cannot wait to be by his side once more. We only knew each other for a short time, and yet in that time he meant so much to me. We were growing so close."

Millay only heard fragments of what Anna said, as Anna was lost in thought and simply spoke the words instead of raising her voice to be heard. Her mind was clearly elsewhere.

Hours passed by as currents and sea life whipped by them as they rode on. The light along the ocean's surface reached its brightest in the day. Anna's stomach grumbled in hunger. *How long will it be before we lessen this fast pace and near Meridia?* She wondered. *I hope we find something to eat before battle. Surely it would be a bad idea to fight on empty stomachs.*

Tao sounded a horn from the front of the traveling sphere, signaling for the group's stop.

"It's about time," Millay mumbled at Anna's side.

Within moments the transparent sphere around the group, which had formed by their sheer momentum, dissipated into the waters about them as they slowed. Kelp flowed like streamers past Anna and Millay's eyes, one piece slapping upon Anna's face like a blindfold. "Now that we're stopping, I hope there's more around here to eat then kelp," Anna said to Millay while wiping the slimy green plant away from her eyes. The piece of kelp rippled off into the waters behind them.

Tao led the group toward an outstretched cavern wall close by, instructing them to flatten into its shadow as much as they could. The entire group could not fit in the shadow of the outward rising stone, but did their best and glided upon their riding-fish while awaiting Tao's instruction.

Tao paced back and forth while riding his riding-fish before them. His bone mask clung sternly to his face.

A little down from where Anna had stopped, she noticed Sebastian watching his father intently.

"We are only a few leagues from Meridia now," Tao spoke only loud enough for the group to hear him. "And so we must be careful not to be heard or noticed by our enemies before the time has arrived to attack. I suggest that the moment to release our enslaved has not yet arrived though, as we are famished from our journey and our bellies need replenishing.

"I have chosen this place to stop for precisely that reason. As we swam a group of four massive whales caught the corner of my eye above. They are large and would serve well to replenish us. They will also provide our weapons with some warm-up work prior to the battle."

Anna looked to the well-lit waters above and behind them and, sure enough, the torsos of four whales glistened in the sunlight rippling about them. Their massive size was betrayed by the fact that they were so far above and away. They appeared to be the size of mere pebbles.

Tao stretched his bone-armor clad arm to the right of him, pointing his finger to the empty waters beyond it. "Sift will lead one third of our group out into open waters in this direction and attack the whales from behind. This will frighten the creatures and cause them to flee closer to our position. The whales will focus solely on Sift's group, not noticing the rest of us sweeping up from beneath them." Tao spun in the waters upon his riding-fish, toward Sift. "Sift, take Sebastian, Anna and the rest of our youth as your group, as we will need the strength of our older warriors to actually take down our prey."

Sift pushed forward with a massive thrust on Lola's back out into the waters. "This a solid strategy sounds," he said. "Young people of Meridia and Baneal to my side come." He waved his massive, noir arm in the currents.

Anna gently kicked the side of her riding-fish. "That's us," she spoke softly to it as it sputtered behind Sift and was quickly joined by Sebastian, Millay, the rest of the youth and their riding-fish.

Sift turned to the group of young warriors behind him. "Are readiness we being?"

Anna smiled to him and braced tight to her shimmering fish. "We're ready."

"Then off we go." Sift faced front once more, before stroking Lola's scaly forehead and riding her swiftly into the waters before him.

The gathering of youth hugged tightly to the path of currents swiveling in his wake.

For seconds currents wove about Anna's skin as she and the others rode forward and slightly upward, not knowing when Sift would turn around and head toward the whales. The ocean became lighter and lighter as they rose closer to its surface.

Sift curled up and back on Lola, darting in the whales' direction once more.

Anna clenched her riding fish's scaly sides with her legs and swam the fish after Sift. The sunlight falling through the waters above twinkled in her eyes.

Whoosh! A school of smaller, ruby red fish gushed past them, bobbing the warrior youths from side to side.

As they emerged from the cloud of fish Anna could see the four massive whales appearing larger and larger before her, un-attuned to what was about to happen to them.

"On them, swarm from above!" Sift shouted in her direction. Lola picked up speed, as the whales were only twenty yards away now.

The seconds passed quickly as Sift and his group bobbed above the whales, thrusting pikes they had strapped to their sides into the Whales' hulls.

"OOOOOOOOOO!" The whales bellowed, temporarily deafening their attackers. "OOOOOOOOOO!" With all the speed their large bodies could muster they fled down and away.

"There they are!" Anna exclaimed, pointing below her as she chased the whales. She had caught sight of Tao and the others rising up to surprise the massive beasts. She halted her fish and let Tao's group do the remaining work.

"OOOOOOOOOO!" The whales cried as Tao and the older warriors surprised them, lunging tridents into their bellies, cutting into their fins and wrapping kelp ropes about their bodies, with weights attached, to help lug them down. The warriors heaved on the ropes while slashing into the whales' underbellies. "OOOOOOOOOO!" The whales cried.

Moments of wrestling with the beasts passed as blood fogged the waters and the whales slowly began to become subdued and die.

Anna felt tears flowing into the currents about her from her eyes as she felt sorrow for the lost lives of the creatures. "Isn't there a better way to do this?" She spoke to Sift as he floated close by.

Sift remained watching the tumbling, moaning whales beneath him. "Before, no better way there was to take them down," he spoke with a hint of what might be his own sadness in his voice. "But now, right you are, a better idea there is."

Sift dove down on Lola's back to where the bone-armor clad Tao dislodged his trident from one of the beasts' sides.

Tao listened as Sift said something. He looked up to Anna and then moved his right arm in the water, instructing four slim men to his and Sift's side. After a moment's coaching the leather-clad men dismounted their riding-fish and swam to the fronts of the whales they had been attacking.

The four men disappeared into the mouths of the whales.

"What are they doing?" Millay spoke from behind Anna as they watched on.

"Haven't you ever seen someone take down a whale?" Sebastian mocked her from her side. "They've sent men into the whales' mouths to invade their bellies and cut out their hearts. It's a much quicker way to put the creatures out of their misery."

"Sounds grotesque," Anna said. "But it's better than what they were doing, I suppose."

"OOOOOOOOOO!" The whales moaned, shaking in the waters about them in an attempt to discourage the warriors attacking them. Then, one by one, the whales' bodies went limp and began sinking to the ocean floor. Moments passed. The four men who had entered the whales' mouths emerged from the whales' limp mouths and kicked free in the waters once more. They were covered in the blood of the whale's mutilated stomach.

Anna's stomach churned at the sight.

The people of Baneal and Meridia led their lifeless prey quickly to the coral dotted sands below where the whales crashed into the coral beneath them, spewing clouds of sand all about their bodies.

The group hugged close to the coral garden as their cooks cut through whale flesh with bone knifes, making deep gashes to free the fatty meat. The chefs heated the meat over cracked malta shells and within the hour, the group was dining on a healthy feast.

Anna paused to whisper something before she began partaking of her portion. "Gelu please take care of these creatures' souls, for they have given their lives for us."

Millay and Sebastian were close to Anna's side.

Millay clasped her hand. "Do you think that once animals die they also go to Gelu's side?"

Anna chewed her first bite and swallowed before answering. It was rich and delectable. "For what they do for us, they deserve to."

"Then they must, I suppose." Millay released Anna's hand and bit into the meat bobbing in the water before her.

As they ate their meals, the sunlight ribbons waving through the waters above became slightly less bright, reminding them that the day was drawing on.

Anna chewed her final bite and waited for the others.

Tao called them closer together so that all could hear him, and began to speak. "It is time for us to venture on the remainder of our journey to Meridia. The daylight lessens and there are only a few hours left for us to fight today if we plan on freeing Meridia's enslaved tonight. Do what you need to do and mount your riding-fish so that we may ride."

The group had finished their meals now and placed their leftovers into the bone hulls of the hollowed whale carcasses. This would stop the small pieces from roaming free in the ocean breeze.

Surely a group of carnivorous fish would come to partake of the remains soon when they scented the whales' blood in the currents.

The group remounted their riding-fish and quickly rode in the direction of Meridia.

The waters whipped briskly across Anna's cheeks as she hugged the ocean floor on Nansk's back. And there it was, rising up slowly from the oceanic sands and mountainous shale walls in the distance, the shimmering spiral iris of Meridia, Cardonea Tower. Her heart beat fast in her chest. She hadn't seen it for months, and yet, in this moment, the sight of her city, called her to its side. A thought leapt into her mind. *If we succeed there today, will I rule there as the heiress to my father's legacy? Would Tao and the others even follow me, or would they secure rule for themselves?*

After all, they hadn't really treated her much like a Zharista since her fleeing from Meridia.

Tao halted the group where they floated, beckoning them as low as they could go to the sands below them. "Meridia is barely over the ridge. Here is where our people who are not warriors must wait for us to succeed and return. Stay low to the sands, and if confronted by the people of Sangfoul, scatter quickly. A small group of our youngest warriors will remain behind to protect you."

Anna knew this meant that her and her friends, along with the rest of the youth that were sent in the first brigade to scare the whales earlier in the day, would be the ones staying. "I will not remain behind," she spoke up. "These are my people we fight for, and though I am not acting as my people's Zharista now, it has been my family who has ruled over them in peace for years. I repay a dept to them by fighting for their freedom."

Tao looked to her. "You don't have to risk your life, Anna. Your people know how much they mean to you and what you would endure to grant their freedom. We all do. But there is no reason to risk the life of the last remaining heir to Meridia's throne."

"Thank you for caring for me." Anna rode her fish to Tao's side. "I have made up my mind."

Sebastian had been looking agitated and red in the face all during Anna's conversation with his father. "I'm not staying behind this time, father," he spoke, not about to let a girl he felt less adept than him, fighting wise, go to battle and not him. "Someday you'll have to let me join you in combat. There has never been a more worthy cause than today."

"Son!" Tao reprimanded him.

"If she goes, I go." Sebastian quickly dove on his riding-fish within a group of older warriors close to Tao.

Tao looked to Millay and the rest of the youth. "Is there anyone else who wishes to charge into battle naively?" The rest of the group was silent. "Very well, you are needed here more then you know, to protect our mothers and children."

Anna looked to Millay a few yards away. "Be safe."

"Me?" Millay laughed. "You be safe! We should be fine." The group of people staying behind hunkered down into a nearby crater, flattening down between flowing kelp swaying within its bowl. Between the kelp they blended in, barely seen.

Tao, Sift, Anna, Sebastian and the hundred or so other warriors faced Cardonea Tower once more.

Tao's eyes fixed on the city before him, contemplating destiny. "We charge into a battle which many of us shall not return from. We will see our brothers and sisters fall by our sides. Our own lifeblood might purge itself into the sea. If there is anyone who wishes to stay behind, do so now. We will not hold it against you." No one moved.

"We stay by your side," A warrior said beside Tao.

Tao began to drift forward on his riding fish. "Then we must move quickly, before the day's light fades," he looked behind him at the others as he spoke. Cool currents swiveled about him. "We will divide into two groups as we approach. I will lead the warriors of Baneal in the first group, and will swoop directly for Cardonea Tower when we enter the city. The second group will be the warriors of Meridia, led by Sift. You will serve as our protection in the back in case we are flanked. Follow us also to Cardonea Tower, but leave space between us so that if we are attacked from behind, you can peal the tail finned ones from our backs. Let us separate into our two groups now."

Sift and the pale, blue-skinned Meridian warriors held back and let Tao and the dark-skinned warriors of Baneal pass in front of them.

Sebastian patted Anna on the back as he hurried past her to join the front group. "You may not have anyone to fight after we get through with them," he blustered.

"I wish none of us had anyone to fight," she spoke back.

Sebastian hollered back as he swept on. "That makes one of us!" He had anticipated battle for years, since his father first began training him.

Tao's group moved a good twenty yards ahead of Sift's. Anna moved on her riding companion's back at Sift's side. Their pace quickened. Cardonea Tower grew larger and larger before them, like a large horn glistening to the ocean's surface above.

A small school of orange fish swam past Anna's cheek as she spoke. "Will he be ok?"

Sift didn't look at her, but instead quickened his pace to match that of Tao's group. "Who? Sebastian? A strong warrior is he, but one of youthful mind. Worry I for the fate of his."

Anna couldn't see Sebastian now in the waters before her. He had moved through the group to Tao's side. Her fingers clutched Nansk tightly. "As do I."

Cardonea Tower rose higher and higher before them as they approached, its windows once specks of blur on its wall, now came to sharpness in Anna's sight. Something was wrong, but what? Nothing moved in the flickering light of the windows. Aside from small schools of fish, nothing moved in the waters about Meridia.

It's a trap, the thought rushed to Anna's mind. *Where are the people of Sangfoul? They must know we're coming if they're not out living their daily lives.* Before she had a chance to share her thoughts with Sift, the sound of rushing currents swept into her ears from somewhere before Tao's group.

They had been about to cross over a cliff that sloped down in Meridia, when instantly a horde of tail finned people of Sangfoul burst up from below them, engaging them in combat. Evanshade led the attackers, his double-sided trident whirling and thrusting against Tao's own. Evanshade's muscles tensed and thrust in the waters with his weapon.

"Ambush!" Tao shouted back to Sift's group as he was pushed back and cut from the longest point of Evanshade's trident.

Anna could barely make out what was happening in the blur of dark skinned and tail finned people.

Sift swept foreword on Lola's back with his trident poised for attack. "To their sides!" he bellowed.

Following closely in his path, Anna's heart heaved in her chest. She could feel her veins pulsing about her pastel blue skin. Minute sands in the waters stung her flesh as she rushed faster and faster toward Tao and the others' side.

Within moments she was engaged in combat with a tail finned man whose eyes were a burnt, hazed-over brown. A scar ran across his forehead that tapered off around his jaw. Her muscles burned as their tridents locked and wrestled. He spun in the currents, almost throwing her from Nansk, then retreated and charged for her, almost running her through.

They locked iron once more, and this time she managed to throw him off guard. She pivoted him downward with her trident, thrusting him toward the sands below. He fled beneath her in frustration, and whipped off to find someone else to battle with, whom he would have more ease defeating.

Anna's stomach churned as she noticed the bodies of several of her comrades limply sinking down to the sands beneath the fighting. Blood streamed out from where they had been wounded. Some twitched as they breathed their final aquatic breathes.

Screams and wails purged the silence that had possessed the waters, mere moments before.

Anna rejoined the fighting with a clench of Nansk's sides, finding herself close to where Sebastian was battling his own opponent.

A tail finned man over twice Anna's size sliced a long sword against her trident. She deftly maneuvered to evade its blade.

"You've found the wrong girl to pick on!" She goaded him while clanging her weapon crisply against his blade several times. "We will free my people! I promise you that!"

The massive hulk of a man beat his thick tail-fin vigorously beneath him, causing the waters beneath Anna to swirl about her. She was swept from her riding fish's back and sucked down in the current's flow as her attacker chased her below.

"Help!" She called to whoever may hear above.

The massive man of Sangfoul loomed above her, his vast body eclipsing the light from the waters above.

Clang!

He slashed for her with his sword and met her trident with swift force. His sword sliced the currents once more as it swept for her neck. "Accht!" he cried as Anna saw three trident spikes protruding through his stomach.

Sift stood on his back with his trident running the man through, and rode him to the sands and hard stone floor below. Sift dislodged the trident, and with a crack, thrust it through the man's skull. "Are alright you being?" He called to Anna.

"Thanks to you I am alive! And that is all that I can ask for right now!" She responded.

Sift quickly swam to her side and together they rejoined the battle. Within moments, they found themselves overwhelmed with attackers and huddled in a group, with Tao and Sebastian close by.

As Anna battled her own foe, she saw Evanshade slay three warriors of Baneal with one keen maneuver of his trident, out of the corner of her eye. "That venomous spawn!" She cursed. "You will die at my hands, Evanshade!" She shouted to him as she backed her young opponent up and Sift ran him through.

If Evanshade had heard her he paid her no mind, gusting with his tail down to a group of Meridian warriors beneath him.

Anna turned, and shivered with shock at what she witnessed.

There was Venge, his sharp pointed teeth and demonic grin thrusting toward them, a shimmering sword clutched in his fists. With a swoop of his blade Venge nearly severed Sebastian's head. Bone crunched against blade. The boy's head spun against a flap of skin still connected. Blood flooded the waters as Venge sucked it within his breath. Sebastian's crippled husk convulsed as it sank.

Venge flipped back and quickly swam away.

"NOOOOO!" Tao screamed, chasing after Venge on his riding-fish.

Anna gasped for breath in the shock as Sift defended her. It was in that moment, after Sebastian's death that a loud rumble echoed and bellowed from beneath the stone and sands below. The ocean quaked about them, causing all who were fighting to lose their balance and separate from their opponents to avoid being hurt.

The loud rumble increased, deafening all in Meridia, as the land split beneath them and caved in on itself around Cardonea Tower. The East and West Shale Walls crumbled into the open ring about the towering iris and then burst upwards in an explosion of air that swept in gargantuan volcanic bubbles toward the ocean's surface.

Cardonea Tower itself began to lean and crack.

"RETREAT!" Evanshade harked to the warriors of Sangfoul. "They have distracted us beyond the city's walls while sabotaging Meridia from below! Gather your families quickly from the tower and retreat to Sangfoul!

The tail finned warriors of Sangfoul quickly scattered, fleeing off either into the unseen distance or for Cardonea Tower to rescue their families.

Only their opponents, the people of Baneal and Meridia, remained.

"Brace yourselves. They may return. This is surely a trap," Tao spoke to his comrades; his eyes alert and fixed on where Venge had fled into the open sea.

They had lost at least thirty of their number since the battle had begun. Bodies from both sides swayed in piles against the ocean floor.

Moments passed.

Large stones broke free from Cardonea Tower in the distance, falling and imbedding themselves in the sands below.

Tail finned people scurried like panicked minnows in the distance to free their people from the tower, before its possible collapse.

Anna watched painfully as Cardonea Tower cracked in three pieces, booming to the sands below. She would never know her Meridia again. All was lost. Sands consumed the waters where the tower had fallen. A gust of cinnamon-hued fog swept all about the ocean, stinging her face before robbing Anna and the others of sight.

21

Rescue

Moments before, the waters about Cardonea Tower

What's happening? Was all Evanshade could think as he burst with his tailfin across the cracking oceanic floor of Meridia while approaching the rising tower before him. *Have to reach Cardonea Tower in time! Have to rescue Illala before it collapses!* Hard sand and stone beneath him burst upward, spewing air bubbles up and about his body.

The sensation of air bursting about his flesh could have been described as tickling, had Evanshade not been in such a state of mental alarm. The stones bursting from below, however, and lodging in his scaly black flesh were excruciating. But his senses would let him register neither sensation. He was too transfixed on his single goal.

THOOM!

As Evanshade neared Cardonea Tower a gigantic stone plunged into the earth beside him. It had cracked off from the tower itself. *Have to find a cage,* he thought, spying one of the large bone contraptions tied with a kelp rope to a hook in the tower wall's base.

His tail-fin pumped from side to side, spinning him in different directions as he dodged smaller stones plummeting down from the tower wall.

Within seconds he reached the cage of bone he had been eying, untying its kelp rope with haste and then looping two whale-leather straps that were at its front, around his shoulder like a pack. This was a cage which enslaved Meridians were transported in from the molten mines to their holding cells.

CRACK! The upper most part of the tower separated from its lower two-thirds, sending a scratching sound through Evanshade's ears as it slid where it had separated and caved downward. It had split off just above Illala's room.

Evanshade's tail had never beaten as quickly as it began to do. His heart raced in his chest, almost bursting, as he swept parallel to Cardonea Tower's wall. He breathed a fresh breath of water through his gills upon reaching Illala's windowsill.

"Evanshade," Illala sighed as she saw his eyes rise above the sill before her. Panic flushed through her face. "What is happening?" She clung to the stone sill as her rotund belly glistened in the sunlight trickling through the ocean outside.

"We must leave quickly," Evanshade spoke to her with both urgentness and love.

"How?" She spoke, knowing that her belly had now grown so large that its weight no longer allowed her the ability to swim. The baby would force its birth any day now.

Evanshade extended his arms to the windowsill. "I will carry you. Step into my arms."

Illala's slim body, with its large belly, climbed through the sill and into Evanshade's arms.

He lovingly cradled her in one muscular arm and opened the bone cage door with another. "Rest in here and I will carry you on my back."

Nervously Illala crept on all fours into the rocking bone cage.

"Wait here," Evanshade spoke as a gnawing thought entered his mind. He tied the cage to the tower wall and swept with his tailfin into Illala's room.

It was dark, possessing a haunting silence. With a push he forced open her door and pivoted down a stairwell to the room below, where he jabbed his double edged trident into the door's lock and ruptured it open. With a swift rush against the door Evanshade burst into the room.

A deformed old man float in the room's center, his fingers bent in different, unnatural directions. The man's expression was both transfixed and that of blank nothing. His leg hung bent at his side.

Evanshade hovered in the doorway and looked upon the man. "This is all I can do for you Amaranth. Free yourself," he spoke. "Meridia is collapsing."

CRACK! The second part of the tower broke free, as the walls appeared to slant in about them. Evanshade left Amaranth to his own devices, hurrying off to Illala's side.

Within seconds he burst into open waters from her windowsill. She huddled in a slanting corner of the cage. He untied her cage from the wall as Cardonea Tower slid to the ocean floor below. He strapped the leather harness to his back and swept toward the realm of Sangfoul.

Whipping brown sands chased him for leagues as he swam with all his sore muscles could muster. Not a soul was in sight.

The cage bobbed behind him.

Huddled against its chilled bone, Illala shivered. Mentally, she was filled with tears.

<u>22</u>

Waft away Realm

The shattered crystal cavern beneath Meridia's depths

As the last bubbles of air fled up the openings in the crystal cavern's shattered ceiling, Maanta decided that now would be the time to make his break for the world of Meridia above the crystal cave. More and more lava was now displacing the cool flowing waters about him. The lava blackened and curled in the cool currents.

With adept speed Maanta pushed up from the crystal wall behind him, maneuvering around branches of lava that stretched and split from every direction. He dodged their fingers as they trickled down after him from above.

Soon he swam through the cavern's ceiling, almost singed by lava oozing out from a split molten vein there. He spun and swam up into a rising tunnel, which had been opened wide by the explosion and the air that had passed through its sides only moments before.

Small stones bobbled down from above as Maanta swam into them, thrusting his arms and legs vigorously in an effort to reach Meridia sooner.

The darkness above stretched on.

Streams of lava trickled down the stone walls about him as he rose.

And then in the distance above he heard a voice, screaming softly. "Help me!"

It was almost as if he was thinking the words, but he knew the noise had been registered in his ears.

Faster and faster Maanta swam until his tunnel opened up into a lit oval cavern. The walls glowed with molten hue.

"Help!" a voice called from nearby.

The oceanic cavern's walls shook about him.

Maanta quickly pivoted in the waters toward the voice. His stomach churned as he saw who had been calling for him. A malnourished, crippled Meridian floated in a locked cell against one side of the room's oval wall. Several of the Meridian's fellows hovered in the room about him, their eyes rolled back in their heads in a state of unconsciousness.

"I'll try to free you," Maanta spoke to the man. "But you have to try and wake the others up while I do so, so that they can swim to freedom by our side."

The crippled man jostled his companions as Maanta tried to think of a way to free them from their cell.

He shook the locked cell's door vigorously. And then in the corner of his eye on the roof of the room he spotted a key dangling from an outstretched hook. Maanta breathed a watery sigh of relief while swimming to the key and clutching it in his fist.

It fit perfectly in the keyhole and Maanta swung the cage door open.

Eight Meridian men and women bumbled free from its opening. They hovered about Maanta, awaiting his direction.

The man who had called for help had successfully brought all but one of the Meridians back to consciousness. This left that one unconscious man floating limply in the cage.

These people barely have any strength remaining in their bodies, Maanta thought. *I can't ask them to carry their companion through the tunnel above to Meridia. But we can't leave him here either.* Maanta pivoted swiftly into the cell and positioned the unconscious man over his shoulder before returning to the others in the center of the glowing room.

"Thank you for freeing us," the one who had called for help spoke to Maanta. "Vast plumes of air blew through the tunnel frightening the guards and sweeping them upward and away from us. We were frightened but had no way of escape from our cell. Thank Gelu you have come to release us."

Gelu, Maanta thought. I haven't heard God referred to by that name in a long time.

"Where do we go from here?" The man asked, with something of shock in his voice that he was actually free once more.

Maanta looked the malnourished Meridian square in the eyes and realized that this man was the only one of the group half conscious of the world about him. "Lead the others through this tunnel to the waters of Meridia above. Then meet me outside Meridia's main city. I am going to search out and free as many Meridians enslaved in these tunnels as I can before meeting you there."

"What of the guards of Sangfoul?" A dark look of apprehension flushed across the man's face.

"Do not fear them," Maanta held the man's eyes as he spoke. "The air which has swept up from beneath us will scare them away from our realm. There may very well be little left of Meridia when you are free once more, but I have a feeling that the people of Sangfoul will flee back to their own realm. They will have no more care for us, only care for what they fear the air will do to their own lungs. If all goes well then all Meridians should be free by the setting of the next sun."

The man swam up to the tunnel above him and then stopped and looked down to Maanta. "You speak as if the air consuming our world has been planned."

"I have released it," Maanta smiled, "to free you."

The man did not return the grin, but instead looked up and jetted through the tunnel above. "Take the tunnel to your left!" He hollered back. "I hope you know what you have done! In freeing our people you may topple our realm and topple all that is left of what Meridians once held dear!"

The man and his group were gone. The heaviness of the unconscious Meridian on Maanta's shoulder weighed him down. *It is not our city, which makes our people,* Maanta thought. *It is our souls.* Maanta could feel the pulse of the Meridian's heartbeat as his body hung limply on Maanta's own.

With a few swift kicks and swoops of his hands Maanta dove into the tunnel to his left. Multiple dark corridors curved in all angles as Maanta made his way to the next room; this one more dimly illuminated then the last.

Dozens of beady eyes followed his movements from the far corner of the room.

"...free us..." They muttered. "...free us...the one has come..."

Maanta found another key dangling from this room's ceiling and dove to the cage imprisoning these beady eyes. Their stares frightened him in a way. Were these truly the eyes of his fellow Meridians?

They are Meridians just like me, he reminded himself. *They have just been forced to endure far worse than I could know. I need to have understanding for what they have been through.* After a twist of the key in the cell's lock he flung its door into the open currents.

The eyes and their bodies burst out in fast quirky pivots around him.

"Go to the waters outside Meridia. I will meet you there," he spoke to them and pointed the way he had come.

Is that someone I once knew? Maanta thought while looking at one of the deformed girls in the group. Her face was bruised and scared. Pus crept from her pores.

With choppy movements the group was gone. Maanta's stomach churned. He looked for another connecting tunnel in the room and found one in the darkness above him. As he swam for its opening, with the unconscious Meridian on his shoulders, the cavern walls shook and rumbled. Lava cracked loose from the tunnel as he entered its lips.

The lava spat in strips through the water about him, singeing his skin as he shot upward to escape its attack. Long moments in the darkness and spraying lava passed as Maanta swam higher and higher.

Suddenly he pivoted around a corner and burst into an illuminated vast open room.

An immense bone imprisoning-cell wrapped about the room's far wall. At least a hundred Meridians were trapped behind its bars.

"Help us!" A female voice shouted from the group.

"Watch out!" A male voice followed.

Maanta swirled in the waters to see what he was being warned of. A massive tail finned man of Sangfoul barreled with a trident toward him. Maanta noticed a key clinging to the man's leather belt.

"Are you the one who brings the air?" The massive serpentine man bellowed out as Maanta dodged the trident's blow.

Maanta dropped the unconscious Meridian he had been carrying on his back in the open waters of the room and quickly swept away. There was a knife in Maanta's pocket. That would hardly be enough to defend against this man's trident but he unsheathed it and swiftly curled around in the room's currents.

The tail finned man slashed at Maanta's legs with his trident.

Maanta curled in a vast loop as he was chased, to avoid being run through. *I can't do this much longer,* he thought. His calves burned with exhaustion.

Another female voice called to him from the cage. "Come to us! We'll protect you!"

Maanta didn't know why, but he believed her. What better option did he have? With a swoop he dove for the bone cage bars where the group of imprisoned had congregated. He clasped the bars tightly with his fists.

The tail finned guard followed and stabbed his trident after Maanta's torso.

With a swirl Maanta dodged the blow and the guard's trident thrust into the cage, almost running one of the prisoners through. Several of the frail prisoners clutched the trident's thick shaft, slowly pulling it into the cage with them.

The guard slapped Maanta with his tail as he attempted to tug his weapon free but with a swirl Maanta was back along his side, unlatching his key.

Arms from inside the cage stretched like octopus tentacles out for the guard's arms and tugged him against its bars.

"HELP!" The guard screamed in agony as the hands of the imprisoned scratched open his flesh and contorted his arms. They ripped his tail-fin from his torso and folded him so grotesquely that they were able to suck him behind the bars with them. His key ripped off and floated to the room's floor beneath Maanta.

Maanta watched in horror at what his fellow Meridians were doing.

They shredded the man's body amidst his dying screams.

"You will pay for what your people have done to us!" Someone shouted behind the bars at the guard.

What have my people become? Maanta thought. He had imagined them weak, deformed and possibly insane, but this was something he had not prepared himself for.

He stared on in blank thought at the atrocity before him.

"What are you waiting for?" One of the men from the far side of the group called to him when the remains of the shredded guard were discarded in the back of the cage. "Grab the key and free us!"

Maanta thought he might prefer insanity to what these people had become. He picked up the key and headed for this cage's lock. No matter what they had become these were still his people and he had come to free them.

The lock clicked as the key twisted in its mechanism and the cage door swung open with a flood of freed Meridians.

One of the last to leave the cage turned to Maanta. His skin was singed and he had a look of old age on his flesh. "We will forever be in your debt for what you have done for us," he spoke.

"You owe me nothing," Maanta returned. "I am one of you. When they tortured you, they tortured me and the rest of us free Meridians by your side."

Maanta dove to the bottom of the room and hefted the unconscious man he had been carrying back over his arms.

A small vibration then ripped through the currents followed by a low rumbling noise. The tunnels beneath Meridia had begun caving in on themselves. The room in which they swam quaked and began crumbling down about them as if repaying them for some unknown discretion.

"Flee for the world of Meridia above!" Maanta shouted as he made his way toward a large tunnel opening in the roof of the room. "The tunnels are collapsing upon us!"

It was a tight fit as the large mass of Meridians swam simultaneously through the gaping tunnel above their imprisoning room. More than once Maanta had thought he would be smashed against the tunnel's cragged wall. Up and up they swam as darkness consumed them and they felt the bodies of their companions bump against them with every movement.

The tunnel's walls shook in the pitch black.

Maanta shuddered as he swore he kicked someone beneath him as he swam. The darkness stretched on. And then he smelled it, Meridia. The scent had changed slightly somehow since he had last been there but the scent of Meridian waters would always be recognizable to him.

It was the scent of home he smelled in the currents as the limbs of his fellow Meridians pumped about him. When you arrive home after a long away-being you can feel it, taste it, smell it in the world about you and yet there will never be a way to describe why you know you have arrived at a place so comfortable to your soul.

Home can be a place like Heaven, refreshing even when in disarray.

Maanta's heart beat softer. His mind calmed. He breathed in the waters about him and reveled in their breath.

And with a thrust he burst forth from the dark overcrowded tunnel into the waters of Meridia above. He opened his eyes in the free flowing currents and choked as he realized his home was gone. What the first man he had saved had said was true; he had destroyed Meridia to save the people he loved.

The waters were no longer a rich deep blue. Curdled brown and gray dust now flowed from the structures which had tumbled in the air bubbles' wake. Lava bubbled up from crevasses cracking along Meridia's ocean floor. A vast chunk of Cardonea Tower lay in the swirling sands beside Maanta. He traced his fingertips along its smooth stone after giving the man upon his shoulders to another to carry. The man's eyes had begun to open and he began regaining consciousness now.

"There is no longer a home for us here," Maanta spoke to the others as they joined him in the waters above the pitch-black tunnel. "We must find the others I have freed and search out the rest of our people who now dwell elsewhere in the ocean. At least our city and people are no longer held captive by the creatures of Sangfoul."

"But how do we live without a place to call home?" A freed man asked him.

Maanta swam up to his side. "We will create a new home, a home free of tyranny."

With swift pivots of his hands and feet Maanta jetted away from the tunnel's opening in the misty dust. The freed prisoners followed him as if in a trance.

No building still rose from Meridia's soil, only crumbled boulders of stone.

Maanta disappeared into the swirling brown haze.

23

Full Circle

Between Meridia's hollow shell and Sangfoul.

It had been days since Cardonea Tower had collapsed and Evanshade had been forced to flee Meridia. And yet still he swam on in the waters toward Sangfoul, harnessed to a bone cage with Illala and her pregnant womb inside.

The rest of his fleeing people had passed him days before because they had more speed without hauling things on their backs. Surely at this very moment they were telling his superior, Venge's father, of his failure.

Evanshade's flesh was worn and sensitive from the constant beatings from the deep-sea tides. His stomach growled from malnourishment. He had given almost all food he had gathered to Illala.

What was he doing?

Why was he returning to Sangfoul? Surely he would be reprimanded for his failure to sustain Meridia after its siege.

An oceanic mountain rose up before his path and he swam above its peak.

Surely they won't approve of my relationship with Illala, he pondered.

Illala's soft voice surprised him from the cage strapped to his back. "I love you, Evanshade."

What is on her mind? He wondered. *Does she know that we may not be welcomed back to Sangfoul?* He feared for her more than anything but where else was he to flee to? Sangfoul was his home. "I love you too." He looked over his shoulder and blew her a kiss. "Do you know that everywhere I go, everything I do, I think of you, Illala? You and our future child are always on my mind."

A school of shimmering blue fish wiggled past him as he swam.

Illala moved up the cage so that she was sitting just behind its front bars and Evanshade's back. She stroked her fingers on his neck as he swam. "I think of you constantly too. I worry about what you may be doing when you are not with me and about whether or not your people will accept our child."

"Why would they not accept our child?" Evanshade asked. He had been so worried about what they would think of him being with Illala that the thought of them not accepting his future son or daughter had not crossed his mind.

Illala traced his back with her fingertips now. "What do you think our child will look like Evanshade?" She asked. "You have a tailfin and I have legs. Your skin is dark as night and mine is blue. Our child will be beautiful to us but if it has legs, such as I do, will they butcher it or enslave it in lava mines when it is older?" As she traced her fingertips along his shoulders, goose bumps rose to her touch.

"I will not let them harm our child. You have my word." Evanshade swam forward, his movements slightly slower and in defeated strokes.

"I love you. I know you won't." Illala sat back in the rocking bone cage now. "But who will protect you when you protect our child?"

Evanshade swam with more determination now. "No-one will harm our child. No matter what happens, I will stop them."

Long moments passed as he pushed forward in the rippling currents, their cool breath licking on his lips and tailfin. He stared at a hammerhead shark high above in the waters as he swam. *We have almost arrived,* he thought. The terrain had become more familiar and hammerheads often dwelled close to Sangfoul.

A large manta-ray stretched its flowing wings beneath him as it burst up from the bed of sand below.

Evanshade squinted. In the distance, the silhouette of Sangfoul rose in jutting spiked spires above the sands where the city had been constructed. He could make out small, tail-fined people, whipping about the structures.

Soon I will have to explain my failures to my people. He thought.

"Uah!" Illala moaned in the cage behind him, sliding against its bone bars.

Evanshade immediately looked to her. "What's wrong? Do you need me to set the cage on the sands?"

Her body quaked against the cage as Evanshade halted it in mid-float. "Uah!" She cradled her rotund belly. "NO!" She shot out at him. "The pain is so great! The baby must be coming!"

Evanshade wanted so badly to let the cage rest on the sands below and hold Illala in his arms to take away her pain but he knew the only cure to her pain would be to reach Sangfoul in time for their child's birthing. There, he could find a healer to help her deliver their child.

"Hold on!" He called back to her. "Sangfoul is not far now! I will get you there in time for our baby to be born! Wait a little longer!"

"Aaaah!" She wailed. "You try holding a child in your body who wants to come out! The baby will come when it comes!"

What if I lose Illala when she gives birth? The horrible thought crossed his mind. He didn't know if he could bear to live without her. Evanshade shut the thought away and focused on what he needed to do for the sake of the woman he loved. "I love you!" He called back to her. "We will make it there in time!"

With all the strength his muscles could muster Evanshade beat his tailfin up and down behind him. He thrust through the currents, moving three times as fast as he had before. All waters before his eyes meshed into a blur. His heart raced and burned inside his chest.

"AAAAH! IT'S COMING!" He heard her scream behind him.

In the blur of the waters before him the dark spires of Sangfoul grew larger and larger until they stretched out so far above him that he knew he was almost to his destination.

A trumpet horn resounded in Evanshade's ears. *They must have noticed me farther out and are announcing my arrival,* he thought. He slowed his speed immediately. His fast beating heart breathed a slower movement as he noticed a group of his fellow soldiers swimming out to greet him.

"Get a healer!" He shouted to them. "Illala is giving birth to my child!"

Immediately one of the members of the group pivoted with his tailfin and swept off toward the city for a healer.

Sangfoul stretched like a dark luminous claw above. The other members of the group quickly swept to Evanshade's side. They joined him in his quick speed toward Sangfoul.

One of the men, a burly man decked in shimmering crimson armor and deep black whale leather, gave Evanshade a panicked look as he swam beside him. "She has died my liege," he spoke to Evanshade solemnly.

Evanshade ignored the man, swimming faster past him in the currents. As he set the bone cage gently down on the sands just outside Sangfoul a healer swept to his side.

The healer was an elderly, wrinkled woman, who was closely followed by three younger helpers holding numerous potions and tools. "We must act quickly," she spoke to Evanshade as he released the cage's straps from his back.

Evanshade choked on his own aquatic breath as he unlatched the cage door and looked upon Illala, crumpled and contorted as she lay against a far corner of the cage wall.

Blood curdled all about her body as it quaked and convulsed. Her eyes had rolled to the back of her head.

"NOOOOO!" Evanshade screamed. What his comrade had said set in. "She's dead." He held his head and wept tears into the ocean waters. His body shook violently. His heart struck with stabbing pains.

As Evanshade wept with anger and horror the elderly healer swam into the cage and pressed her fingertips to a vein on Illala's neck. "She is alive, my liege!" She called back to Evanshade but he did not hear her through his own distress.

The healer grabbed a green bottle of liquid from one of her helpers outside the cage and pressed the small bottle to Illala's lips, forcing her to breathe it into her gills.

Illala's glazed over eyes returned to look forward and her limbs regained movement. Her own pre-birth blood swayed in the currents before her eyes. "Uh," she moaned. "I'm in such pain. Where am I?"

The healer brushed Illala's hair away from her face. "That is not important now. You are giving birth. Pay attention to me and do exactly as I say."

"Uh," Illala moaned. "I am so weary."

The healer moved down to Illala's thighs and massaged her tense muscles. "Push!" She called to the girl. "Push!"

Illala pushed with what little strength she had, but her body was exhausted from the combination of the waters beating against her as Evanshade swam and the contractions which reaped their way painfully through her body. "Uah!" She moaned.

"PUSH! Damn you, girl!" The healer called to her. "This child will not be born without a little effort and pain! PUSH!"

"AAAAAAAAAAAH!" Illala pushed continuously now, anxious to birth her child and be free of this anguish.

Evanshade had heard her scream and looked up from his own distraught thoughts to find her still alive and the healer down by her open legs, massaging Illala's thighs. *I never thought I'd be so happy to hear her voice, let alone her scream,* Evanshade thought as he raced to the cage's side.

"It's coming!" The healer exclaimed excitedly. "I can see the baby's head crowning! One more push!"

"AAAAAAAAAAAAH!" Illala screamed as a tiny baby slipped into the currents from her body into the healer's cupped hands. Illala's tense body relaxed against the cage and sand beneath her.

The baby cried and squirmed in the old healer's cupped hands. A tailfin wiggled from the child's waist. Its skin was a dark navy-blue. Beneath the top of the baby's tailfin there was a small bulge.

"It's a boy." Evanshade smiled and reached his arm through the cage bars to Illala's shoulder. "We have a son."

Illala reached her arms out to the baby. "Please," she said to the healer, asking for her child. "He is so beautiful."

The healer took a sharp tool from another of her helpers and carefully cut the baby's umbilical cord before passing the child to its mother.

In Illala's arms her son cooed and squirmed gently. Its beautiful deep blue eyes looked up at her own, causing her heart to melt. She kissed him tenderly on the forehead and tilted her head to look back at Evanshade behind her. "He looks like you," she said. "We have been blessed."

Evanshade had a proud, fatherly grin, on his face. "We have."

"What should we name him?" Illala stroked the baby's soft skin.

"I have an idea." Evanshade kneeled down on his tailfin and hugged her with the bone cage between them. "I haven't told you this but when I was first born my parents gave me a different name then the one I have now. My name was changed to Evanshade when I became a warrior. My birthing name was Equilious."

Illala smiled and kissed his hand. "What a handsome name."

"I've always wished it was still my own," Evanshade admitted.

"Then it will be our son's." Illala rocked their baby in her arms. "Welcome to the world, Equilious." She kissed the baby's adorable bald head gently.

Equilious cuddled up warm to his mother's bosom.

"We should get you inside and clean you up," the elderly healer swam outside the cage as she spoke to Illala.

Evanshade opened his arms from his embrace with Illala. "We'll take her to my quarters. There she can rest, and we both can enjoy the company of our baby boy."

Illala tried to swim upward but couldn't. She was too exhausted from the journey and giving birth.

"Rest your body, Love," Evanshade spoke. "We will carry you in the cage to my windowsill."

Illala rested back against the sand and cage floor beneath her as Evanshade summoned a few of the strong men in his welcoming party to his side.

"Each one of you grab an edge of the bottom of the cage and follow where I direct you to my quarters," he instructed them. He grabbed hold of the cage directly above Illala's head and lifted it, with the others, high above his head in the currents.

With thrusts of their tailfins, the group swam the contraption high above the ocean floor to a room almost at the tip of one of the spiked towers that stretched before them.

As they reached his room's windowsill Evanshade halted them where they float. "Move the cage's door against that sill there," he spoke. "Hold it still, and I will carry Illala and my son out of the cage and into my room. After we are out take the cage to the slave yard."

"We will," one of the younger men replied.

Evanshade let go of his grip on the contraption and pushed with his tailfin to the door in its front. He unlatched the door's lock and swam inside to Illala, swooping her and Equilious up in his arms. "Soon you will be able to rest." He kissed her on the cheek and swam from the cage, through the windowsill and into his bedroom.

When he turned to look out the window once more the cage was gone.

The room was dark as Evanshade wrapped Illala and baby Equilious in warm, woven-leather sheets, and gently let them float in a corner of the room. "I will make some light, Love," he spoke to Illala while swimming to an intricate crimson vase aside a coral desk along the far wall.

After reaching his arm inside the vase's opening Evanshade withdrew it with three malta-eggs clenched in his hand. He broke them open onto dishes sitting on pillars about the corners of the room. A molten glow illuminated the walls.

Evanshade watched Illala's eyes as she took in the space.

He had commissioned a slave once to carve scenes of battle in every inch of stone on the faces of the walls about him. The slave had done a magnificent job. Evanshade had dreamt of and lived battle his entire life and could think of no better way to decorate his room.

He smiled with pride as Illala took it all in. And then something happened inside him, something that had happened a few times lately, a realization came to him like a swift crack in stone.

By having scenes of war carved into my walls I have paid tribute to the very way of life that will inevitably be the end of me, he thought. He was ashamed. *This battle-hungry thirst in my spirit led to the deaths of Illala's family. How do I keep it from leading to the deaths of Illala and my son? I have given Equilious my name. How do I assure he is not doomed to relive my fate?*

Evanshade dove to Illala and held her in his warm arms. His lips kissed Equilious's forehead. "These depictions on my walls are not who I am," he spoke to her. "They are what I once was. Once you are healed we will find a safe place to live outside of the realm of Sangfoul," he promised her.

Illala half-smiled at Evanshade's attempt to calm her thoughts. "How will you do that when my people will surely be looking to take revenge on you for the heartache you have caused them? And surely your ruler would come searching for us."

"We will find a way." He held her close as she rocked Equilious. "I will find a way."

There was silence then as Illala found comfort in Evanshade's strong arms.

"We should clean you up," Evanshade broke the silence as he realized her clothes were still tainted with blood that had come forth from her body in the birth. "Equilious could use a cleaning as well. Wait here."

With a swoop of his tailfin he swam to the vase once more where he retrieved kelp-cloths to clean his family off with. He warmed them over the cracked malta-shells and returned to Illala's side. "We need to get these clothes off of you," he said. "Once you are clean I have some garments that you can wear until we can buy you more in market."

Equilious cooed in his arms while Illala disrobed. *She is so beautiful,* he caught himself thinking as she slipped her loose fitting leather garments from her body. Her cool blue skin was supple. Her breasts glowed in the room's crimson light. Evanshade marveled at how much smaller her belly had instantly become after giving birth.

But her pregnancy bump was one of the most beautiful parts of her body out of them all.

Her pure eyes looked into his as she reached out her arms to hold her child. Evanshade placed Equilious gently back in her cradling arms and began to move the warm kelp-towel across her smooth body.

Droplets of blood disappeared from her skin and into the towel as it brushed beneath Evanshade's fingertips along her body. He kissed her as he did so. He couldn't help but enjoy the sensation. But he didn't make an advance toward her. He restrained himself.

When she was clean he retrieved a fresh towel and cradled baby Equilious in it in his arms' embrace. He wiped the child off gently and wrapped him in yet another fresh kelp-towel.

Equilious wiggled in the cloth as Evanshade handed him back to Illala.

Next, Evanshade swam to a coral chest along one of the walls and retrieved a set of his clothes for Illala.

He cradled Equilious as she put them on. Equilious' tender body in his arms was comforting somehow.

Evanshade looked up and smiled at Illala's beauty. She was beautiful even in his clothes that were tailored, not just for men, but also for people with tailfins. The fancy skirt he had given her usually was worn around the top of his tailfin but fit her body just right. "You look amazing even in my clothes."

She rolled her eyes and gave him a grin. "You'd think I look amazing in anything. It'd be nice if we could go to market tomorrow and at least get some clothes for a female to wear. We need to get some things for Equilious too. Besides, I'd like to see a little of what your realm looks like."

Evanshade swam to her and gave her a kiss. "If you feel up to it then it sounds like a plan to me, Love."

THOOM! THOOM! THOOM! A booming knock echoed through the room's door.

"Who is it?" Evanshade called back, surprised that someone was interrupting him so soon after his arrival. He spun in the waters and swam to the door.

A youthful male voice responded from the other side. "I am Calpis, a page of Lord Malistour's! He summons you to the Hall of Reckoning!"

Evanshade turned to Illala, a worried look in his eyes. "Malistour is Venge's father. He is ruler to our race. His only superior is the Dark Master himself. If he summons me I must go. Do you wish me to request someone to stay here with you?"

"No. I should be fine." Illala kissed him once more. "Gelu knows I was alone enough in Meridia that you should not start worrying about leaving me alone now. Be safe Evanshade. I love you."

Evanshade kissed his son once more on the forehead before pushing open his large stone door.

Calpis hovered on the other side, his tailfin beating gently. His clothes were tattered, eyes were sunken in and Evanshade thought he looked malnourished as well.

Malistour's pages always look like this, Evanshade thought. *If he'd just treat them better they'd be healthier and of a lot more use to him.*

"Follow quickly. Malistour is waiting," Calpis choppily said before spinning and swimming off quickly down the hall.

Evanshade was surprised at Calpis' speed but kept close as he led the way to the Hall of Reckoning. This was an insult, Evanshade realized, and Malistour was keeping a close eye on him. Evanshade knew the way to the hall. He had no need of an escort. "What is this all about?" He questioned Calpis as they swam.

"Ask Lord Malistour," was the only response Calpis gave him.

The halls swerved and turned in all directions and even led straight up at one point. Then, halfway down the core of the massive black spike tower, Calpis swerved quickly left and into the Hall of Reckoning. Evanshade followed just behind.

Evanshade had forgotten the morose grandeur of this great hall. It was haunting, even to those who ruled here. Its dark black stone was lit only by a few malta shells cracked in the center of the room. The space itself was immensely vast in width and length.

Malistour hovered in the waters on the far end of the open space. From tail to head he stretched 12 feet and his girth matched his rippling muscle. His body seemed to rip from his leather garments. His cheeks were drawn and ridged. To his left and right were two sets of massive guards, but in their girth they were only half his size. "YOU HAVE FAILED US!" Malistour bellowed from across the hall as Evanshade entered. "WHAT HAVE YOU TO

SAY ABOUT LOSING MERIDIA?" A trident with a shaft as thick as a dolphin's body was grasped in his fists.

"Losing Meridia was not my failing!" Evanshade shouted to the looming man as he approached. Malistour made Evanshade nervous because he was massive and unpredictable but Evanshade was damned if he was going to let the tyrant see fear in his eyes or hear it in his voice. Evanshade shivered though as he noticed something in the dark distance to his left and right. He could barely see the silhouettes of Sangfoul guards as they held something on iron leashes before them. The things bared their teeth viciously as they attempted to swim forward.

"I SEE YOU HAVE NOTICED MY NEW PETS!" Malistour laughed. "DO YOU LIKE THEM? I HAVE BEATEN BANEALIAN SLAVES INTO BEING MINDLESS ATTACK CREATURES!"

Evanshade remained silent. The Lord of Sangfoul disgusted him. He halted in the waters yards from Malistour.

Calpis scurried behind his master.

"SO THE LOSS OF MERIDIA WAS NOT YOUR FAILING? EXPLAIN!"

Evanshade took a silent gulp. "Surely you have heard from your son who has no doubt already arrived! We were attacked by warriors of Baneal and some of the escapees from Meridia's original siege but were winning the battle when suddenly an eruption of air burst through Meridia's soil, toppling Cardonea Tower and Meridia's East and West Shale Walls! I do not know if the burst of air was our foe's doing, but I can tell you there was nothing left and no use in staying!"

"YOU SHOULD HAVE STAYED AND PROTECTED OUR CLAIM! IT WAS NOT YOUR RIGHT TO DECIDE THAT MERIDIA IS WORTHLESS TO US NOW! IT IS NOT EVEN MY RIGHT! THAT CAN ONLY BE DECIDED BY THE DARK MASTER!"

"What would you have had me do?" Evanshade swam forward and upward, anger pulsing across his face. "Would you have had me stay and risk the lives of our people for a barren stretch of sand? Would you have had me risk your own son's life?"

Malistour was outraged and swooped down like a giant toward Evanshade to skewer him on his pillar of a trident. He halted though and quenched his anger with another response. His weapon burned in his fists as they pulsed with red. "YOU TAUNT ME EVANSHADE! DO NOT TEMPT ME TO HAVE YOU SLAIN! VENGE WOULD HAVE SURVIVED!" Malistour swam within a breath of Evanshade's face. His head was twice Evanshade's size and he grabbed the man's face with his massive hands and shook it.

The slaves growled in the dark recesses of the room as they bit at their restraints.

Evanshade shivered with fear.

"YOU DID NOT FLEE TO PRESERVE MY SON'S LIFE!" He breathed his sour, fish-egg breath, into Evanshade's nostrils as he almost deafened Evanshade's ears. "YOU FLED TO PROTECT THE LIFE OF YOUR MERIDIAN WIFE!"

Evanshade almost fainted in Malistour's grasp.

"IS THAT NOT TRUE?"

Evanshade writhed to free himself. His sight began to fade to black. And then Malistour's massive hand let loose his face.

"I ASKED A QUESTION! ANSWER! IS THAT NOT TRUE?"

Evanshade sank in the waters as he struggled to gain full grasp on his consciousness. He choked as he breathed water into his gills. His muscles tensed. His tail flipped back and forth instinctively.

"SO HELP ME EVANSHADE FROST!"

Evanshade's body stilled and he stuttered as he began to speak. "Sh sh sh she is not my wife."

"SHE MAY AS WELL BE!" Malistour struck his trident into the floor. The room shook. "YOU HAVE A CHILD WITH HER, DO YOU NOT?"

Evanshade cupped his eyes as he curled in the fetal position. "I... I have..."

"A CHILD WITH A TAINTED, LEGGED MERIDIAN! WHAT WERE YOU THINKING? YOU KNOW OF COURSE THEY MUST BOTH DIE!"

Evanshade straightened himself out and looked Malistour directly in his irises. A newfound strength exuded from his body. "No," he breathed in determination. "You will never take their lives. I will not let you."

"HA!" The massive hulking creature grabbed his rotund stomach. "NO! I WON'T MURDER THEM! YOU WILL SLAY

THEM BOTH, AND IN THE END GROVEL TO ME FOR YOUR OWN LIFE!"

Evanshade burst forward at Malistour with hatred boiling from his eyes.

With one swift movement Malistour grabbed both Evanshade's wrists and stretched his arms to their full span. Evanshade's back bones cracked and echoed throughout the hall.

"YOU WILL BEG ME FOR FOREGIVENESS!" Malistour flung Evanshade's limp body like a rag doll into the swaying aquatic darkness of the hall.

24

Her Finding

Outside the crumbled shell where Meridia once stood

The cinnamon-hued fog of dust and sand whipped and stung Anna's eyes as she huddled in a tight group with her comrades. Her trident braced to her side. She smelt blood in the currents from the battle.

"Stay close," Tao's voice warned her and the others as the sound of whirling sands clicked about them.

She could not make out the bodies of Tao and the others, only their silhouettes. And something slick skimmed along her calves as she tread water. "Did you feel that?" She asked to whoever would answer.

"What?" One of the others replied.

"Probably an eel," Tao spoke up.

She was being paranoid.

"Don't break formation until the sands clear," Tao's voice came again. "They could attack us again at any moment."

The sands whirled before her sight for long moments before dissipating faintly. The shadows of her comrades beside her comforted her. She had begun to be able to make out their features now. Sift's strong body was immediately to her left.

She found it interesting that in front of her she could still see nothing though.

A gust of dark and light sands swept before Anna and green hues now mixed within the breeze. Then instantly the sands slowed and began to dissipate again.

What was that dark shadow coming closer and closer to her through the sands? It moved quickly and had a human-like form. "There's something coming toward us," Anna whispered to the others. She held her trident tight in her fists, preparing to strike the thing.

The sands dissipated more and more now so that she was almost able to make out the person's features. And then it hit her. Her approacher's tone, slim build, and charming smile struck her mentally and drew breath from her heart. He had been ripped away from her in her life's most intimate moment of passion. "Maanta?" She gasped, letting her trident go slack in her hands. "Could it be you?" He approached quicker now and her heart was consumed by warmth. He was more handsome than she had even remembered and his body had matured since she had last seen him.

She longed to hug him close and not let go.

25

His Return

Outside the crumbled shell where Meridia once stood

Maanta's legs beat slowly in place as he hovered in the sandy waters outside where Meridia had once stood. He had met up with the almost 200 Meridian slaves he had freed after releasing the air pocket but had decided to keep the group close to the city until the sands dissipated and they were able to see their hands before their faces once more.

After all, what was the point in being freed if only to charge blindly into the unknown to be devoured by creatures of the deep you could not see? The tail finned people of Sangfoul might also be searching for them close by. The whipping sands in the waters about him were so thick that he could not see even a finger before his eyes.

Where is Archa? He questioned in his mind. *She knew I was coming to Meridia. She should have arrived by my side by now.*

The others about him jostled and whispered to each other. He could hear them in the storm of sand. "Be silent," Maanta spoke to them. "We do not know who could be listening. Wait until the sands clear to speak."

With a hush they silenced their lips.

And then amongst the silence and clicking sand winds he heard other voices, fainter voices then the hushed whispered tones he had heard from his group.

One of the voices was deep and that of a male. "Stay close," it said. Maanta could barely make out the sound.

Maanta cupped his hand next to the ear of the Meridian beside him and whispered to her that he wanted them to stay there while he investigated. He instructed her to whisper this in the same way to the others.

Silently Maanta swam away from the freed Meridians. He moved so slowly as to not be heard with the movements of his legs and hands, and listened so intently to the waters about him, that he heard every pulse of their movements.

A female voice glided across his hearing from the distance. Once again it was barely audible. "Did you feel that?" It asked.

That voice, Maanta thought. *It's so familiar. Where have I heard it before? Anna?* His heart raced. *Could she be here?* He quickened his pace to get close to the voice sooner. *Surely it's her,* he thought. Her voice was unmistakable to his mind.

He heard the first voice a little louder this time. "Probably an eel," it said.

Maanta longed to hear the female voice once more. He was certain it was Anna's. Through the sands the features of a young woman slowly became visible as a silhouette before him. Surely that wasn't the young woman who had spoken with Anna's voice.

When he had last been with her, Anna's curves had been slimmer than this girl's and she had been shorter as well. He swam quicker and as he did so the sands dissipated some before his eyes.

The girl's features shone through the aquatic sand breeze. Her curly red hair flowed in the waters behind her as her emerald eyes looked longingly into his own. Those were Anna's eyes. He knew them instantly. She had matured and was more beautiful then ever. It was her.

"Maanta?" Anna's beautiful voice called to him. "Could it be you?"

Maanta rushed to her now with no caution to be silent anymore. Anna was the only thing on his mind. He wrapped his pale arms around her pastel-blue waist and back. "It's me," he spoke in her ears. "I've missed you so much."

Others were speaking to him now but he paid them no mind, focusing solely on Anna.

"I feared you dead," Anna wept into the waters. "Where have you been? Why didn't you come to me? I'm so happy you're alive!"

Maanta held Anna close, not wanting to let her go. He traced his fingers through her hair and along her head as she moved closer. "I have seen so many things and been so far." He could feel her warmth joining his own as he held her close. "There is so much to tell you. When we've settled in some place tonight I promise I'll share it all with you. I'm just so happy to be by your side once more."

"Did you think of me where you were?" Anna brushed her cheek against his own.

Maanta's thoughts went back to the mountain when he was daydreaming about Anna so much that he fell from its cliff. "Sometimes I could think of nothing but you."

She kissed his lips and he held her cheek with his hand. It was a deep passionate kiss that they held for long moments before looking into each other's eyes once more.

Maanta stared into Anna's warm, pure emerald eyes, and marveled at the strength, purity and passion within them. He still held her cheek with his hand. "I love you, Anna." The world about him seemed surreal as he said the words. He had wanted to say them so badly in Orion's Birth before he had been swept away to the world of air.

"Oh Maanta!" Anna hugged him even tighter than she had before and kissed him deeply again. "I love you too!"

"AHEM!" The loud, grunt-like noise came from somewhere close by and finally registered in Maanta's hearing and thoughts. "If having a reunion like this, she gets, dread I the reunion receive will I." Sift's dark muscular body hovered slightly beside Anna's in the swirling sandy waters.

Maanta kissed Anna once more and then went to shake Sift's hand. "It's great to see you again too, Sift." Maanta gave him a hug too. He petted Lola on the head where she floated close by. "I can't wait to hear all about what has happened with Anna, you and the others since I have been away."

"Nor can, waiting we be, to hear what done have you my friend." Sift waved some of the Meridian warriors and Tao over to his side now to also greet Maanta. "Although, as must you have guessed, Meridia and our enslaved there have, I fear, been lost."

Most of the Banealian and Meridian warriors were paying attention to Maanta now, a few of them shaking his hand and giving him their best regards. Tao looked distant and stared off into the blank and distant sandy fog.

Maanta's heart raced. He couldn't believe he had waited so long to tell them about the good news. "It is true Meridia seems to be lost." He gave Sift a heartening grin. "But the slaves of Meridia live. I freed them from the prisons beneath Meridia before the city's collapse."

"Do not lie to us, boy!" Tao snapped at him with a dark look in his eyes. "They are all dead! How could they have survived?"

"Tao," Sift gave his comrade a stare. "If Maanta says free they be, then free they be."

"Then where are they?" Tao looked dark and lost again.

"Follow me. I'll show you." Maanta swam forward and began to disappear in the sandy fog before them.

"Toward Maanta we follow!" Sift shouted and waved his armored arm in the currents as he mounted Lola once more.

The group mounted their riding companions also and swiftly followed in Maanta's wake. Anna and Sift were at the lead. The only one who didn't come was Tao. Instead he swam down to look for the beheaded body of his son that had sunk to the ocean floor during the battle.

"Venge will pay," Tao cursed beneath his breath. A lost and blind hurt consumed him.

The sands whipped and curled before Maanta's eyes as he swam to where he had left the freed slaves. In truth they were only 15 or so whale lengths away. Soon their faces and bodies became visible in the now settling sandy fog. They stretched like a large circular wall in the waters before him. He wasn't able to see how many there were through the sands until just now. *It was worth the sacrifice of our city,* he thought. *Thank goodness they are all now free.*

Maanta swam into the group and was about to tell them about his discovery of Zharista Anna and the others close by when the Banealian and Meridian warriors burst through the sandy fog.

"My people!" Anna cried as she raced to them, hugging each one of them she was near as she arrived to their side.

Other cries of jubilation could be heard over and over again in the coming moments as warrior Meridians met up with loved ones they had long believed dead.

"Candinar!" One man called out as he rushed to a freed Meridian's side. "Brother!"

A female warrior noticed her malnourished husband in the mass of freed slaves and rushed to be with him, kissing him repeatedly.

The warriors of Baneal smiled and cried as they embraced the previously enslaved who had no family here to greet them.

It was a bittersweet reunion, because for each person who was now here reuniting and celebrating their freedom, at least 20 more had died in the massacre, the enslavement and battles. And that didn't even include the numbers of enslaved people of Baneal who were dying or had perished in Sangfoul.

The reunited kissed, held and comforted one another until the light streaming through the surface of the water above began to set and fade.

Sift suddenly appeared by Anna and Maanta's side as they spoke with the first slave Maanta had freed. They had discovered his name was Medvedev.

Medvedev spoke of how he had been forced to mine the lava by hand from the caverns beneath Meridia. His hands were crippled and black as coal. He also told the heroic tale of how Maanta had freed him after the air had burst through the tunnels. "But I fear our people's spirit will not be repairable after losing Meridia to the sand and coral ocean floor," he spoke.

Maanta put his arm around the man. "It is our souls, Medvedev, that make who we are, not the place where we were born."

Medvedev had a blank stare as he spoke. "But you must remember, at least for many of us who were enslaved, our souls have been broken. Without our homeland, where will we heal them?"

Sift broke in to the conversation and spoke to both Anna and Maanta at once. "Getting dark it is, and we have left many of our people who, not warriors are, a good distance away from here. Return to them before nightfall, we should."

"Good point," Anna agreed. "We should be heading back to them." She took a conk-shell that Sift had had strapped to his side and held it to her lips. "My fellow Meridians and Banealians," the noise echoed through the spiraled shell, "it is getting dark and we must return to others of our people we have left beyond these waters!"

The now massive group stopped their talking to listen to her words. There was barely any sand left to block their sight in the waters.

"Travel closely!" Anna spoke. "For the people of Sangfoul may still lurk about us!"

Within moments they grouped together and began heading back toward Tao. Once more Sift, Anna and Maanta led the group.

At first when they came to where Tao should be they did not see him.

"This is where he was?" Anna questioned Sift.

"Yes," Sift answered while looking about him. "And we must find him. For cannot, we leave him behind."

"I wouldn't dream of it," Anna assured him.

The waters were relatively clear now so Tao should have been easily visible but darkness was also falling and Maanta realized, as he searched too, that it was possible the darkness was shading Tao from them. It was bizarre though, if Tao was here, that he hadn't swum to them the second they arrived. Their group now numbered close to 300, once combined, and would be easily noticed by anyone close by.

Then, beneath them on the still-stirring sandy oceanic floor, Maanta noticed a body curled and cupping its hands to its face. "Tao!" Maanta shouted down to him before showing Anna and Sift where he was. "Tao!" Maanta called again.

At first Tao paid them no mind. He didn't even look up, but after Sift also called for him he swam slowly upward.

When Tao arrived to their side his eyes were sunk with darkness and depression. "They're gone," he spoke with disparity.

Maanta couldn't understand why Tao seemed so dark and lost. He should be joyous that the enslaved had been freed.

"True it is," Sift responded to Tao. "Evanshade and the others of Sangfoul appearing are to be nowhere about."

"Not them," Tao spoke angrily now. "The bodies of our slain are gone, swept away by the currents which churned in the falling of Meridia. My son is lost. He should not have died this way."

Tao's son, Maanta thought. Why was this sparking a memory? *The boy,* he remembered. *Tao's son was the boy who greeted me in Baneal and begged to come with us to Orion's Birth. He must have come here with the others to fight the people of Sangfoul and free our Meridian slaves.* "I'm sorry for your loss," he said.

"Don't be." Tao's voice was crisp and harsh. "He gave his life for a just cause." Tao was trying to justify losing his son, Maanta could tell, but the look in Tao's eyes said something different. They spoke of hate.

And hatred can bring nothing of goodness to our world, Maanta thought. *We have to help him try to move past his son's death and find some other light in the world. Otherwise it will consume him and could bring harm to us all.*

Sift put his arm around Tao. "Tonight, hold we will a memorial for him and our other lost brothers."

Tao looked distant and did not respond.

Sift petted Lola's smooth scales with his strong hands. "Now, leave we must for the group which, left we did in the waters outside Meridia."

"Agreed," Anna moved forward before looking back to Maanta. "Join me on my riding fish until we find you another riding companion or Archa meets up with us again."

Maanta swiftly swam up and mounted the riding fish while hugging close to Anna's waist.

The group traveled slowly through the currents as they made their way back to Millay and the Meridians and Banealians they had left behind. The recently freed slaves had no riding companions and so wherever they went they would have to move at this slow speed.

Maanta enjoyed it though. It had been so long since Anna had been by his side and he was enjoying each moment closely holding on to her.

"How far off is the group we're looking for?" He asked her while holding tight to her waist. Cool currents zipped along his body as he and Anna led the group behind them. Sift rode Lola at their side.

"Not far, only a little ways." Anna took a hand from the riding-fish and caressed his hand where it touched her side. "But I'm not in any hurry. I like having you close like this."

"Maybe I can hold you close as we sleep tonight." Maanta smiled and caressed her fingertips. Anna's back was warm against his chest.

The remains of Meridia were out of visibility as the group rose and dipped across a hillside in the quickly darkening night. The coral, fish and terrain seemed to glow about them as the group swam, like ghosts.

As they swam above a swaying kelp field, illuminated by the paled light of the descending sun above the ocean, Anna slowed her and Maanta's riding fish, turning her head in Sift's direction. "Wasn't this the place?" She asked him.

"Thought I that it was so." Sift looked carefully below them, squinting his eyes. "If here they are then a grand job have they done of hiding."

Anna halted their riding fish. "Then why haven't they seen us and come to our side?" As she asked this, the field of illuminated kelp swayed and parted as hands pushed at the dense kelp leaves.

Bodies shot up from the kelp basin and swam quickly toward them. One particular female body headed in Maanta and Anna's direction.

"Anna!" Millay called up in joy. "Thank goodness you have returned. We feared the worst when a fog of sandy currents consumed the waters about us. We didn't know what it could mean."

"Meridia has fallen to a rising pocket of air that rose from beneath the seafloor," Anna smiled. "But there is fantastic news. The tail fined people of Sangfoul fled as Meridia fell, and Maanta has freed the once enslaved of our people."

"Maanta?" Millay hadn't noticed him before, behind Anna, but as Anna spoke his name he caught her eyes. "You have come back to us, Maanta." She hugged the boy that she did not yet know. "I assumed you dead but Anna was always convinced you were alive. If you freed the enslaved of Meridia then you must be a great boy indeed!"

The other people who had glided up from the kelp basin were now welcoming their warriors back and greeting the freed slaves. In the darkness, all movements and facial features could barely be seen.

"I am not great," Maanta said. "I have done nothing hard or difficult that someone else could not."

Sift had been listening to their conversation and spoke to Maanta now. "But thought of an idea, you did, and put it to action where all others did not. In truth, certainly brave this is. Be not so modest, Maanta."

Maanta blushed but tried to hide it from the girls by sitting up straighter on the riding fish. "Thank you, Sift. I appreciate the compliment. I will never see myself as great though."

"As you shouldn't," Sift patted Maanta on the back, "for seeing yourself as great, to arrogance can lead. Greatness in truth can only exist in modest souls without corruption overcoming."

Moments of silence passed as the group thought about what Sift's words meant. Sift dove off in the currents to greet others rejoining them.

Millay's facial expressions turned concerned. "How did Sebastian fair in battle?" She asked. "Why is he not by your side? Does he ride with Tao?"

"He was killed in battle," Anna reached her hand out and held Millay's.

It was as if Millay's heart dropped. "I knew we would lose warriors in combat. It is unavoidable. But I never thought it could be Sebastian who would fall." She bit her bottom lip as she thought she would cry. "How is Tao?"

"He is not taking it well," Anna spoke. "He seems to be slipping into despair."

"I will go to his side and try to comfort him." Millay looked worried. "It's so good to have you back safe. I don't know how I would have taken it if you would have fallen as well." Millay swept off in the currents to look for Tao.

As darkness fell to its pure black night the group decided to rest in the kelp basin until morning when they could mourn their dead and decide what was to be done next.

Millay and Sift slept close to Tao and tried to comfort him before his thoughts traveled to the world of dreams.

Maanta held Anna in his arms at the edge of the kelp basin, slightly away from the others. Kelp swayed and clung to their bodies as they stared up to the moonlight shimmering across the ocean's surface above.

Anna turned and whispered in Maanta's ear. "We have laid down to rest now." She kissed him softly. "You told me you would tell me tonight of the places you've been and the things you've experienced since we were last together."

"You won't believe me." Maanta traced his fingertips down the bare of Anna's back.

"I will believe whatever you tell me." Anna laid her head on his strong, pale chest. "I trust you. No matter what you say I'll know it is true."

A cool hush of currents sent goosebumps up both of their bodies.

"It all began when I was ripped away from you by the gust of air in Orion's Birth," Maanta began. He told her about how Noah and two of his sons had rescued him after he had come to float on the crest of the ocean. He recited Noah's story for her about God's flooding of the world and about how he had learned to breathe air along with the other ways of the people of land.

She cringed when he told her of how he had choked up his gills from his mouth and she was shocked to discover that Noah was the man called Noa she had heard so much about as a child.

"How could he still be alive?" Anna asked.

He told her that he didn't know but that Noah was now over 900 years old.

"Gelu must be strong in him!" She exclaimed.

From there Maanta told her of the letter he had received from Amaranth and about the symbiotic creatures which he eventually tucked in his cheeks to assist him in his breathing underwater again.

She hadn't expected him to tell her that he was the one who had released the air pocket from beneath Meridia that had toppled her kingdom, but she surprised him by thanking him because without the loss of Meridia her people would have never been freed.

"I wanted to return to you so many times before now but I knew the only way to free our people was to release the air pocket as Amaranth had suggested." Maanta's fingertips traced Anna's curly red hair. He kissed her forehead.

"It was worth the wait." Anna smiled. "But what are we to do now?"

"I've been thinking about that." Maanta still stroked her hair. "The people of Sangfoul will never rest until our people and the people of Baneal are either completely enslaved or annihilated. But before I left the world of air and land I spoke of our dilemma with Noah and his sons and I think there is a way for us all to live free and without fear of the people of Sangfoul."

Anna raised her head and rested her arms on his chest. Her pure emerald eyes peered into his own. "What way is that?"

"If I was able to breathe air and learn to walk and live on the land above our waters then surely all our people can do the same." Maanta put his arms behind his head and smiled back at her. "And the people of Sangfoul could never again torture us because even if they were able to learn the ways of breathing air they could never walk because they have tailfins instead of legs."

Anna thought for a moment, still looking in Maanta's eyes through the flowing dark currents. "It would work. But we would have to convince the others that it was a good idea and they may be harder to convince of the truth of your story then I was. I would never be able to leave them behind."

"Neither would I." Maanta held her close in his arms as the two closed their eyes and drifted warmly off to the world of sleep.

In the morning they would tell Sift and the others of their idea.

The darkness drew Maanta downward to dream.

26

A Realization

Inside Maanta's Mind

Two nova white eyes glared at him, a chill breath rippling upon his neck, as he lay bound in molten chains to the darkness, his arms singed and a foreign mind clawing, dragging at his soul. His stomach went clammy. Maanta was alone, not knowing where, but alone. Somehow this was familiar. Where was he?

"Come to me," the spoken sounds seared within his mind. "Come and be adorned."

"Who's there?" Maanta replied. "What do you want of me?"

"I am power. I am strength. I am darkness." Sizzling, the nova eyes glared at him as the words were spoken from the darkness beyond them.

"What do you want of me?"

"I am lust. I am hatred. I am fire."

A shiver swept through Maanta's body. What truly was this thing speaking to him? What was happening?

"I am denial. I am jealousy. I am fear. Do you fear me?" It spoke in low ominous tones. "Come to me! Come and be adorned."

Maanta huddled in a corner of the darkness with the light of the reflecting nova eyes shimmering across his face, unable to speak. Waters began to sizzle about him, forming boils upon his flesh. Tears flowed from his open eyes.

And then Maanta realized where he was. His eyes dried. He had been here before. It was a dream. The boils on his skin and the burning scars about his body disappeared and the nova white eyes took a shape before him.

"Do you know what I am?" The thing hissed in Maanta's thoughts. Its serpent body swirled in the blackness.

I do, Maanta thought, *and yet I can't say the word.*

"You know me?" The serpent laughed wickedly.

"Lucifer!" The word leapt from Maanta's lips.

The serpent coiled and its shimmering white eyes flinched. "Join me!" It hissed to him. "Together we can rule the depths!"

"Never." Maanta floated stilly in the darkness. A massive opal trident appeared in Maanta's hands.

"Then one of us must die," the serpent hissed. "And it will not be me!" It leapt at Maanta and was skewered upon the tips of his trident.

Maanta plunged the weapon deeper into the squirming thing's body. "You will never again harm my people," he said before shuddering as the trident took on a serpent form of its own and became one with the attacker.

The bright-eyed serpent hissed and cackled as it pulled back from Maanta once more. "You cannot defeat the darkness!" It writhed and grew three times its original size before lunging for Maanta's waist and ripping both it and Maanta's intestines in half. Maanta's mind and sight went blank. A heat ripped through his soul. His eyes cooked like fish eggs and burst into the open darkness.

27

A Divide

The kelp basin

Sunrise filtered through the ocean's surface above.

As Maanta awoke in the barely-lit kelp basin he felt something smooth bobbing against his hand. He flinched at the thing's touch. Maanta was red with exhaustion and was shaking with fear from his dream. Anna still lay in slumber on his chest.

The smooth thing bobbed against his hand once more. He pulled his arm away and swam up quickly in the waters while holding Anna closely to his body.

Anna groggily awoke as Maanta searched for what had been rubbing against him. He knew what he had just experienced was only a dream but he was making no assumptions that what had just been rubbing against him was merely a fish.

"Wha?" Anna sleepily questioned as her eyes squinted in the slim pastel light of morning.

Where is it? Maanta thought as he searched the waters below him. *Whatever it is it must have gone.* And then he saw it quickly approaching him.

It moved swiftly, with smooth gray skin, fins and a body that pulsed up and down as it swam. A blowhole sat in its forehead and its long mouth grinned at him as it approached. "Ooooaaaaaoooooo..." it sang.

"Archa!" Maanta exclaimed. "Anna, it's Archa. She's returned to us."

Anna was fully awake now and Maanta released her from his arms. She kissed him quickly before Archa barreled into his chest.

He hugged Archa tightly and the two went swirling off into the waters before returning once more to Anna's side.

"Where have you been, girl?" He asked Archa while mounting her back. His hands stroked her forehead. "I thought you would meet up with me in Meridia.

"Ooooaaaaoooooo..." she sang.

"Never mind where you've been." Maanta kissed her forehead. "It's just good to know you're safe and that you're here with me again."

Soon the remaining Meridians and Banealians awoke and dined on the kelp they had been sleeping amongst. It wasn't the most delectable breakfast Maanta had ever had, but it would provide his body with the necessary nutrients he would need for the day ahead. Maanta also cooked a few minute sand dwelling fish on cracked malta shells for himself and Anna.

Toward the end of their meal, Tao swam above them in the basin and sounded his conch shell horn. The entire basin of Meridians and Banealians turned their attention to him.

Maanta couldn't help but note that Tao looked now as if he had regained a confidence in himself he had lost. *He still appears troubled though,* Maanta thought.

"My fellow Banealians and Meridians," Tao bellowed. "Today is a day of both great joy and sorrow! We have been reunited with many of the people of Meridia we had feared lost to enslavement, and at the same time we have lost many of our number in combat.

"We find comfort that we are reunited and yet Meridia is eternally lost to us and Banealians are still enslaved in Sangfoul! We search for rest, and yet can we ever truly believe the people of Sangfoul will leave us to survive in peace?"

The group in the basin was silent.

Tao floated above them and appeared to stare down each of their eyes. "That is why, when we speak of what to do next, I have a proposal for us all! I say we head for Sangfoul, free the enslaved of Baneal and take our revenge on the people of Sangfoul! We slaughter them where they live, as they have done to us! Then and only then can we find peace without fear!"

Many of the basin's crowd roared with approval. "Revenge!" They chanted. Maanta was surprised to see that the ones roaring in response were mostly the Meridians he had freed from the lava mining caverns.

Surely they are ready for peace and not warring now, Maanta thought.

Many more of the crowd held silent while others mumbled to companions close to them.

No one was responding in opposition to Tao's plan.

Something must be done, Maanta thought. *Someone has to say something to bring these people to their senses.* Maanta swam swiftly above the basin, yards away from Tao. "No one can deny that the people of Baneal should be freed," Maanta spoke to him loud enough for the people in the basin to hear. "But revenge is not a just reason to do so, and to immediately go to Sangfoul after we are so weary from battle would be suicide.

"You speak of slaughtering their people, if we best them in combat, so that they can never attack us again. Would you murder their elderly and children as they did to us? Would we not be becoming what we hate most?"

The crowd below listened intently.

Tao's face grew angry and ridged. "They deserve it for what they have done to us! They murdered my son!"

Maanta stared into Tao's hateful glare yards away. "You speak blindly and in despair, Tao. What you propose would lead to breeding of sin in us all, and to our ultimate destruction. I have a plan that would free us and would leave us with no more reason to fear the people of Sangfoul. We do not need to charge blindly into Sangfoul or slaughter their young to find peace once more."

"We have no need of your plan!" Tao thrust his arms and fists into the swaying oceanic currents, not providing Maanta with the opportunity to voice his plan. "Revenge!" He chanted. "Revenge! To Sangfoul!" He pivoted, mounted his riding-fish and sped off in the direction of Sangfoul.

"Revenge!" Many people in the basin chanted back, swam up and followed in his body's wake. Most of those who followed him were the Meridians Maanta had freed.

The remaining Meridians and Banealians stared up from the kelp basin toward Maanta, their minds in shock.

Sift swam quickly up from the basin to Maanta's side. "Go on," he spoke to the boy. "Tell us what consists of your plan."

"What just happened?" Maanta asked Sift. "Why did he leave like that and why are they following him."

"Overcome him, insanity has," Sift spoke softly to Maanta. "And those that follow him, the same way, must be. Truth there is in what spoken you have. Another way must there be than slaughter and death. Speak of your idea to us all."

Maanta took a moment to collect his thoughts and then spoke once more to the remaining people in the basin. Archa swam to his side to comfort him. "I have been to the world of air above our waters," he began. He told them all what he had told Anna the night before. Then he told them of his idea that they should return to the land above the waters where they could all learn to breathe air, and where the people of Sangfoul would never be able to reach them.

"He is as insane as Tao!" A voice called up at him from the basin.

"No! I have heard stories of others of our people adapting to breathe air!" Another voice from the basin called upward. "If he knows the way to the world of land and air, then we must go!"

"The air will drown us all and we will die!" A third voice called.

Anna rose up from the basin on the backside of her riding fish and joined Maanta and Sift. "Listen to me, people of Meridia and Baneal," she spoke to the group below them. "I know Maanta well and if he says he has been to these places and done these things, then he speaks the truth. Do not doubt that. Meridians, I remain your Zharista and I say we follow him to the world of air with our fellow people of Baneal."

I hope they listen to her, Maanta thought.

Anna spoke to them again. "But there is one more thing I feel we should do before we leave the waters. The people of Baneal have fought valiantly by our side to free our enslaved, and we owe it to them to try to release their people also."

The crowd below cheered.

"But I do not propose slaughter or even killing," she continued. "Instead, we should approach Sangfoul and, as the city sleeps, send a few of our number behind their walls to stealthily free the enslaved Banealians. Then we shall follow Maanta to the world of land, air and freedom above our waters."

Sift spoke softly so that only Maanta could hear. "She speaks wisdom," he said.

"She does," Maanta agreed, before riding Archa to Anna's side.

The crowd was speaking inaudibly amongst themselves again.

Sift spoke up now. "People of Baneal, assisted in leading us well, Tao has for years, but insanity it is which has overtaken his soul. If follow him, bring we would death and sin upon us all. Speaks in truth, Anna does, and such valiant an idea she has for freeing our enslaved. To join her, I say, the people of Baneal should!"

The Banealians in the crowd below cheered.

"Will you follow me to free the enslaved Banealians in Sangfoul and then to freedom and peace in the world of air?" Anna asked the Banealians and her Meridian subjects below.

"Yes!" Millay hollered up from the crowd.

"Yes!" Another call followed.

"We will!" A Banealian voice called out. The crowd was cheering and clapping again now.

Maanta smiled as he watched the group cheering on their leaders. *We are no longer Banealians and Meridians,* he thought. *We are now one.*

Sift swam quickly down to rejoin the group in the kelp basin. "Prepare your belongings quickly you must. Shortly leave we should if wish we do to free the enslaved Banealians before Tao attacks Sangfoul."

Within the hour they gathered their supplies and prepared their riding fish for the travel to Sangfoul. They formed in a square traveling formation, much like a blanket, that would hug the terrain beneath them as they moved. Their group was smaller now but would still be easily detected if they traveled much above the sea floor. Not only could the people of Sangfoul be looking for them, there was no way of knowing what Tao's reaction would be if he noticed them moving behind him. Sift would lead with Anna, Maanta and Millay from the front.

"To Sangfoul!" Sift called back over the crowd as they perched, some two per fish, on their riding companions.

With a thrust, the group burst up from the kelp basin toward Sangfoul. A group of small shimmering jelly fish scurried from their path.

Maanta hugged tight to Archa's smooth muscled body as waters whipped vigorously past his form. "Oh how I've missed this feeling!" He called to her.

They would travel for days, hugging the ocean floor over mountainous terrain and deep caverns. They dined on whatever sea life they came across, sometimes whale, sometimes squid, sometimes kelp, coral and oceanic worms. Not once did they see Tao and the others ahead in the distance. The people of Sangfoul also were nowhere to be seen.

Maanta couldn't shake the feeling though, that they were being watched. Something was following them. Flickering shadows in the caverns played tricks on his mind. But when he would swoop away from the group's formation to check, nothing was there.

On their fifth day of travel, as a large mountain of the ocean floor rose above them in the distance, Sift instructed them all to stop. "Here we shall remain," he told them. "Sangfoul lies just beyond the yonder mount. Of ages has it been since enslaved I was here but know I this to be the place."

What was moving at the oceanic mountain's base? Maanta squinted his eyes. *Tao,* he thought as he spied a better view of his old comrade and the others that had followed him after his mad rant. They had camped in close to the mount's base and scurried about it like tiny minnows in the distance. The light of the day was fading now.

"Do you think they see us?" Maanta asked Sift as they hovered in the waters upon their riding companions.

"Not likely," Sift replied. "Immersed they have their minds in warring thoughts and vengeance. Look they ahead to battle and an enemy which beyond the mountain waits, not back to ones which, know they not, do trail them." Sift waved his arm in the currents to the others behind, and turned to address them. "Rest here we will tonight," he called to them. "And tomorrow discuss we shall on how, free the people of Baneal, we will."

As darkness laid its full cloak upon the ocean's depths that night, Maanta and his companions settled in as close as they could to the sands beneath them so as not to be discovered by Tao or the people of Sangfoul.

Maanta held Anna close in his arms once more, as small fish flittered across his sight. Nearby he heard Archa breathing as she dreamed. He closed his eyes, opened them, and closed them again as he simply embraced the warmth of Anna's head resting on his shoulder.

It would take him hours to get to sleep, because every time he was on the brink of slumber, he thought he heard an unwelcome presence moving in the darkness just beyond the group.

Maanta was the last to find sleep that night. But eventually he convinced himself he was hearing things and he allowed his mind to rest.

After he and all the others' minds were lost away in the realm of slumber, something whispered in a cracked voice.

"...odyssey..." It spoke.

<u>28</u>

Night Visitors
Inside Maanta's Mind

Two nova white eyes glared at him, a chill breath rippling upon his neck, as he lay bound in molten malta chains to the darkness, his arms singed and a foreign mind clawing, dragging at his soul. It hissed. His stomach went clammy with blood's pulse. Maanta was alone, not knowing where, but alone. Somehow this was familiar. Where was he?

"Come to me," the spoken sounds scathed within his mind. "Come and be adorned."

"Who's there?" Maanta replied. "What do you want of me?"

"I am power. I am strength. I am darkness." Sizzling, the nova eyes glared within him as the words were spoken from the darkness beyond them.

"What do you want of me?"

"I am lust. I am hatred. I am fire. I am sin."

A shiver swept through Maanta's body. What truly was this thing speaking to him? What was happening?

"I am denial. I am jealousy. I am fear. Do you fear me?" It spoke in low ominous tones. "Come to me! Come and be adorned," it hissed and roared at the same time.

Maanta huddled in a corner of the darkness with the light of the reflecting nova eyes shimmering across his face, unable to speak. Waters began to sizzle about him, forming boils upon his flesh. Tears flowed from his open eyes.

And then Maanta realized where he was. His eyes dried. He had been here before. He had been here many times. This was the dream. The boils on his skin and the burning scars about his body disappeared and the Nova white eyes took a shape before him.

"Do you know what I am?" The thing hissed in Maanta's thoughts. Its serpent body swirled in the blackness. Steam seamed to curl from its eyes.

I do, Maanta thought. *And yet I can't say the word.*

"You know me?" The serpent laughed wickedly.

"Lucifer," the word leapt from Maanta's lips.

The serpent coiled and its shimmering white eyes flinched. "Join me!" It hissed to him. "Together we can rule the depths!"

"Never." Maanta floated stilly in the darkness. A massive opal trident appeared in Maanta's hands. It was ridged to the touch. *How did the dream end last time?* He thought.

"Then one of us must die!" The serpent hissed. "And it will not be me!" It leapt at Maanta and then time and motion seemed to stop. The glowing-eyed serpent stopped in mid water. All was still.

Another voice entered Maanta's mind. This voice had no form. **"To best the Devil, one must be above its tricks and sins,"** the voice spoke. **"If you do not hate, do not lust, are not gluttonous, have no greed and do not kill then the Devil cannot exist."**

Time, space and matter remained still. The serpent was a foot from Maanta's chest and Maanta's heart felt as if it would explode.

Everything evaporated into tiny bubbles and darkness consumed Maanta's dream.

<u>29</u>

A father, A mother & Freedom at last

Outside Sangfoul where Sift and the others slept

Maanta awoke with a shiver and nervous fear clutching his body. The entire camp around him slept. The sun was rising through the ocean's surface above and Anna rest closely upon his chest.

He couldn't explain it, but he felt drawn to somewhere beyond the rising mountain, high above the ocean's depths in the distance. He had to follow the feeling. Something was waiting for him out in the distant waters.

Slowly, he moved Anna from his chest and helped her slumbering body to rest upon the sandy oceanic floor. He kissed her gently on the forehead and then mounted Archa before darting off in the waters toward the place he felt called to. Why he felt the need to leave Anna and the others, he did not know. What was happening to him?

Maanta rose on Archa as she swam through the waters over the mountain before them. The black spike spires of Sangfoul rose in dreadful glory ahead of Maanta now.

***

Anna awoke as Maanta kissed her forehead. The kiss was comforting and made her smile. But she did not open her eyes. Why was he setting her on the sands? His chest had been so strong and warm. At any moment he would lay down beside her again and they would warmly cuddle back to sleep.

But he didn't return to her. Instead she heard him mount Archa beside her and swim away in the waters.

As she opened her eyes, Anna saw Maanta riding Archa quickly toward the mountain in the distance. *Where is he going?* She wondered as he moved farther and farther away. She had already lost him once, unexpectedly. She wouldn't let it happen again.

Slowly, as not to wake the others, she mounted her riding fish and swept off after Maanta. The sunrise-lit morning waters swept coolly past her as she followed him over the mountain ridge.

Sangfoul's deep black spiked structures shocked her as they came into view. They stood like tombs above the ocean floor. Surprisingly, no tail finned people swam about Sangfoul's black rising horns.

Maanta and Archa swam quickly past Sangfoul's structures and then on toward a series of caverns that seemed to exist in rising stone walls not far away.

Anna kept her distance, so that Maanta would not know she was following, and as she rode her riding fish through the black horn buildings, something caught her eye in a window in one of their high rooms.

There, in a barely lit room, a young girl with pale pastel blue skin cradled an adorable baby in her arms. She looked familiar. Anna swept past, continuing to follow Maanta. *Illala!* Anna realized. *She's alive! After I discover what Maanta's up to, I'll have to come back and try to convince her to come with us. Are they using her as a babysitter to watch over their children? How bizarre.*

Anna had long thought Illala dead and could never have guessed that she would have had a child with Evanshade.

Anna moved on the riding-fish's back quicker now as she saw Maanta disappear into a pitch-black cavern beyond Sangfoul. The cavern was high in elevation, higher than any of Sangfoul's horns rose, and Maanta disappeared into its lips of darkness.

She arrived at the cavern's entrance shortly and halted, not entering. Voices inside startled her. One voice was that of Maanta. Whose voice was the other?

***

Sunrise was brighter now as Maanta advanced on Archa's back toward the dark cave before him. Archa shivered beneath him as if she sensed something in the cave he did not.

But do I really not sense it? He asked himself. Something was drawing him in. It was as if a magnetic force in the cave was pulling him into its grasp. And he knew what it was too, who it was. *Why have I come here? Why did I not just stay with the others?* Maanta dipped into the darkness of the cave. He felt himself pulled to a force close by.

Blinding light stunned his eyes and then darkness resumed in the cave's waters, leaving a glistening figure in its wake. The shimmering thing was a man draped in a shining white cloak. Fig leaves were sewn into the man's garment and the stitched-in form of an apple tree stretched across the man's chest. The handsome man's soft blond hair flowed in the currents of the cave. "Welcome my son," the man greeted Maanta and stretched out his arms to offer an embrace. "Come to me. Come and be adorned."

Maanta halted on Archa's back in the waters and examined the glowing man before him. "I am not your son," Maanta spoke in a steady tone.

The glowing man approached Maanta. "You are my son. All people of the waters are my sons and daughters. Do you know what I am?" The man spoke in a warming tone.

Maanta held his place. "How could I not know what you are? You have haunted my dreams again and again. But you are not my father. Gelu is my father."

The glowing figure chuckled lightly. "God? Your father? Would a father drown all but one family of his sons and daughters, just because they did not please him? No. He is not your father. But I am, because when God decided he did not like the people of the world and tried to drown them, I rescued them and helped them to adapt to breathe water. He would murder his children when I would save them."

Inside Maanta's heart hatred brewed, but he shut it down and replaced it with love for his friends and Anna. He knew that to hate Lucifer would give Lucifer strength. "Gelu drowned the sons and daughters of the world because their souls had become corrupt beyond repair. They had become lustful, greedy, gluttonous and murderous. And you are the one who showed them and convinced them to be that way. You may be the father of Sangfoul, but you are no father of mine.

"And because the people of Meridia and Baneal have replaced sin with love and caring in their souls, Gelu has given us the chance to live our lives once more in the world of air. We will be safe from you there."

The heavenly-looking man's eyes and body contorted and twisted until he took the shape of a crimson-red serpent man in a tattered black cloak. Horns protruded like vines from his forehead. His fingers twisted and curled as he spoke. "You will never be rid of me," he hissed. "Even if you do reach the world of air, there will always be sin in the souls of man, and I thrive where sin survives." A scaly trident formed from the tip of his arm and he swam toward Maanta with great speed.

Maanta clutched his own trident tightly in his hands. He shivered in fear. He then remembered the second voice that had spoken to him in last night's dream and let his trident sink from his grasp to the cavern floor below.

The serpent man struck his trident upon Maanta's chest and then evaporated into a smoke of aquatic dust.

The cavern was dark as coal once more. Maanta stroked Archa's smooth head as she bobbed gently in the currents.

The exact words he had heard the night before resonated in his ears and he spoke them aloud in remembrance. "To best the Devil, one must be above its tricks and sins. If you do not hate, do not lust, are not gluttonous, have no greed and do not kill then the Devil cannot exist." Maanta smiled. "Sin cannot overcome sin. To kill the devil, all you need do is exist without him."

"What?" Anna's worried voice called from outside the cave.

"Anna!" Maanta swam quickly to her. "I didn't expect you would follow me here."

She gave him a look as he exited the cave, a 'You should have woken me so that I could come with you.' look. But she said something different. "What are you doing? Are you alright?"

Maanta leaned over from Archa's back and kissed her. "I wasn't, but I am now. Thank you for looking out for me."

Anna looked warily back on Sangfoul behind them. "We should be returning to the others. Surely Sangfoul will awaken soon and it would not be wise to be discovered before we have freed the Banealian slaves. There is also something I wish to do before we return."

"What is there to be done?" Maanta skimmed Sangfoul with his eyes for tail finned people stirring. In the center of the city, close to the seafloor, he noted nets with dark hued arms and legs protruding from their holes. "Those must be the slaves we have come to free." He extended his pale arm and pointed down to the dozen or so nets.

"We'll have to tell Sift of their location when we return." Anna also looked to the nets. "There is something I need to tell you. When I was following you, I made a discovery in a room high up in one of the dark horn towers. Barely lit by the rising sun, Illala was cradling a baby in her arms."

"Illala?" Maanta had not expected that Illala was still alive, let alone here. "Are you certain it was her?"

"It's been a long time since she's been with us, but it could have been no other but her. We must go and free her before the city wakes."

Still no one stirred outside the structures of Sangfoul, and the sun became brighter in the waters as the day began. Anna and

Maanta rode their riding-companions quickly to the window where Anna had spied Illala.

They peered above the windowsill and looked upon Illala as she cradled the child, cooing at it softly. The room she was in was encased in carved red stone.

"Illala?" Anna called inward. "Is that you?"

Illala turned in the waters and was surprised to see Anna at her windowsill. "Anna?" She asked. "What are you doing here? They'll kill you if they find you. Come into my room quickly."

Without hesitation Anna and Maanta swam into the room. Anna hugged Illala around the baby, whose bottom half was covered by a kelp blanket.

Illala rocked the baby gently. "Meet my son, Equilious."

"Your son?" Anna asked in shock. "Who's the father? Is he still alive?" Anna then noticed a dark figure crouched in a corner of the room. Its lowered head rose to look at her slowly as she spoke. "Evanshade!" Her heart jumped as she recognized her enemy only feet away.

Maanta swam before her in a protective stance.

"I am Equilious's father," Evanshade said in a deep, sad voice. "Please, stay and say what you have come to say to Illala. I give my word I will not harm you."

"Illala," Anna stuttered. "How could you? He murdered our people and your own family."

Evanshade ground his teeth as his tailfin seemed to shiver beneath him.

"I love him," Illala spoke. "I do not need to explain our love to you." Equilious began to cry and Illala calmed him by rocking him. "Why have you come here?"

Anna looked leeringly to Evanshade and then back to Illala once more. "Is it safe to speak in front of him?"

"Yes." Illala looked in pain. "You have my word."

Anna and Maanta swam out of the way of the window's view. "I'll trust your word," Anna spoke. "We have come to Sangfoul to rescue the enslaved Banealians here. After the slaves are freed, we will travel to Orion's Birth where we have found a way that will take us to the world of air. Maanta has discovered that our bodies can adapt to breathe the forbidden fluid." She flashed another worried look toward Evanshade, but was sure that since he had not yet attacked her, she must be safe. "Once we live in the world above water, we will be safe from the people of Sangfoul. They have no legs and could never survive there."

Illala kissed Equilious's forehead. "Then why have you come to me?"

"Because we saw you through your windowsill and wish to convince you to come with us."

"I can't." Illala looked to the weary looking Evanshade. "I could never leave him."

Evanshade looked up quickly and locked eyes with Illala. "No," he said with determination in his voice. "You have to go."

"But our family?" She gave him a questioning look.

Evanshade rose and thrust his tailfin in the waters until he was side-by-side with the woman he loved. "You do not know the things I know Illala. Malistour wishes you and our son dead. He'd have me kill you myself, but when I will not do it, he will no doubt send someone else for his murderous task. You must go with them."

"But our son, his tailfin," Illala uncovered Equilious's swirling appendage. "He could never live in the world of air. You've heard them."

"They will find a way for him to survive and he would not survive much longer here." Evanshade hugged Illala and their new son warmly. "I will discover where you are and rejoin you in time."

Illala looked deep in thought.

Evanshade turned his eyes to Anna and Maanta. "You must leave with urgency. There will be no time to free the slaves."

Maanta swam closer to Evanshade now. "Our group will not leave without them. Our plan is to rescue them tonight while your people sleep and then we will be on our way."

Evanshade swam to the windowsill and looked out over the city below. "Tonight will be too late. Malistour has discovered both Tao's group and what I'm assuming is your own. He will attack by midday and slaughter all in his way."

Turning back to Maanta and Anna, Evanshade realized by the look in their eyes that they would not abandon the slaves. "If you have to free them, then sneak around the city and free them as we attack Tao. You may have just enough time to free them and get away. I'll do whatever I can do to keep my people from catching up to you."

"Why are you doing this?" Anna asked. "Why destroy our world and then turn on your own to save what is left of us?"

Evanshade turned to look out the window once more. "I am a different man than I was when we first met. I have fallen in love with one of you. I have realized the wrongs of my soul." He swam back to Illala and then gave her a deep kiss. His eyes remained dark and forlorn looking. "Now you should go, before Sangfoul awakes and you cannot flee the city. Our army will surely begin to gather within the hour."

For a short while more Illala fought with him to stay, but eventually Evanshade convinced her that this would be the only way for their family to survive. He would find her again, he reassured her.

They both cried as Maanta cradled Equilious for Illala, and Evanshade pulled her close. "I love you," Evanshade whispered in her ear.

The only thing Illala brought with her, as she and Equilious left with Maanta and Anna, was a rope bag filled with kelp and whale-leather diapers.

Maanta slipped out the windowsill first and was relieved to see that the people of Sangfoul were not out and about yet.

Anna, Illala and Equilious were soon to follow. Illala rode the backside of Anna's riding-fish with her and cradled Equilious close in her arms.

They moved swiftly in the currents out of Sangfoul.

Evanshade watched them from his crimson room in the black spiked tower. He had told Illala he would be with her again one day. He doubted that was the truth.

Currents and minute particles of sand whipped past Maanta as he clutched close to Archa's torso and they dove above and below the mountain's tip near Sangfoul. He was once again not visible to the people of Sangfoul and this brought a feeling of safety to him, even if he now understood that the tail finned people knew of his group's presence there.

He glanced below him to Tao's group at the mountain's base, as Archa swam past above them. A few members of the group pointed their arms up at him, Anna, Illala and Equilious as they jetted past on their riding companions, but Tao seemed to pay them no notice. He either hadn't seen them, or was too fixated with his obsession of revenge on the people of Sangfoul to care.

Maanta refocused his sight to where Sift and the others were camped close to the ocean floor. Once again, they had embedded themselves into oceanic coral and kelp and were barely visible.

With a swoop, Archa and Maanta dove until he was just above Sift and the others.

Sift darted up on Lola's back to meet him. "What place of going have you been?" He questioned Maanta harshly. "When awoke we did this morning, nowhere to be found were you or Anna. What thought you of what we would imagine?"

Maanta squeezed his legs against Archa's side and halted her before Sift. "It's hard to explain why we left without saying anything, but we have returned with information and someone I think you'll be happy to see." Anna, Illala and the young baby quickly joined Maanta's side.

Sift rode Lola closer to them. "Illala?" He asked in surprise. "Could it be you? Where did you find her?"

Anna spoke now. "We discovered her in a room in one of the towering spikes of Sangfoul, and encouraged her to come with us to the world of air. She has also brought her child with her."

Illala had covered Equilious's head with the kelp blanket he was wrapped in, while they had ridden away from Sangfoul, but she now pulled the blanket down to reveal Equilious's adorable eyes and smile. He squirmed and curled against her.

"And a baby?" Sift dismounted Lola and swam directly to their side. "Can cradle I the young babe? So long has it been since held I one of such youth."

Illala passed the adorable baby into Sift's strong arms where he gently held it to his chest.

"He's so light," Sift said as Equilious sucked his thumb in the man's arms.

Maanta dismounted Archa and floated in the waters just behind Sift. He watched the baby as it smiled. *What a beautiful sight,* he thought. "We come with news also Sift, and I wish it could wait but it can't. By mid-day the people of Sangfoul will pursue an attack upon Tao. They know of our presence and will surely come for us when they are done with him and his makeshift army."

Sift passed Equilious back to his mother. "Then prepare we must ourselves, quickly to free our enslaved people. But how will we succeed? In daylight, suicide this will be. Approach, no doubt we'll have to, with only a small group to stand a prayer of being not noticed. The fact that preparing for battle, they are, will be in our favor, because the slaves will still be in their nets instead of out working the lava mines."

Maanta decided he would not tell Sift that the idea he was about to share with him, and the information, had come from Evanshade, because Sift might view Evanshade's words as treacherous and untrustable. "I have an idea," he said. "If we send a small group around to the backside of Sangfoul, we can free the slaves when the people of Sangfoul attack Tao. Their attention will be distracted. We will have to free the slaves quickly and return to our group before Tao is defeated."

Sift rubbed his fingers across his chin as he thought. "Your plan sounds the best which we could have," he said. "With quickness must we leave, and hide behind the city of Sangfoul. But of whom do we take upon our mission?"

Maanta looked at his companions and then to the people in the group of Meridians and Banealians below them. "Three people would be harder to notice then five or ten. What if me, you and Anna went?"

"A solid number, three seems, but of the three you have chosen I am not sure." Sift looked to Anna. "Surely, needed by her people, Anna would be if return we do not. Rule she could if found we were and killed. Left behind, she should be."

Anna didn't like the idea of remaining behind or the idea of being separated from Maanta but she had to admit Sift had a point. "Agreed," she simply said. "And we are Illala's only friends here now. It would not be right of us all to leave her just as she arrives."

Sift eyed the people below. "But who should be our third?"

"Millay," Anna said instantly. "She is swift and well trained for fighting should you face a confrontation. She is also silent in her movements."

"No objections have I." Sift looked to Maanta. "And you?"

Maanta looked below where the curly haired Millay was trident practicing with another member of their group. Millay seemed to have the upper hand. "I know little of her, Sift, but if Anna recommends her, then I'd say she's our best choice. She seems talented with her trident."

"Then the three of us it is." Sift remounted Lola and began to descend to the rest of the group once more. "Speak we must as a group, and then with quickness, on our way be."

It didn't take long for Sift and Maanta to explain their plan to Millay and she was excited that she had been chosen as the third person for the mission.

"Dangerous it will be," Sift said to her.

"We have been through much as a people," Millay looked at him as she spoke. "I no longer have fear of danger."

Maanta and Millay rode Archa and Millay's riding-companion off to find food for them before their mission, as Sift explained to the remainder of the group what was going on.

He didn't spend long talking, only giving them the basic idea of what he, Maanta and Millay would be doing.

"Swim shortly away from here, as free the slaves, we will," he told them. "And if return we do not, before the people of Sangfoul defeat the warrior's which Tao's are, then flee you must for Orion's Birth after Anna's lead. Fear not, for catch up we shall." Shortly after he had finished speaking, Sift rode Lola off to where Maanta and Millay were feeding their riding-companions.

Anna instructed the rest of the group to begin preparing their riding-companions for the journey to Orion's Birth.

Within moments, Sift, Millay and Maanta swept on their riding-companions toward the oceanic mountain that separated them from Sangfoul. They skimmed the sandy ocean floor, churning sediment in puffs in their wake.

Sift led Maanta and Millay.

"How will we avoid being seen?" Maanta called up to Sift as they went. "Surely the people of Sangfoul will be amassing at the other side of the mountain's base by now! If we come down on the other side of the mountain surely we will be seen!"

"Another way is there!" Sift called back to Maanta and Millay from Lola's back as they swept along in the waters. "Follow me and show you I will!"

Sift curled swiftly to their left as they neared the mountain's base. Tao's group of warriors was far to their right side and had not seen them.

As they moved closer and closer to the mountain's base, they still hugged the ocean floor and were now surrounded by fields of coral and shimmering fish which swam about it. The ocean floor beneath them slowly became an open cavern of darkness where an earthquake had once split open its sides. The light blue of the sunlit ocean faded to pitch black in its depths.

"Found here, we have, our way of stealth traveling!" Sift called back to them before dipping Lola quickly down into the darkness. "Fish noises make, as traverse through the darkness cavern we do, so that know we do where each other are!"

Maanta dipped Archa swiftly down in the darkness next. She followed Sift and Lola with no hesitation.

Millay's riding-fish on the other hand balked as she attempted to get it to follow the others, but she was eventually able to get the fish to go the way she desired.

At first Maanta was apprehensive about where he had followed Sift. They had no source of light and if one of them were to get separated from the others here, there would be no way of finding their way out of the cavern beneath the ocean floor. The darkness closed in on his sight, giving him a feeling of claustrophobia. He closed his eyes and saw no more darkness than he did with his eyes open. Something warm and slimy brushed past his face and was quickly gone. Where was he going?

"oooooo" Sift's fishy note caught in Maanta's ear and he felt a little more comfortable understanding better how they would keep track of where each other were.

If they were to speak to each other, it was possible that the people of Sangfoul would hear them and know something was amiss.

"oooooo" Maanta sang back as he followed Sift's voice.

"oooooo" Millay also sang behind him. Her sweet female voice carried a soothing tone.

"oooooo" They sang back and forth through the darkness as they followed each other's fish calls.

The darkness which had caused Maanta to shiver with unknowing when they had first dipped within its depths now became a sort of exciting music-box for him. The notes they called back and forth to each other seemed to dance in the darkness before his eyes.

"oooooo" Sift sang in his hopping low tone and Maanta swept Archa after him.

"oooooo" Maanta sang purely.

"oooooo" Millay soothingly replied as she swept quickly behind.

They swerved and turned many times and were never discovered by anyone else in the aquatic cavern tunnels. They didn't even know if anyone else was actually there with them at all.

They spent no more than twenty minutes in the darkness before a shimmer of light shone down upon them from above their heads. They could see each other, glowing as they swam.

"Upwards," Sift whispered back to Maanta and Millay. They barely noticed his mouth move.

He swept up into the light above and Maanta and Millay followed closely. They halted just below the open mouth of another crevice in the ocean floor.

Sift held his finger to his lips to instruct the other two to remain silent and he cautiously raised his eyes out of the crevice to inspect the waters around its mouth for people of Sangfoul. "There's no one close by," he spoke softly to Maanta and Millay.

They each raised their heads out of the mouth of the crevice and looked around. Towers of spiked black rose above them. In the distance they could see a massive army preparing themselves for battle along the base of a mountain. Tailfins wiggled beneath their torsos.

"We've reached the other side," Maanta spoke softly. "How did you know the crevice of darkness would lead us here?"

Sift's sight remained on the amassing army. "Before released I was from slavery here, this cavernous tunnel once for enslavement was used. Father which once mine was died when heart his was, was pierced upon this crevice's walls."

Maanta felt sad for Sift but did not reply. *Some things are so hard to find the words for,* he thought. He almost wished he hadn't asked.

"Feelings of sadness feel not for me," Sift lowly spoke. "Past a long time ago it was."

"Who's that?" Millay softly asked as she pointed to a massive figure in the group of Sangfoul warriors. His body was twice as large as the others and his strength could be seen from this distance.

"The name his is of is Malistour," Sift said as he watched the massive man in the distance. He seemed to shiver as he spoke. "And rules he does Sangfoul with Evanshade being his right hand man and the Darkness Master ruling above him. Best he can any warrior in combat. Slaughter he does their souls."

"Then Tao and the others?" Maanta asked.

"Bury they should their bodies in the sands now," Sift said with a blank look in his eyes. "Stand they not a prayer." Sift turned his sight now from the congregating warriors to the black buildings that rose above them in another area in the distance. He extended his arm to point across the crevice toward the rising black towers. "Shall not it be long now. In the center there is of those towers the slaves, netted will be. As battle begins between the people of Sangfoul and Tao, swiftly move we shall to free the slaves."

They sat upon their riding-companions for what seemed like an hour in the dark crevice of ocean floor.

The sun shimmered at its peak of heat through the ocean depths and Maanta found he was restless. He tapped his fingertips in a swift rhythm on Archa's backside. He stared at the group of Sangfoul warriors and wondered when they would make their move.

Suddenly Malistour bolted across the length of the group and then back again. His tailfin seemed to Maanta to have the girth of a whale and his voice bellowed across the waters.

Maanta couldn't make out his words but a loud tone of anger carried through the currents from Malistour's lips.

Malistour's colossus form then burst through the middle of the army and charged up the mountainside. His tail fined warriors swam vigorously behind him.

Maanta squinted his eyes. He could barely make out Evanshade's form just behind Malistour as they dove over the mountain's peak toward Tao's camp. *If Evanshade truly despises his people and Malistour then why is he still fighting by their side?* Maanta wondered. *Can I trust his advice?* He wondered if he could truly trust anything Evanshade had said.

"Now!" Sift's voice quickly directed him before he jetted up from the crevice on Lola's back and rocketed toward the base of the rising black spike towers. "Not much time do we have!"

Maanta and Millay followed him quickly on their riding-companions, currents whipping about their forms. Millay sped before Maanta. Her curly hair whipped behind her in the waters as she moved.

As Maanta met up with Sift and Millay in the center of the rising black towers he scoped out his surroundings. A dozen thick braided nets were strung from hooks on the inner sides of the towers, hanging the nets midfloat between the structures. They looked as if they were meant to hold maybe three or four people but there were at least ten slaves tightly strapped in each net. Their legs and arms dangled like dead spider legs from the net holes.

Their faces squeezed tight against the nets in places.

"My People!" Sift called out to them. "Come have we to free you!"

The limbs in the nets began to stir, flapping wildly from the net holes. The people's eyes opened and their bloodshot stares sent shivers through Maanta's body.

One man whose neck was twisted bizarrely away from his body recognized Sift. "Friend?" He called to Sift. "You have come for us, but surely they will capture you."

"We will see." Sift rode Lola to his side, unsheathed a bone knife and began sawing at the thick rope. "With this net help me!" He called to Maanta and Millay. "Once freed some are give we can knifes to them and free others with more quickness!"

Maanta rode Archa to the same net and began sawing with his own shark tooth knife on the rope.

Millay did the same.

The rope was stiff because the net was so packed with slaves, and it hummed in Maanta's fingertips as he sawed. At first it would not fray, but after long moments of work that made his arms extremely sore, hairs of rope cut free. "It's breaking!" Maanta called to Sift.

"It is here too!" Millay called out as she sawed with all her might. The muscles in her forearms tensed as she moved.

"Good! With working keep on!" Sift replied.

Strand by strand the rope broke beneath Maanta's knife. The slaves in the net barely moved. *They must pack them so closely together so that they cannot attempt escape*, Maanta thought. *It seems as if they can barely breathe.* More and more of the rope broke beneath his blade until all at once the three places where they were sawing burst open and eleven Banealian slaves burst out from the net cage.

They curled as their bodies cramped and they attempted to catch their water-breath.

Maanta, Sift and Millay were also sent tumbling in the waters as the force of the breaking net flung against them.

One slave, who had apparently died since he had been strung up in the net, lay limp on the ocean floor.

"Quick! On another net work!" Sift called to Maanta and Millay as he swam to the freed slaves who were working out their cramps.

Maanta and Millay rode their riding-fish to the closest net and began to saw on its own taut, thick braids.

Sift unsheathed the seven extra knives he had brought with him and handed them out to the freed slaves who seemed to have the most mental and physical strength in their bodies. "All which free now be join us!" He spoke to them. "Free, we need to the others, before returning are the warriors of Sangfoul!"

Several of the freed slaves swam to Maanta and Millay's side and began working on the net they were slowly sawing apart. The others followed Sift's direction and began swift work on two of the other tightly drawn nets.

WHOOSH! With another gust of water and broken net, the new net Maanta and Millay had been sawing burst open and more anguished slaves burst from its clutches.

The newly-freed group also clutched their sides from cramps and Maanta, Millay and the other slaves with knives who had been helping them went on to the next net.

WHOOSH!

WHOOSH! The two other nets Sift and the others had been working on burst free.

There were eight nets left now, and with four nets worth of freed slaves to assist them their work went quicker then before. Some of the slaves without knifes retrieved sharp stones and shells from the ocean floor and began sawing away at the thick braids, while others simply pulled as hard as they could at the ropes while the others sawed.

The pastel blue light of aquatic day played across their faces. Somewhere far above them toward the ocean's births a school of sharks swam. Their shadows would have been barely seeable above, had anybody looked.

WHOOSH! WHOOSH! WHOOSH! WHOOSH! WHOOSH! WHOOSH! WHOOSH! Seven of the remaining eight nets burst open.

Maanta's arms burned in pain from the exhausting work.

"Quickly, to the final net move!" Sift bellowed out.

In a rush Sift, Maanta, Millay and the entire mass of already freed slaves swam to the final net. They sawed on its ropes and tugged at its sides. Not a single net hole was unmanned and it took no more then three minutes to open. *WHOOSH!* It flushed open into the currents and they all now floated freely in the ocean currents, some still clutching their sides.

For a second, Maanta took a breath of water and looked at the slaves about him. They were scarred and bruised and some were missing limbs. All of their eyes were bloodshot and their ribcages pressed through their dark flesh. The imprint from where the nets had encaged them was also still on their skin.

"Where do we go from here?" One of them asked Sift urgently. "The people of Sangfoul will surely be back shortly."

"We have to get as far away from them as possible," another freed slave said.

Sift rode Lola to Maanta and Millay's side. "Of which route should we take in returning to the others?" He asked them.

Millay spoke first. "If we go over the mountain, then the people of Sangfoul will surely see us with the freed slaves and send a group to deal with us and recapture them."

"True." Maanta looked past the upward-stretching black spiked towers and back to the dark crevice in the ground they had come from. "And if we travel through the dark crevice beneath the city and mountain then we risk some of our group getting lost in the darkness. Either way we will have troubles."

Sift thought about this for a few moments. The broken nets wafted in the currents and hung from the rising towers about them. "Take we shall the crevice and tunnels. Tis true some lost could become there but if seen we were while swimming over the mountain sure failure could befall our souls. And something else have thought of I. If after long years of freedom from this place still remember I the way through the crevice's depths then surely those who have worked it more recently shall the way know. Move slower, we shall have to, because these freed slaves no riding companions have."

Sift rode Lola quickly away from the towers towards the crevice they had come from. "Follow me!" He waved back to the others as Maanta and Millay followed close behind. "Shall lead for you, we will, the way to freedom!"

The 100-plus freed slaves followed quickly after them.

Sift spoke to Maanta as they both dove on their riding-companions into the dark crevice and tunnels. He spoke lowly so that the freed slaves could not hear as they swam into the mouth of the tunnel. "May notice you something about these freed Banealian slaves of difference from the freed slaves of Meridia. Whence the Meridian slaves freed were, revenge implanted itself upon their souls. Because, this is, the people of Sangfoul stripped them of their freedom and life and yearned they did to have it back. Bitter they were from what they had lost.

"Slaves these are of Banealian relation, and however, were birthed into slavery and known they have never a thing other. Know they not of freedom or peace. Know they not what missed they have and will wish not to return to the people of Sangfoul for any reason, be it revenge or any other. Know I this for truth, for I was one of them."

The two men skimmed in the darkness now upon Lola and Archa's backs, followed closely by Millay and the released slaves.

"Then why has Tao become the way that he is?" The cool cavern currents skimmed along Maanta's face. "Wasn't he also born and brought up as a slave here in Sangfoul?"

"Tis truth he was," Sift's voice came from paces before Maanta's now. "But once released, learn he did the breath of freedom, and twas the killing of his sons which consumed his now darkened soul with the scent of revenge."

30

Extinguish

Between the aquatic mountain and Sangfoul

A fire burned in Evanshade's heart as he lined up with approximately 400 of his fellow soldiers and prepared to attack Tao at the mountain's other side. His hatred was not for Tao or any of the freed Meridian slaves that now served as much of Tao's pitiful makeshift army. The hatred in Evanshade's soul was for himself and his people, not for what they had become, but instead, for what they had always been.

But have we truly always been this? He thought. *Or were we born different? Did we have different souls at birth and chose to be murderous at heart?* He stared down at his tailfin, something he knew he had been born with. But a tailfin didn't make him a serpent, did it? And even serpents weren't evil unless they chose to be.

Malistour swam up behind Evanshade, startling him as he spoke. "WHAT OF YOUR WIFE EVENSHADE? HAS SHE BEEN FELLED BY SOME UNKNOWN ILL?" A clumsy grin crept across the massive man's face.

Evanshade gritted his teeth and clenched his double bladed trident strong in his hands. "You know very well what has become of her and my child. Do not goad me Malistour."

"YOU HAVE TAKEN THEIR LIVES THEN! VERY WELL! I DID NOT KNOW IF YOU STILL HAD IT IN YOU!" Malistour swam away quickly to inspect the rest of his warriors, but sliced Evanshade slightly in the back before thrusting away.

Evanshade stared ahead, not flinching but instead nullifying the pain with thoughts of Illala and Equilious.

Venge floated in the waters beside him, adorned in black spiked armor. He laughed at Evanshade's expense. "You should never have kept that wench!" Venge smiled his grin of sharpened, pointed teeth. "Why would you take in one of a lesser race? It's like fucking with one of the slaves!" He laughed wickedly again.

Evanshade yearned to run him through right there and then, but he knew if he did, Malistour would have his head for it. Venge was Malistour's son and dealing with both of them would have to wait. *If loving Illala makes me lesser in their eyes, then I am proud to be so,* he thought. And then, after a few moments, something else came to his thoughts. *Even if I was born as sin-filled as my people are, Illala has helped me to become a better being than that.* He bickered with himself in his own mind. *But if I am truly a better person, then why am I accompanying my people in attacking Tao? I should have left with Illala when I had the chance.*

Daylight in the waters darkened and then lightened as Evanshade looked down at the trident in his hands. *Who's blood will spill upon this weapon before day's end?* He thought.

Malistour burst through the crowd behind Evanshade, his massive tail whipping and beating against the warriors he passed. "MAY THE BLOOD OF ALL LEGGED CREATURES SPILL UPON OUR WEAPONS THIS DAY!" Malistour shouted as he charged up the mountain before them, rising quickly toward its peak. "MAY THE BLOOD AND FLESH OF OUR ENEMIES WITHER IN OUR HANDS!"

All 400 of Malistour's army charged up the mountainside behind him, and Evanshade and Venge swam at their lead.

To Evanshade, Malistour's body looked like a massive half-shark, half-whale as it curved and dipped over the mountain's peak. Soon Evanshade followed Malistour with Venge and led the rest of the army in their wake.

Tao and his makeshift group were barely visible now at the bottom of the mountain before them. They bustled back and forth as they saw Malistour leading the overwhelming army toward them. They had not expected an attack unless it was on their own terms.

The tail fined people of Sangfoul blanketed the mountainside as they swept down.

"SPARE NO LIFE!" Malistour boomed back to his followers behind him before charging into the group of legged creatures before him. He stabbed one Meridian who had been freed from the slave camp through the heart, then twisted another man's head clear off of his shoulders with his other hand. With a spin of his trident he sliced off the legs of two other men. They writhed while sinking to the depths below. "IS THIS WHAT YOU BRING ME, TAO?" He laughed deeply as spit flung from his lips into the waters about him.

Evanshade watched close by as he dueled with another freed Meridian slave. He attempted not to injure the man while keeping his own body from harm. Tao was dueling with two warriors of Sangfoul not far away and seemed to meet his eye. No, it wasn't him he was looking at, it was Venge.

"Come to me, coward!" Tao called out to Venge as he stabbed one of his attackers in the shoulder and caused him to retreat. "You murdered my son, but now I come for you. Today you will pay for my son's death!"

Venge grinned through his sharp teeth. "Palistaise!" He yelled to Tao's other opponent. "Let the old man through. Today the father also will die at my hands!"

Tao's second opponent swerved and swam off to attack another legged-opponent close by. Tao's comrades were being skewered and beheaded all around him now, their screams echoing through the depths. It had become a slaughter.

Tao bolted for Venge.

"NO!" Malistour grabbed Tao's neck with his massive fist and ripped the man's trident from his hands. "YOU ARE MINE, TAO!" He bent Tao's legs behind his back and cracked his spinal cord in half before raising Tao high above his head. The man's legs hung limp beneath him and he screamed inaudible noises into the waters. "YOU DARE TO ATTACK ME? YOU MAY HAVE BESTED EVANSHADE IN MERIDIA, BUT HERE YOU DIE!" Malistour stretched Tao out like taffy before him, swept his massive tailfin up and slammed it down, slicing Tao's torso in half.

Blood spat into the waters.

Bile churned in Evanshade's stomach as he watched Tao's hate riddled eyes roll in the back of his head and his separated body descend to the depths below.

"KILL THEM ALL!" Malistour screamed.

For short moments more the warriors of Sangfoul slaughtered the remainder of the Meridians and Banealians in Tao's group. In those moments screams echoed all about the mountain wall, and then silence filled the depths.

Tao's followers were slaughtered in what seemed to be a blink and a breath.

Malistour grinned while wiping crimson blood from the tips of his trident. "IS THAT ALL THE FIGHT MERIDIA AND BANEAL HAVE TO OFFER?" He spun and peered around the waters in hopes that he would find a survivor somewhere that he could bloody his trident on once more. "I DID NOT THINK MUCH, BUT I THOUGHT BETTER OF THEM THEN THAT!" He turned to his son. "VENGE! COME TO ME!"

Venge dove to his father's side quickly.

"WHERE IS THIS SECOND GROUP YOU DISCOVERED? I SEE THEM NOT ON THE HORIZON IN THE DISTANCE!"

Venge's tongue seemed to swirl behind his sharpened teeth as he spoke. As arrogant as he was, he bowed to his father as he replied. "I see them not either, father. They must be hiding upon the seafloor in the distance or in one of the series of caves and tunnels which surround our land."

A light flickered in Malistour's eyes. "PERHAPS I HAVE SPOKEN TOO SOON! THEY MAY NOT PUT UP A FIGHT, BUT IT APPEARS WE HAVE A TREASURE HUNT ON OUR HANDS! THIS DAY COULD YET PROVE INTERESTING!" He thrust upward quickly with his tailfin so that he could better address his people. "SEARCH ALL THE WATERS BEYOND THIS MOUNTAIN AND THE CAVES AND TUNNELS THOSE WATERS LEAD TO! THERE IS YET A GROUP OF MERIDIANS AND BANEALIANS WE HAVE NOT SLAIN, AND I WISH TO HAVE THEIR HEADS BY NIGHTFALL!"

The warriors of Sangfoul stilly watched their leader.

"WHAT ARE YOU WAITING FOR? FIND THEM! REPORT HERE WHEN YOU DISCOVER WHERE THEY ARE!"

Quick as they could, the warriors of Sangfoul scurried into groups and swam off to hunt their second group of prey.

Evanshade led a group of three. Neither of his companions was experienced or even warriors he had known before. That was fine because he knew that if they did happen to come upon Illala and the others, he would have to sacrifice their lives to keep them quiet.

Only Malistour and Venge waited behind.

Once Evanshade's trio had swam beyond earshot Malistour spoke as quietly as he could to Venge. "Follow Evanshade," he instructed his son. "I do not trust him. He knows things he has not shared."

"Yesss father," Venge hissed through his teeth. "If he deceives us, his blood will be mine."

31

Orion's Birth Bound

The cavernous tunnel beneath Sangfoul's mountain

With such great speed Maanta and the others swam through the dark, chilled cavern that even the darkness seemed to blur before their sight. They knew there would only be a short timeframe they would have to meet up with Anna and the others before the warriors of Sangfoul would defeat Tao and come looking for them.

"Do you think we will reach them in time?" Maanta asked Sift quietly.

"Speak not," Sift replied. "The end of the cavern soon we'll reach and for all we know our enemies could be near."

Slowly, a soft light spread in the darkness before them as they rose up toward open water once more.

The lips of the crevice opening brought hope to Maanta's heart. Soon they would be in open waters and could travel in a direct shot to where they thought Anna and the others would be.

They moved closer to the shining cavern opening on the ocean floor and then a group of shadows moved in the light's path. "Something moves down there," one of the shadows said.

"It's probably an eel. Let me see," another shadow responded.

Sift halted Maanta, Millay and the slaves behind him. Some of the slaves made sharp noises as they rammed into those in front of them in the darkness.

The first shadow entered the cave now. "That was no eel!"

Maanta's heart pounded in his chest.

Sift led them forward once more. There would be no turning back now. They had come too far to retreat back to Sangfoul's inner city.

Maanta clutched his trident tight in his hands as he rode Archa's back up through the darkness.

The second shadow called to another hidden companion. "Evanshade come here! I think they're hiding in this crevice-cave!"

Evanshade, Maanta thought. *Are we saved? Or has he played me and the others as fools all along?* He wanted to say something to Sift but knew he would be heard.

They were close now and light began to fall on Sift and Maanta's faces.

"It's them!" The first shadow called out before being skewered from behind on Evanshade's trident and then tumbling into the crevice hole.

Evanshade quickly dispatched his other companion's life as well.

Sift burst from the cave crevice's opening, taking Evanshade by surprise and pinning him against the coral and kelp-covered ground with the bar of his trident. Maanta and Millay rose from the cave into the light blue waters shortly after and were followed by the enormous mass of Banealian slaves they had freed.

"Closely stay to the coral and kelp so as not to be seen by others," Sift told them as they emerged from the cavern. Evanshade lay motionless beneath his trident's shaft.

"I am not your enemy, Sift," Evanshade spoke slowly and cautiously. "Did Maanta not tell you I am realizing my wrongs and no longer wish you ill? Why else would I have killed my fellow warriors?"

"Hatching you could be a more sinister scheme." Sift still pinned him hard against the ground. "Not to be trusted are you."

Maanta came quickly to Sift's side, thankful that battle had been averted.

"It may be true," Maanta said as Archa nudged Evanshade's arm. "I hadn't told you before but Evanshade was there when we rescued Illala from Sangfoul and Equilious is his son. He even told us when they would be attacking Tao and suggested that we free the slaves when the people of Sangfoul and Tao's group were locked in combat."

Sift looked to Evanshade as if pondering his fate. "You stay with us now and unarmed you come." He stripped the double-edged trident from Evanshade's grasp and placed it in Maanta's hands. "Give your own trident to one of the slaves and this one carry," he instructed Maanta.

Maanta passed his trident along.

"Cross us not, Evanshade." Sift pressed the bar of his trident with a burst of force against Evanshade's chest, causing him to choke before allowing Evanshade to rise. "Lucky are you that we do not shackle you as once you have done to me. It is by Maanta's honor that allow you we have to survive."

"You will not regret your forgiveness." Evanshade turned to Maanta as he finished his sentence. "Your people will arrive safely to Orion's Birth."

They traveled quickly then, assisted by Evanshade's knowledge of the seafloor beyond Sangfoul. They hugged to patches of oceanic vegetation so as not to be seen and traveled as closely as they could to the sands beneath them.

And the feeling he was being followed returned to Maanta's mind, but somehow in a different way this time.

They passed where they had originally camped when they had arrived to the outskirts of Sangfoul, and Maanta noticed a small group of tail fined warriors skimming the area and talking back and forth.

They passed unnoticed.

Thank Gelu Anna was wise enough to start heading for Orion's Birth, Maanta thought, realizing that since she was not here, she must have left with the others.

It would be at least the same distance they had already traveled again before they would finally rejoin Anna.

Darkness had begun to set for the day as Maanta noticed movement along the barely visible sand and kelp in the ocean before him. "That's them," he spoke to Sift who was close to his side. They appeared to be moving slower then Maanta and Sift's group and would be easy to catch up to now.

"Cautious be," Sift warned Maanta. "Warriors of Sangfoul could they be to cut us off." Sift turned a wary look back to Evanshade.

As they came nearer, though, Maanta noticed legs moving in the group as they swam. It had to be them. The people of Sangfoul didn't have legs.

"Anna!" Maanta called to the group moving in the aquatic foliage before them.

The group stopped its movements. Maanta could barely make out a female form rising on her riding-fish out of the kelp pocket they had been traveling in.

"Maanta?" Anna's beautiful voice called back to him. "Is that you? We saw the people of Sangfoul dip over the mountain to attack Tao and decided it was time to begin heading for Orion's Birth! I'm so happy to have you safe and back with us again!"

Another voice called out from the group hidden by the kelp in the darkness. "They've freed our people!"

Several of the Banealians hidden in the kelp before them rose out of it quickly and swam to the freed slaves traveling with Maanta and the others to greet them.

Anna rode her riding-fish quickly to Maanta's side, touched his cheek with her hand and kissed him. It felt good to feel her touch again, even if he had only missed it for a short while.

Soon they had come together as one group again in the darkness and had welcomed the freed Banealian slaves warmly. Evanshade had also found Illala quickly in their number and embraced her and baby Equilious in his arms. He kissed the soft head of his baby boy as he held them both.

They couldn't rest though, Sift insisted, the longer they stayed in one place the sooner the warriors of Sangfoul would discover them.

"It's true," Evanshade assured them. "The warriors of Sangfoul are searching for us."

The entire group seemed to look upon Evanshade with fear and distain. Illala assured them Evanshade was not the murderous man they knew him to be, but no one in the group, except Maanta and Anna, wanted anything to do with him. They insisted he continue traveling unarmed and far behind them in the waters.

Soon they were off again, traveling low amongst the kelp, coral and pits of the ocean floor with a soft sheen of aquatic moonlight barely glistening upon the world about them. Far in the distance behind them, Evanshade followed with Illala by his side. Equilious was cradled in her arms and the baby cooed softly against her chest.

Through the night they traveled to reach Orion's Birth quicker. It had taken five days to reach Sangfoul after leaving Meridia but Orion's Birth was a closer distance from Sangfoul than Meridia was, and on their way to Sangfoul they had traveled slower than they now were. If they were able to keep up this pace and travel through the nights, then they would be able to reach Orion's Birth around the time when the sun would rise for the second time.

Night gave way to day as they pressed on with no sign of their enemies. The sun rose like a beacon over the ocean's horizon above.

Instead of meals, which they would have had to stop for, they began catching whatever small fish they could find swimming in and out of the kelp close by. They would rely on these small morsels to keep their energy up as they traveled on.

Early morning passed to noon and then to sunset as time passed by. The sounds of whales calling to each other in the distance danced through their ears.

As the sun spread a crimson glow across the waters in its setting Evanshade heard something. It was a low booming noise coming from far behind him. He couldn't make out what it was but he recognized the noise's pitch. He would know it anywhere. "Malistour!" He said, as he spun around jerkily with his tailfin and saw a large mass of movement coming quickly toward them from behind. "Someone must have discovered us and alerted him of our location. They will be upon us within the hour."

Illala stopped with him and gave him a worried look. "What do we do?"

Evanshade kissed her tenderly. "You rejoin the main group with our child and continue on with the others. I will remain here and attempt to stall them."

The worry in Illala's eyes beamed. "But they will kill you! Surly they know you have betrayed them?"

Evanshade stared at the approaching mass behind. "It's true. I will probably die, but I could have no life in a world of land and air anyway."

"And what of our child? He needs a father and he too has no legs! We need you, Evanshade!" Illala hugged him.

"There is no other way. Go to them and warn them to move more quickly. I will meet you at Orion's Birth if I survive." For a moment more he hugged her and then kissed her with a desperate passion.

"You will always be my Love," she told him before swimming toward the rest of the group which moved before them.

Evanshade admired her beautiful back as she swam away and looked into the eyes of his son, who looked back at him as he was cradled in Illala's arms. "We will all die," Evanshade spoke to himself. "I will die here first, and then they all will be slain before they ever reach Orion's Birth. What did I invoke on us all, Illala, by attacking Meridia?"

Dread filled his heart and clotted in his throat as he floated in the currents, watching Illala and the others swim out of sight in the distance before him, and the warriors of Sangfoul come closer and closer to him from behind.

They were almost there now. Any minute they would be upon him.

And then something rustled in the kelp below. A pair of eyes flickered and glistened in the darkness and moonlight that was filtering through the ocean depths once more. "…come for what it stakes to take does Malistour or so it thinks but reckoning must us with it soon for such not will it fink our room…"

Evanshade stared into the shimmering eyes below. "Amaranth?" He asked. "Is that you?"

A cragged old body swam up from the kelp below. One of its legs seemed to flap contortedly at its side. Scars maimed its body. Its eyes flashed back and forth at what appeared to be nothing. "…amaranth of not I am but odyssey sir sam I am…"

How did he survive the fall of Meridia? Evanshade thought. "The people of Sangfoul are coming Amaranth," Evanshade spoke to him quickly as he watched Malistour and the others growing larger and larger before him. Malistour had now recognized him in the distance and shouted something to him just out of earshot. "Hide back in the kelp and coral, old man, and spare your own life before they arrive."

The crinkled old Amaranth didn't heed his advice and instead, came to his side. There was nothing Evanshade could say or do that would persuade him to leave.

"…in endings of Meridia was a soul did change and free this was and so I trek to by your side to save the souls thine came to prize…" Amaranth's fingers popped as he curled them inward and stared ahead in determination. Small blue orbs glowed upon his palms.

Evanshade looked at Amaranth bizarrely. "I don't know what you say or do old man, but it's good to have you by my side."

Malistour was only a half-mile away now and the anger in his eyes directed toward Evanshade was ferocious. "YOU HAVE BETRAYED US!" He bellowed. Within minutes he closed the distance between them, his massive army close behind. "WHAT FILTH WOULD BETRAY HIS OWN PEOPLE FOR THE MIRE OF THE LEGGED RACE?"

"A man who has learned the error of his ways," Evanshade spoke to himself as he stared defiantly ahead. What was he doing, remaining behind here? He didn't even have a weapon to defend himself.

Malistour rushed forward, his arm outstretched to choke Evanshade.

Then suddenly, a white shield of flickering light leapt forth from Amaranth's hands and stretched for the length of the ocean, protecting them both from the coming army and Malistour's outstretched hand.

Malistour's hand bounced off the shield and seared over where it had touched.

"BLASPHEMY!" Malistour cursed. "WHAT SOURCERY HAVE YOU BROUGHT WITH YOU? REVEAL YOUR MAGE!"

Malistour sent his most muscular warriors careening into the wall of light in attempts to break its defensive shield. They curled over in pain.

Evanshade turned to Amaranth. *They can't see him,* he suddenly realized. "Are you a ghost whom only I can see?" He whispered to the deformed old man but Amaranth didn't answer, only glared ahead in the direction of their attackers. His eyes glowed transparent blue.

"WHO ARE YOU SPEAKING TO, COWARD?" Malistour ranted. He struck the light field with his trident and spun back from electrocution.

Several more warriors charged into the wall, all to no avail.

Malistour pointed one of his massive fingers toward Evanshade's eyes. His tail beat below him rapidly in agitation. "WE WILL LEAVE FOR NOW, EVANSHADE, BUT MARK MY WORDS, WE WILL DISCOVER A WAY AROUND THIS WALL AND WHEN WE DO, WE WILL PLACE YOUR HEAD UPON A STAKE!"

Malistour and his army swam off down the wall's side in one direction in search of its end.

"Thank you Amaranth," Evanshade said while watching the army of Sangfoul swim away. "I don't know if you are a ghost or what your purpose is, but thank you for rescuing me and for stalling Malistour and his army."

"...amaranth I am not instead am merely odyssey..." Amaranth said while still staring blankly ahead, the light shield flickering forth from his palms. "...for on this place your saving makes but yet of thus another waits and yours the life that place will take for thus this is nil your time..."

"Come with me to find Illala and the others once more." Evanshade placed his strong hand on Amaranth's bony, malnourished shoulder.

As he did so Amaranth faded and disappeared in the currents, only his light shield still remained to prove that he had been there.

Evanshade dove off in the currents with as much haste as he could muster to catch up with Illala and the rest of the group heading for Orion's Birth.

32

Arise

The waters nearing Orion's Birth

The second dawn was rising now in the waters since Maanta had helped free the slaves caged in nets in Sangfoul, and he had not slept since that time, but it seemed eons in the past. Orange and yellow hues of the rising sun above the ocean danced in his sight as they dispersed the darkness of night from the depths.

And in the distance those beautiful dancing hues skipped across a marble structure which rose up from the ocean floor.

"Orion's Birth," Maanta breathed. "Orion's Birth!" He called to all the group of about 200 he was traveling in now.

They cheered in response and quickened their pace.

Anna looked to Maanta and smiled. "We are here," she said as she rode quickly on her riding-fish's back. "We are too close for the people of Sangfoul to stop us now. We are free."

They swam closer and closer in the open waters before Orion's Birth, their hearts beating faster and faster as they knew they neared salvation. Soon they were at its rising, shimmering outer marble wall and pillars.

The group gathered around it in a large mass and awaited Maanta's instruction.

"What do we do from here?" Anna asked him. "You know more about this place and its workings than any of us."

Maanta rose up on Archa's back above the gathering of Meridians and Banealians and took a conk shell from Sift as he rose. "When bubbles of the transparent fluid air begin to rise from the center ring of Orion's Birth's walls, go to that air and it will carry you up to salvation and the world of air and land above," he turned as he said this, speaking to all their people and connecting with their eyes. "We will have to enter in waves, as we cannot all fit in Orion's Birth's center ring at once, but we will meet again where the currents of air take us."

One woman in the group below sounded her voice. "When will these currents of air come?" She asked.

"I have no way of knowing," Maanta told her, "but I have faith in Gelu, that they will come to take us away soon."

A noise rumbled beneath them, shaking the ocean floor. Tiny air bubbles began rising from Orion's Birth's center marble ring and the runes covering its walls shimmered and radiated light.

"There!" One of the Banealian men said while pointing at the rising spheres of air.

"Now quickly fill Orion's center ring with as many people as we can," Maanta instructed them.

People dismounted their riding fish and began swimming cautiously into the structure's center ring.

Quickly the air bubbles turned to streams of air rising upward, carrying the pastel blue and black skinned Meridians and Banealians up toward the ocean's crest.

More and more people followed and were swept up in a symphony of rising bodies in the gushing air currents. Only half of them had yet to enter, but Maanta, Anna, Sift, Millay, Illala and baby Equilious still all remained behind.

Millay swam in to the rising clear fluid, her curly hair flowing behind her, and was swept away in a blurring gust toward the world of sky above. More people followed her and were swept up in a dance in the clear stream.

The air stream's noise echoed loudly in the waters about them.

Maanta then noticed Illala swimming away from the rising air column with Equilious cradled in her arms. "Where are you going Illala?" He called to her.

She was shouting something in the direction she was headed, but he couldn't make out her words over the sound of Orion's Birth's rising air.

Out of the corner of his eye Maanta then saw Evanshade swimming with his tailfin from the distance toward her. And beyond him, not far off, was Malistour's army. "Evanshade, they're following you here!" He shouted to the man, but Evanshade did not hear his call.

Sift swam to Maanta's side. "With quickness go to Orion's Birth's flowing currents with Anna," he encouraged him. "See I will to Illala's safety."

Maanta gave Sift a worried look. "Don't take long," he told his friend. "The rising air currents of Orion's Birth will not arise much longer."

"Safe I will be. Now go!" Sift curled away upon Lola's back and charged toward Illala as she now ushered Evanshade quickly toward Orion's Birth.

Maanta and Anna rode their riding-fish close to the rising stream of air and dismounted. Anna rubbed the scaly back of her fish as Maanta kissed Archa's forehead lovingly.

He glided down and looked into Archa's eyes. "As we are swept up to the world of air, leave quickly," he told her. "Meet me again on the shore of earth and air where you discovered me before."

"Arch! Arch!" Archa bobbed her head in understanding.

"Are you sure we can breathe in the world of air?" Anna's eyes looked scared now as she looked into Maanta's own.

"You can trust me." He kissed her deeply. He then looked into her eyes to show her how sure he was that they'd be fine. "Ladies first!" He swept his pale arm toward the rising air pluming up beside them.

She smiled. "If there's one thing I can always be sure of, it's you, Maanta," she said and then swam into the rising column of air.

It lifted her up and away quickly and Maanta swam into the rising air column just behind her.

The ocean about him blurred as he shot up in the rising air. He could see nothing beside him but blurs of blues, grays and yellows. But above him, in perfect clarity, he saw Anna's strong slim legs, gorgeous back, outstretched arms and beautiful curly red hair flowing backward in the wind of the air column. The blurs about him became lighter and lighter.

He breathed the air about him into his lungs and marveled at the fact that at one time, he felt as if he were dying when air filled his body, and now it felt refreshing. The creatures tucked within his cheeks sucked at the mists he still consumed in the air. Wind blew against his body and he marveled at the way it whipped about him.

Suddenly the air shot him above the vast ocean of water he had come from, thrusting him high up in the sky. A beautiful red, yellow and orange sunrise shimmered across the beach and lush green trees in the distance. The ocean beneath him glistened in its light. *What beauty!* He thought, as the momentum that had built up in the column of air stopped pushing him upward in the sky and he hovered for a moment in suspended animation.

He caught a glimpse of Anna beside him. His heart stopped. She was choking on the air and seemed to be feeling the burn of the sunlight on her body. She dropped quickly toward the ocean once more.

Maanta hadn't warned the others of the pain and grueling experiences he had gone through in order to breathe air and function properly above the water. He had been afraid that telling them would have discouraged them from coming with him, and now his heart burned because he knew what they were going to go through.

After hovering for only a few seconds high up in the sky above the ocean, Maanta too, plummeted down toward the ocean's rippling crest.

His body cracked against the ocean's firmament and he almost lost consciousness, but he kept moving his arms and legs, looking in all directions at the Meridians and Banealians floating in the rippling waves of the ocean, unconscious.

How long did I float in the waters, halfway between water and air? He wondered. *How long was it before Noah came to my rescue?* He swam to Anna, who wasn't far away, grabbed one of her pale blue arms with his own and began swimming her toward shore, about a half-mile away.

Maanta smiled as he recognized Noah, Japeth and Shem racing down the beach to help him with the others. It would take much of the rest of the day to swim the others to shore, and months of work would have to be done to teach their bodies to breathe and show them the ways of living on earth.

"Thank you God for giving us this second chance," Maanta said as he swam Anna toward shore.

33

Bath

Orion's Birth

Beneath the depths Orion's Birth's rising column of air still pulsed upward but its flow was lessening now.

Sift urged Illala, who was cradling Equilious, and Evanshade toward it.

"I can't go with you," Evanshade was telling Illala. "I would never be able to survive on land without legs. I only caught up with you again, after my escape from Malistour, to tell you I survived and that I will always love you."

Tears flowed from Illala's eyes into the ocean. Her face was pale with sadness. "And what of our son? He has a tailfin. What makes you sure I am not bringing him to his death? We should stay behind with you."

"Your God will find a way for him to be alright." Evanshade caressed her hand as they swam closer to the rising currents of air.

Malistour and his warriors swept across the ocean floor close by and would soon be upon them.

"EVANSHADE!" Malistour boomed. "TRAITOR! YOUR HEATHEN FRIENDS MAY HAVE ESCAPED BUT YOU WILL NOT FIND YOURSELF SO LUCKY!"

Sift float, directly by the currents now. "Quickly come, Illala!" He called to her. "Death is upon us! With haste embrace we must the currents of air!"

She wouldn't listen to him, still arguing with Evanshade and trying to convince him to come with her.

"Illala!" Sift called to her close by. She didn't even turn her head. Did she even hear him?

Within seconds Malistour would be upon them. He charged like a massive whale toward their diminished rank of four.

Instinctively Sift grabbed Illala's arm and pulled her toward the rising column of air with Equilious. Illala squirmed against his strength to free herself of his grasp, but soon he was in the column of air itself and tried to pull her in with him.

Sift's body shot upward in the air currents. Just as he did so, Illala broke free of his hand's grasp and swam back to Evanshade's side.

"Go!" Evanshade told her. "I love you! If I can, I'll try and find a way to you someday! Take our child to freedom! His life is more important than yours or mine!"

Malistour was almost upon them now and Evanshade lifted Sift's discarded trident from the sands below them in Orion's Birth.

Malistour careened into him and they locked tridents in combat. Evanshade was being pushed slowly back. "GO!" He screamed to Illala. "I don't know how much longer I can hold him off!"

Venge swept around Malistour, out of the massive group of warriors following him, and spun for where Illala was.

"I love you!" Illala called to Evanshade before swimming into the rising air and escaping Venge's thrusting trident. She rose quickly in the air with Equilious tucked close to her chest. In seconds she was out of sight in the air column above Orion's Birth.

"Flee, legged-whore!" Venge called after her before turning and running Evanshade through his back. The tips of Venge's trident protruded from Evanshade's chest. Globules of blood wafted in the water's currents up from them.

Evanshade curled over in pain, and as he did so, Venge's trident twisted at his insides. "AHHHHHHHHHHHHHH!" He screamed.

Malistour laughed heinously. "TO SEE YOUR DEATH IS ALMOST WORTH THEIR ESCAPE," he bellowed, and all the warriors of Sangfoul joined in laughing and mocking Evanshade. "LET HIM JOIN HIS FRIENDS!" Malistour instructed Venge.

Venge's tongue licked the tips of his fanged teeth as he swayed Evanshade into the massive flowing currents of air on the trident's prongs.

Both Venge and Malistour held the trident down so they wouldn't lose it or Evanshade's body in the rising air, and watched as blood spewed up from Evanshade's pores, spraying up in the air.

Evanshade was unconscious now and his flesh ripped from the muscle beneath it. The air seemed a crimson red hue as his blood and guts spewed up about it.

And so it was that Equilious's birth into the world of air would come in a bath of his father's blood.

34

Birth of Oceana

In the sunrise, on the firmament of the ocean

The sun played across his arms and warmed him as Maanta swam Anna toward shore. The others speckled the waters in all directions about him.

Noah, Japeth, and Shem leapt into the ocean from the beach before him and they were calling to him in greeting as they swam to start pulling people ashore.

Sift? Maanta thought and turned to look upon the column of air which still shot up out of the ocean. Mist and sprays of water leapt up where the air spouted up from the ocean. It made the sound of a soft waterfall as it trickled back down across the waters. *Sift, please be alright and bring Illala and Evanshade safely to us.*

Sift's body burst up in the rising air, somersaulting and soaring into the sky before being tossed to the side and then crashing into the top of the ocean.

Maanta breathed a sigh of relief. *Where are Illala and Evanshade though?* He wondered. *Has something happened to them? Why would Sift come without them?*

The column of air lessoned and Maanta held his breath. Where were Illala and Evanshade? To his relief a slim female figure shot up out of the spout of air but he was horrified to see something small fling from her hands as she twirled unconscious in the sky. "The baby!" Maanta yelled.

Illala dropped to the waters below with a splash of water that sliced into the sky and baby Equilious was flying through the air in Maanta's direction.

He can't survive a collision with the ocean's surface! Maanta thought as he let go of Anna's arm and swam with all his strength toward where baby Equilious seemed to be falling.

The baby's tailfin flapped in the open air as it plummeted down like a falling star. Its eyes were wide with fear.

Maanta swam a few yards in what seemed like seconds before scooping his hands out to catch the baby in his arms. He attempted to cushion the baby's fall as much as he could by moving his arms and hands downward as he caught it. Equilious wiggled in his hands and flopped there with his tailfin. Maanta gently set Equilious in the ocean. "I'll have to keep an eye on you until your mother can again," Maanta spoke to him.

Blood drifted in the waters from Equilious's tender baby body.

No! Maanta thought. *Where is he hurt?* Equilious hugged gently to Maanta's body as Maanta searched him for injuries, but found none.

He then looked at the rising column of air. It sprayed red into the sky until the air ceased to pulse upward and the ocean rippled with waves. A pool of red flowed where the air column had risen up from the waters.

Evanshade, Maanta thought. *He must have given his life to save Illala and Equilious.* He watched the baby wiggling its tailfin in the waters and felt its tender body cuddle against his chest. It made him want to have a child of his own one day. He wanted to feel the feeling Evanshade had felt as the father of this child. "Thank you for giving your life for him and us, Evanshade," Maanta spoke to the open air and hoped that somewhere in the cosmos Evanshade heard him. "I will watch over him, I promise you."

He swam back to Anna's side with Equilious cradled in his arms and brought them both to shore. He laid Anna's unconscious body upon the warm sandy beach and kissed her forehead before heading to Noah's house, filling his tub, and setting Equilious inside.

For the remainder of the day Maanta, Noah, Japeth, Shem and their wives brought the bodies of the ocean's people to shore. Most were unconscious but some struggled against them as their bodies squirmed in the sun's rays.

In the coming months they would feed them, give them drink and teach them all how to adapt to the ways of the world of earth and land.

35

La Fin

Years later
On the porch of a an oak house along the seaside in the crisp
morning breeze

The sun was rising crisply in the morning's warm waters as Maanta leaned back in a wooden chair on the front porch of the beachside house he and Anna had constructed for themselves to live in, many years ago.

The sounds of chirping birds sang through the morning air and Maanta squinted to see perfectly where the sun rose up from the rippling ocean in the distance.

What a world, he thought. *How blessed I am to be here. There is beauty in everything.*

A family of deer nibbled at the branches of a tree not far away.

Maanta looked to Noah's house down the beach. The old man had faded a little as the years aged on but he still breathed strong breath in his lungs. More than anything, Maanta was grateful that Noah had been there to pull him ashore all those years back.

That was ages ago, Maanta reflected as he thought of Anna's beautiful form still asleep on the soft bed inside their home. *I love her so much. There is no way that I can give thanks enough to God for giving us the chance to live in peace and love together.*

Maanta's eyes then looked out to the shimmering ocean once more. A man with a tailfin, Equilious, leapt out of the waters, then dove and splashed back into them playfully.

And thank goodness Equilious survived. He reminds me so much of myself, with his adventurous ways.

The noise of tiny footsteps on wood then scampered up behind Maanta.

"Father..." A young girl's voice said.

People

Meridians
Ailoo - one of Zhar Nicholea's three daughters

Alexandra – Zhar Nicholea's wife and also one of the rulers of Meridia

Amaranth – a magician and scholar of Meridia

Anna – one of Zhar Nicholea's three daughters

Illala – a young Meridian girl

Lilya – one of Zhar Nicholea's three daughters

Maanta – a young Meridian boy

Medvedev – a freed Meridian slave

Millay – a young Meridian girl who befriends Anna

Nicholea – the ruler of Meridia and its surrounding waters

Psyol – Nicholea's son

Banealians
Ailcalm – Tao's deceased son

Leil – a Banealian warrior

Sabastian – Tao's son and a young Banealian warrior

Sift – one of the leaders of the Banealian people

Tao – one of the leaders of the Banealian people

People of Sangfoul
Calpis – one of Malistour's servants

Equilious – a baby boy, half Meridian and half person of Sangfoul

Evanshade – the third in charge of Sangfoul

Malistour – the second in charge of Sangfoul and Venge's father

Venge – Malistour's son

Others
Gelu – God

Ham – one of Noah's sons

Japeth – one of Noah's sons

Lucifer – an angel God banished from heaven

Noa – Noah

Noah – God's chosen one to build an ark to save the animals of the earth when the earth was flooded to punish humanity for its sins

Shem – one of Noah's sons

Places

Ar'arat – the mountain Noah's ark eventually came to rest on when the flood waters subsided

Baneal – an underwater city erected by the Banealian people after their escape from enslavement in Sangfoul

Cardonea Tower – the tower in Meridia where its ruling family lives

The East Shale Wall – a mountainous cliff of shale to the east of Cardonea Tower. The people of Meridia live in rooms carved into the wall.

Meridia – a peaceful underwater city ruled by Zhar Nicholea and his family

Orion's Birth – an underwater rune covered structure made up mostly of marble. Air sporadically erupts from its center and rises toward the births of the ocean.

Sangfoul – a city ruled by a vicious race of mer people with tail fins

The West Shale Wall - a mountainous cliff of shale to the west of Cardonea Tower. The people of Meridia live in rooms carved into the wall.

Riding Companions

Archa – a dolphin that carries Maanta throughout the ocean

Lisaly – a small fish that carries Illala throughout the ocean

Lola – a large shimmering fish that carries Sift throughout the ocean

Miscellaneous Words

Corundum Scribing Claw – corundum is an extremely hard mineral and mer people use pieces of it shaped like claws to write with on kelp scrolls. The claws are heated by lava first and write on kelp by searing it with their heat.

Forbidden Fluid – air, It is called the forbidden fluid because it is what humans breathed before God flooded the earth and all mer people believe that if any of it gets in their lungs they will die.

Kelp Scroll – a sheet of kelp used to write on

Malta Shell – a hardened stone with warm lava filling its insides. Mer people crack them open and let the lava flow out. The lava can either be used to light the darkness or sea life can be cooked in the heat about an open malta shell.

Riding Companions – fish that mer people with legs ride on like we ride horses in order to get places quicker

Runes – symbols carved into stone, often possessing mystical powers

Made in the USA
Charleston, SC
07 March 2011